Richard Laymon was born in Chicago in 1947. He grew up in California and has a BA in English Literature from Willamette University, Oregon, and an MA from Loyola University, Los Angeles. He has worked as a school-teacher, a librarian, a mystery magazine editor and a report writer for a law firm. He now works full-time as a writer. Apart from his novels, he has published more than sixty short stories in magazines such as *Ellery Queen*, *Alfred Hitchcock* and *Cavalier* and in anthologies, including *Modern Masters of Horror*, *Book of the Dead*, *Stalkers*, *Under the Fang* and *Dark Love*. His novel *Flesh* was named Best Horror Novel of 1988 by *Science Fiction Chronicle* and also shortlisted for the prestigious Bram Stoker Award, as were *Funland* and his short story collection, *A Good, Secret Place*. Richard Laymon is the author of many acclaimed novels of horror and suspense, including *The Cellar*, *The Stake*, *Savage*, *Island*, *Body Rides* and *Bite*. He lives in California with his wife and daughter.

# Fiends

## Richard Laymon

HEADLINE
FEATURE

First published in Great Britain in 1997 by
HEADLINE BOOK PUBLISHING

First published in paperback in 1997 by
HEADLINE BOOK PUBLISHING

A HEADLINE FEATURE paperback

10 9 8 7 6 5 4 3 2

ISBN 0 7472 5525 3

Typeset by Avon Dataset Ltd, Bidford-on-Avon, Warks

Printed and bound in Great Britain by
Mackays of Chatham plc, Chatham, Kent

HEADLINE BOOK PUBLISHING
A division of Hodder Headline PLC
338 Euston Road
London NW1 3BH

This book is dedicated
to the
'Pink Tea'

Warner Law
Clayton Matthews
Arthur Moore
Gary Brandner
Jack Matcha
Charles Fritch
Leo Whitaker
Bob Colby
Marshall Oliphant
Dan Marlow
Francesca Colby
Patricia Matthews
Carol Law
Marilyn Granbeck

And the good old days

'So we'll go no more a-roving
so late into the night'

# Table of Contents

# Bibliographic Information

Fiends — First appears in this volume.

Kitty Litter — © 1992. First appeared in *Cat Crimes II*, edited by Edward Gorman and Martin Greenberg, published by Donald I. Fine.

The Bleeder — © 1989. First published in *New Blood*, Winter, 1989 issue.

Desert Pickup — © 1970. My first professional sale, published in the 'Department of First Stories', *Ellery Queen's Mystery Magazine*, November, 1970 issue.

The Mask — © 1993. First published in my limited edition short story collection, *A Good, Secret Place*, Deadline Press, 1993.

Eats — © 1985. Originally published in *Mike Shayne's Mystery Magazine*, July, 1985 issue. Reprinted in *The Second Black Lizard Anthology of Crime*, edited by Ed Gorman and Martin Greenberg, 1988. Reprinted as a cartoon in *The Bank Street Book of Mystery*, a Byron Preiss Book published by Pocket Books in 1989.

The Hunt — © 1989. Originally published in *Stalkers*, edited by Ed Gorman and Martin Greenberg, Dark Harvest, 1989.

Slit — © 1993. Originally published in *Predators*, edited by Ed

# INTRODUCTION
## The Fox in the Chicken Suit

### by Dean Koontz

At the moment Richard Laymon was born, a mysterious rain of one million frogs fell on Cleveland, Ohio, and over seven hundred citizens were severely injured by large plummeting amphibians. In Tibet, at that same hour, the Dalai Lama suddenly levitated twelve feet off his monastery floor and, seized by Tourette's syndrome, began barking like a dog and shouting the word 'gravy' in seventy-nine languages. While the holy man was aloft and shrieking, two archaeologists, at work outside Jerusalem, un-earthed the altar of a third-century devil-worshipping cult on which was carved an image of Satan that bore an uncanny resemblance to the Warner Brothers' cartoon character Yosemite Sam. Even as the doctor slapped Richard Laymon's butt and the author's first cry echoed through the hospital delivery room, a group of Carmelite nuns in Boston inexplicably fell into a ferocious hysteria and, racing through the streets of that city, set fire to anyone they encountered who was named 'Herman'. In London, the Queen's favorite feathered hat exploded for no good reason, causing no harm to her august personage but putting her in such a foul mood that, forgetting what century she was in, she ordered the royal hatmaker beheaded. In zoos all around the planet, elephants broke out of their enclosures and squashed anything cute and furry that they could find; for a few minutes, bears addressed startled onlookers in clear, grammatical English, speaking with better diction and projection than the greatest stage actor who ever lived – although according to all reports, none of them had anything interesting to say; and gorillas performed entrechats with a grace that made a ballerina weep. Perhaps the greatest mystery of that fateful day was the bewildering presence of so damn many ballerinas in so many zoos.

Then the world settled into its usual routines. Frogs stopped falling from the sky and were only seen in French restaurants, where they belonged. The Dalai Lama floated back to earth, stopped shrieking about the gravy, and returned to his usual pursuits: prayer, meditation, and betting on the ponies. Wiping the bloodied remains of squashed bunny rabbits off their thunderously huge feet, the elephants ambled back into their enclosures. Their passion for ballet forgotten, the gorillas just ate bananas and stood around scratching their asses. Calm ensued. Peace reigned on God's good earth.

But all the while, Richard Laymon was quietly growing up.

With his sunny face, disarming manner, unfailing cheerfulness, and singularly good humour, he passed through high school and college as smoothly as a fox in an exceedingly convincing chicken suit could pass through a flock of Prozac-numbed hens – that is, of course, if foxes were sufficiently talented tailors to make chicken suits and if hens were able to obtain Prozac prescriptions. If you met Richard Laymon (who, for some reason I don't fully grasp, is known as 'Dick' to his friends) he would strike you as one of the most amiable men you have ever met. He is one of those guys who – were he a movie actor – would most often play the best buddy of the male star: in comedies, he would be lovable and bumbling; in romances, he would be lovable and adroit at bringing the estranged lovers back together after they had quarreled over one stupid misunderstanding or another; in police action pictures, he would be the lovable partner who would be shot stone-cold dead by the villain at the end of act two, sending the star on a flinty-eyed, tight-lipped race for justice and vengeance; in a horror movie, he would be eaten alive. Thus, he was able to appear sufficiently mild-mannered to obtain a job, after college, as a ninth grade English teacher in a Catholic girl's school. The nuns adored him – and they weren't those crazy damned nuns in Boston who set fire to anyone named 'Herman'; these were *nice* nuns. The students thought Dick was just swell, and their parents thought he was a particularly wholesome young gentleman.

But all the while, Richard Laymon was quietly writing.

Later he worked in a library at Marymount College, where he probably wore a bow tie, a jacket with leather patches on the elbows, and a look of bookish bemusement. There, I imagine, he kept the card catalogue in impeccable order, dusted the shelves, staffed the lending desk, regretfully sent out overdue notices, murmured of Socrates and Plato to his patrons, and gently reminded boisterous students to whisper at all times. If he were a fox, he would have sewn for himself a chicken suit so thoroughly convincing that any farmer would have reached under him in search of eggs.

He married Ann in 1976, as sweet-tempered and gracious a lady as you would ever hope to meet. In 1979, Ann gave birth to Kelly, a blonde little girl who appeared to have been modeled after the cutest cherubim in certain paintings in the Vatican. No one could look upon this young family without smiling approvingly and feeling that all was right with the world.

In 1980, however, Richard Laymon published his first novel, *The Cellar.* No doubt every nun who had ever known him began to pray for his soul, and every library patron who had ever been alone with him among the stacks at Marymount felt a chill along his or her spine, and all the Catholic school girls to whom he'd taught English said, 'Hey, *cool*!' *The Cellar* was the scariest, fastest-paced, darkest, just-plain-nastiest thriller in years. In that debut, he established a style that has often been imitated but never equalled: plunging, pull-out-all-the-stops, no-limits, in-your-face, shock-packed, take-off-the-top-of-your-head, gonzo suspense and horror that will appal some people and exhilarate others.

Over the years, in nearly thirty novels and numerous short stories, Dick has never compromised his unique vision in order

3

to please the marketplace, yet he has found an audience of devoted readers. Curiously, as I write this, he is better known and more widely admired in England than here in his native country. This situation arose, I believe, because many American editors favored the light diet of 'quiet horror' rather than the meaty stew that Dick cooked up, and along with *good* novels of quiet horror, they shoveled into bookstores uncountable self-conscious pseudo-literary exercises in obscurantism by writers who had yet to learn correct grammar and syntax, books that gave quiet horror – *all* horror – a bad name. Those unreadable tomes, combined with the usual yearly total of 3,568 vampire novels, virtually destroyed the genre on these shores even while Dick was trying to build a career doing something different from the work of others.

He has survived, however, and prospered, because a significant number of readers like a bowl of stew in their literary diet from time to time. By being politically incorrect in his fiction and singularly clear-eyed and cold in his portrayal of evil, he writes stories that read like the work of no one else – which is essential if a writer is to stay afloat in the sea of sameness that is modern publishing. Now that he has written so many books, however, he has revealed himself and can never again quite squeeze all the way back into that chicken suit.

Indeed, when Gerda and I go to the Laymon house for dinner, we sometimes wonder if Ann is really the gentle lady she seems to be or if she is engaged in a masquerade as clever as her husband's. When she's cooking, I pop into the kitchen unannounced – just to be sure that she's adding only herbs and spices to each dish and not anything lethal. When she picks up a carving knife, I ease to the edge of my chair, prepared to leap away from the table and throw myself out of the nearest dining-room window if she should move in my direction instead of toward the turkey or roast. Several times, I've been a bit too edgy, misjudged her intention, and hurled myself through a pane of glass, only to look back into the house from the lawn and see her standing over the roast, looking astonished and bewildered. Too embarrassed to admit my suspicions, I always claim to have been catapulted out of the room by a catastrophic muscle spasm, and I think she buys that story because she keeps giving me the names of medical specialists who might be able to help me – though lately they have all been psychiatrists.

I keep a sly watch on Kelly too. When she was a tiny little girl, she was so cute you could have dangled her from one of the branches of a Christmas tree, and everyone would have been so dazzled by her that they wouldn't have noticed any other decorations – yet she always had an unexpected wit that was more sophisticated and astringent than the average child's sense of humor. One night, when six of us adults sat around the Laymon dinner table, having a grand good time, Gerda realized that Kelly was standing in the doorway, in her pajamas, quietly commenting on our conversation; Gerda nudged me, and when I tuned out the adults and tuned in Kelly, she was funnier than any of us – even though we thought ourselves reasonably amusing. Not long thereafter, during a visit to an amusement park with the Laymons, as we were suddenly swept up in a surging crowd, little Kelly – then no bigger than an elf – reached for my hand, gripping it tightly, and I was touched by her genuine vulnerability and more deeply touched by the fact that she trusted me to keep her safe; yet this *same* little girl eschewed the usual doll house and played, instead, with a miniature haunted castle full of monster figures and beheaded victims. That is a fact, not a comic exaggeration. Now, many years later, Kelly is a young lady of seventeen, quieter than the sprightly imp of yore, even demure. Nevertheless, she is her father's daughter, with those strange genes, and if at dinner some evening she were to say, 'Let *me* carve the roast, Mom,' I'm certain that I'd have another catastrophic muscle spasm and wind up on the lawn amidst shattered window glass.

I hope that you enjoy this collection of stories as much as I have enjoyed it. I only wish all of you could have the additional pleasure of knowing Dick Laymon and his family as well as I do. In truth, the strangest thing about them is that they tolerate me as a friend.

# Fiends

## 1

Willy had left the window pane for last. Now it was done. He stepped backward, careful to keep his bare feet from landing on pine cones, and looked at it.

Great. Real class. Best damn shack in Wisconsin.

And he didn't look to bad, himself, in the window's reflection. A little bony, but what the hell?

'What a fuckin' stud,' he muttered.

Then he whipped his putty knife at a dead, barkless poplar far across the clearing. It struck blade-first, glanced off, and disappeared into the thick undergrowth near the tree. Turning, he hurled the putty can high toward the lake. It plopped into the lily pads just beyond the shore.

He picked up a red bandanna and wiped the sweat off his face. A mosquito lit on his arm. He watched it for a moment, then rolled it under his fingertip until it disintegrated into a red smear.

'That'll teach you, y'little turd.'

He went into the one-room shack. It still smelled of mildew, but what could you expect from a place that'd been boarded up for three years? Besides, he'd be gone tomorrow.

The mattress in the corner was cluttered. He tossed his handcuffs onto a table in the middle of the room, set his flashlight and pocket knife on the floor, and sprawled backward.

A piece of paper crunched softly as his head pushed it against the mattress. He raised his head and picked up the paper.

It was brown with age. Creases from many foldings obliterated some of the lines.

Holding it above his face, he read the headline:

## NORTH GLEN GIRL RAPED, KIDNAPPING FOILED

Foiled, all right. Thanks to that fucking neighbor.

*Fix her wagon.*

Taking care of that snoopy old bag would be kicks. He looked forward to it.

But not as much as he looked forward to Martha.

Marty.

She'd only been fifteen, way back then. Fifteen and cute and fresh and a virgin.

She had changed a lot since that morning ten years ago when he'd nailed her.

But not her address.

# 2

After the curtain slid shut and the lights came on in the movie theater, Dan let out a sigh of relief.

'Unimpressed?' Marty asked.

'It was better than a hangover, but just barely.'

'That good?' Grinning, she pulled her hand away from him and stood up. It felt good to get out of the seat. Straining upward on tiptoes, she enjoyed the luxury of stretching her muscles. 'Hope the second show is better.'

'Couldn't be worse. Hungry?'

'For what?'

'How does popcorn sound?'

'Popcorn. Sounds great.' Turning around, she scanned the people in the rear part of the theater. She had spent most of her twenty-five years in North Glen, and knew most of the faces.

'You want the butter flavoring?' Dan asked.

'But of course.'

'What size Pepsi?'

'Medium.'

'For an extra twenty-five cents, you can get a large.'

She laughed and said, 'Medium will be . . .' Her voice stopped dead as the man near the back of the theater smiled at her and she suddenly recognized him. She sat down fast and scooted low in her seat until the back of her head was against the cushion. She propped her knees against the sticky metal of the seat in front of her. She folded her arms across her belly.

'What's wrong?' Dan asked.

'Nothing.'

'You sure?'

'I'm sure.'

'Okay. I'll be right back.'

She grabbed Dan's arm. 'No. Wait. Don't go.'

He frowned and looked worried. 'What is it?' he asked.

'Do you think we could just leave?'

'You don't want to see the second show?'

'I'm not . . . I feel sort of icky.'

'We can go.'

'You won't mind missing it?' she asked.

'Hell, we can always rent it from Blockbuster if we really want to see the thing. We can leave.'

Dan got to his feet and Marty followed him, sidestepping carefully, trying not to tread on feet, tumble over knees, or bump into heads along the row in front. At the aisle, she took Dan's arm and looked down so she wouldn't have to see that face again.

She kept her eyes fixed on her sandals and the carpet until Dan pushed open the door and they entered the lobby. The lobby lights seemed very bright. Fighting the impulse to look behind her, she hurried with Dan to the exit doors.

'Wait,' she said, and took off her yellow pullover sweater. 'Won't need this outside.'

Dan pushed open the door. The chilly air from the theater followed them outside until the door shut. Then the muggy night settled over them.

9

Marty took hold of Dan's hand. They walked down the block and round the corner. Dan's old Ford was squeezed into a stretch of the curb between two driveways. He opened the passenger door for Marty.

She climbed in. The air inside was stifling. While Dan walked to the other side, she rolled down the window.

'I'll have the air-conditioning going in a minute,' he said as he dropped into the driver's seat.

'Yeah, right. Mother Nature's air-conditioning.'

'The best kind. Doesn't deplete the stratosphere.'

Marty managed to smile.

When the car was moving, a warm breeze came in through the window. Marty let her arm hang outside and leaned against the door to feel the air's calm touch. 'It's a beautiful night,' she said. 'I love it when it's hot like this. Makes the night seem so . . . friendly. Sort of friendly and quiet.'

'And romantic,' Dan suggested.

'Why don't we go somewhere?'

'Do you feel up to it?'

'I think so,' she said.

'Where to. My place?'

'Nah. This is too beautiful a night to be cooped up.'

'Cooped up?' He put an arm around her shoulders and reached down to her breast. 'I'm not sure I like the sound of that.'

Marty moaned at the gentle pressure of his hand.

'I hate bras,' he said.

'They come off.'

'I wish you wouldn't wear them at all.'

'My parents.'

'I know. Your parents. Christ. You're twenty-five.'

'Am I?'

'You oughta get a place of your own.'

'So I hear.'

'It isn't normal.'

'So you keep telling me. And like I keep telling you, I don't see any reason to move out. I like it there. They like having me.

10

And I don't see any reason to find a place for myself until I'm ready to start a family of my own.'

'Is that a proposal?' Dan asked, not sounding especially amused.

'*This* is my proposal – let's go to the lake.'

'Okay, okay.'

Outside town, the road had no lights but Dan drove fast as if he knew every twist and curve and bump, and he was taking them by instinct.

'The air-conditioning works really good out here,' Marty said.

'Open your vent?' Dan suggested.

Marty opened it. A warm breeze rushed suddenly up her legs and under her skirt. She kicked off her sandals. The floor mat was gritty under her bare feet.

'Can I ask you something?' Dan said.

'Anything you want.'

'What was bothering you at the show?'

The question hit her like a blow to the stomach. She wanted to double over and hold herself.

'You weren't sick, were you?'

'Not really.'

'You were scared. That's why you wanted to get out so fast. Something scared the hell out of you. What was it?'

Marty turned her face away and gazed out of the open window. Her arms felt cold. She rubbed them, trying to get rid of the goosebumps.

'Tell me.'

'I saw this guy.'

'Who?'

'Someone I used to know.'

'You saw him during intermission?'

'He was sitting near the back.'

'An old boyfriend?'

She shook her head.

'Was he an old boyfriend?' Dan repeated.

She looked at him. His eyes were on the road and the rearview mirror. He hadn't seen her silent answer. 'No' she said. 'Not a boyfriend. I don't think I want to talk about it, okay?'

'Fine,' he muttered.

'I'll tell you sometime,' she said quietly. 'But not now, okay?'

'Fine. I just wondered if it might be him in the car that's following us.'

Marty groaned. She twisted round and looked out of the rear window. She could see nothing except the curving two-lane road, most of it hidden in shadows cast by the tall forest on both sides. 'Where?' she asked.

'About fifty yards back. No headlights.'

She kept studying the road behind them. And finally she noticed a dark shape against the lighter darkness of the blacktop, moving along like a low, hunching shadow.

# 3

Near Gribsby, four hundred miles above North Glen, a young man paced the end of a creaking pier.

'About time, huh?' he heard.

He looked toward the shore and saw Tina. She stopped beneath a light, waved, and ran up the pier to meet him. 'Whew!' she said. 'I didn't think I'd ever get away. Relatives can be such a pain in the butt, you know that?'

'I know that,' Brad said. 'The good Lord willing, we'll never be relatives.'

'I didn't mean *that*.'

'I know.' He held out his arms. Tina stepped into them and he kissed the tip of her nose.

'Lousy aim,' she said.

He kissed her mouth. Her lips were warm and open, dry at first, then slippery. He moved his hands on her back, feeling her ribs through the soft thickness of the old sweatshirt that was far too big for her. The sleeves were cut off. He stroked her bare upper arms and slipped his hands into the sleeve holes and rubbed her shoulders. Tina hugged him more tightly.

'I could stay like this forever,' she said.

'We wouldn't get much fishing in.'

'Creep.'

'Ready to go?'

'Nope.'

'Yep.' He kissed her forehead, then pushed her away. 'Climb aboard.' Squatting, he gripped the gunwale and held the boat steady while Tina boarded.

'It's a beautiful night,' she said. 'Get a load of that moon.'

He watched Tina instead. She stood on the deck with her bare feet apart, her hands on her hips, smiling as she looked from the full moon to the bright path it made on the lake.

'Isn't it something?' she said.

'*You're* something.' Brad climbed onto the deck. 'You look like a pirate.'

'Yo ho ho and a bottle of rum.'

'Except for your fanny.' He patted it.

'What about my fanny?'

He stepped back and inspected it, frowning thoughtfully like an artist examining the lines of a statue. 'Nothing is wrong with it . . . exactly.'

'Oh, thank you.'

'But it's not the fanny of a pirate. They've got big, broad butts. Yours is much too graceful and delicate.'

'Sorry.'

'I'll just have to grin and bear it.'

'Bare it?'

The way she smiled made Brad pull her close, holding her lightly, kissing her, finally pushing his hand down the back of her jeans and feeling the cool smooth skin of her buttocks.

Tina squeezed him tightly, and let go.

'Shouldn't we be shoving off?' she asked.

'Should we?' he murmured against the warm curve of her neck.

'The fishies are waiting.'

'Very true. Thanks for reminding me.'

He let her go. Together, they untied the mooring lines. Then Brad turned on the ignition key and pressed the starter button.

The twin inboard motors thundered into life. Tina came up beside him. He gave her a swat on the rump.

'If you break it, you buy it.'

'How much?' he asked.

She held onto him as the boat lunged forward. 'You probably can't afford it,' she said.

The bow lifted above the waves.

'You're forgetting, I'm a wealthy man.'

'Right. Your dad owns a bait shop.'

'There are different kinds of wealth,' he said, grinning.

'You're wealthy in worms.'

'How about ten bucks? Is that enough?'

'Plenty.' She smiled up at him. 'You get a discount 'cause I love you so much.'

Brad put a hand on her shoulder. 'Have I wished you happy birthday yet?' he asked.

'No. What're you waiting for?'

'Happy birthday. The big seventeen.'

'Yeah. I'm ancient.'

Brad throttled down. The roar of the motors diminished to a sputtering whisper and the boat slowed, its bow slowly lowering into the waves. 'Time for your party,' he said, and killed the motors. 'We'll let her drift for a while.' He lifted Tina onto the pilot's seat. 'Just sit tight on your priceless fanny.'

'Ten bucks isn't priceless.'

'Right back,' he said, and went below. In the galley, he opened his ice chest. Two glasses were tucked into the crushed ice along with two bottles of champagne. He left one bottle behind and hurried topside.

Tina grinned. 'Hey! Champagne?'

'Happy birthday.'

'Shouldn't you have a towel to wrap round the bottle? They always have towels.'

'A towel, a towel. Good idea. Hold these.' He gave the bottle and glasses to Tina, then rushed below and found a beach towel. It was still damp and smelled of sun tan oil. He tucked it under his arm and picked up a flat, gift-wrapped box. As he reached the top of the steps, he heard a pop. A cork shot past his ear. It thumped the window.

'Almost gotcha!' Tina blurted.

'Good thing you missed.'

'Yeah?'

'How far can you swim?'

'Far. Very far.' She scanned the shores. The nearest was at least a quarter mile away. 'I could make it,' she said.

'This wouldn't.' He tossed the gift sideways. Tina gasped, but he snatched it out of the air with his other hand.

'What if you'd missed?' Tina asked.

'I never miss.'

'But what if?'

'Seriously?'

'Seriously.'

'I would've dived in after it. There's no way I'd let *this* get away. No way in the world.'

'It's something pretty good, huh?'

'It's something *wonderful*.'

'Gonna give it to me?'

'Later. First, we've got to toast the birthday girl.'

# 4

'Why would he want to follow you?' Dan asked without looking away from the dark, twisting road.

'I don't know,' Marty said.

'You'd better tell me. I've got to figure out how to handle this.'

'Can you lose him?'

'Maybe. For tonight. But he can always go after you tomorrow. He can wait around till he finds you alone. Do you want that?'

'Of course not.'

'Then tell me what he wants.'

'I don't know what he wants. I testified against him once . He went to prison.'

'What did he do?'

'Never mind.'

'Thanks for all the information. At least we know one thing; if it *is* your friend back there, he probably doesn't plan to shake your hand.'

'That's for sure.' She looked out of the rear window and gazed down the road, searching the shadows.

'I'll take you to my place,' Dan said.

'No, not your place.'

'I've got a gun.'

'No!'

'Why the hell not?'

'You want to *shoot* him? That'd be great.'

Dan glanced at her, smiled with one side of his mouth. 'It might not come to shooting.'

'But it might.'

'In that case, may the better aim win.'

A few minutes later, he slowed down in front of his house.

'Keep driving,' Marty said. 'If you get your gun, someone might end up getting killed.'

'Damn right.'

'Keep driving, or you can just let me out and I'll take my chances walking home.'

He made a snorty sound, then muttered, 'I just hope your friend isn't armed.'

Two hundred yards farther, he swung the car sharply onto the narrow road leading to Wilson Lake.

'What are we going to do?'

'I've got a little plan.'

'Dan?'

'Nothing to worry about.' He looked at her and grinned. 'Dan's plans never fail. What does this guy look like?'

'Let's go to the police.'

'I can take care of it.' He slowed down and peered into the rearview mirror until the other car turned. 'He's following us, okay.'

'Dan!'

16

'Don't worry, everything's fine. How about getting me a flashlight?' He pointed to the glove compartment. Marty opened it, took out the flashlight and snapped the compartment shut.

The flashlight had a ribbed metal casing.

Near the shore, the road widened into a parking lot. Dan steered onto its hard dirt. As he cruised past several dark cars with couples inside, he kicked off his sneakers, reached down and pulled off his socks.

'Going for a swim?' Marty asked.

'You never know.' He stopped beside a pickup truck and cut the engine. 'Place is sure crowded tonight.' He slipped his bare feet back into his sneakers and stuffed one of his socks into his pants pocket. 'Okay, lets go.'

'Go where?'

'Out there. For a walk. Too many people around here, even if they *are* too busy to see anything. Hand me the light, honey.'

She gave it to him, shouldered open her door, and stepped onto the dirt of the lot. The ground felt nice and cool under her feet. But she put her sandals on, anyway, feeling too vulnerable without them. For a moment, she even considered putting her sweater back on, though the night was balmy and her clothes were sticking to her back and buttocks.

'Shall we take a stroll along the shore?' Dan asked.

'Are you kidding?'

'No.' He looked over his shoulder. Following his glance, Marty saw the dark car turn slowly onto the parking lot. 'Let's go,' Dan whispered, and pulled her hand. 'Don't look back. We don't want your friend to know we're onto him.'

At the edge of the lake, Dan turned on the flashlight.

'What's that for?'

'To see where we're going.'

'There's plenty of moonlight.'

'Your friend has to see where we're going, too.'

'Could you stop calling him that. My friend? He isn't my friend.'

'If you say so.'

17

She pulled her hand away. It was wet. She wiped it on her skirt.

'What if he's got a knife?' she asked.

'That'll be his tough luck.'

'I like your confidence.'

'No, you don't.' He led her onto a path. To their left, down a steep grassy slope, the water lapped against the shore. The woods pressed close on their side, forcing them to walk single file. They had to duck under low branches.

'Couldn't ask for a better place,' Dan said.

'To hide?'

Dan chuckled, then swung the flashlight so its beam swept across the water. 'Think he saw that?'

'How could he miss it?'

Dan turned off the flashlight and began to unscrew its base.

'What're you doing?'

'Taking it apart.'

'Nice,' she muttered.

'Here, let's get into these bushes.' He dropped two batteries into his palm and pushed Marty. 'You get over there behind that tree.'

'Where'll you be?'

'Right here.'

'Dan . . .'

'I'll just have a chat with this guy. What'd you say his name is?'

'Willy. You aren't going to do something stupid, are you?'

'Me?' He laughed and patted her back. 'Get over there and hide, and don't make a sound. If things get out of hand, try and sneak back to the car. I left the keys under the front seat.'

'Whatever you have in mind . . .'

'Over there. Hurry.'

Marty hesitated. Dan took a quick step toward her, so she turned away. She stepped through the underbrush, feeling its damp leaves cling to her legs, until she came to a birch tree. She crouched behind it to wait, but couldn't see Dan. So she stood up and leaned against the trunk to watch.

Dan was busy doing something with the flashlight and sock. Dropping the batteries into the sock. Knotting it.

Suddenly, he stopped.

Marty heard nothing but the usual summer sounds of crickets and frogs.

Without a sound, Dan stepped into the path. His right hand, down at his side, swung upward. The flashlight glinted moon like the broad blade of a knife as it plunged upward into the man's belly.

# 5

Something shiny swept up out of the darkness. Willy slashed at it with his knife, but missed. A cold, numbing force crushed his breath. His arms dropped. His knees hit the shoreline path. Dirt and gravel scraped his hands. He tried to gasp, 'Shit!' but couldn't. No air.

No fucking air at all.

# 6

From behind the tree, Marty saw Dan kick one of the arms. It collapsed, and Willy fell face down.

'Roll over,' Dan said, barely loud enough for Marty to hear. After giving the command, he waited a second. Willy didn't move except to squirm on the ground. 'I said to roll over.'

The gasping shape still didn't do it.

Dan swung the sock with the batteries in its toe. He whipped it against Willy's shoulder. It made a dull thump, and Willy cried out.

'Now, roll over.'

This time, Willy obeyed.

'Why were you following us?'

Willy gasped something that Marty couldn't make out.

'Flattery won't get you anywhere,' Dan said. He walked around to Willy's side and knelt down to look him in the face. 'God, you're an ugly asshole. Why were you following us?'

Willy raised his head, but only for a moment because Dan pushed it back down with the bottom edge of the flashlight. 'Don't move.'

'You're gonna . . .'

'I'm gonna what?'

Marty couldn't quite hear the answer.

'Is that so?' Dan smashed the head of the flashlight against Willy's face.

'I'm gonna cut off your . . .'

Dan stuck the bottom edge of the flashlight under Willy's nose. 'Sharp, isn't it? If I ever run into you again, I'll put your nose where the batteries go.' From the squeal of pain, Marty thought he was already doing it. 'You understand?'

Willy muttered something.

Then shrieked.

Then, sobbing, said, 'I understand.'

'Good. Very good.' Dan stood up, wiping the edge of the flashlight on his pants. 'Just remember, okay?' He whirled the sock until the weighted toe picked up momentum, then crashed it against Willy's head. 'Good night, now,' he said. Willy looked unconscious. 'Come on, Marty. Time to go.'

She stepped out from behind the tree, shaking.

'That should give Willy some second thoughts,' Dan said.

'You bastard,' Marty said. 'You didn't have to . . . torture him!'

'I wanted him to get the message.'

'God, Dan . . .'

'You think I liked doing that?'

She gazed at his face. It was pale in the moonlight. Reaching up, she brushed his messy hair away from his eyes. His forehead was hot and damp under her fingertips. 'Yes,' she whispered. 'I think you liked it. A lot.'

Dan made a sound that was almost like a laugh.

A nasty laugh.

Then he untied the knot from his sock and dumped the batteries into his hand. He slipped them into the metal cylinder

20

and screwed the bottom into place over them. With his thumb, he flicked the switch. Nothing happened. 'Look at that,' he muttered. 'The fucker broke my flashlight.'

Marty walked behind Dan, staring at the ground to keep from stumbling even though her mind paid no attention to the dips and turns and sudden rises of the trail. She didn't hear the water caressing the shore, or the summer night sounds of small animals. She didn't see the lightning bugs that drifted among the bushes, silently glowing and fading. She knew they were there; they always had been. But now she didn't care.

When Dan opened the car door for her, she muttered, 'Thanks,' and climbed in.

'Amazing,' Dan said, sliding into the driver's seat. 'A person could get murdered here and nobody would even notice.'

'They're busy,' Marty muttered.

Dan pushed the key into the ignition, but he didn't turn it. Instead, he stared at the dashboard. Marty wondered what he was waiting for. She said nothing, though. She felt as if he'd turned into a stranger.

Letting go of the key, Dan moved toward the middle of the seat and put his arm across her shoulders. When she faced him to protest, he kissed her.

She pushed him away. 'Cut it out.'

'What the hell's wrong with you?'

'Wrong? You just beat a man senseless.'

'So?'

'And you enjoyed it.'

'Yeah?'

'Yeah!'

'I didn't *exactly* enjoy it. More like, it gave me a nice feeling of accomplishment. You know? Like throwing a touchdown pass.'

'This isn't football.'

'That's right. Maybe I'd better go back and finish him off.'

'Great. Wonderful. Why don't you just do that?'

'He wouldn't ever scare the hell out of you at the movies again.'

'That's a great reason for killing a guy.'

'What did he do to you?'

She said nothing.

'How did he make you so afraid of him?'

'None of your business.'

'I just beat the crap out of the guy for you. Don't I deserve to know why?'

'I didn't ask you to do that. You did it because you wanted to.'

'Crap. That's crap. And don't go around trying to read my mind. This character did something to you. I don't know what he did, but you're my girl and I'm not about to let some asshole go around intimidating you. Clear?'

'Yes,' she said quietly, rubbing her face. 'It's clear. But Dan, don't you see that it's wrong? You can't go around *hurting* people.'

'You can try.'

She turned away from him. 'Take me home. Please.'

# 7

'This stuff really hits the spot,' Tina said.

'That's what it's for.' Brad refilled both glasses with champagne. He set down the bottle, clamping it between his bare feet to keep it from following the roll of the deck, and put his free arm around Tina.

'You sure know how to throw parties,' she said.

'Better than your parents?'

'Better than the one they threw *me*, that's for sure. Which was no party at all, if you wanta know the truth.'

'I'm sorry.'

'That's okay. I haven't had a party since I was eight. Till now.'

'Ready for your present?' Brad asked.

'Sure.'

He took the package off the seat and handed it to her. 'Happy birthday, Tina.'

She set down her glass and began working on the ribbon. She slipped it off, then unfastened the tape at each end of the package and removed the paper without tearing it.

'Going to save the wrapping?'

'Sure.'

'So you can re-use it sometime?'

'No! I wouldn't re-use it. I'll save it for a keepsake.'

'Oh,' Brad said, and felt a tightness come to his throat.

Tina held the flat, rectangular box by its lid and shook it until the bottom fell onto her lap. Then she folded back the tissue paper inside. 'Brad! Oh, it's beautiful!'

'The saleswoman called it paisley. That's the pattern, I guess. Real colorful and everything, but you can't see it much in this light.'

The dress unfolded as Tina lifted it from the box. She stretched her arms upward, holding it under the moonlight. 'It's just gorgeous! Look how it shines! Oh, thank you. It's wonderful!'

She hugged him tightly, awkwardly, squeezing his neck. But the hug only lasted a moment. Then Tina put the box and wrappings on Brad's lap. 'I'll be back in a jiffy,' she said, and hurried across the deck, the dress in front of her like a wispy dancing partner. Once, she made a dizzy sidestep and almost fell. Brad jumped up to help, but she stayed on her feet and vanished below.

He sat at the stern, waiting.

Finally, the cabin door opened, then latched shut. Brad watched Tina's dark form rise and step into the moonlight.

'What do you think?' she asked.

'Very nice.'

'It's absolutely beautiful in the light. All gold and red and blue. I guess you know that, though.'

'Does it fit all right?'

'Does it?' She posed for him.

'Looks great to me. Is it supposed to cling like that?'

'Sure.' She walked toward him, keeping a hand on the gunwale to steady herself.

The fabric, glossy in the moonlight, sheathed all the rises and hollows of her body until it stopped partway down her thighs.

'It makes me feel naked,' she said. 'Naked and covered with something like baby oil so I'm all slick and shiny.' She rubbed a

23

hand over her ribs. 'Feel,' she said, and stepped into Brad's arms.

Her back was a curving sleekness under the cloth's lubrication.

She moaned. 'It feels so good.' She squeezed him extra hard, grunting with the effort. 'This is just the nicest gift anyone's ever given me.'

'Like it, huh?'

'I love it. Here, you feel.' She tugged Brad's T-shirt off, embraced him and moved lightly against him. The fabric was warm with the heat of Tina's skin, a slippery film between her body and his.

Then Brad noticed that the dress was gathering above his hands. He rubbed upward on her sides, working the dress higher, and slid a hand down until the silken fabric ended and he felt the bare skin of her buttocks.

'Lift your arms,' he whispered.

She raised her arms and he pulled the dress over her head. He draped it across the stern seat. Then he held her hands and looked at her.

He swallowed, trying to get rid of the lump in his throat. 'You're so beautiful,' he said.

'I love you so much,' she said. 'I love you more than anything.'

'I love you, too,' he said.

She moved in against him and unfastened his jeans.

# 8

When Marty awoke in the morning, the drapes above her bed were bright with sunshine. The drawcord was just out of reach, so she got up quietly and opened the drapes, freeing the sunlight to slant downward onto her bed.

She lay down, closing her eyes against the brightness and enjoying the feel of the heat as she listened to the house. Her mother and father were not yet stirring. She sat up and slipped off her nightgown. As she pulled it over her head, the sunlight touched the skin of her back, warming and soothing, draining away all desire to move. Elbows resting on the knees of her

24

crossed legs, she hung her head and let the sun sink in.

Things should always be this way, she thought.

And her stomach knotted as she half expected to hear the doorbell ring – just as it had rung that other morning, a sunny morning so much like this – when she was fifteen years old.

A warm, summer wind had been blowing through her room that morning, whipping the drapes above her bed and making the light flutter on the pages of *Jane Eyre*. The breeze smelled of flowers and freshly mowed grass, and hinted of a blistering day.

When the doorbell rang downstairs, she didn't want to answer it.

But if she didn't get the door, nobody would, and maybe it was something important.

Rolling reluctantly out of bed, she pressed the open book face down on the sheet to keep her place, then hurried across the carpet to the closet door and pulled her robe off its hook. As she slipped her arms into her robe, the pajama sleeves were shoved up almost to her elbows.

The doorbell rang again.

She fastened the top button of her pajama shirt, hitched up the drooping pants, and tied the robe shut.

The bell rang once more before she got downstairs.

She opened the door. Seeing a total stranger took her by surprise, but there was nothing menacing about his skinny body or his crew cut or his black eyebrows meeting above his nose. His big ears made him look funny.

'Good morning,' he greeted her, bowing his high, narrow head. 'Can I talk to the master of the house?'

'He isn't home right now,' she said.

'When do you expect him back?'

'What's this about?'

'I do odd jobs.'

'Well, I don't know if he'd . . .'

'Can I talk to your mother about it?'

'She isn't . . .'

25

Marty suddenly realized that she shouldn't be saying such things to a stranger.

'She isn't home,' he said. It wasn't a question. 'I know.' His thin lips curled into a grin. 'They shouldn't have left you alone.'

The door crashed into her. She tumbled backward as the stranger rushed in.

Looking up from the floor, she saw the knife in his hand.

'Stand up,' he said, waving it.

'What do you want?'

'I want you to stand up.'

It was hard getting off the floor because her bones felt soft and wobbly. But she did as she was told.

'Your bedroom's upstairs, right?'

She nodded.

'I know. I know all about you, Marty. I've been keeping an eye on you for a long time. Ever since I saw you at the car wash with your old lady. You had on white shorts and a red blouse. I wanted to rip 'em off you and fuck you right there. But I'm not stupid. I waited for just the right time. And guess what? This is it. Let's go upstairs.'

'I don't want to.'

'Start walking.' He waved his knife under her chin.

She began to cry.

He walked behind her, the knife point biting through her robe and pajamas, nipping her back. Up the stairway. Down the hall. Into her sun-bright bedroom.

When he began to strip her, she said, 'Don't. Please.'

He didn't bother to move *Jane Eyre* before shoving her backward onto the bed. By the time he finished, the book's slick dust jacket was ripped off. The covers were broken. The spine was split, and loose pages were scattered over the sheet, spoiled with blood and semen.

Lying back, Marty covered herself with a sheet, curled up on her side, and watched her forefinger draw a line along the edge of the mattress pad.

*Why did he have to come back? What does he want?*
*Me.*
*He wants me.*
*Again.*

# 9

The parking space in front of Willy's motel room was empty. He pulled into it.

With a grocery bag in one arm, he opened the door of his room. Air-conditioned. Nice and cool.

He dumped the bag onto his bed. Out fell a plastic bottle of aspirin, his filthy wadded T-shirt, and a coil of clothesline.

He pulled off his boots and jeans, staggered into the bathroom.

In the mirror there, he saw what had been done to him. The crusty gash at the base of his nose. The bruises.

*I'll kill his ass, the cocksucker.*

Willy took four aspirin tablets, washing them down with handfuls of water. Then he made his way back to the bed. He threw off the blankets and crawled in naked between the sheets.

And moaned.

Slowly, his pain faded.

Everything faded.

In half-sleep, he saw Marty sprawled on a bed, her arms and legs tied to the corners, the sunlight golden on her bare skin.

She looked fifteen for a while.

But then he imagined her changing, growing, getting better, until she became the Marty he'd seen last night.

Before sinking into deep sleep, he made her scream.

# 10

A young woman named Peggy climbed out of her car. She rubbed her damp hands on her shorts and took a deep breath. Then she walked to the screen door of Mickey's Bait Shop, dust rising behind her white sneakers.

A bell jangled when she opened the door.

'Be right with you,' a voice called from a back room. It wasn't the voice she expected.

Not Mickey's.

But at least it belonged to a man.

She shut the door and hooked it. With a flip of her right hand, she reversed the cardboard sign so it read OPEN on the inside.

The shop was shadowy. It smelled of damp earth, fish, and something else. Machine oil? It smelled good – fresh and masculine.

Boots thumped on the hardwood floor. Cowboy boots, probably. Seemed like half the guys in Wisconsin dressed like cowboys.

'Hi, there,' this one said as he took his place behind the counter.

A good-looking guy, couldn't be older than twenty. His faded blue shirt was open at the throat. From the look on his face, he liked the looks of Peggy.

She took off her sunglasses.

'Can I help you?' he asked.

'I was looking for Mickey.'

'Dad? He was taking a group out on the Eagle Lake.' The son checked his wristwatch. 'He should be back any time, though. You might try the motel.'

'My name's Peggy.'

'Hi. I'm Brad.'

'Nice to meet you, Brad.'

'Is there something *I* can help you with?'

'I could use some bait.' She looked over her shoulder and spotted several tackle boxes on shelves near the door. 'And how about one of those tackle boxes? My old one's all rusted out. Would you show them to me?'

'Happy to.' Brad came around the end of the counter. He wore cowboy boots, all right. And old, faded blue jeans. When she looked at his face, she caught him checking the front of her T-shirt.

'How's life at Camp Wahtooki?' he asked.

'A little lonely.'

'You a counselor there?'

'Yep.'

'Well, what sort of tackle box did you have in mind?'

'Who says I've got a tackle box in mind?'

'You?' he asked, and grinned.

'Me?' Gazing into his blue eyes, she reached forward and gently squeezed his crotch.

His eyes suddenly got very wide. 'Jeez,' he said.

'Let's go behind the counter.'

Brad glanced at the screen door.

'That's taken care of,' Peggy said.

She led him around the counter, knelt in the narrow space behind it, and pulled off her Camp Wahtooki T-shirt. Brad stared. She helped him take off his shirt, then embraced him. When she sucked on his mouth, he finally started to move.

He stroked her breasts.

She lay on the cool floor. It was rough and hard beneath her shoulder blades. Brad unfastened her shorts. Knees up, she raised her buttocks off the floor. Brad pulled the shorts up to her knees, down to her ankles. She kicked them away. Brad opened his jeans and crawled between her legs.

He was big. Even bigger than Mickey. So big it hurt. Stretching her, filling her. She dug her nails into his back, crushed her mouth to his, and met each hard thrust with one of her own. Again and again. Clawing, groaning, together pounding him high and deep.

A face appeared above the counter. A girl's face. She looked sixteen or so. A beautiful face. A horrified face.

It watched.

Somehow, the watching excited Peggy even more.

She didn't care where the girl came from. Maybe from a rear entrance. It didn't matter.

Nothing mattered except Brad inside her.

'God, darling!' she gasped, clutching his buttocks.

29

Nothing but Brad.

His teeth clamped on her shoulder as he plunged.

Nothing.

The girl looking down from above had tears in her eyes. She lifted a hand to wipe them off. Her short sleeve was a shiny swirl of color.

Didn't matter. Nothing mattered.

*Nothing, nothing, nothing!*

*Just THIS!*

Peggy's breath caught. She arched against Brad, quaking inside, feeling his wild spurting throbs. 'God!' she cried out. 'Oh God! Yes!'

As she came, she watched the girl's face.

The face suddenly lurched away and was gone.

A while later, Peggy said, 'That was fantastic, Brad.'

'Yeah.'

'Problem?'

'No. It was great. Really.'

'You busy tonight?' Peggy asked.

'Well . . . yeah, I am.'

She ran her hands through his hair. 'Another girl?'

He looked solemn. 'Yeah. My . . . actually, my fiancée. We're . . . we got engaged. Just last night. I don't know . . . I shouldn't have . . . I don't know what the hell I'm doing here with you.'

'Fucking.'

She squeezed his buttocks with both hands. Tightening muscles inside, she squeezed his penis.

It was still big.

It started getting bigger.

'Just once more, darling.'

'No, I don't . . .'

'You want to. I know you do.'

'It . . . isn't right.'

'She'll never know.'

30

# 11

Four hundred miles south of Mickey's Bait shop, Willy was driving past the front of Marty's house. A white Pontiac stood in the driveway. The garage door was open. He saw a Volkswagen inside.

Would've been handy if the Pontiac was already gone. But this was fine. This was how he'd figured it. He'd figured on having to wait. In a way, he'd hoped for it.

Gave him time to finish another piece of business.

He turned right, then right again, and came down the back side of the block. The fourth house from the corner was directly behind Marty's place. Only hedges and a drainage ditch stood between their back yards. Both yards had plenty of trees for cover. Willy got out, leaving his rope under the front seat. He walked to the end of the block and turned the corner.

He came to Jefferson, Marty's street, and crossed it.

The house he wanted was the third one up, a small place surrounded by lavish gardens.

That's two things H. Dunning's got, Willy thought. A green thumb and a big nose.

He walked quickly toward the house, keeping his eyes on Marty's place across the street. Bad news if she'd happen to look out and see him.

He hurried up H. Dunning's driveway and took a cobblestone path to the front door.

The doorbell had a weathered note tacked below it. Willy could hardly read the faded ink, but it seemed to say, 'Bell not working. Please knock.'

He knocked.

'Who's there?' called an old voice from inside.

'Bill Smith. We haven't met, but I live down the block. I was passing by, and happened to notice your beautiful azaleas.'

The door opened.

He knew it would.

'Mr Smith?' The short, smiling woman offered her hand. 'I'm Hedda Dunning.'

31

Willy took her hand, gripped it tightly, and threw his forearm against her chest. He shoved her backward into the house and followed her, clutching her wrist. He shut the door.

'Young man! What're you . . . ?' She squealed when he twisted her arm. It was an old arm, bony and brown. Willy wondered if he was strong enough to break it off.

Probably.

Sobbing, Hedda blurted, 'Leave me alone! Don't hurt me!'

He grinned and took off his sunglasses.

The old woman's weeping eyes narrowed. 'I know you,' she said. 'You're that William Johnson who molested . . .'

'Good memory for an old bag. I've got a good memory, too. Like, I remember your testimony. You fucked me good.'

'Don't you use that language with me, you no-good snake.' She tried to jerk her arm free. She kicked. The toe of her shoe hit Willy's shin.

'Do you think that hurt?' he asked.

She kicked him again.

His fist doubled her. She wheezed and choked as he dragged her into the kitchen. There, he picked her up. Clutching the back of her collar, he opened the refrigerator door. He shoved her head in. He slammed the door on it.

Eggs fell out of the holder in the door. Two of them broke on the back of her head. Willy had to laugh.

Then he stretched her out on the kitchen floor and stripped her naked.

Later, he wanted to see if he really was strong enough to rip off her arm.

He was.

He tore the other arm off, too. But her legs were tougher, and he was a little worn out by the time he got to them, so he gave up after doing no more than breaking the left one out of its hip socket.

He took a Pepsi out of her refrigerator, popped it open, and sat down at the kitchen table.

From there, he had a fine view of Marty's house.

32

# 12

Marty's hands were soapy when the telephone rang.

'It's for you, dear,' her mother called from upstairs.

Marty rubbed the sponge once more over the slick surface of the plate, then rinsed off the soap and stood the plate upright in the drain rack. After wiping her hands on a towel, she picked up the phone. 'I've got it,' she called. Then she said, 'Hello,' into the mouthpiece.

'How you been?' Dan asked. There was a flatness in his voice. He sounded weary.

'Not too great. How about you?'

'Well . . .' He was silent for a few moments, then said, 'I'm sorry about last night.'

'Are you?'

'I shouldn't have fought with you like that.'

'Are you sorry for what you did to Willy?'

'He got what he deserved.'

'It wasn't . . .'

'Damn it, Marty!'

'I know you think you did it for me. But you didn't have to brutalize the man.'

'Shit.'

'Dan!'

'When are you gonna grow up? You meet violence with bigger violence. That's how it works.'

'You're wrong. You're so wrong.' Marty's chin started trembling. Her eyes filled with tears. 'I know you did it for me, to protect me. I know that. But it was . . . so horrible! I . . . I just don't know . . .'

There was a long silence on the phone.

'Dan?'

'Yeah?'

'I don't like . . . this other side of you.' Sobbing, she waited for him to speak. But he didn't. 'You tortured him, Dan. You *tortured* him.'

33

He didn't try to defend himself; he hung up.

Marty put down the phone and stood there, gazing at the wall. Then she ran upstairs to her bedroom, flopped down on her bed and sobbed into her pillow.

Soon, the pillow was warm under her face. Warm and wet. Her body, tired from crying, relaxed. Sleep washed all the pain away as it came down on her, pleasant and heavy, an old friend bringing peace.

When she woke up, she listened to the house. It was silent except for the electric hum of her alarm clock. She glanced at the clock. Almost seven.

Her face felt tight where the tears had dried. Rubbing it with both hands, she thought back to dinner. Her parents had mentioned going over to the Bransons tonight.

Seven-ish.

The house sounded empty. Apparently, they'd already left.

Marty sat up on the side of her bed, wondering what to do. She couldn't stay alone in the house – not with Willy out there someplace.

*If he isn't in a hospital.*

*Or a morgue.*

*No, he couldn't be dead. Dan hadn't hurt him enough to kill him.*

She kicked off her sandals, unfastened her belt, and slipped off her shorts. Standing, she looked out the window. The neighborhood looked deserted. No kids were playing in the street or yards. Nobody was mowing grass. Even Hedda was missing from the chair on her front porch where she always planted herself after dinner to watch whatever might be going on within eye range.

Marty shut the drapes, then took off her blouse. As she took off her bra and panties, she thought about Dan.

*Don't wear any. Give him a big surprise.*

*Sure thing. No way.*

She put on a fresh pair of panties and a new bra. Then she put on a fresh white blouse and a bright yellow skirt that Dan liked.

*'Cause it's so short.*

34

*He'd have me bare-ass naked if I'd let him.*

I must be nuts, she thought as she picked up the phone beside her bed and tapped in Dan's number.

I'm not nuts, she told herself. Everything was fine till last night. Everything was great.

*Mostly.*

After the fourth ring, his answering machine picked up. The sound of his voice almost made her start crying again.

She waited for the beep, then said, 'Hi. It's me. Are you there? Anyway, I'm sorry about . . . everything. I don't want to lose you over a thing like this. Okay? Anyway, I'm alone and I was thinking maybe you could come over. But I guess you're not home? Anyway . . . give me a call or something. Bye.' She hung up.

*Where are you?*

She went down the hall to the bathroom. Grimacing at herself in the mirror, she muttered, 'You really blew it, champ. Congratulations.'

She washed her face and brushed her hair, then headed downstairs. On the kitchen table was a note:

Dear,

We're off for the Bransons. Won't be home till late. If you go off somewhere, be sure and leave a note.

Love,

Mom

Marty went to the sink. Empty. The counter, too. Someone had finished the dishes for her and put them away.

She checked the kitchen door to make sure it was locked. Then she made a tour of the house. The front door was locked. She crossed the living room and checked the sliding glass door to the back yard. When she pulled, it rumbled open. No real surprise; the thing was a devil to get locked.

She pushed it with all her strength and pressed the metal switch. Then she tugged again at the handle. The door stayed shut.

After making sure the rest of the house was secure, she returned to the living room. She sat on the sofa, picked up the TV remote, and thumbed the power button.

The television stayed dark.

'Great,' she muttered.

She tried a few other buttons, in case someone had pushed something by mistake. But they didn't help.

Putting down the remote, she got to her feet and stepped over to the television. She braced herself against the walnut top of the console, bent over, and peered down behind it.

The power cord was unplugged.

'Huh?'

*How the hell could that happen?*

Marty stretched herself across the top of the set and reached down for the cord.

A hand grabbed her between the legs.

# 13

With his one good eye, Homer Stigg saw a girl up ahead. Seemed funny, a young gal like that walking south this time of the evening. Next town, Mawkeetaw, was a good twenty miles. Not so much as a gas station till then. Nothing but road and forest.

Well, he was heading for Mawkeetaw.

His insides seemed to twist up and quiver.

*No, best leave it alone.*

Such a pretty young thing. Those legs. That golden hair hanging way down her back. And that dress. That dress wasn't decent. Those colors, though.

Homer had never seen one so shiny and bright. It put him in mind of Joseph's coat of many colors.

Oh, now she was turning around, looking straight at him.

Her face so sweet and lovely. Her dress sticking to her in front. Plain as the nose on your face, she didn't have on a stitch of clothing underneath that dress.

Now her thumb was out and she smiled at him.

Homer's foot lifted off the gas pedal. He felt so tight inside that he thought he might get sick. He hunched over the steering wheel.

*Keep on driving, boy. It ain't right to give rides to such sweet young gals.*

*But what if you leave her there? If you leave her, won't be long before another fella comes along. Maybe a fiend who'll violate the temple of her body.*

So he stopped.

Turning his head, Homer watched the girl hurry toward the car. Her dress, all green and red and blue and golden, rippled and shimmered as she came.

Homer leaned across the seat and opened the door for her.

'Thanks,' she said, bending down to look in. 'Where you heading?'

'Down Mawkeetaw. Hop on in, if you wanta go that way.'

She nodded her head and started to climb in. Homer turned away as she reached a leg into the car and her dress started sliding up her thighs.

'That where you live?' he asked. 'Mawkeetaw?'

'No.' The door thumped shut.

'Where you call home?'

'Up north,' she said. Her voice had a hard edge.

Homer pulled onto the road. 'What's your name?' he asked.

'Nothing.'

'Don't you defy your elders, girl.'

After a few moments of silence, she muttered, 'Tina. My name's Tina.'

'Tina what?'

'Never mind.'

'Where's your manners, girl?'

'I'm sorry,' she said, sounding like a little child.

Homer looked at her. Her head was down, her face solemn, her hands folded on her lap. The dress barely covered her lap. Her legs were tawny and smooth.

He wanted to touch them.

Looking away quickly, he leaned forward to ease his tight, sick feeling.

But he was afraid she might get suspicious if he stopped talking. So he said, 'You got family in Mawkeetaw?'

'No.'

'Friends?'

'I've been there a few times for the fair,' she said. Her voice was very quiet.

'You from Gribsby?'

'I never said that.'

'You running away from home?'

'Never mind.'

'I've got me half a mind, girl, to turn this buggy around and take you back. I'll bet Sheriff Diggins, he could find your folks in no time flat.'

'Don't you dare try it,' she said. Her voice was a taut whisper.

Homer looked at her. She met him with steady, narrowed eyes. Her face looked as if it expected a punch, but wouldn't budge an inch. 'I'm not going back,' she said. 'Never. You just try taking me back and see what happens.'

'Keep a civil tongue in your head, girl.'

'I'm not going back.'

'Maybe you are, and maybe you aren't.'

'What do you mean by that?'

His heart was suddenly pumping madly. What *did* he mean by that?

*Lord, so confusing.*

'I shouldn't have picked you up,' he said. His voice had a dry, raspy sound that frightened him.

'You didn't have to,' Tina said.

'Oh yes, I sure did. I had an obligation. A Christian obligation. It was my duty. I have to save you.'

'Save me?'

'That's right.'

'From what?'

'Fiends. There's all kinds of fiends in this world. Fiends just

38

waiting to get their filthy hands on the sweet, young flesh of girls like you.' He cleared his throat, but the scratchy sound wouldn't go away. 'Just couldn't leave you there on the road. Fiends'd get you for sure.'

She looked at him.

She looked wary.

'Now don't fret, Tina. I won't let them get you. I'll protect you. I sure will.' Reaching out, Homer ran his fingers through her hair.

So soft. Soft and golden, like her skin.

# 14

When the hand grabbed her, Marty jumped and banged her head on the wall. Then she looked over her shoulder.

Willy grinned.

She kicked and tried to shut her legs, but his hand stayed between them, clutching her, hurting her. An arm wrapped around her hips. It pulled her off the television. When she started to scream, Willy flung her to the floor and dropped on top of her, crushing out the scream.

He rolled Marty onto her back.

She reached for his face, fingers hooked for clawing, but he grabbed her wrists. Pressing them to the carpet, he straddled her hips and sat on her.

Marty bucked and twisted, trying to throw him off. Then she saw his strange grin, so she stopped moving.

'C'mon, horsy! Gideeyap!' He bounced a couple of times.

Marty's knee took him square in the back.

'Naughty horsy!' he bounced harder.

She shot her knee up again. This time, Willy shifted enough to keep it from landing solidly. Then he leaned forward until his face loomed directly over Marty. 'Give Willy a kiss to make up,' he said.

'Go to hell.'

He bent lower and tried to kiss her mouth. She turned away.

He pressed his mouth to her cheek and slobbered on her. 'Aren't you glad to see him again?'

'Get off me!' She felt the spittle roll toward her ear. 'What do you want?'

'You'll see.'

'Get off!'

'I plan to.'

'Bastard!'

'I'll let you up. But if you move, I'll kill you.'

He climbed off Marty and stood up.

With his weight gone, her body felt strangely light. She tried to rub the pain out of her wrists, then scratched the backs of her hands. They were itchy and red, the carpet's pattern imprinted in her skin.

As Willy walked toward the hall closet, Marty raised her head. Her blouse had come untucked in the struggle, but its buttons were still fastened. Her skirt was gathered above her waist, exposing her white panties.

She straightened the skirt as Willy came out of the closet.

He had a coil of rope in his hand.

Kneeling beside Marty, he tied a slip knot into one end of the rope.

'Can I sit up now?' she asked.

'Be my guest.'

She sat up and asked, 'What's that for?'

'Hanging you.' He dropped the noose over her head. Reaching behind her, he lifted her hair from under the rope. His hand paused, caressing her neck. Marty felt goosebumps rise under his touch. She heard herself make a tiny, whimpering sound.

'Scared?'

She tried to talk, but couldn't.

Willy laughed. He slid the knot against the front of her throat, then backed away from her and tugged the line. Her head jerked.

'Ow!' she gasped.

'Up.'

Marty slowly got to her feet.

*Stall! Do something! Oh, God!*

She straightened her blouse and skirt. She scratched her left shoulder as if she had an itch there. Willy watched.

'Another minute,' he said, 'it won't be itchy anymore.'

She shoved her fingers inside the noose and pulled it open.

Willy was too quick.

He tugged his end of the rope and the noose whipped shut, jerking at the back of Marty's neck and flinging her headlong into his arms. He hugged her tightly against his body, gave her rump a painful squeeze with one hand, and said, 'Nice ass.'

'Fuck you.'

'Let's go over to the stairs,' he said. Releasing the grip on her buttock, he stepped backward, paying out rope. Then, using the rope like a dog leash, he led her toward the stairway.

'You won't hang me,' Marty said.

'Don't think so? Maybe you'd better hope I do, honey. 'Cause you know what? I've always known I'd come back and pay you a visit. I've had a lot of years to daydream about it and think about all the things I'll do to you. It's how I used to fall asleep at night in my cell. You were always the last thing on my mind at night. Every night. And I always fell asleep with a boner.'

At the foot of the stairs, he told Marty to stand still. Then he climbed up the stairway backward, paying out rope and keeping the line taut.

'Willy, don't,' she said. 'They'll send you back to prison. You'll spend the rest of your life there. Do you want that? The entire rest of your life?'

'That's if they catch me. But they won't.'

'Yes they will. If you . . . everyone will know you did it. They'll catch you, all right.'

He reached the top of the stairs.

'Willy? Don't do this.' She tried to sound brave, but it didn't work well.

'What'll you give me?' he asked.

A few strides along the upstairs hallway, and he would be standing directly above Marty.

'Anything,' she said. 'Just don't . . . don't hang me. Please. Don't kill me. I'll do anything. Please.'

And then she started to cry.

# 15

'I want out,' Tina muttered, pressing herself against the passenger door. 'Stop and let me out.'

'As soon as we get to Mawkeetaw,' Homer said. He patted her knee. She pulled it away. 'Scare you? All that talk about fiends?' He forced himself to laugh. His face felt very hot. 'I reckon I oughta apologize, but I won't. Know why? 'Cause I want you scared. Yes, I do. You're a sweet child, and I want you scared. Graveyards, they're full of fearless, sweet young girls.'

'Oh, Christ.'

'Watch your tongue, girl. Take not the name of the Lord thy God in vain.'

Her lower lip started shaking. Then she began to sob.

'Aw, now, don't cry. Nothing to cry about. I'll take good care of you. I sure will. Nothing to fret over, long as you're with Homer.'

He shook his head, upset that he'd let his name slip out.

'Let me go,' Tina said. 'Please?'

'Can't do that. If I let you go, sweetheart, why, a fiend might come by and snatch you up. You don't want that to happen.' He reached a hand toward her. She slapped it away.

'Don't *touch* me!' she blurted.

'Didn't mean nothing by it.' He frowned at her. Tears streaked her face. She sucked in a deep breath and held it, biting her bottom lip. Her arms were crossed in front of her body, hiding her breasts. She was tilted awkwardly to keep her legs out of easy reach. 'Say, you don't think I'm a fiend, do you? I'm not a fiend. Heck no.'

'Then let me go.'

'Can't. Wouldn't be safe. Do you know what they do to pretty girls like you? The fiends?'

So confusing. That awful tightness, his heart thumping, his

breath coming so loudly. 'They start with your clothes. Rip them right off you.'

She jerked at the door handle.

Homer jammed his foot down on the brake pedal. The tires screamed as the door flew open and Tina dropped backward through it.

In the rearview mirror, Homer saw her tumbling along the pavement. By the time he had stopped the car to watch, she was no longer rolling. She lay motionless in the grass alongside the road. Her dress of many colors was twisted high. Leaf shadows, stirred by the evening breeze, trembled on the white skin of her buttocks.

Homer pulled her door shut. He pushed the gear shift into reverse.

His hands clenched the steering wheel and he pressed his forehead against it, shaking.

All so confusing.

*Never should've stopped.*

*Never should've picked her up.*

*Never!*

He looked at the rearview mirror.

The girl was on her hands and knees, slowly crawling toward the edge of the forest.

'I'm *not* a fiend!' he cried out. 'I'm *not!*'

He shoved the shift forward, jammed the gas pedal to the floor, and sped away.

# 16

'Anything?' Willy asked from the top of the stairs.

'Anything!' Marty cried. 'Anything! Just please don't do it! God! Don't! Whatever you want! Anything! Just please please God, don't hang me!'

'Okay. Here's what. Phone that prick boyfriend of yours and tell him to haul ass over here.'

'What?' She sniffed and wiped her runny nose. 'What do you want with him?'

'A little payback.'

'Okay. Okay. I'll do it. I'll call' – she dropped backward – 'him.' Dropped backward grabbing the rope with both her hands.

Willy let go of his end to keep from being tugged off the top of the stairs, and Marty sat down hard. An odd, tickling pain jolted through her.

Before Willy could bring in the slack, she jerked the noose off her head. She got to her feet and ran for the door. Her hand found the knob. She twisted and pulled. The door swung open. Looking over her shoulder, she saw Willy leaping down the stairs three at a time.

She slammed the door and sprinted across the lawn.

At the street, she turned around. The front door opened. Willy stepped halfway out, then took a backward step and shut the door.

*He's staying inside!*

Afraid to come out and chase her?

She supposed he would probably sneak out the rear of the house.

Unless . . .

*He knows I'll have to come back, sooner or later. What if he decides to wait?*

No, he'd be crazy to stay inside. He would have to figure she would call the police.

Marty started running toward Hedda's place. She could phone the cops from there.

As she started to cross the street, Dan's car suddenly rounded the corner and pulled to a stop. 'Where you going?' he asked, reaching across the front seat to open the door.

'No place special.'

'Can I give you a lift?'

'Yeah. Okay.' She climbed into his car and pulled the door shut. 'Did you get my message?'

'Message?'

'Guess not. I called you about . . . ten minutes ago?'

'Really? No, I didn't get any message. I thought I'd drop by and . . . you've been crying.'

'Yeah.'

'What's wrong? It's not because of our . . . ?'

'Yeah. Of course it is.'

He shook his head. 'I was just coming over to see if we couldn't manage to straighten things out.'

'Nice idea. I had the same thing in mind. That's what I phoned about.'

'You must've just missed me.' He smiled at her. 'Well, where to? Your place?'

'That wouldn't be a good idea. Mom and Dad are there. I want to be alone with you.'

He put his hand against the side of her face.

'How about your place?' she suggested.

'My place it is.'


An hour later, Marty was stretched out face down on the bed, naked and sweaty. She felt languid and wonderful. Willy seemed like a problem from long ago and far away.

Dan, sitting on her rump, had been gently rubbing her back for the past few minutes. Now, he swept her hair sideways so it fell over her shoulder.

She was glad to have the hair away from the hot nape of her neck.

She supposed Dan was about to kiss her there.

But he asked, 'What's this?'

'What's what?'

'This mark.'

She suddenly felt sick.

'I don't know,' she said.

'Marty?'

'It's nothing.'

'It looks like a rope burn.' His hands clamped the tops of her shoulders. 'How did it get there?'

'I don't know.'

'Tell me!'

'I don't *know!*'

'It *is* a rope burn, isn't it?'

Marty didn't answer. Dan's fingers tightened on her shoulders.

'That hurts,' she said.

He squeezed harder. 'Who did it to you?'

'Stop that!'

'Who?'

'Who do you think?'

'He put a *rope* around your neck?'

'It doesn't matter. I got away.'

'*When? Tonight?*'

'Yes, tonight. Forget about it, okay? It doesn't matter.'

'When tonight?'

'Damn it . . .'

The hands clenching her shoulders suddenly jerked up and down, shaking her.

'Damn it!' she cried out.

'Just before I showed up, wasn't it?'

'Let go of me.'

'The motherfucking bastard. Where was he?'

'I'm not telling you anything. He wants to kill you, you know.'

'He was in your house, wasn't he?'

'No.'

'That's why you were out in the street. That's why you wanted to come over here. Your parents weren't in the house, *he* was.'

'Go to hell,' she said.

Dan climbed off her. 'You stay here,' he said.

Rolling over, she watched him scurry off the bed. He rushed about, snatching his clothes off the floor and putting them on. When he was dressed, he pulled open a drawer of a nightstand beside the bed. He took out a holstered revolver.

'No, don't,' Marty said. 'Put it away. Don't go over there. We can call the cops and have them . . .'

'I'll handle this bum. What the fuck was he going to do, *hang* you?'

'He's probably gone by now.'

Dan took a box of ammunition out of the drawer, opened it, and

46

grabbed a handful of cartridges. He dumped them into a front pocket of his jeans. Then he met her eyes. 'What else did he do?'

'Nothing.'

'Did he rape you?'

'He didn't do *anything*. I got away. Don't go over there, Dan. He wanted me to call you. He *wants* you to come over. I think he wants to kill you.'

'Good. Hope he tries. You stay here till I get back.' Leaning over the bed, he hooked a hand behind her neck and drew her toward him.

She resisted for a moment, then leaned forward and kissed him. 'Be careful. Don't let him hurt you.'

'I'll be fine,' he said, and then he was gone.

Sitting cross-legged on the bed, Marty listened to his footsteps. The front door shut quietly. For a few moments, only the chirping of crickets came to her through the open bedroom window. Then she heard Dan's footsteps by the road. The car door thumped shut. The engine whinnied and started. Gravel crunched under the wheels and the sounds of the car began to fade away.

# 17

Willy sat in the darkness of Hedda's kitchen, watching. He'd been sitting there for a long time. He didn't mind the wait.

Marty would have to come back. Wherever she'd gone after running off, she couldn't stay away forever. Sooner or later, she'd come home.

Then he would have her.

*Nice of her not to call the cops. Stupid, though. Maybe she went off to find that prick boyfriend of hers, get him to handle it.*

Willy hoped so.

He got up from the table, stepped over Hedda, and went to the refrigerator. Not much inside. He grabbed a package of cheese, swung the door shut, and returned to the table. There, he unwrapped a thin slice of cheese and began to eat it.

He was working on his fifth slice when a car stopped in front of Marty's house. A Ford. The same Ford that he'd followed to the lake last night.

Willy pulled the plastic wrapping off another slice of cheese as the headlights died and a man climbed out of the car.

The prick.

And he had something in his right hand. A gun?

*Figures. Cocksucker likes to play hardball.*

Willy folded the slice of cheese in half, then folded it again, making a small, thick square. He stuck it into his mouth.

Across the street, the prick was rushing across Marty's front yard. He disappeared around a corner of the house.

'Gonna sneak up on me?' Willy asked with his mouthful of cheese. 'Real tricky, you dumb-ass shit.'

He got up from the table. His fingers were slippery from the cheese. He wiped them on his jeans and headed for the door. 'So long, sweet stuff,' he said to Hedda.

Outside, the hot night air smelled like moist grass. A welcome change from the bad air of the kitchen.

The prick was nowhere to be seen.

Walking with a casual pace, Willy crossed the street.

He opened the back door of the Ford, climbed in, and shut it quietly.

Kneeling on the floor, he peered out the window at Marty's house.

A light came on in an upstairs window.

Marty's window?

Willy couldn't remember what her bedroom had looked like, that morning ten years ago. He only remembered that it had been very sunny. Very bright and sunny, making Marty's hair shine. Her face had gotten sweaty. There were tiny specks of sweat above her lip. They glistened in the sunlight. She had tears on her cheeks. Her eyelashes stuck together, making little, curly points.

The light in the upstairs window went off.

Willy took the knife from his pocket and opened its blade.

## 18

'What the hell?' Roger Sanderson knew it was no mirage. It was a real live girl walking slowly through the darkness, her head down. She wore a paisley dress that was torn behind the right shoulder. Roger slowed down and pressed a switch to lower the passenger window.

The girl turned her face toward him and smiled.

'You lost?' he called.

'Me?'

He laughed. 'Climb aboard, mate, and I'll see you to a safe port.'

He watched her get in. Her knees were scraped and filthy. Her dress was very short.

'Nice car,' she said.

'Nice dress.'

She pulled the door shut, and the overhead light went off. 'You like it?' she asked.

Roger switched the light back on. 'Sure looks good on you.'

'Thanks.' She smiled and blushed. Her face was dirty. Tears, dry now, had drawn streaks down her cheeks. 'I'm afraid it got ripped,' she said. 'Back here. See?' She leaned forward and turned her back to Roger. Her skin, where it showed through the rip, was scraped raw.

'How'd that happen?'

'I fell out of a car. Well, actually, I jumped.' Her smile vanished. 'Crazy old guy went weird on me.'

'Had to hit the silk, huh?'

'Oh, it's not silk,' she said, looking down at her dress. 'It's like polyester or something. But it feels like silk, I guess.' She rubbed the glossy fabric and frowned at Roger.

'Hit the silk is a figure of speech,' he said. 'It means to bail out with a parachute.'

'I bailed out, all right. No parachute, though.'

'Did the crazy guy hurt you?'

'Nope. It was the road that banged me up. He just made a few grabs, but you should've heard him talk. Gave me the willies.'

Roger turned off the overhead light, and started driving.

'So, are you a teacher or something?' the girl asked.

'A teacher? What makes you think so?'

'Your lesson about hitting silk. Plus, nobody but teachers talk about stuff like figures of speech.'

'Sorry, Holmes, but I'm a sales rep.'

'I'm not Holmes, I'm Tina.'

'Pleased to meet you, Tina. I'm Roger.'

'I think I like you, Roger.'

'Thank you. I do believe I like you, too.'

# 19

After Dan left, Marty lay down on his bed and stared at the ceiling. She should've stopped him from going. Somehow, she should've stopped him. It was insane, going after Willy with a gun.

She spent a long time lying there, thinking about it all and worrying.

Finally, she got up, went into the kitchen, opened the refrigerator and took out a can of beer. She carried it into the living room and sank onto the sofa.

And gulped the beer.

*Damn him anyway.*

*Has to prove what a tough guy he is.*

*It'd serve him right if . . .*

*No!*

*God, Dan, you idiot. Who the hell do you think you are, Rambo?*

When the can was empty, she flung it across the room. It bounced off the wall and dropped to the carpet.

Then she went into the kitchen and found herself another can of beer. Sipping it, she wandered into the bathroom. She placed the can on the edge of the sink, then sat down on the toilet and urinated. When she stood up and saw herself in the mirror, she shook her head.

Her hair was dark and stringy. Her face was speckled with sweat. She looked down at herself. She was sweaty all over. Her pubic curls were matted down.

She felt pretty sticky down there, too.

So she decided that a shower would be a good way to pass the time while she waited for Dan's return.

If he *does* return, she thought.

*Stupid macho jerk.*

She picked up her can and took it with her to the bathtub. Squatting beside the tub, she had a couple of swallows, then reached out with one hand and turned on the faucets. While the water rushed out of the spout, she tested its heat with one hand and drank beer with the other.

The can was still pretty full by the time she was ready to step in, so she took it with her.

Holding it above the spray, she raised her other hand to close the shower curtain.

She watched the way her arm angled up to the curtain. It was slender and lightly tanned, and it glistened with wetness. She felt a drop of water slide along its underside, tickling.

The curtain's metal rings clamored along the shower rod as she pulled it shut.

Then she faced the heavy, warm spray.

The water pelted her, flooded her open mouth, spilled down her chin. It drummed her closed eyelids until her eyes ached. Then she bowed her head. It pounded down, matting her hair, streaming down the sides of her face, into her eyes and along her lips and chin. It ran down her shoulders and breasts and belly.

It felt great.

But she wanted to use soap and get herself clean.

Hard to do that with a can of beer in one hand.

So she turned away from the shower. With the spray splattering her back and sliding down her buttocks and legs, she tilted the can to her mouth and drank.

Gulped it down.

All of it.

Then belched.

From the other side of the shower curtain, Willy said, 'Excuse you.'

Marty jumped and her feet slipped out from under her.

# 20

As she started to fall, she dropped the beer can and made a grab for the curtain rod. It broke loose and she followed it sideways over the edge of the tub. She landed on her back, both legs propped up by the tub.

'Nice fall,' Willy said. 'Nice view.'

She swung her legs down to the floor, clamped a hand between them and crossed her other arm over her breasts. Raising her head, she looked at Willy.

He stared down at her, grinning. 'Pretty as a picture,' he said. 'Wish I had me a camera.'

'Where's Dan?'

'Who?'

'Dan.'

'Oh, the prick?' Willy spread his arms. The front of his T-shirt was soaked with blood. 'I stabbed him with my little knife. Took his billfold. He didn't have much cash to speak of. A shitty thirty bucks and change. You really oughta go out with a better class of guy. Like me.'

'You . . . killed him?'

'Maybe yes, maybe no.'

'God.'

'You really shouldn't have sent him after me, honey.'

'I didn't.'

'Bitch.' Willy took a wallet out of his back pocket and threw it at Marty. It slapped her bare shoulder and bounced off. 'Time to go.' He slipped a faded blue towel off its bar and flung it. It dropped across Marty's knees, but she didn't make a move to take it. 'Now,' he said.

Sitting up quickly, she grabbed the towel.

'Don't just sit there, dry yourself.'

Holding the towel against her body, she carefully got to her knees.

'Now!'

'Turn around,' she said.

'My ass. I'll give you five. One.'

Clasping the towel to her breasts, she reached out sideways with her free arm. She groped blindly, keeping her eyes on Willy.

'Two.'

Her hand found the side of the bathtub. She braced her palm against it and pushed herself up.

'Three.'

She stood up straight.

'Four.'

She glanced from side to side, looking for a weapon. Anything heavy or sharp. Nothing.

'Five.'

She backed away as he came forward.

'You know what happens now?' he asked. 'I'm gonna dry you myself.'

'No.'

'Yep. You had your chance. I counted five. Lucky me.'

'Please.'

Her jerked the towel away from her. 'Nice. Real nice. Last time I saw you stripped, you didn't have hardly any tits at all. Look at 'em now.'

She tried to push past him. He shoved her backward against the wall. With the towel in both hands, he started rubbing her.

'Stop it! Don't!'

'Real nice.'

'You damn bastard!'

'I'm not hurting you.'

'Stop it!'

'How does that feel?'

'You . . . !'

'Honk honk!'

'Bastard!'

He laughed.

Marty drove her knee up, changing his laugh to a squeal of pain. As he started to fold, she shoved him. He fell backward. She leaped over him and ran for the bathroom door.

She rushed through the door and threw it shut. A moment later, a blast slammed the air. A bullet knocked through the door, throwing splinters into her forearm.

As she ran across the front room, she snatched her blouse up off the floor. She thrust her wounded arm through a sleeve. Some splinters caught the cloth. Others flattened down. She hardly noticed the pain as she made for the front door.

She flung it open. As she raced outside, she got her other arm into its sleeve.

A car was parked along the roadside. Willy's Chevy.

The street was deserted. The nearest building, half a block to the south, had no lights in its windows. A couple of hundred yards up the road, the woods began.

The woods and Wilson Lake.

*If he catches me there* . . .

But it seemed like the only place to go.

The rough asphalt was hot under Marty's feet as she sprinted up the road. She pumped her arms, throwing out her legs as far as they would stretch, her bare feet reaching out but never far enough. Never fast enough.

She kept running, taking gulps of air in quick gasps, her open blouse flapping behind her.

Soon, she felt an unusual warmth inside her legs. In the muscles of her thighs and calves. Though she tried to work them as fast as before, they began to feel tired and heavy. She swung her arms harder to make up for it. The weariness started inside them, too.

But she kept running.

As she took the turn into the woods, she glanced back.

Car headlights came on.

She tried to run faster. With every stride, her arms and legs

54

struggled against the heaviness. Her lungs burned.

But still she kept running.

Finally, she came to the parking lot by the lake.

Last night, it had been crowded with teenaged lovers in cars. Tonight, it was empty.

Nobody to help her.

Marty dashed for the far side of the lot. She heard the racing engine of the car. Blocking her way was a fallen, long-dead tree. She planted a hand on it, kicked her leg into the air, and vaulted it just as the headlights started sweeping the lot.

She squatted with her back against the trunk and shut her eyes. Her hands were slippery against her knees. Sweat streamed down the burning sides of her face. She took deep, painful breaths, hoping to recover quickly enough to do some good.

Then she turned around and looked over the top of the tree trunk.

Willy was out of his car, walking along the other side of the parking lot, peering into the darkness, pausing to listen.

It wouldn't take him long to find her. A few minutes, maybe. *Gotta do something!*

Then she saw the silver path of the full moon shining on the lake.

# 21

Ahead of him on the dark road, Roger saw a neon sign flashing, WAYSIDE MOTOR INN. The pale blue lights below it read 'Vacancy.'

'Hey hey!' he said. 'A port in the storm.'

'Hope they've got food,' Tina said. 'I'm starving to death.'

'Mah dear, ports in the storm are renowned for their cuisine.'

He pulled to a stop in front of the motel office. 'You can wait here,' he said. 'I'll be back in a flash.'

Inside the office, he asked for a room with twin beds. The manager, a stooped and bony old crone losing the last of her white hair, squinted out the office window.

'My daughter,' Roger explained. 'The spitting image of her mother, God rest her soul.'

The old woman's watery eyes narrowed at him.

Roger solemnly shook his head. 'Life is so fleeting,' he said. 'Feeble candle flames are we, snuffed, perchance, by a vagrant breeze.'

The old woman seemed to shrink. 'Forty bucks,' she said, and pushed a registration card at him. 'Fill this out.'

As he wrote the requested information on the card, he asked. 'How late does your cafe stay open?'

'Never closes.'

He paid, and she gave him a room key.

Back at the car, he climbed in and said, 'All set. Room sixteen.'

He looked through the cafe windows as he drove by. A lone man sat at the counter. Two couples and a family of six sat at the booths along the wall. 'It doesn't appear crowded. The food's probably greasy enough to lubricate a fleet of Lincolns.'

'I hope it isn't closing.'

'The manager informs me that it stays open continuously.'

'Thank goodness.'

'Thar she blows!' Roger spun the steering wheel. The head-beams lit the side panel of a station wagon, glanced with a blinding flare off the picture window of Room 16, and came to a stop on the brick wall and door. 'We have arrived,' he announced.

'I hope they've got chicken in a basket.'

'Bet they do. I'll just set the luggage in our room, and we'll be off. Unless you want to wash up first.'

'Let's eat now.'

'Do you want to see the room first?'

'I'd sure like to eat.'

'Then eat we shall, without further ado. Or further a-don't.'

'Huh?' Tina asked. Then she grinned and said, 'A joke.'

Roger laughed as he hopped from the car. He hurried around the front and opened the door for Tina. She reached out a hand. Roger helped her out. He held her hand all the way to the cafe,

56

where he let go and said, 'We've got to act properly, now. I'm passing you off as my daughter.'

'Sure thing, Pops.'

He laughed.

Inside, Tina walked briskly to a booth and scooted across it. She patted the cushion beside her and said, 'Sit here, Father.'

'I'll sit over here,' he said. He went to the other side of the table. 'And please take it easy on the father routine.'

'Why don't you sit by me? Do I smell bad?'

'You smell fine.'

'Then why?'

'View's better over here.'

She smiled and nodded. 'Do you think I'm pretty?'

'You're a thing of beauty.'

'A *thing*?' She wrinkled her nose.

'That's poetry. John Keats. "A thing of beauty is a joy for ever." '

'Yeah? That's kind of nice.'

She was a joy, all right. Roger watched her pick up the menu and study it, her brow furrowed with concentration. Serious blue eyes, a sweet clear face still lined where tears had washed channels through the dirt, hair the color of gold.

And her body. The way the paisley dress was clinging, he could see that she had a very fine body indeed.

'Look!' She beamed at him. 'Southern fried chicken.'

'This is your lucky day.'

'Sure is.' Her eyes suddenly went sad, and Roger realized that today, perhaps, had not been especially lucky for her.

'Mine, too,' he said.

'Huh?'

'My lucky day. Meeting you. I'm not in the habit of picking up strangers, you know.'

'I didn't know that.'

'Too dangerous.'

'Why'd you pick *me* up?'

'You don't look dangerous,' he said. 'Not dangerous at all, just very lonely and helpless.'

57

'I'm not all that helpless.'

'Glad to hear it.'

'You might be right about the lonely, though. You're lonely too, aren't you?'

'Sometimes.'

The waitress arrived. He ordered the fried chicken for Tina and a patty melt for himself. Tina asked for a coke, and Roger ordered coffee.

When the waitress was gone, Tina said, 'Do you really think I'm pretty?'

'Very.'

Leaning across the table, she whispered, 'What about my figure?'

'From all appearances, it's in fine shape.'

She nodded in agreement, sat back, and grinned mysteriously. 'Know something?' she whispered.

'What?' His mouth was dry.

'Make a guess.'

'Beauty is truth, truth . . .'

'No. Guess again, silly. Guess what I'm wearing under this flimsy little dress.'

He smiled. 'I don't know. What?'

'Skin. Nothing but skin.'

'Fancy that,' Roger said, and took a drink of water.

# 22

'Stop!' Willy shouted.

Marty's feet slapped into the water, splashing its coolness high against her body. She waded out until it reached her thighs, then gulped in a deep breath and dived. She stayed below, swimming furiously, until her lungs couldn't hold the air any longer. Then she blew it out in a gush of bubbles and skimmed to the surface. Air! It was fragrant with the night smells of the woods along the shore.

When her breathing became more regular, she trod water and listened. It was difficult to hear much beyond her small area of swirling water and thudding heartbeat and breathing, but she heard enough to know that Willy wasn't swimming after her.

Not on the water's surface.

She squinted at the shore, hoping to see him, but only spotted the top of his car. A chill scurried up her back. Suddenly, she half expected a cold hand to clutch her ankle and drag her down. She thrashed out, flattening into a crawl as her legs rose to the surface. She kept her face down for speed. Her legs kicked, tight and fast. Her arms darted forward, reaching her cupped hands far out and sweeping them down through the water.

She swam hard until she heard Willy's voice from far away.

'Hey out there!' he called.

She said nothing.

'I'd come out and join you, but I haven't got time.'

*He doesn't know how to swim?*

*Either that, or he's just chicken.*

'You better come back. Right now.' He said nothing for a while. Then he called, 'Did you hear me? Come outa there!'

She continued to tread water and say nothing.

'Look, you better come out.'

Marty could hardly see him. He probably couldn't see her at all.

*If he can't see me, he can't shoot me.*

*Probably wouldn't be able to hit me, anyway. Not with that pistol.*

Marty didn't know a lot about handguns, but she knew they were meant for nearby targets. If you wanted to shoot someone this far away, you should be using a rifle.

*And maybe he's scared to fire because of the noise.*

'I don't see you coming in,' Willy yelled.

And he wouldn't, either.

*I'll just wait him out.*

'By the way,' he called, 'I guess I forgot to tell you something about your prick boyfriend. I didn't kill him. All I did was bonk him on the head.'

Marty's mind seemed to freeze.

'He's in the trunk of my car.'

She couldn't think.

'So you better come in now, or I'm gonna open up the trunk and shoot him in the eye.'

Marty buttoned her blouse as she waded out of the lake. When she reached shore, Willy clutched her upper arm and pulled her to his car.

'I want to see Dan,' she said.

'Fuck you.'

He opened the passenger door and shoved her in. The seat felt scratchy against her naked buttocks. Willy shut the door.

She sat up straight and arranged the front of her sopping blouse so it covered her lap.

Willy climbed in and shut the door. 'I like your outfit,' he said.

'Bastard.'

'You wouldn't call me that if you knew the great little place I'm taking you to. Nice little cabin off in the middle of the woods. Stocked up with the best canned food you ever tasted. I fixed the place up real nice for you. It's got real class. Great spot for a honeymoon.'

'*What?*'

'Honeymoon,' he repeated. 'You know. No, I reckon you don't – you still living with your mommy and daddy like a little kid. How come you aren't married, huh? Never found the right man? Guess I set too high of a standard and none of these pricks can live up to me. That right?'

'Go to hell.'

'Anyway, I don't aim to marry you. Thought we'd have us a honeymoon without. We're gonna have a great old time.'

'Eat shit and die.'

'That's no way to talk after all my kindnesses to you and Danny. I could've killed him if I'd wanted. And I could've blown *your* head off.'

'You tried.' She wiped a drop of water off her chin.

'Not hardly. I tried to miss you, that's what I tried to do.'

'Sure.'

'I'm a dead-on shot. You might find that out, sometime, if you give me much more grief.'

A car swung into the parking lot. Marty watched it creep along. It stopped beside them, only a few yards away from her door.

The driver glanced at her, then took off his glasses and turned his back. He scooted toward the girl in the passenger seat.

'Aren't we lucky?' Willy said. 'Hope the girl ain't a pig.' He reached under his seat and picked up Dan's revolver.

'What are you going to do?'

'Just gotta get you something to wear.' He climbed out, shut his door quietly, and walked around the front of his car, the revolver swinging at the end of his lanky arm.

Inside the other car, the couple were embracing, unaware of Willy's approach.

'Watch out!' Marty yelled. 'Get out of here!'

The girl with her back to the passenger door saw Willy approach the driver's window. She stopped moving. For a moment, the boy continued to squirm against her. Then he looked over his shoulder.

'Oh, hello,' he said. He sounded embarrassed and very young.

'Out of the car.'

'Yes, sir.' The boy fumbled along the top of the dashboard and found his glasses, then looked down at his open shirt.

'Get out,' Willy commanded.

'Just a . . .'

The girl said something to him.

The boy reached for the ignition.

Willy stuck the gun muzzle against the boy's ear. 'Out. Now.'

'What do you want?' The kid no longer sounded embarrassed; he sounded terrified.

'You'll see.' Willy opened the door for them, and the interior light came on.

Marty saw how young they were. Sixteen, maybe. The girl might've been even younger – fourteen, fifteen?

The boy climbed out of the car. His fingers moved quickly to button his shirt as if it were very important.

'You, too.'

The girl pressed her back against the passenger door.

'Willy!' Marty said. 'Let her alone.'

'Shut up.'

'Do you want money?' the boy asked.

'Yeah. Good idea.'

The boy reached into his rear pocket. He slid out a wallet. Marty could see his hand shaking.

Willy jerked the wallet away.

'Hey!'

'Shut up, kid.' Willy leafed through some bills, then shut the wallet and stuffed it into his pocket. 'You're filthy rich, you little shit.'

'I'd like to have it back,' the boy said. 'Please? Keep the money, but I'd like to have my billfold back. It was a present.'

'Tough titty,' Willy said.

The boy's eyes narrowed behind his glasses. 'Give it over.'

Willy laughed.

Suddenly, the boy went for him, face turned away, windmilling with aimless fists, crying out, 'Give it you lousy son-of-a-bitch motherfucking bas . . . !'

The gun barrel crashed against his skull.

Marty cringed at the sound of it.

The boy staggered on wobbly legs.

Willy hit him again on the head. Marty turned away.

When she looked back, the boy was lying on the ground and Willy was leaning into the car. 'Your turn, hot stuff,' he said to the girl. 'Come on.' He grabbed one of her hands and dragged her across the front seat.

Her free hand caught hold of the steering wheel. Willy tugged until she let go. Gasping with alarm, she tumbled backward out of the car. She landed on her back, legs in the air.

Making a show of gallantry, Willy helped her stand up. He turned her around and brushed the dust off the back of her knit shorts and jersey.

'Real cute,' he told Marty, looking over his shoulder and

beaming her a smile. 'Real class.' He patted the girl's rump. 'You'll look great in this outfit, honey. Think it'll fit? She hasn't got much in the tit department. What do you think?'

'Just leave her alone, Willy.'

'That's twice you've said my name, you dumb fuck.' He faced the girl. 'Take your clothes off.'

The girl stood rigid.

'Come on, hot stuff, strip.'

'The boy's clothes will fit me better,' Marty said.

'Shut up.'

'They will!'

'Strip,' he told the girl.

Marty threw open the door and started to climb out.

Turning, Willy pressed the muzzle between her eyes. It made a subtle ache, way back behind her eyes, like something she felt once while trying on the glasses of a friend. She sat back down in the car, but left the door open and kept her feet on the ground.

Willy jammed the barrel down the back of his jeans. He grabbed the girl's jersey at its waist and tried to lift it. She clamped down both arms, holding it in place.

'Get your arms up.'

She pressed them closer to her sides. Her mouth was a tight line.

'Okay,' Willy said. He let go of her. Taking out the pistol, he knelt by the unconscious boy. His thumb drew back the hammer. 'I'll give you five. Start stripping.'

The girl didn't move.

'One.'

She still didn't move. Marty glanced at the revolver. Its hammer, at full cock, looked like a vicious mouth about to snap shut.

'Two.'

The girl crossed her arms and gripped the bottom of her tight jersey. She peeled it off in a quick, fluid motion.

Marty felt sick for her.

'Three.'

She tucked the jersey under her chin and unbuckled her belt.

'Come on.'

Her fluttering hands opened her waist button, found the zipper tab and pulled.

'Four.'

The jersey fell, but she didn't stop to pick it up.

'Real nice,' Willy said.

Both her hands tugged the tight shorts down her legs.

'Five.'

'There!' she cried out. Naked except for her panties, she hugged her breasts and sobbed loudly. 'There! I'm done! There!'

Willy lowered the hammer with his thumb, then stuck the revolver into his jeans again. He picked up the girl's clothes, shook the dust off them, and tossed them to Marty. 'Get them on,' he told her.

'I'll have to stand up.'

'So stand up.'

He went to the girl and put his hands on her shoulders.

'Keep your mitts off her,' Marty said.

'Shut up and get dressed.'

Holding the clothes, Marty watched him slide his hands down the girl's arms. They moved down her sides. They caressed her hips. They clutched and rubbed her buttocks. Then they tore off her panties.

The girl tried to push him away.

'WILLY!'

He threw her to the ground.

'DON'T!' Marty shouted as he dropped on top of the girl. 'Stop it! Get off her!'

She dropped the clothes, grabbed Willy's arm and tried to pull him away. It was slippery with sweat. He got it free and swung at Marty. The girl under him lashed out with one hand, fingers hooked and spread like claws. Willy pulled up short on his swing at Marty and blocked the girl's attack.

Then he drove a fist down.

Marty heard it connect with the girl's nose. The naked body gave a grotesque lurch and lay still.

Willy got between the girl's legs.

Marty dived, tearing him off her. They rolled on the ground. When they stopped rolling, Willy was on top. He sat on Marty's chest, pinning her arms under her knees. With one hand, he pulled her hair until she gasped with pain. When her mouth opened, he jammed the gun barrel in.

It was thick and cold, and tasted of oil. Its front sight cut the roof of her mouth. It pressed far back toward her throat until she gagged.

# 23

'Lucky for you a stiff's no fun in the sack.' Willy laughed and pulled the gun out of Marty's mouth. Its front sight chipped a tooth. He climbed off her. 'Get dressed.'

Marty rolled over, choking, spitting gritty bits of tooth into the dirt.

'Now.'

She got to her feet and picked up the girl's shorts.

'Put them on.'

They fitted snugly. After she picked up the jersey, she knelt by the boy. He looked very still. Through the thin fabric of his shirt, she felt his body heat and the rise and fall of his breathing.

'Knock it off,' Willy said.

Ignoring him, Marty went to the girl. In the moonlight, her face looked black with blood. The nose was mashed sideways, its ridge broken.

'Put on her top.'

Marty turned her back to Willy and started to unbutton her blouse.

'Don't be shy,' he said. 'Just think of me as your guy. Which I am. The only guy you're ever gonna have.'

She didn't move.

'Turn around right now or else.'

She turned around. Facing him, she took off her wet blouse. Willy stared at her. Not drying herself, she pushed her hands through the jersey sleeves and pulled it over her head. It stuck to her wet skin.

Willy reached out a hand.

Marty backed away from him. And kept backing away until the side of the car stopped her.

'Sit down,' Willy said. 'Right there. On the ground. Better still, lie down.'

'What for?'

He grabbed the neck of her jersey and pulled. She went to her knees.

'Lie on your stomach.'

She did.

'Now stay that way.'

Kneeling down, Willy went through the boy's pockets. There was only a handkerchief and comb.

'Give him back his wallet,' Marty said.

'Shut the fuck up.'

He climbed into the car, found the girl's leather purse on the floor and dumped it on his lap. Marty, on the ground, couldn't see what fell out. But she saw Willy pick up a billfold and look inside. He grinned. 'Not bad. Kid's got rich folks.'

'Maybe she works.'

'Maybe we'll take her with us.'

'Great idea. Hold her for ransom?'

'Nope,' Willy said. He dropped the purse. 'Ransom, that'd be too much trouble. I'll just take her along for a little variety.'

'Broken nose and all?' Marty asked.

Not answering, he climbed out of the car and went to its front. There, he opened the hood. Her jerked a hose loose and threw it into the lake.

'Finished?' Marty asked.

'Not just yet.' He stepped over the unconscious boy and squatted beside the girl. 'See that? Look at the number I did on her nose.'

'I saw.'

'A real ugly mess, huh? But it's just from the neck up, and that isn't the part that counts. Know what I mean?' He reached down and patted the girl's right breast. 'Guess I'd better not take her with us. Not with her nose like this. People'd wonder.'

'They sure would.' Marty spat out a fleck of tooth. 'They'd ask a lot of questions.'

'Well, since I'm not taking her...' He picked up the girl's legs and turned her until the top of her head was toward Marty. Then he dropped her legs and got on his knees between them.

'Willy! No!'

'Yes, yes.' He pulled the pistol out of his belt and aimed it at Marty.

'God, don't.'

He laughed. 'Think I'm gonna pass up a piece like this?' He unzipped his jeans.

'Do me instead.'

'Thanks anyhow.'

'Willy, I'd be better. Hell, she's out cold. She'll just lie there.'

'You're for later. She's for now.'

'Don't do this to her.'

'Jealous?'

'Please.'

Willy, grinning, pulled his penis out of his jeans. It was big and upright.

'I'm not going to let you.'

'Can't stop me.'

'We'll see about...'

In the distance, a car engine rumbled and sputtered.

They both looked toward the entrance to the parking area. So far, there was no sign of headlights.

'It'll be here in a minute,' Marty said. 'It'll be the first of a whole bunch. The movie probably just got out. Pretty soon, this place will be crawling with horny teenagers.'

'I'm not quitting now.' Willy started to lower himself onto the girl.

Marty scurried backward, half expecting a bullet to smash through her body. She crawled to Willy's car, stretched across its

67

front seat and reached to the steering wheel.

As she shoved, the blare of Willy's car horn sounded through the night.

# 24

The driver's door flew open. The revolver came in, swinging. Marty jerked her hand away an instant before the barrel hammered the steering wheel where her fingers had been. The horn went silent.

'I'm gonna fix you for that. Fix you real good. Sit up! We gotta get out of here.'

He jumped into the car and slammed the door.

'Shut your door, damn it! I could've fucked that girl, you stupid bitch. Shut it!' His fist shot sideways, pounding Marty's arm as she leaned away. She pulled the door shut. Willy started the engine and backed up.

The headbeams lit the boy and girl. Their bodies were motionless, but Marty knew they were alive.

Alive and lucky.

Willy's car rolled over the bumpy road, out of the woods, onto the main road.

'Where'd that other car go?' Willy asked.

'I wouldn't know.'

'It was coming.'

'Maybe it turned off.'

'You said a whole bunch were coming.'

'Maybe I was wrong.'

'I oughta kill you.'

She looked out her window. There was nothing to see but dark woods.

She looked at her forearm and saw several places where splinters from the door had torn into her skin. She didn't seem to be bleeding, but the area around the cuts felt tender and sore.

Compared to the rest of her body, her arm was in good shape. Dizzying throbs pounded through her head. The roof of her mouth, cut by the gun sight, felt ragged and painful at the touch of her tongue. The front tooth was crooked and sharp. Her stomach seemed hollow and sour. Underneath the jersey and shorts, her skin itched because she'd still been wet when Willy made her put them on.

*You're in great shape, kid.*

*At least he didn't rape the girl.*

*Thank God.*

Marty slipped a hand down the back of her shorts and scratched her buttocks. They felt clammy.

'Do you mind if I get in the back seat?' she asked. 'I want to lie down.'

'Go on.'

She turned around, crawled awkwardly over the back of the front seat, and dropped onto the rear seat.

'Don't try and pull anything,' Willy warned. 'Remember who's in the trunk.'

'I remember.'

Putting her back to Willy, she curled onto her side and pillowed her head on her arm just above the splinter cuts.

She wanted to take off the damp clothes so that she could get dry.

But she didn't move.

*He'll look around and see me.*

So what? she thought. This wouldn't be the first time he's seen me naked. Anyhow, he'll only be able to see my back. And what's he going to do about it?

Trembling slightly, Marty struggled out of her jersey. Then she pulled the shorts down to her knees.

The warm night air blowing through the windows rushed against her skin, soothing it, caressing away the itchy dampness.

Willy didn't make a comment, didn't touch her.

*He doesn't even know.*

The air kept blowing against her, and soon the pains of the body no longer mattered. Only the warm dry smoothness of the moving air mattered. After a while, she fell asleep.

In her dream, Dan was late coming home from work. Apparently, she was married to him. And he was late. And she was worried. But suddenly the front door opened, and Dan came into the bright sunny room. He was naked.

'Where are your clothes?' Marty asked.

'I had to take them off and leave them in the trunk. They're all bloody.'

Now she noticed that Dan was all bloody.

'What happened?' she asked, not terribly concerned. But curious.

'Oh, I had a little run-in with one of your old boyfriends.'

'So, it's *his* blood?

'Mine. But I'm all right.'

He came toward her, arms spread out to hug her. His blood would get all over her. But she didn't mind. She was naked, too. She could simply take a shower. So she opened her arms for him.

Instead of stepping into her arms, he moved a hand up the back of her leg.

Which seemed an odd trick, since he was in front of her.

His fingers delved into the crevice of her rump.

Marty suddenly woke up and felt a hand back there. She flinched rigid. A finger thrust at her anus.

'Bastard!' she yelled.

Willy laughed.

Marty swung an arm down behind her, grabbed Willy by the wrist and jerked his hand away. Still clutching it, she flopped onto her back. Willy was twisted sideways in the driver's seat, watching her over his shoulder.

'Let go,' he said.

Clutching his arm with both hands, she tugged it down and backward.

Willy cried out and seemed to rise higher in his seat.

'Fucking bitch! I'll kill you.' Then he suddenly turned his head forward and yelled, 'SHIT!'

The brakes shrieked.

Marty flew forward and let go of his arm.

The car jerked, throwing her off the seat. She landed on the narrow floor. As she tried to get up, a whining skid sent her sprawling.

Somewhere, a horn blasted. A cry of brakes surged through the night.

But not from Willy's car.

*Toward* Willy's car.

Marty braced herself for the impact.

It didn't come.

Silence came instead.

The car stopped.

She took deep breaths, trying to calm down.

Nearby, two doors slammed. Then boots scuffled across the asphalt.

Marty thought about getting up from the floor.

But then the footsteps halted near Willy's side of the car and a man said, 'Look what we got here! Got a babe here, butt-naked.' He sounded excited.

'Sure as hell,' said a second voice, also male. It came from the passenger side of the car. 'Hey, honey,' it said. 'Honey, you all right there?'

She didn't move, didn't say a word.

'I think she's out of it, Stu.'

'So's this guy.'

'How come? We didn't hit 'em.'

'Reckon they're stoned.'

'Yeah, bet that's it.'

'Damn near got us killed, fuckin' drug fiends.'

'Let's fix 'em.'

'Fuckers damn near killed us, we oughta fix 'em good.'

The door at Marty's feet opened. Rough hands grabbed her ankles and started dragging her out.

She tried to kick free.

Still dragging her, the man called to his friend, 'Hey, this one's awake!'

'Good deal.'

'Come on over here and gimme a hand.'

He dragged her the rest of the way out of the car. As she fell to the pavement, a blast slammed through the warm night air.

He let go of Marty and called, 'Stu!'

Pushing herself up to her hands and knees, Marty saw her man start backing away fast, holding out his hands. He was a bald, skinny guy, maybe forty years old, and didn't wear a shirt. He made little whimpery sounds as he backed up.

The next shot from Willy's gun punched a hole in the middle of his chest.

# 25

Roger opened his eyes. Apparently, he'd dozed off. He rolled onto his side. Tina smiled at him. She looked very fresh and young in the mellow lamplight. Her body was a curved mound under the sheet. Her upthrust shoulder was bare. The fine, downy hair on her arms was golden.

'Did you like it?' she asked.

Roger smiled. 'Did I like what?'

'Remember?'

At the touch of her fingers, he squirmed and sighed. 'It's coming back to me,' he said.

'Was I good?' Tina asked.

'Ah, yes. As good as good can be.'

'Be serious.'

'Serious?'

She took away her caressing hand. She snuggled against Roger and pushed her forehead against his chest. 'Be very serious,' she said. She sounded as if she might start crying. Roger held her gently. 'Was I good really?' she asked again.

'You were fine.'

'Only fine?'

'You were fantastic. You *are* fantastic.'

'Really? Don't kid me. Tell me really.'

'Fantastic. Absolutely.'

'How many women have you been with?' she asked, her breath tickling his chest.

'I don't know.'

'Tell me,' she said. Her fingernails lightly scratched his hip.

'Oh, six or seven. Seven, I guess. You're number seven.'

'Now, tell me the truth.' Her fingernails stopped moving. Her hand flattened, warm on his skin. 'How was I? Compared to the others.'

'The best.'

'The very best?'

'Far and away the best. Easily. No comparison.'

'Cross your heart?' Her lips brushed the skin of his chest.

'Cross my heart and hope to die.'

Roger felt her hand move down from his hip. He moaned as her fingers curled around his penis.

'You sure I'm the best?' she asked.

'No doubt about it.'

For a long time, she said nothing. Her fingers continued to hold him. He grew harder and bigger. After a while, she said, 'There's nothing wrong with me?'

'Of course not.'

'Then why?' Her hand went away.

'Why what?'

She didn't answer. She rolled face down and pressed the pillow over her head.

Hearing her muffled sobs, Roger put a hand on her back.

# 26

Marty didn't know, until she woke up, that she had passed out after the shooting.

Even before opening her eyes, she knew that she was not in Willy's car. This car's engine was quiet. Its air was cool. Too cool. She put a hand on her thigh and felt goosebumps. She moved her feet. The shorts were down around her ankles.

Opening her eyes, she saw the jersey wadded on the seat

73

between her and Willy. She reached for it. Willy's hand came down on hers. He grinned at her. She jerked her hand away, taking the jersey. As fast as she could, she put it on and pulled up the shorts.

Willy laughed.

Marty said nothing. She sat motionless, arms folded across her chest, and wondered if Willy had raped her while she'd been passed out.

No, she didn't think so.

'Real class, huh?' he asked.

'What?'

'The car. Real class. Air-conditioning, the works.'

'How long was I out?'

'Who knows? I didn't time you. Did you see the way I capped those motherfuckers?'

'I saw enough.'

'What a kick.'

She closed her eyes and rubbed her face with both hands.

'Too bad you weren't awake when I moved your Danny boy.'

'Convenient,' she muttered into her hands.

'Huh?'

'I just happened to be unconscious when you changed cars.'

He laughed. 'Not my fault you faint at the sight of a little blood. What, you worried I didn't put Danny boy in our trunk?'

'I don't think he was ever in *any* trunk.'

'Think whatever you want. He's in the trunk.'

'Then stop and show me.'

'Get fucked.'

'You killed him, didn't you?'

'If you say so. See if those bozos got any maps in the glove compartment, huh? I'll show you where we're going.'

'I don't care.'

'Sure you do.' He punched her in the arm. 'Open it.'

She opened the glove compartment.

'What's in there?'

'Some maps, gas receipts, Kleenex.'

And a fifth of Kentucky bourbon that she decided not to mention.

'What about a Wisconsin map?'

She pulled out the stack of maps, found the Wisconsin map and put the others away.

'Open it up.'

She spread the map open.

'Okay. See a town called Marshall up to the left?'

'I can't see anything.'

Willy turned on the ceiling light. It cast a dim yellow glow onto the map.

'Look near the top. A couple of inches from the top. Marshall.'

'I don't see any Marshall. There's a Gribsby here.'

'Down the road from Gribsby.'

'Mawkeetaw?'

'Down a bit more. Marshall. See it?'

'Yeah.'

'Okay. Now, there's a lake over a bit to the right.'

'Cricket?'

'That's her. See a little blue dot beside Cricket?'

'No.'

'A little tiny dot. A speck.'

'I don't see anything there.'

'Well, some maps show it, some don't. Anyhow, that's where we're heading. For the speck.' He turned off the overhead light. 'A real nice little lake. More like a pond. And you know the nice thing about it? Nobody ever goes there. Not a single motherfucking soul.'

'Why not?' Marty tongued her chipped tooth.

'Fishing stinks. You can't ski 'cause there ain't enough room. And it's harder than hell to find. There's only one way in. You gotta take this shitty little dirt road that's so fucked up you can hardly drive on it. Won't be easy to find at night.'

'Am I supposed to be your navigator?'

'Yep. But we still got a ways to go. You can put it away for a while.'

She folded the map, but did it wrong.

'Nobody ever teach you how to fold a map?' Willy asked.

'My education has been sadly neglected.'

He laughed. 'Bet you learned a thing or two tonight.'

She dropped the map to the floor, and turned her face to the window. In her mind, she saw the shirtless man get knocked off his feet, a hole between his nipples.

'Yeah,' she muttered. 'I learned a thing or two.'

Suddenly, her stomach twisted.

*He's a murderer.*

It changed things.

Before, she had been a victim for Willy to kidnap and rape and brutalize any way he wanted. Bad enough.

Plenty bad enough.

But now, she was a witness to two murders.

*He has to kill me.*

*I've gotta get out of here!*

*What about Dan? If he's alive in the trunk . . .*

*I have to save him.*

She took a deep, shaking breath, and said, 'Thirsty?'

'Huh?'

She opened the glove compartment and took out the heavy glass bottle of bourbon.

'Holy shit! Good deal!'

Marty unscrewed the plastic cap, tilted the bottle to her mouth and took two quick swallows.

'Save some for the fishies!'

She handed the bottle to Willy.

He drank. Then he said, 'Good stuff.'

'Sure is,' Marty agreed. She smiled at him. The bourbon seemed to be burning out the bottom of her stomach.

Willy offered the bottle.

'Thanks,' she said, taking it.

'Just don't make a pig outa yourself.'

She tilted the bottle up.

The bourbon splashed against her tight lips. None got into her

76

mouth. She lowered the bottle, wiped her lips dry, and handed it back to Willy.

'Why don't we listen to some music?' she suggested, and reached for the radio.

The bottle knocked her hand away. 'I don't like music.'

'It'd be nice and relaxing.'

'We can relax at the cabin,' he said, and took a swallow. 'Just a couple more hours.'

'Can't we listen to music?'

'Music sucks.'

'Then is it okay if I take a nap?'

'Sure thing. Wanta take off your clothes again?'

'No.'

He laughed.

Marty made a show of stretching and yawning. Then she leaned against the passenger door and lifted her legs onto the seat. She wiggled as if trying to find a more comfortable position, and let her bare feet slip out from under her. They touched Willy's hip.

''Nother drink?' he asked.

'Sure.' She stretched out her arm, pressing her feet harder against him. She pretended to take a swig.

'Have more.'

She pretended to swig again. Then she handed the bottle back to Willy, and sighed loudly.

'Lucky for you my hands are full,' Willy told her.

Grinning, he took a drink.

Marty curled her toes against the side of his leg. She bent toward him. He gave her the bottle. While she lifted it to her mouth, Willy's free hand caressed her legs. She lowered her feet to the floor and scooted a little closer to him. His hand moved up her thigh, but she set down the bottle in its way. Laughing, he took hold of the bottle and picked it up. 'What'll you do when it's empty?' he asked.

'I just don't know,' she said.

'You'll get fucked, that's what.'

'Oh, yeah?' She started to move away from him.

He planted the bottle between his legs and threw an arm across her shoulders, stopping her. She relaxed against him. He lifted his arm off her, retrieved the bottle and drank several large swallows.

He clamped the bottle between his thighs again, and returned his arm to her shoulders.

'Let me.' She reached over and plucked out the bottle. When she raised it to her mouth, Willy's arm pushed downward between her back and the seat. She leaned forward, sipping. His hand went under her jersey.

Marty didn't resist.

She drank, instead.

His hand moved slowly up her side. It was warm and dry. The fingers were long. They caressed her skin as they roamed higher.

Marty took a big swallow of bourbon when the hand found her breast.

It tickled, it massaged, it squeezed.

Lowering the bottle, Marty clutched his hand and pressed it harder against her breast. She moaned. Clamping the bottle between her legs to free her other hand, she grabbed Willy's thigh.

'Go for it, honey,' he said.

Marty squeezed his thigh until it must've hurt. Groaning, Willy dug his teeth into her shoulder. The car swerved. His groaning changed to a gasp of alarm. The hand under Marty's jersey went still as he focused on steering.

When the car straightened out, he laughed and yelled, 'Yeah!' and gave her breast a tweak.

Marty flinched and grabbed his wrist. 'Quit it, now,' she said.

'Yeah?'

'Yeah. I've been through a hell of a lot with you, Willy. I'll probably go through lots more. But not, if I can help it, a windshield.'

'Maybe I'd better pull over, huh?'

'Maybe so,' Marty said.

But he didn't.

## 27

Roger stroked the length of Tina's back, and kissed her shoulder. Still she continued to cry. He started to ask her what was wrong, but stopped himself. He was tired of asking, and tired of being answered with speechless sobs.

'I wish you'd stop that,' he finally said. 'I hate it when a woman cries. Is it something *I* did?'

A muffled 'No' came from under the pillow.

'Something I *didn't* do or say?'

'It isn't you.'

'Well, that's nice to know. I wish you'd told me that half an hour ago.' He pulled the pillow off her head. She looked up at him. Hair hung in her eyes. She pushed the hair away, and her eyes were red.

'What is it?' Roger asked. 'I mean, you don't have to tell me, but maybe I can help. You never know. I'll help you if I can.'

'Thanks,' Tina said.

'Do you want to talk about it?'

'I don't know.'

'You might feel better if you talk about it. That's what they always say, anyway. I don't know how true it is.'

She sniffed and said nothing.

'Is it a guy?'

She nodded.

'What did he do? Did he hurt you?'

She rolled onto her back and looked at the ceiling. 'I found him with . . . making love with somebody. Right in the store. Right behind the counter. He was going to marry me.' A tear trickled from the corner of her eye, down her temple and into her ear. With a fingertip, she rubbed it out of her ear. She wiped her eyes.

'Who was the girl?'

'I don't know. Someone from Camp Wahtooki. It's a summer camp down the road from town. A *girl's* camp. She was maybe a counselor, or something. She had one of those camp station wagons, so I guess she must be a counselor. The bitch.'

'Do you think the guy is serious about her?'

'It looked serious to me. Brad was screwing her.'

'I mean, have they been seeing each other?'

'I don't know. How should I know? He's with me nearly all the time when he's not working. Maybe she visits him at the bait shop every day. I don't know, I just walked in on him. It was like one of those dumb things that happens on TV. But, hell, you know, I drop in on him all the time and . . . I've never caught him doing *that* before.'

'Did you talk to him about it?'

'Are you kidding?'

'No. Maybe it was completely innocent.'

'How could it be innocent? He was *humping* the bitch.'

'What I mean is, maybe it didn't mean anything.'

'It means plenty when you get down on the floor and stick your weenie in a woman. Doesn't it?'

'Usually,' Roger admitted. 'But the thing is, any normal guy is going to do it to a good-looking gal if the opportunity presents itself. Especially if he's not married. Even if he is, maybe, depending on the guy.'

'God, that's nice.'

'It can be nothing more than a physical thing. There doesn't always have to be a big emotional involvement.'

'*We were going to get married!*'

'So?' Roger said.

She glared at him.

'I'm not claiming it's right. I'm only saying it sometimes will happen, and maybe the guy really does love you and just got . . . involved, carried away. It happens. It almost happened to me. Several times.'

'Almost?'

'I guess the Boy Scout in me won out against the lech. I was married then. Somehow, I always managed to resist the temptations. It wasn't easy. Some of those gals . . . Now I sometimes wish I'd gone ahead. Faithful, boring Roger should've put it to every babe in sight. If I'd known what my dear wife was up to, I would've had myself a field day.'

'She was playing around?'

Roger couldn't answer. He lay on his back and rubbed his face. It made him feel weary and sick to remember. Finally, he said, 'I wanted to kill her when I found out.'

'I wanted to kill myself,' Tina said.

'Instead, we both ran away.'

'Yep.'

'That's because we have high moral character.'

'Is that why?' Tina asked, and smiled.

'But of course. What'd you say the guy's name is? The guy that cheated on you?'

'Brad.'

'Tell you what, why don't you give him a call?'

'I can't do that.'

'Sure you can. I told you that I'd help, didn't I? Well, this is my help. Advice based on years of wisdom. Phone Brad. Give him a chance. Give yourself a chance. Just call and see what happens.'

'I don't know.'

'Go ahead. The phone's right there beside you.'

'I can't just *call* him.'

'Sure you can.'

She shook her head.

'Go on. You want to. I know you want to.'

'I guess so, but . . .'

'Then do it.'

'Well . . .'

'I'll go into the bathroom if you don't want me to listen.'

'No, stay.' She rolled onto her side, facing away from Roger.

He put his hand on her bare shoulder.

She swung her feet off the bed and sat up. Leaning forward, she reached to the telephone and lifted its handset.

'Do you know his number?' Roger asked.

She nodded.

'Probably press nine for an outside line, then do the area code and number. That's how these things usually work.'

'Should I reverse the charges?'

'This is on me.' He put his hand on her shoulder again. He could feel her trembling. 'Just go ahead,' he told her.

She tapped in the numbers, and waited.

They both waited.

Then she said, 'Hi, it's me.' Silence. Then, 'I don't know, somewhere down south. Near a place called Wayside, I think . . . I managed . . . Yes, I thumbed . . . I know how dangerous it is. So what? A lot you care . . . You know what I mean. I saw you with her. Behind the counter . . . Yes, that.'

There was a long silence. As she listened to the phone, Tina began to cry softly. Roger kissed the back of her shoulder.

'I don't know,' she said into the phone. 'It hurt, Brad. It really hurt . . . I love you, too . . . Sure, I do . . . You don't have to do that. Just go to bed and I'll see you in the morning . . . The same way I got here . . . No, don't. I'm starting back now, so if you drive down we'll probably miss each other . . . Yes, I'll be careful. Could you give my parents a call and tell them I'm okay? . . . I love you, too.'

She hung up. Then she eased down onto her back, reached up and curled a hand behind Roger's neck. She drew his head down and kissed him on the mouth. 'Thank you,' she said.

'My pleasure.'

Then she got off the bed and picked up her paisley dress.

'What are you doing?' Roger asked.

'I'm going back to Brad.'

'Now?'

'Yup.'

'Why wouldn't you let him pick you up?'

She pulled the shiny dress over her head, saying, 'I can't let him see me like this.'

'Like what?'

'I'm a mess. My dress is torn.'

'How do you plan to get home?'

'Hitch a ride.'

'At this hour?'

'I'll manage.' She buttoned the front of her dress.

'It's too dangerous. Let me drive you.'

'Nah. I'll be fine. It'd be all out of your way, and . . .'

'I don't mind.'

'Thanks, but . . . nah. I'm going back to my *guy*, you know? Wouldn't be right, you taking me. Not after what we did.'

'But it's the middle of the night.'

'I can take care of myself.'

'Why don't you at least stay here till morning? Maybe we can find somebody in the coffee shop. Somebody nice and reliable to give you a lift home. Preferably of the female persuasion.'

'I can't wait that long.' Done with the dress, she stepped over to Roger. 'Thanks so much for everything. You've been great, really great.' She bent over and kissed him.

He didn't let himself enjoy the soft touch of her lips or the warmth of her body. In minutes, she would be gone. He would probably never see her again. It was better, now, to let himself get no closer to her. 'I hope everything works out,' he said.

'Thanks.'

'You really ought to wait for morning.'

'I know, but I can't.'

'It won't be safe out there. Everybody in the world isn't . . . there are lots of nuts out there.'

'Fiends, too,' Tina said. She smiled gently and pushed her fingers through his hair. 'I'll always remember you, Roger.'

'I'll remember you, too. Sure will.'

'You go to sleep, now.'

After watching her leave, he rolled to her side of the bed, reached up and turned off the lamp. Then he lay back. He stared for a long time into the darkness, wondering about what he'd just lost.

# 28

Willy took a long pull at the bourbon and gave the bottle to Marty.

She pretended to drink while Willy drew his fingernails up the inner side of her thigh. The nails made her squirm with a sickish, hurting tingle. Then his hand pressed between her legs and rubbed her through the soft cloth of the shorts.

The headlights caught a road sign. Willy's hand stopped moving and he read aloud, 'Wayside. Pop, a thousand 'n twenty-two. Issa biggy.'

There were a few homes scattered along the roadsides, most of them dark at the windows as if abandoned to the night. At the edge of town, the Dairy Queen was open and crowded.

'Lookit all the babes!' Willy slowed down and stared out at them. 'Nice. Really really nice. Hey, lookit the titties on that one!'

'Want her instead of me?' Marty asked, trying to sound annoyed. 'You can take *her* to your cabin.'

'Shit, I'd take ya both. Wouldn' mind that. Wouldn' mind at all. Not a bit. Little variety . . . I'd screw ya one adda time, 'n both at once. Wouldn' mind that.'

But he kept on driving. Past a closed gas station, into the town's business district. All the stores were closed. Some kept their signs turned on, but most didn't. Every store had a light inside casting a dim, lonely glow onto the deserted sidewalks in front. The marquee of the movie theater near the end of town was dark. Its ticket booth was empty. Through the glass doors of the lobby, Marty could see a man in a purple coat talking with a uniformed girl at the snack counter.

'How come you didn't stop for that queen of tits at the Dairy Queen?' Marty finally asked. 'Thought you wanted . . .'

'You'd of tried to get away.'

'No, I wouldn't. Not anymore. I've been . . . remembering. How it was the last time.' She rubbed his hand against her groin. 'How good it felt.'

'You were screaming.'

'Just 'cause I was scared. But I loved how you felt. Inside me. I *want* you inside me. Just like before.'

'Liked it, huh?'

'It was the best ever. If we weren't in this damn town, I'd make you pull off the road right now and fuck me.'

84

'We'll be outa here in a minute.'

'Hurry.' She stood the bottle on his leg. Willy took his hand away from her and lifted the bottle to his mouth. As he drank, Marty squeezed the front of his jeans. His penis was hard. She felt it move under her hand.

The tires bumped over railroad tracks at the end of town.

Pretty soon, Marty thought. Can't let the town get too far behind.

There were houses on both sides of the road. Then an open gas station, a cafe called Bab's Burgers, a motel with its big sign flashing 'Wayside Motor Inn'.

'A motel!' Marty blurted. 'Why don't we go in and get a room?' She gave him another gentle squeeze. 'Think how nice it would be. We'd have a bed.'

They had already left the motel behind, but Marty didn't give up.

'Come on, Willy. It'd be great. You oughta turn around. We'd have a big old bed. And a shower. We could take a shower together. Have you ever done it in the shower? We'd both be all slippery...'

'Shit!' Willy blurted. 'Lookit *her*!'

Marty saw her, and groaned.

It was a girl, probably no older than sixteen, slim and blonde and walking backward along the roadside, her arm out, her hand closed, her thumb pointing behind her. She wore a paisley dress skimpy enough to guarantee rides from men.

Willy's foot lifted off the gas pedal.

'Don't stop,' Marty whispered.

The girl took a wide stance, her dress drawing taut across her crotch.

'Shit!' Willy said.

Now the girl was behind them, and Willy's foot was lowering onto the brake pedal.

'Don't stop, honey. You have me.' Marty capped the bourbon bottle and set it on the floor. 'You don't need anyone but me.'

'Need her.'

The car stopped. Marty looked over her shoulder. The girl,

bathed in the eerie redness of the rear lights, was starting to jog forward.

*So young . . .*

*Too damn young! Just a kid.*

'Drive,' Marty said.

She jerked open Willy's belt, unbuttoned his jeans and pulled the zipper down. He had no underwear on. His penis was a thick, pale column tilting upward, its tip almost touching the steering wheel.

Marty heard footfalls in the gravel. In the side mirror, she saw the girl hurrying toward them.

Closer and closer . . .

Only a few strides away . . .

'Drive!' Marty said and dropped down toward Willy's lap and took him into her mouth and sucked.

Willy stepped on the gas.

'Hey!' the girl yelled.

Willy sped away from her.

Marty slid her mouth, licking and sucking.

'Uhhh, yeah,' Willy gasped. 'Yeah. Oh, babe! Suck me off. Do it, do it! C'mon!'

She had saved the girl.

*He might go back to her if I stop.*

She kept on.

*Gotta get him into the woods. Away from the car and Dan.*

*If Dan's even still in the trunk.*

*If Dan's even alive.*

If she finished Willy with her mouth, he might not bother taking her into the woods. He might take her straight to the cabin.

*Don't wanta go there.*

She tried to take her mouth away, but Willy gripped the back of her head and held her down.

Pushed her down, ramming deep.

She gagged and struggled to pull away but Willy only forced her head down harder.

*Bite him!*

*He'd kill me for sure.*

But she was choking. It was blocking her throat. She tried to breathe through her nose, but couldn't.

Her hand reached up and found the steering wheel.

She grabbed the wheel and tugged.

Willy's hand leaped away from the back of her head.

Marty, still clutching the wheel, resisting Willy's efforts to turn it, shoved herself up until her mouth was empty.

She was still choking when the car swerved to the side of the road and skidded to a stop.

# 29

'Coulda got us killed,' Willy said. 'That's twice . . .'

'I'm sorry, sweetheart, but I couldn't breathe. I didn't mean to grab the wheel.' She leaned against him, kissed him, and lowered her hand onto his lap. She lightly wrapped her fingers around him. He was as big as before, wet and slick from her mouth. 'Let's go in the woods now,' she whispered.

'Sure. Why the hell not. Where's the bottle?'

Marty found it under the seat, and sat up with it. Shaking it, she heard sloshing sounds; some bourbon still remained in it.

Willy finished fastening his jeans. Then he shoved the car keys into his right front pocket. He climbed out, the revolver in his hand, and pushed its barrel down the front of his waistband. 'Bring the bottle with ya,' he said.

Marty opened her door. The night air rushed in. It was cooler than before, but felt balmy after the chill of the air-conditioner. She climbed out and shut the door.

Willy came over to her side of the car. 'Let's go this way,' he said. He draped an arm over her shoulders and she led him down a grassy embankment. At the bottom, the ground was springy and wet. Water pressed up between Marty's toes. But the ground was dry on the slope. She climbed higher. Just beyond the top of the ditch, the trees began.

'Don' wanna go far,' Willy said, pulling back at the edge of the forest.

Marty kissed him on the mouth. 'We wanta get away from the road, don't we? 'Case somebody comes by?'

He answered by squeezing her breast. Then he said, 'Gimme the bottle, honey.'

She handed it to him, then led him forward. They walked past tree trunks, clumps of bushes, more trees, deeper and deeper into the woods, farther from the car. Farther from Dan in the trunk.

*If he's in the trunk.*

Finally, they came to a small, moonlit clearing. 'How about here?' Marty asked.

Willy swung her around. She hugged him. One of his hands slipped under the back of her jersey and roamed her bare skin. The other, holding the bottle outside her jersey, pressed her tightly against him.

The revolver dug into her belly.

*Get my hands on it . . .*

She lowered a hand, squeezed Willy's thigh, raised her hand to the hard bulge, squeezed and fondled him there as his mouth pressed her lips roughly and his tongue pushed between her teeth. Sneaking her hand sideways, she felt the steel barrel through his jeans.

'Wrong gun,' he gasped into her mouth.

She pulled his zipper down and reached into the open fly.

His hand was no longer under her jersey. It bumped against her hand, and she wondered for a moment what he was up to.

As she slipped him out through his fly, he unfastened the front of her shorts.

*That's what.*

She raised her hand to his belt buckle.

Her knuckles brushed the wooden grip of the revolver.

*Now! Do it now! Grab it!*

But her hand wouldn't move. It stayed at the belt buckle, trembling.

Willy started tugging at her shorts. They were tight. He jerked and dragged at them until he got them down around her knees.

They were loose there. When he let go of them, they dropped to her ankles.

He pushed his hand between her thighs.

*Grab his gun!*

A finger slipped into her.

With a gasp, she staggered backward. The shorts caught her ankles. Caught and held and tripped her.

Willy held on.

Held on and went down with her as she fell and smashed her hard against the ground.

The pistol butt rammed into her belly.

The bottle under her back broke.

From the clink it made before bursting, Marty guessed it had struck a rock.

The back of her jersey was suddenly soaked with bourbon. And maybe blood. She felt glass in her skin.

'The bottle broke,' she said.

'Yeah?' Willy pulled his arm out from under her.

'I'm cut,' Marty said. 'It's under my back. It's in pieces. It's cutting me. You've gotta get off.'

'Yeah?'

'Please.' There were pieces buried in her skin. She felt numb in places. Other places were starting to sting, and streams of blood were tickling along the arch of her back. 'Just get off me for a second . . .'

Willy pushed himself up and sat across her hips.

She started to raise her back off the ground, but he clutched her throat and held her down.

'Please, Willy.'

Grinning, he shook his head. Either he was too drunk to understand or care about the glass under Marty, or he liked the idea of grinding her into it.

Pleading, she thought, might only make it worse.

Willy pulled the revolver out of his jeans, tossed it on the wet grass about six feet away, and unbuckled his belt.

'Honey,' Marty said, trying to stay calm. 'Let go of my throat, okay?' She crossed her arms over her belly and started to pull up the jersey. 'I can't get it off without sitting up.'

He leaned back, taking his hand from her neck, and finished opening his jeans. Then he took off his shirt and threw it aside.

As Marty slowly raised her back off the ground, she pulled the jersey up. It was sticky with blood. Shards of glass pulled loose from her back, dropped and tinked against others. When the jersey was off, she flung it away. Sitting upright, she wrapped her arms around Willy and hugged him tightly . . .

And twisted to the left so they tumbled sideways, rolling.

She came down on her side. Though she felt no broken glass, she knew it couldn't be more than a few inches away. So she wrestled Willy onto his back. Stretched out on top of him, she pushed her open mouth against his.

Reaching out with one arm, she patted the dewy grass. Stretched her fingers.

Then had to look.

The revolver lay three or four inches beyond her fingertips.

Willy squirmed beneath her, trying to force her legs apart.

They suddenly rolled onto their sides. Farther from the gun.

Marty swung a leg over him and forced him onto his back again. Straddling him, she reached out for the revolver.

He clutched her buttocks and thrust.

Marty grabbed the gun by its barrel.

Willy's penis rammed deep into her, throbbing and squirting.

She swung the pistol and clubbed the side of his head.

Willy yelped. His body jerked rigid, and he suddenly went limp. Except for the part that was buried in Marty.

Still rigid, it kept jumping and spurting for a few seconds after the rest of Willy seemed to be unconscious.

As fast as she could, Marty climbed off.

On her feet, she took a couple of steps backward, then stopped and reversed the revolver and took aim at Willy.

He wasn't hard any more.

He lay motionless on the ground.

Marty felt blood running down her back, her buttocks, and the backs of her legs. She felt semen dribble out of her and trickle down her left thigh.

Soon, Willy moaned and pressed a hand against his ear. He squirmed a little.

When he opened his eyes, Marty thumbed back the hammer and aimed at his face.

'Don't,' he said. The word came out like a groan of pain and fear. 'Please, don't shoot me.'

'Dirty rotten bastard,' she said.

'Please.'

'Don't move.' Keeping the gun leveled at him, she crouched and picked up his shirt. She wiped herself with it and flung it at him. He cringed as if he expected the shirt to burn him. When it fell onto his legs, he flinched.

'Don't move,' Marty repeated.

Trying to keep the revolver aimed at Willy as much as possible, she put on her shorts. Then she picked up her torn, bloody jersey. She put the gun through its right sleeve and used her left hand to pull the jersey up her arm and over her head. For a few moments, she was blind. But when she could see again, Willy was still on his back.

She changed the gun to her left hand, worked it under the jersey and out through the left sleeve.

'Okay,' she said, the jersey still rucked up above her breasts. 'Pull your pants up.'

As he drew the jeans up his legs, Marty tugged her jersey down. It felt heavy and wet and sticky against her back. It hurt her cuts, but she was glad to be dressed.

She waited for Willy to finish with his jeans. Then she told him to put on his shirt.

When he had it on, she said, 'Stand up.'

'Where we going?' he asked.

'Back to the car. Let's go.'

Trying to get to his feet, he staggered and fell down. But he tried again. This time, he made it.

'Walk ahead of me,' Marty told him.

He turned his back to her and started walking. He walked awkwardly, sometimes stumbling.

Marty followed him, staying a few paces back and out of reach. Soon after they entered the thick trees, she uncocked the gun to prevent it from going off by accident.

It seemed to take a very short time to reach the edge of the woods.

Marty followed Willy down the grassy slope to where the ground was soggy, and up the embankment to the road. Willy stopped beside the car and turned around to face her.

'Open the trunk,' she ordered.

'Okay,' said Willy. But he didn't move.

'Now.'

'Whatcha gonna do if I don't?'

'Shoot you and open it myself.'

'You ain't gonna shoot me.'

'Just open the trunk and . . .'

He lurched toward Marty, reaching for the gun.

She pulled the trigger.

Nothing happened.

Willy grabbed the barrel. As he jerked the gun away from her, he punched her in the face.

Marty dropped to her knees.

'It's single action,' he said. 'You dumb fuck. Gotta *cock* it.'

His fist came in, smashing her face again. And again. And again. She slumped backward.

Willy said something, but she couldn't hear him through the ringing in her ears. She tried to get up. Her legs were bent behind her and her arms wouldn't work right.

Willy walked toward the rear of his car.

Marty struggled to her knees. Her head drooped. It felt as heavy as lead. The side of her face was burning from the punches. She wanted to let her arms fold, to stretch out on the ground and lie there, on and on.

Instead, groaning with pain, she raised her head. She saw Willy open the trunk of the car. She wanted to ask him what he was doing, but she didn't have the strength. Then she saw him raise the revolver, cock it, and aim into the trunk.

'NO!' she screamed.

The gun blasted, leaping in his hand.

Marty struggled to her feet and staggered to the back of the car. Before Willy could grab her, she glimpsed Dan's face in the darkness of the trunk.

The top of his head was partly gone.

'NO!'

She kicked and squirmed in Willy's arms, but couldn't get loose until her teeth found his ear and she bit it hard. His yell of pain stunned her for a second. Then she realized that he had let go of her.

She dashed to the edge of the embankment and jumped as far as she could. She made it almost to the bottom before her heels hit the wet grass. Her legs flew forward and her rump hit the slope. She slid the rest of the way down, then scrambled to her feet and ran, splashing through the soggy grass.

'Stop!' Willy shouted.

Her legs chugged, carrying her up the rise on the other side of the ditch.

From behind her came the sound of a metallic *clank*.

The gun hammer dropping.

But there must've been no live round in the chamber, because there was only the *clank* and no blast.

She reached the top of the slope.

Broke into a sprint for the woods.

A root snagged her foot.

As she lurched forward, falling headlong, a gunshot split the night.

# 30

Willy grinned when he saw the girl walking backward alongside the road ahead, her thumb out. The same girl he'd tried to stop for, back near that town.

She must've passed his car while he'd been out in the woods with Marty.

She'd gone a pretty good distance, too.

A mighty quick walker.

He stopped his car beside her. 'Want a lift?' he called out the passenger window.

'Man, oh man, *do* I!'

The light inside the car came on when she opened the door, and Willy got a good look at her.

Nice. Real nice.

He always did like the young stuff, and the way this gal's dress was clinging to her skin . . . He watched it slide up her thighs when she climbed into the car.

'Where're you headed?' he asked.

'Gribsby.'

'I'm going as far as Marshall.'

'Oh, that's fine.' Her voice seemed awfully cheerful for so late at night. 'That's great. I'm sure I'll be able to find a ride from Marshall.'

'Probably.'

She sighed loudly with relief or pleasure.

She folded her arms below her breasts, slouched down in the seat, and smiled at him. 'This is great,' she said. 'It sure feels good to be heading home.'

# 31

Rolling over, Marty crossed an arm over her face to block the bright sunlight. Then she opened her eyes. When the air touched them, they felt raw and burning. She saw that she was stretched out along the edge of a forest.

For a while, she didn't remember. Then it all came back. She moaned as it poured into her like a foul liquid, burning and nauseating.

Suddenly, she sat up. She could see the road.

The road, but no car.

Willy was gone!

The quick movement did it. She twisted sideways and threw up. When the convulsions stopped, she crawled away from the mess.

She heard a car coming. Afraid Willy might be returning, she flattened herself on the ground. After it was gone, she got slowly to her feet. She leaned against the trunk of a birch tree and felt blood begin to trickle down her back.

The forest seemed safer than the road, so she walked into it. Walking hurt badly. Her head was the worst part. It jolted with each step and throbbed madly every time she bent to pass beneath a low limb.

At last, she came to a sunny clearing. Maybe the same clearing as last night. She couldn't be sure. It didn't matter, though. The clearing was bright and well hidden. She only cared about that.

Lying face down on the tall grass, she found it softer than she hoped. It didn't even feel scratchy on her bare arms and legs. It simply matted down under her, soft and dry, as if it had been put there especially to serve as her bed.

She lay with her eyes shut, half awake, half dreaming, and at first she thought that the quietly approaching footsteps were part of her dream. Then she opened her eyes and saw a pair of moccasins.

# 32

Willy stretched and groaned with lazy pleasure. The sun felt so hot and good. If it weren't for his bastard of a headache, life would be perfect.

The bitch had really given him a wallop with that gun.

He grinned. He'd really given her a wallop, too. With a different kind of gun.

He opened his eyes, lifted his head and looked down his sweaty body at it. Wouldn't do at all if it got sunburned. Especially not now, with so much good stuff ahead.

*Speaking of which* . . .

He got off the blanket and walked to his shack. 'Here I am,

sweetums. William the Conqueror.' He posed in the doorway flexing his muscles.

The girl in the shadows shut her eyes. She lay curled on her side on the mattress, naked, her arms handcuffed behind her back.

Reaching high, Willy plucked a key down from the top of the doorframe. 'Have you been a good girl?' he asked, walking toward her.

'Yes,' she muttered.

'Do you want William to let you go?'

Her eyes opened and she nodded.

Willy leaned over her with the key, opened the left cuff, then the right. His fingers came away bloody. He wiped them on the white skin of the girl's buttocks.

'Now put on your beautiful dress,' he told her.

She sat up and brought her arms slowly in front of her. She frowned at her raw, bloody wrists.

'Oh, did I have the cuffs too tight?' Willy asked.

'Where are we going?' the girl asked.

'It's a surprise.'

She tried to pick up her shining, paisley dress, but her hands wouldn't work. The dress fell. Willy picked it up. She raised her arms, and he put it over them. It drifted down her body.

Willy helped her to stand. Then he fastened every button on the dress.

'Let's go outside,' he said.

As she stepped out the doorway, she raised an arm to shade her face from the noon sun.

'Bright, huh?'

She said nothing.

Willy picked up his handcuffs and rope, then followed her outside. 'Go over to that dead tree,' he told her.

She looked around at him. She glanced at the rope and cuffs in his hand. Then she looked toward the woods that began several yards to the left of the white, barkless poplar.

'Don't try to run,' he said. 'I'll just chase you down, and then I'll *really* have some fun with you.'

She walked to the dead tree.

'That's right. Good girl. Now put out your hands. That's a good girl.'

Her eyes stayed on his eyes, making him a little nervous as he handcuffed her wrists. He knotted the rope to the chain between the bracelets, then flung the coil over a high, thick branch of the poplar. It dropped on the other side. He took the end and began to pull, raising the girl's arms.

'I haven't given you any trouble,' she said quietly. 'I've done everything you asked, no matter how . . . no matter what it was. Why do you have to hurt me?'

''Cause I like it.' He tied the rope to the trunk of the dead tree. 'See how nice I am? I'm leaving you on your feet. Or would you rather sort of *dangle*?'

She shook her head.

'Now guess what I'm going to do,' he said.

Staring into his eyes, she said, 'I don't know.'

'Come on, guess.' His hands roamed the shiny, slick cloth. It was already hot from the sun. He felt her body through it.

The girl gritted her teeth.

'Gonna rip the dress off you,' Willy said.

'No, don't. Please. It was a present. Don't wreck it.'

He slapped her face.

Then, growling like a dog, sometimes biting the skin underneath, he slowly shredded the dress with his teeth. The girl cried as he ripped. When she finally was naked, he took her from behind with quick hard thrusts that rammed her up off her feet.

Later, he left her hanging in the sun.

He rested in a shaded place near the car and enjoyed the view.

# 33

When Marty opened her eyes, there was no longer a headache behind them. The curtains rustled with a mild breeze. Light slanted down through the window, laying a slab of gold on the floor. A clock by the bed showed 3:15.

Sitting up, she looked in front of her. A dresser, a closet. Heavy hiking boots stood on the closet floor next to a pair of sneakers. On hangers, she saw a plaid lumberjack coat among many shirts, a dark suit, a colorful sport coat and a white terry-cloth bathrobe.

She got up. The mirror above the dresser threw back her reflection, stunning her. She hardly looked like herself. Her face was swollen and discolored. Her hair was a wild tangle.

Well, her right profile didn't look too bad. Willy had only struck the left side of her face.

*Why did he leave me?*

She didn't want to think about it.

She opened the bedroom door. The living room was darker and cooler than the bedroom. 'Jack?' she called softly. No answer came. 'Jack?' Nothing. She walked across the rug, then out the front door. He wasn't on the porch.

*He was gone?*

Back inside the cabin, she shut the door and locked it . Then she ran to the kitchen and locked the back door. She peaked inside a utility closet. She checked the bathroom. A closet in the living room. Behind all the furniture.

Not looking for Jack anymore.

Searching for Willy.

Shaking and chilled, she shut herself into the bedroom.

'You're a fine specimen,' she told the face in the mirror.

The normal side of her face smiled nervously; the swollen side hardly moved.

Turning around, she stared over her shoulder at the mirror's image of her back. The knit jersey was torn in a few places midway down. It was stiff and brown near the rips.

She took it off.

The large, square bandage – applied by Jack after carrying her to his cabin – was white except for a tiny dot of blood in its center. All around the bandage, her skin was stained. All the way down to her waist. The shorts had soaked up a lot of blood. She took them off.

Dropping the clothes in a heap, she stepped to the closet. She took down the robe. Its hanger fell, making a tinny *ping* when it hit the hardwood floor. She crouched to pick it up, being careful to keep her back straight so the cuts wouldn't pull.

It was then that she saw the dark, glossy stock. She pushed some clothes aside. Propped against a back corner of the closet stood a double-barreled shotgun. Sweeping hangers away, Marty pressed between two clean shirts. They felt cool and fresh on her skin. She hoped that the blood stains on her back were dry.

Her hand closed around the wide, side-by-side barrels. She lifted. The shotgun was heavy. With her arm outstretched, she could barely raise it off the floor. So she dragged it out of the closet.

The shotgun had two triggers. It also had a hammer at the back of each barrel. There was a lever between the hammers. She pressed it sideways with her thumb.

The barrels suddenly dropped, nearly wrenching the weapon from her grip. They hung toward the floor, connected to the stock by a hinge. In each chamber was a round, brass disk with a little nub in the center.

*It's loaded.*

Marty rested the barrels against the floor, then lifted the stock until the latch snapped. The shotgun was whole again. She returned it to the closet and straightened the hangers in front of it.

Then she put on the robe. It was far too big. She rolled up its sleeves and tied its cloth belt.

Jack was still gone when she went into the bathroom. She took a long shower. Then she dried herself carefully, surprised by the number of cuts and bruises she discovered.

She put on the robe and tied its belt snugly. There was a comb by the sink. She did the best she could with her hair, and opened the bathroom door.

Jack looked up from a magazine. 'How you doing?' he asked.

'A lot better than a few hours ago.'

'Glad to hear it.' He unrolled a leather pouch and started loading tobacco into his pipe.

'Sure is nice of you to help me.' She sat on a rocker across from him. 'Do you mind me borrowing your robe?'

'Not at all.'

'My things are a mess.'

'I noticed.' He struck a match and sucked its flame down to the surface of the tobacco. 'Did you sleep well?'

'Great.'

Jack tamped down the loose ash in his pipe and lit another match. As he drew the flame into the briar bowl, he looked at Marty and raised his eyebrows. He blew a cloud of smoke.

'Smells like a cake baking,' Marty said. 'A chocolate cake.'

Jack shrugged.

'Would it be all right if I use your telephone? I'd like to call my parents and let them know I'm okay.'

'Help yourself.'

'I'll call collect.'

'No need.'

The telephone was on a lamp table at the end of the sofa. Marty stood up and went over to it. She picked up the handset, then tapped in the numbers.

Sitting down on the sofa, she listened to the ringing.

Someone picked up. 'Hello?' asked her father. He sounded tense.

'Hi, Dad.'

'Marty! My God! Are you all right?'

'I'm okay.'

'What in the name of God . . . ?'

'I was kidnapped.'

'*Kidnapped?*'

'I just got away a little while ago. I'm all right. You and Mom can stop worrying about me.'

'We've been basket cases.'

'It's all right now. I'm not sure when I'll be home, but . . .'

'Where are you? Where are you calling from?'

'A place in the woods. Anyway, I'm fine. I've got to get going, now.'

'Marty . . .'

'Give my love to Mom.'

'Marty, for . . .'

'Bye for now, Dad,' she said, and hung up.

'Short but sweet,' she said to Jack, and tried to smile. 'I just didn't want to get into it, you know?' She made a small laugh. 'Besides, it was long distance and you were paying.'

'You were actually kidnapped?' Jack asked, and puffed on his pipe.

'Yeah.'

'Guess we'd better make a call to the police.'

'Could it wait? I'm still . . . I don't know. I feel like I need some time, or . . .'

'The sooner you get to the police, the sooner they'll put your kidnappers out of commission.'

'Kidnapper. Only one.'

'Don't you think you should call the police?'

Marty looked into Jack's eyes. They were gentle, confident, comforting. He seemed like a man who *knew* things and could handle tough situations. She would be safe with him. 'How about tomorrow?' she asked.

'Fine with me.'

'Can I stay here till then?'

'You're welcome to stay as long as you want.'

'Really? As long as I want?'

'Sure.' He grinned and puffed his pipe. 'Long as you behave yourself.'

# 34

Willy took a red bandanna out of his jeans and wiped the sweat off his face. 'Hotter than boiled piss,' he said.

But the shack was just ahead. He would be there in a minute or so. About time! Two hours was too damn long to be tromping through the boonies, especially in this kind of heat.

He was glad he'd done it, though. Now he was sure they were alone. No sign of humanity anywhere nearby. He sure had found

101

himself a great place for a hideout – or Dewey had.

I oughta drop Dewey a card, he thought. 'Hello from your old stomping grounds,' he said aloud.

The girl, apparently hearing him, lifted her head. She was still standing, arms high, under the tree. And still on her feet to keep her weight off the handcuffs.

'Hi, sweet stuff. Miss me?'

She squinted at him and said nothing.

'Looks like you got yourself a little sun,' Willy said, and laughed.

Where she'd had a tan before, her skin now had a deep, rosy glow. Where her skin had been white, she now appeared to be wearing a bright red bikini.

Willy dragged a fingernail down her breast.

She flinched and made a hissing sound between her teeth.

The scratch from his fingernail looked blue-white for a moment, then went red.

'Hurt?' Willy asked.

'Yes.'

'Tough titty.' He laughed.

# 35

'Are you hungry?' Jack asked. 'I picked up a couple of steaks in town this afternoon.'

'Great. I'm starved.'

'Okay. Why don't you go on and get dressed, and I'll start the barbecue?'

Marty felt her skin heat with embarrassment as she thought about the torn, filthy rags on the bedroom floor. 'Won't this do?' she asked, glancing down at the white robe.

'We don't know each other well enough,' he said.

Marty smiled. 'Oh. I see.'

'Go change,' he said.

She went into the bedroom. On the bed lay two green shopping bags. Inside them she found a white blouse, a pale blue skirt, panties and a bra, and a shoe box containing a pair of white sneakers.

All brand new, the tags still on them.

Blushing, she called out, 'Thank you, Jack! They're great!'

'You're welcome,' he called from somewhere beyond the shut door.

Marty took off the robe. She hung it in the closet, glimpsing the shotgun's stock before she turned away. Then she removed the bandage from her back and made a new one. After that, she removed the tags from the clothes. She started to get dressed.

The bra was slightly too large.

'Wishful thinking,' she muttered. Laughing quietly, she put it on anyway.

Everything else fit well. Looking at herself in the brand new clothes, she felt clean and fresh and very safe.

The night with Willy seemed far away.

Until she saw her face in the mirror.

That brought it all back. Her stomach twisted. She crouched on the floor, shivering, hugging her belly. Then, like an icy wind, it passed. She hurried outside.

The afternoon sun was hot and calming.

She found Jack behind the cabin, standing at a red brick barbecue.

'The clothes are wonderful,' she said.

'You look great.'

'If you're into battered, bruised and ugly.'

He laughed. 'I must admit, I would be interested in seeing what you look like when you haven't just been beaten to a pulp.'

'Consider it done. It's the least I can do for you.'

# 36

Willy came out of the shack. He was naked. He held his red bandanna in one hand, his leather belt in the other.

The girl raised her head and opened her eyes.

'This is gonna hurt, sweetie. But don't scream too loud, or I'll have to gag you. You wouldn't want that. My hanky's got boogers in it.'

Her dry lips stuck together when she tried to open her mouth. Then they peeled apart. She licked them, and asked in a raspy whisper, 'Why are you doing this to me?'

'Because I can?'

He began to swing his belt.

# 37

When Jack drove her into the town of Wayside that evening, it looked different from the night before. Golden in the lowering sun. Busy, yet peaceful. And crowded. A dozen people stood in line at the movie theater.

'Would you like to see a show?' Jack asked.

'Would you?'

'Sure.'

Jack parked the car, and they walked to the theater. Inside, they found seats near the front. The lights faded out. And the previews started.

Marty could hardly believe that she was safe and watching a movie.

Only two nights ago, she'd been in a theater with Dan.

She'd spotted Willy . . .

For the next couple of hours, she stared at the enormous screen but noticed little that was on it. She dwelled on the screen in her mind, the one that played a horrible film about Willy.

In that film, she relived it all.

Again and again.

Marty was pulled out of it when the lights came up. She found that she was squeezing Jack's hand.

On the way out of town, Jack asked if she would like some ice cream.

'Sure,' she said.

They stopped at the Wayside Motor Inn, and each had a hot

fudge sundae at its all-night burger joint.

Then they were in the car again, rushing along the dark, twisting road.

'Gives me the creeps,' Marty said. She slid across the seat, close to Jack. He put an arm across her shoulders.

'You don't need to be afraid.'

'He's still out there,' she said.

'But he doesn't have you. Not anymore. And tomorrow we'll go to the police.'

'Will you come with me?'

'Of course.'

'What if Willy comes for me tonight?'

'He won't.'

'He might already be at your cabin waiting for us.'

Jack's hand went to the back of her neck. Gently and firmly, he rubbed her there. 'He won't get you. Not tonight. Not while I'm around.'

# 38

'You look good in stripes. Anyone ever tell you that?' Laughing, Willy scraped the bottom of his chili can. Then he licked the spoon. 'That was funny. Why aren't you laughing?'

The girl, sitting on the mattress with her legs crossed, said nothing. She gazed sullenly down at the can of chili in her hand.

'By the way, sweetie, what's your name?'

She scooped a spoonful of chili into her mouth.

A flashlight lay on the table beside the big, battery powered lantern that lit the center of the room. Willy picked it up, turned it on, and threw its beam in her face.

She shut her puffy eyelids.

'What's your name?' Willy repeated. And then he remembered a game he used to play when he was a kid. He put down the flashlight. He went to the bed and knelt on it, facing the girl. She smelled like sweat and sex. 'Now,' he said, 'what's your name?'

'Tina,' she said.

'You lie!' he blurted, and smacked her hard in the face with his open hand. The blow turned her head sideways. 'What's your name?' he asked again.

She looked at him. She pressed her lips tightly together. They were cracked and bleeding. She said, 'My name's Tina.'

'You lie!' he yelled, and smacked the other side of her face. 'What's your name?'

She glared at him. She said nothing.

'YOU LIE!' He swung. His hand clapped her cheek so hard his fingers tingled and blood flew off her lips.

# 39

'I'll be just outside the door if you need me,' Jack said from the bedroom doorway.

'I need you,' Marty said.

He grinned. 'Maybe some other time. Goodnight.' He shut the door as he left.

Marty turned off the bedroom light and stood in the darkness. She thought about going out to Jack. But she didn't want to seem pushy.

*Some other time*.

She took off her clothes and climbed beneath the sheet, wishing he was there beside her, holding her close and warm. His strong arms around her. Caressing her. Not doing anything funny, just being gentle and safe . . .

She woke up with a start.

Her heart was slamming. Her bangs were plastered to her forehead with sweat and the bed was soaked beneath her. She lay there motionless, wondering what had shocked her awake.

The room was pale with a creamy glow of moonlight. The door was still shut. Between the door and the dresser fell a shadow. The shadow was too small to conceal a person. But the open closet made a large darkness.

*He's in there.*

*No, he's not. Don't be ridiculous.*

*He is!*

The sweat seemed to freeze on Marty's skin. She pulled her top sheet up tightly under her chin.

The only sound she could hear was her own loud, thudding heart.

She glanced at the nightstand. There was no lamp on it.

Scissors.

After bandaging her back that morning, Jack had put them in a drawer of the nightstand. She'd used them, herself, just before supper.

*Now, where'd I put them?*

*On the dresser.*

But the dresser stood beside the open closet.

*I'll never make it. He'll jump me before* . . .

*Nobody's in the closet!*

*Willy is.*

Marty inched her leg toward the side of the mattress. After a long time, her right heel dropped over the edge. She kept moving her leg sideways, slowly, slowly, until it was off the mattress all the way to her rump. Her foot on the floor, she started sliding her left leg over.

Eyes on the dark, open closet.

*He's watching. If he starts coming, run for it.*

At last, both her feet were on the floor.

She raised her back so gradually that the bedsprings hardly made a sound. They were nearly silent, too, when she leaned forward and eased her weight off the bed. She stood up straight, staring at the black closet.

Nothing seemed to move in there.

With six slow, careful steps, she reached the dresser. Her hand patted the top of it.

And found the scissors.

Picked them up. Clenched them tight.

With the tightness of a scream growing in her chest, she

sidestepped to the closet. Raising the scissors high, she lurched into the darkness. She drove them down, hard and silent.

Pain seared her thigh.

She tried to stifle her yelp of hurt surprise.

Waving her other hand in the air, she caught the dangling string and pulled. The closet light came on.

Nobody there.

Nobody except Marty.

Marty, naked and sweaty and shaking. Marty, scissors in her hand. Marty with a ragged red gash ripped across the inner side of her right thigh.

She had a sudden urge to sit down on the closet floor and cry. Sit there and cry till dawn.

Instead, she bandaged her leg.

Then she got dressed, putting on the stiff, filthy shorts and jersey that Willy had stolen from the girl by the lake.

Then she took the shotgun out of the closet.

Sneaking through the dark house, she found Jack asleep on the living room sofa. She set down the shotgun. She found his trousers draped over a nearby chair.

His keys were in the right front pocket. His wallet was in the left rear pocket.

She took out a five-dollar bill and slipped the wallet back into his pocket. She kept the keys.

She was tempted to kiss him before leaving.

But she didn't dare.

He might wake up and not let her go.

# 40

Thrusting and shuddering, Willy erupted inside Tina. Then he relaxed on top of her.

Somewhere along the line, she had fainted.

Just as well. Willy hadn't liked the way she'd just taken it, never saying a word even when the pain made her twitch and weep.

He pulled out and sat back.

A breeze was blowing through the open door and window, giving him goosebumps. He got up and shut them both. The handcuffs lay open on the table. He picked them up. Then he turned off the lantern and made his way through the darkness. He found the mattress, got to his knees, reached out and touched Tina. Her skin was hot. From its sticky ridges, he knew he was touching her back. He slid his hand down her rump and down the back of her leg to her ankle.

He cuffed her left ankle. After sitting beside her, he attached the other cuff to his own left ankle. The bracelet was almost too small, but he managed to get it on.

Then he unfolded a blanket and lay back, covering himself. He stared at the dark ceiling.

It had been a great day.

Even if the girl wasn't Marty.

*At least Marty got what was coming to her.*

He'd scared the shit out of her with the noose.

He'd killed her boyfriend. Twice. He grinned. Not every prick gets to die twice.

He'd fucked her. Got her in the mouth, too – almost.

And he'd shot her dead.

*That old hollow-point sure made a mess of her back.*

He grinned, remembering how she'd been sprawled out in the moonlight, the blood all over her back.

Too bad he'd had to kill her, though.

He'd wanted *Marty* here, not *Tina*.

*Not that there's anything wrong with Tina.*

*Except she ain't Marty.*

He sighed. *Oh, the stuff I would've done to her . . .*

# 41

The attendant at the all-night gas station raised his red, chubby face out of a comic book when Marty stepped up to the window. She smiled at him and slipped a five-dollar bill into the trough under the glass.

'Pump number two,' she said.

He took the bill and nodded.

'Could I ask you something?' she said.

He shrugged.

Before she could start to ask for directions, he frowned and said, 'What happened to your face?'

She shrugged. 'A guy hit me.'

'Slugged you?'

'Yeah. A few times.'

'Sheesh. He really creamed you.'

'I noticed. I felt it.'

'What'd he wanta do that for?'

'He's just a jerk who likes to hurt people.'

'Does it hurt a whole lot? Your face?'

'Some.'

'Guy must be a real creep.'

'He is.'

'Somebody oughta fix his wagon for him.'

'Somebody plans to. Do you know where Cricket Lake is?'

'Sure. You going there?'

'Not exactly. I'm looking for a place close to Cricket, though. It's a small lake. I don't know its name, if it even has one.'

'We got lakes like that all over the place.'

'This one's just west of Cricket.'

'West?'

'Yeah. It has a dirt road leading to it, and one cabin.'

'Oh, I bet you mean the Dewey place.'

'Maybe.'

'The place that Jason Dewey hid out. A little shack by this lake. Jason Dewey, he hid out there . . . guess it must've been three summers back.'

Marty shrugged her shoulders.

'You know about Jason Dewey?'

'No, but . . .'

'He's the guy that chopped up that family down Hingston way. You must've heard about it. Made all the news. He hacked up the

110

mother and father and all the kids, two or three kids – and the family parrot.'

'A parrot?'

'Yeah.' He grinned. 'He *ate* the parrot. Wild, huh? A real nutcase.'

'He had a hideout somewhere near Cricket Lake?'

'Sure did.'

'How do I find it?'

He gave her directions, but explained that she should wait for morning. 'You ain't gonna find the turn-off in the dark. But if you wanta wait till morning, I'll take you out there myself.'

'I have to go right now.'

He looked disappointed. 'You sure you can't wait?' he asked.

'Sorry. But I've got a wagon to fix. Thanks for the information.'

'Welcome.'

'Pump number two,' she reminded him.

'Five bucks worth.'

# 42

Two miles west of Cricket Lake, Marty swung the car onto a meager dirt road and stopped. Turning sideways in her seat, she reached up and removed the plastic cover from the dome light. Then she twisted the bulb loose. She put the cover and bulb into Jack's glove compartment, then started driving forward.

The road, little more than a couple of wheel ruts, was hard to drive on. It threw the car around as if trying to rip the steering wheel out of her hands. She held on tightly, fighting to keep control.

A rough bump jolted her teeth together and she bit her tongue. Tears blurred her vision. She didn't dare let go of the wheel, so she tried to blink them away. It didn't work. Tears still blinded her. So she gripped the wheel as hard as possible with her left hand and used her right to rub her eyes clear.

Just then, the road turned.

The car swerved out of the shallow ruts.

She grabbed the wheel and steered along the overgrown center strip, bushes scraping against the right side of the car until she guided the tires again into their twin paths.

She slowed down and took the road more carefully.

*Just take it easy. No big hurry. I've got all night.*

*Just so I get there before morning.*

*Catch him in his sleep.*

*If he's there.*

*God, I hope he's there . . .*

# 43

'Hey,' Willy heard. Something shoved his shoulder. 'Hey, wake up.'

'Huh?' he asked. 'What?'

'I've got to go,' Tina said.

'What?'

'I've gotta go to the bathroom.'

'Shit. You gotta go *now?*'

'I can't help it.'

'Shit,' he said again. Then he said, 'Okay, so I guess we gotta get up. We're cuffed together, case you didn't notice.'

'I noticed.'

Slowly, awkwardly, they both stood up in the darkness. Willy got behind Tina and steered her to the table. There, he turned on the lantern. 'Okay, now we go outside.'

'Together?'

'If you think I'm gonna take off the cuffs at this hour, you're outa your fucking mind. Let's go.'

As they walked in tandem toward the door, Willy saw their reflection in the window. It was the brand new window that he'd installed just before taking off to get Marty. 'Hold it,' he said, and grabbed her shoulders. 'Get a load of the lovebirds. Almost as good as a mirror,' he said.

'Can we go?' Tina asked.

'When I say so.'

In the reflection, he watched his hands vanish behind her

112

shoulders. They reappeared under her arms, then covered her breasts. Her breasts felt hot and slippery. He watched himself squeeze them, watched his fingers pinch her stiff nipples.

She squirmed and made odd little noises in her throat, but didn't protest.

He'd grown hard. He rubbed himself against her back.

In the reflection, he saw one of his hands glide down her belly. It continued downward and went too low to be seen in the window.

He felt her moist curls.

Then his fingertips spread her and slid in.

He saw her smile in the glass.

'Feels good, huh?' he asked.

'This does,' Tina said.

The portrait shattered. Jagged shards exploded into the night outside. Others dropped from above. They plunged down like broken slabs of ice, stabbing and slicing her outstretched arm.

Willy jerked her away from the broken window.

'You bitch!' he yelled as they both stumbled backward, cuffed at the ankles. 'You stupid bitch! You busted my fuckin' window!'

When they fell, Tina landed on top of him. She squirmed and thrashed. Her back and buttocks were hot and slippery. Willy liked how they felt, sliding against his skin.

He didn't know that she was clutching a spike of broken glass until she started to use it on him.

# 44

After what seemed like more than an hour of slow driving through the woods, Marty rumbled down a slope and spotted a rock, pale in the moonlight, resting in the strip between the ruts.

She jammed on the brakes.

Not quick enough.

The rock scraped and thundered against the car's undercarriage.

When the noise stopped, she wiped the sweat out of her eyes. She eased her foot onto the gas pedal. The car started slowly forward.

Then she saw it.

Ten feet ahead, shining in a stray slant of moonlight, was the rear window of another car.

Willy's car. The one he'd taken after killing the two men on the roadside last night.

Marty hit the brakes and turned off the engine. She opened her door, glad she'd taken care of the ceiling light.

She climbed out and dragged the shotgun after her. Propping its stock on the ground, she crouched behind her open door. She cocked both hammers.

Looking over the top of the door, she could only see the back of Willy's car. She gazed at its trunk. Beneath the dark curving metal, Dan lay dead.

Unless Willy'd moved him.

*Dan*.

She turned her eyes away from the trunk.

To each side of Willy's car, she could see woods. But not much else, not from her crouched position behind the door. She didn't want to stand up. She liked it fine behind the solid, protective door. But there was no choice.

Slowly, she stood up straight.

She gazed into the darkness, half expecting a gunshot to crack the silence.

No, she thought. He won't shoot me.

He had shot at her before, but only to stop her from escaping. This time, she wasn't trying to escape; she was *coming* to him. He would want her alive.

Hefting the shotgun, she rushed, crouching, to the front of his car. There, she knelt down by the tire. After taking a moment to catch her breath, she raised her head and looked up the road.

The shack, less than fifty yards away, was probably no bigger than her bedroom at home. The walls looked like pale, weathered wood. From where she crouched, she could see a door and a window. The window was lit by a dim, hazy glow. As if a flashlight might be on inside the shack.

She shivered and felt the hairs rise on the back of her neck.

Is he up? she wondered. At this hour?

*Up or not, this is it.*

'Here I come, Willy,' she whispered. 'Ready or not.'

And she was up and running, shotgun heavy in her hands, pine needles crunching under her shoes, running, fingertip sliding through the trigger guard, running, stopping at the shack's wall, thrusting the barrels in through the broken window ...

# 45

Willy, standing naked only a few feet away, grinned at her. He was bloody from head to toe. His arms were high as if he might be hoping to surrender.

Before he had a chance to say anything – before he had a chance to dive for cover – Marty fired.

With a harsh roar, the shotgun spat flame and jumped in her hands and slammed back against her shoulder.

The blast caught Willy in the middle of the chest. It hit him like a hard wind, lifting him off his feet, hurling him backward.

But he didn't go down.

In the light of a battery lantern on the nearby table, Marty saw him, still grinning, start to glide back toward her.

A deathless thing, still up and coming.

She glimpsed shiny, broken rib bones in the pulpy clutter of his chest.

She let out a scream that scorched her throat.

And she thought, *Go for the head!*

She aimed for Willy's face as he came gliding toward her.

It was only then that she noticed the shiny blades of glass jutting out of his eyes. And the wide wedge of glass jammed into his mouth, giving him such a big, strange grin. And the slash across his throat.

She held fire.

A ceiling beam creaked, and Willy began to glide backward again.

Marty suddenly realized that he was suspended by his wrists.

He swung back and forth below the rope like a mutilated Tarzan.

Lowering her gaze, Marty saw that his genitals were gone.

So was his left foot.

When she was done throwing up, Marty entered the shack and looked around. She tried not to look at Willy.

Nobody else seemed to be there.

She found lots of blood, especially on the floor near Willy's dangling body. And on the wall and floor near the broken front window. And on the mattress.

There was a lot of semen on the mattress, too.

*He must've brought someone here. Grabbed some other poor girl after I got away . . .*

*Someone tougher than he counted on.*

*Tough enough to take him out.*

'Hello?' she called.

No answer came.

'Anybody here?'

Still, no answer.

'Whoever you are . . . if you can hear me, thanks. I came here to kill the bastard, but you beat me to it.' Marty suddenly found herself smiling. 'You did a good job on him! You did a *great* job!'

After a few moments, she called, 'Do you need a ride out of here? Or help? Are you hurt? Do you need medical attention? Hello? I'll do anything I can for you!'

Nothing.

She spent a while longer looking around – hoping Willy's tough victim – his killer – might return.

She searched the entire shack.

As she walked out with the shotgun slung over her shoulder, she wondered what had become of the person.

She also wondered what had become of Willy's left foot and his genitals.

She climbed into the car, turned it around, and headed back for Jack's place.

116

## 46

The next morning, Tina walked out of the woods and onto the road.

She was barefoot.

She was clean from soaking in the lake last night. The lake water had sure felt good on her sunburn and on a lot of places where Willy had hurt her. She supposed she might've stayed in it all night, but her hands and arms kept on bleeding.

So then she'd waded out and hunted around until she found the remains of her paisley dress under the tree where Willy had torn it off her. Willy had ruined it, shredding it with his teeth like that.

But the shreds had turned out to make very fine bandages. She'd bound the cuts on her arms and hands with bright, shiny rags.

She'd tied a piece around her left ankle, like a broad bandage, to conceal the handcuffs there.

And she'd made herself a bikini top by knotting a few pieces together.

After sunrise, she'd returned to the shack. Willy was anty, and he stank. She'd gotten out as fast as she could.

Outside, she'd used Willy's pocket knife to take the legs off his jeans and make herself a pair of cut-offs to wear. She'd put on the shorts, then dropped the knife into her pocket.

The knife had come in mighty handy in the shack last night. Without it, she'd *still* be cuffed to Willy.

She planned to keep the knife forever.

And keep it always ready, just in case.

Now, walking alongside the road, she heard the sound of an engine. Turning around, she watched a bright blue pickup truck come around a bend.

She put out her arm to hitch a ride.

It was no surprise when the pickup stopped for her. No surprise at all. Not the way she was dressed.

She bent toward the passenger window.

The driver, a nice-looking young man, smiled at her. He wore a T-shirt and tan shorts. His smile looked friendly. 'Can I give you a lift?' he asked, and glanced at her flimsy, makeshift bikini top.

'You aren't some kind of pervert or fiend, are you?'

He suddenly blushed. 'Me? Nope.'

'Better not be,' Tina said. 'I'd hate to have to kill you.'

'You and me both,' he said, and laughed a little.

Smiling, she climbed in.

'Where to?' he asked.

'Home,' she said.

# *Kitty Litter*

'She's here for a kitty!'

My flinch came to an end before the second word was out of her mouth, but my heart still thudded fast and hard. I'd thought I was alone, you see. I was stretched out on my lounger beside my backyard pool, surrounded by redwood fence, enjoying a new *87th Precinct* paperback, savoring the feel of the sunlight and the warm breeze.

The invasion took me by complete surprise.

After the jolt by the imperious voice, I jerked my head sideways and saw the girl.

Already, she was inside the gate and marching boldly toward me.

I knew right away who she was.

Monica from down the block.

Though we'd never actually met, I'd seen Monica around. And *heard* her. She had a loud, nasal voice which she operated primarily to snap back at her poor mother and berate her little friends.

I knew her name because she was often the subject of shouted warnings and threats. I also knew it because she used it herself. She belonged to the odd tribe that refers to itself in the third person.

She was about ten years old, I suppose.

If I had not been so unfortunate as to observe her behavior on previous occasions, I certainly would've been struck by the beauty of the girl striding toward me. She had rich brown hair, gleaming eyes, excellent facial features, a flawless complexion, and a slender body. She didn't look beautiful to me, however.

Nor did she look cute, though she wore a delightful outfit comprised of a pink cap with a jauntily upturned bill, a denim pinafore dress, a white blouse, white knee socks and athletic shoes of pink to match her cap.

She was neither beautiful nor cute because she was Monica.

To my way of thinking, there is no such thing as a beautiful or cute snot.

She halted beyond the foot of my lounger and scowled at me. Her eyes flicked up and down my body.

My swimsuit had never been meant for public inspection. I quickly sheltered myself with the open book. It lay like a pitched roof atop my lap.

'You *are* Mr Bishop?' she demanded.

'That's right.'

'The man with the kitties?'

I nodded.

She nodded back at me. She bobbed on her toes. 'And you're giving them away for free?'

'I'm hoping to find good homes for them, yes.'

'Monica will have one then.'

'And who is Monica?' I asked, though obviously I knew the answer.

She pumped a small thumb against her chest, dead center between the denim straps of her dress.

'You're Monica?' I asked.

'Of course.'

'You want one of my kittens?'

'Where are they?'

In spite of my dislike for this particular child, I was eager to find homes for the kittens. My ad in the newspaper, and the fliers I'd tacked to several neighborhood trees, had not been greatly successful. Of the four kittens born to the litter, I still had three.

They were not getting any younger. Or any smaller.

Soon, they would pass out of the cute, romping, frisky kitten

120

stage altogether. Who would want to adopt any of them, then?

In other words, I had no wish to be choosy. If Monica wanted a kitten, a kitten she would have.

'They're in my house,' I said. 'I'll bring them out for you to . . . inspect.'

As I leaned forward on the lounge and wondered what to do about my immodest swimsuit, Monica scowled across the pool at the sliding glass door of my house.

'It isn't locked, is it?' she asked.

'No, but you stay . . .'

Ignoring me, she skipped off along the edge of the pool.

I took the opportunity to stand, set down my paperback, and snatch my beach towel off the lounge pad. Quickly, I wrapped the towel around my waist.

Corner tucked under to hold the towel, I hurried after Monica. She was already striding briskly past the far end of the pool.

'*I'll* get the kittens,' I called to her. 'You wait outside.'

I did not want her in my house.

I did not want her to ogle my possessions. I did not want her to touch them or break them or steal them. I did not want her to leave the taint of her pushy, pestilent *self* inside the sanctuary of my home.

She reached for the handle of the sliding door. Clutched it.

'Monica! No!'

'Don't have a cow, man,' she said. And then she rumbled open the door and entered.

'Come out of there!' I yelled.

She hadn't gone far. Stepping over the runner, I spotted her standing near the center of my den. Her fists were planted on her hips as she swiveled her head from side to side.

'I asked you to stay outside.'

'Where are they?'

I shrugged and sighed. She was in. There was no way to undo it. 'This way,' I said.

She followed me toward the kitchen.

'Why are you wearing that towel?' she asked.

'Because it suits me.'

'Where'd your suit go?'

'It didn't go anywhere.'

'Did you take it off?'

'No!'

'You'd better not've.'

'I didn't. I assure you. I also assure you, young lady, that I'm on the very verge of asking you to leave.'

A small wooden gate was stretched across the kitchen doorway to keep the kittens corralled. I hiked up my towel as if it were a skirt, and stepped over the gate.

I turned around to watch Monica. 'Careful,' I warned.

It would serve her right to fall and mash her impish little nose flat, I thought. But she swung one leg, then the other, over the top of the gate and made it to the other side without misadventure.

She sniffed. Her upper lip reached for the bottom of her nose. 'What's that stink?'

'I don't detect a stink.'

'Monica may barf.'

'You might be smelling the litter box.'

'Yug.'

'There it is, now.' I pointed at the plastic tub. Its desert landscape appeared a trifle bumpy. 'You'll have to get used to some rather unpleasant aromas if you wish to keep a cat in . . .'

'Oh! Kitty!'

She rushed past me, dodged the table, and pranced to the far corner of the kitchen where the cats were at play on their blanket.

By the time I caught up to her, she had already made her pick. She was on her knees, clutching Lazzy to her chest, stroking the little tabby's striped head.

Lazzy had a rather frantic look in her eyes, but she wasn't struggling much.

The kittens rubbed against Monica's knees, purring and meowing.

'She'll take this one,' the girl said.

'I'm afraid she won't.'

Monica slowly twisted herself around. Her eyes said, *How dare you!* Her mouth said, 'Oh, yes she will.'

'No. I offered you one of the kittens. That isn't one of the kittens.'

'Oh course she is! She's the tiniest, cutest little kitty of the bunch, and she'll go home with Monica.'

'You may have one of the others.'

'Who wants them? They're big! They aren't cute little kitties. *This* is the cute little kitty.'

She nuzzled her cheek against Lazzy's face.

'You don't want that one,' I said.

She started to get up. I grabbed her shoulder and pushed her down until she was on her knees again.

'Now you're in trouble,' she said.

'No doubt.'

'You touched Monica.'

'You're a trespasser in my house. You came in uninvited even after I told you to stay out. You were preparing to leave with property that belongs to me. So I had every right to touch you.'

'Oh, yeah?'

'Yeah.'

'You'd better just let Monica take this cat home, right now, or else.'

In spite of what I'd said about trespassing, etc., her threats could not be ignored. Here I was, a thirty-eight-year-old bachelor wearing next to nothing, alone in my house with a ten-year-old girl.

It wouldn't look good.

The notion of facing accusations sickened me.

'All right. If you want that cat, she's yours. Go on, take her and get out of here.'

With a victorious grin, Monica rose to her feet. 'Thank you,' she said.

'If you want to know the truth, Lazzy always did give me the creeps.'

'The creeps?'

'Never mind.'

Monica narrowed her eyes. 'What's wrong with her?'

'Nothing.'

'Tell. You'd better tell, or else.'

'Well . . .' I dragged a chair away from the kitchen table, swung it around, and sat down on it.

'Is this going to take long?'

Ignoring her question, I said, 'It all started with Lazzy falling in the toilet.'

She gasped as if the cat had suddenly turned white-hot, and tossed her aside.

Lazzy let out a *reeeeooow!* as she twisted and rolled through the air. But she did a quiet, four-point landing. Heading for the blanket, she glanced over her shoulder and gave Monica a look that was clearly miffed.

'You didn't have to throw her like that,' I said.

'She fell in a *toilet*!'

'The toilet had nothing in it except for clean water. Besides, this was some time ago.'

'You mean she isn't dirty any more?'

'She's perfectly clean.'

'Then what's the big deal?'

'She drowned.'

Monica tucked her chin down and gazed at me as if peering over the top of invisible eyeglasses. She folded her arms across her chest. I wondered if she had picked up the stance from an elderly relative. 'Drowned?' she said. 'Puh-leese.'

'I'm serious,' I said.

Monica tilted her head to one side. 'If she drowned, she would be dead.'

I chose not to argue. Instead, I proceeded with the story. 'It began when Mrs Brown gave birth. She was a tabby who belonged to my friend, James, in Long Beach. When he told me about the litter, I expressed an interest in taking one of the kittens off his hands. Of course, I couldn't take one immediately. I needed to wait until they'd been weaned.'

Monica narrowed an eye. 'What does that mean?'

'A kitty can't be taken away from its mother right away. It needs the mother's milk.'

'Oh, that.'

'Yes. At any rate, we set a date for me to visit James and select a kitten. Do you know where Long Beach is?'

She rolled her eyes toward the ceiling. 'Monica has been to the Spruce Goose and the Queen Mary . . . oh, so many times that she is totally *bored* by them both.'

'Then she knows that the drive takes about an hour from here.'

She nodded. She sighed. She looked over her shoulder, apparently checking up on Lazzy.

I went on with my story.

'I drank quite a lot of coffee before setting out in the morning for Long Beach. By the time I reached James's house, I was very uncomfortable.'

This won her attention away from the cat. 'What?'

'I had to pee. Badly.'

'Oh, for heaven's sake.'

'I hurried to the front door and rang the doorbell. I rang it again and again, but James didn't answer. As it turns out, he had forgotten about our date, and gone shopping. I didn't know that at the time, however. I knew only that the door was not being opened, and that my teeth were afloat.'

'You should not be talking to a child about such things.'

'I'm afraid the condition of my bladder is integral to the story. Anyway, I was becoming frantic. I pounded on the door and called out James's name, but to no avail. I considered rushing over to a neighbor's house, but the idea appalled me. How could I ask a stranger for the use of a toilet? Besides, who would allow me inside for such a purpose? There were no gas stations, restaurants, or shopping malls near enough . . .' Monica interrupted me with a sigh. 'Anyway, I had no choice but to let *myself* into James's house. It was either that or . . .'

'You are a very crude person.'

'Not so crude that I wanted to pee outside. And fortunately,

125

matters didn't reach that stage. At the back of the house, I found an open window. The screen was in my way, of course. But I was too desperate to care about niceties. I fairly tore the screen from its moorings, boosted myself through the window, tumbled onto the floor of James's bedroom, and raced for the bathroom.

'As it turned out, the bathroom was where James had been keeping the new litter – with the door shut, you know, so they wouldn't scamper all over the house. And to confine the aroma of the litter box, I'm sure.'

'This is a *very* long story,' Monica complained. 'Long *and* gross.'

'All right. I'll make it quick, then. I burst into the bathroom, pranced about to avoid mashing several kitties underfoot, and prepared to relieve myself. But when I looked down into the toilet bowl . . .'

'Lazzy,' Monica said.

'Lazzy. Yes. Though, of course, that wasn't her name at the time. At any rate, she must've climbed onto the rim of the toilet for a drink, and tumbled in. She was floating on her side, her little face down in the water. I had no idea how long she might've been that way. But she wasn't moving at all. Not of her own accord. She was turning slightly as if being spun by a very slow, lazy whirlpool.

'Well, I fished her right out and laid her out on the floor. She looked horrid. Have you ever seen a dead cat?'

'She was *not* dead. She's right there.' Monica pointed, her arm so straight and stiff that it seemed to be bent just a bit the wrong way at the elbow.

Lazzy lay on her side, head up, licking one of her forelegs.

'She doesn't look dead now,' I agreed, 'but you should've seen her shortly after I pulled her out of the toilet. She had that *awful* look – fur all matted down, ears flattened back. Her eyes were shut, so all you could see were dark slits. And she looked as if she'd died snarling.' I bared my teeth at Monica to give her the idea.

Monica was doing her best to appear bored and annoyed and

126

superior to all this. In spite of her efforts, however, she had a rather slack look to her face.

'The kitten was cold,' I said. 'Sopping. The feel of it sent chills through me. But that didn't stop me from examining the poor thing. It had no heartbeat.'

'I'm sure,' Monica said. But she was definitely looking a trifle distressed.

'The little kitten was dead.'

'No, it wasn't.'

'It had drowned in the toilet. It was as dead as dead can be.'

'Was not!'

'Dead dead dead!'

Monica pounded her fists against her thighs. Red-faced, she snapped, 'You're an *awful* person!'

'No, I'm not. I'm a very nice person, because I brought the dead kitten back to life. I rolled her onto her back and covered her little mouth with my mouth and breathed into her. At the same time, I used my thumb to push at her heart. Have you ever heard of CPR?'

Monica nodded. 'CPR was a robot in *Star Wars*.'

I was glad to find that she was not quite as smart as she thought she was.

'CPR stands for cardiopulmonary resuscitation. It's a technique used to revive people who . . .'

'Oh, *that*!' She suddenly looked very pleased with herself. And very prim and very superior. Her head dipped from one side to the other while her shoulders oscillated. '*So*, the kitty *wasn't* dead. Monica *told* you she wasn't dead.'

'Oh, but she was very dead.'

Monica shook her head. 'Was not.'

'She was dead, and I brought her back to life with the CPR. Right there in the bathroom. Pretty soon, James came home. I told him what had happened, and he let me have the kitten I'd saved. So I named her Lazzy, short for Lazarus. Do you know who Lazarus was?'

'Of course.'

'Who?'

'None of your business.'

'Whatever you say. Anyway, I brought Lazzy home with me. And do you know what?'

Monica sneered at me.

'Lazzy never grew any larger after the day I brought her back from the dead. That was six years ago. She has been the size of a little kitty, ever since. So you see, she's my pet. She's not part of the litter I want to give away. She's the *mother* of the litter.'

'But she's *tinier* than they are!'

'*And* she's been dead.'

Monica stared at Lazzy for a long while. Then she turned to me, no longer looking the least bit shaken. 'She isn't *either* the mother. You made the whole thing up just so you could keep the cute one.'

She rushed over to the blanket, snatched up Lazzy and hugged her and kissed the dark brown M on her honey-colored brow.

'Put her down,' I said.

'No.'

'Don't make me take her from you.'

'You'd better not.' She glanced at the kitchen doorway behind me. 'You'd better get out of my way, or you'll be in very very bad trouble.'

'Put down Lazzy. You may still take one of the other kittens, but . . .'

'Get out of the way,' she said, and walked straight toward me.

'As soon as you've . . .'

'Mr Bishop said, "Come into my house. I have a little kitty for you." ' She halted and leered at me. 'But when Monica went into his house, he told her a urine story and he took off the towel he was wearing and he said, "This is the little kitty I have for you. His name is Peter." '

I could only gasp, 'You!'

'And he told me to pet Peter and kiss Peter. I didn't *want* to do it, but he grabbed me and . . .'

'Stop it!' I blurted, and stumbled sideways out of her way.

'Take the cat! Take her and get out of here!'

As she strutted by, taking away my Lazzy, she winked at me. 'Thank you so much for the kitten, Mr Bishop.'

I watched her leave.

Just stood and stared as she sashayed through the den and stepped over the threshold of the open sliding door. Immediately after setting foot on the concrete, she burst into a run.

Apparently afraid I might find a smidgen of nerve and attempt to retrieve my cat.

But I didn't move a muscle.

An accusation such as she had threatened to make . . . How does one disprove such a thing? One doesn't. Such an accusation, once made, would cling to me like leprous skin for all the days of my life.

I would forever be known as a pervert, a child-molester.

So I let her *steal* my dear Lazzy.

I stood frozen with terror and *let* her.

And from outside came a familiar *reeooow!* followed by a quick harsh yelp – the sort of yelp a girl might make if the cat in her arms decided to claw its way to freedom – followed by a thudding splash.

I still stood motionless.

No longer terrified.

Amused, actually.

The poor dear. Fell and got herself all wet.

Lazzy leaped over the threshold and came scampering through the den, fur abristle over the ridge of her spine, her tiny ears swept back, tail curled up in a small, bushy question mark.

She slowed down, then rubbed her side against my bare ankle.

I picked up my tiny little cat. I held her in front of my face with both hands.

From outside came more splashing sounds.

Cries of 'Help!' and 'Help!'

Was it possible that Monica's bag of tricks did not include swimming?

I dared not get my hopes up.

There were no more cries for help. I did hear some choky gasps and quite a good deal of splashing, however, before silence replaced the disturbance.

I carried Lazzy out to poolside.

Monica was at the deep end. Face down, arms and legs spread out, hair drifting above her head, blouse and jumper shimmering slightly.

She rather looked like a skydiver enjoying a freefall, waiting for the very last moment to pull her ringcord.

'I suppose I ought to pull her out,' I told Lazzy. 'Give her some CPR.'

Then I shook my head.

'No. Not a good idea – a man my age putting his hands on a ten-year-old girl? What would people say?'

I headed for the sliding glass door.

'Why don't we go pay a visit to James? Who knows? Maybe someone will be lucky enough to find Monica while we're away.'

Lazzy purred, her little body vibrating like a warm engine.

# The Bleeder

The spot of wetness on the sidewalk at Byron's feet looked purple in the mercury glow of the streetlight. It looked like a drop of blood.

He squatted down and peered at it. Then he pulled a flashlight out of the side pocket of his sport jacket. He thumbed the switch. In the bright, somewhat yellowish shine of its beam, the spot appeared crimson.

Might be paint, he thought.

But who would be wandering around at night dripping red paint?

He reached down and touched it. Bringing his fingertip close to the flashlight glass, he inspected the red smear. He rubbed it with his thumb. The stuff was kind of watery. Not gooey enough for paint. More like blood that had been spilled very recently.

He sniffed it.

He could only smell mustard from the hot dog he'd eaten during the last show, a smell strong enough to overpower blood's subtle aroma. But it wouldn't have masked the pungent odor of paint.

Byron wiped his finger and thumb on his sock. Still squatting, he let the beam of his flashlight drift over the concrete ahead. He saw a dirty pink disk of flattened bubble gum, a gob of spit, a mashed cigarette butt, and a second drop of blood.

The second drop was three strides away. He stopped above it. Like the first, it was about the size of a nickel. Sweeping his light forward, he found a third.

Maybe someone with a nosebleed, he thought.

Or a switchblade in the guts.

No, a *real* wound and there'd be blood everywhere. Byron remembered the mess in the Elsinore's restroom last month. During intermission, a couple of teenagers had gone at each other with knives. He and Digby, one of the other ushers, had broken it up. Though the kids only had minor wounds, the john had looked like a slaughterhouse.

Compared to that, this was nothing. Just a drip once in a while. Even a nosebleed, he thought, would throw out more gore.

On the other hand, the person's clothing, or a handkerchief, might have soaked up most of it – so that only a fraction of the spillage actually hit the sidewalk.

Just a little drip now and then.

Just enough to make Byron very curious.

The trail of blood was going in his direction, anyway, so he kept his flashlight on and kept a lookout.

'What, the streetlights aren't bright enough for you?'

He turned around.

Digby Hymus, known to the gals who worked the refreshment stand as the Jolly Green Dork, came striding down the sidewalk. The thirty-year-old retired boxer had removed his green usher's jacket. Its sleeves were tied around his neck so he looked as if he were giving a piggy-back ride to someone who'd been mashed by a steam roller. His arms were so thick with muscle that they couldn't swing close to his sides when he walked.

'Hate to tell you this, By, but you look like a goddamn retard with that flashlight on.'

'Appearances are often deceiving,' he said. 'Take a gander.' He aimed his flashlight at the nearest spot of blood.

'Yeah? So what?'

'Blood.'

'Yeah? So what?'

'Don't you find it intriguing?'

'Probably some babe sprung a leak in her . . .'

'Don't be disgusting.'

'Hey, you're the guy so interested in blood. You've got a real ghoulish streak, you know that?'

'If you can't say something nice, don't say it.'

'Screw you,' he said, and walked across the road to his parked car.

Byron waited until the car sped off, then continued to follow the trail of blood. He stopped at the corner of 11th Street. His apartment was five blocks straight ahead. But the drops of blood went to the right.

He paused for a moment, considering what to do. He knew that he ought to go on home. But if he did that, he would always wonder.

Maybe the bleeder needs help, he told himself. Even a slow leak could be fatal if it went on long enough. Maybe I'm this person's only chance.

Maybe I'll be a hero, my story will be on the news.

Then guys like Digby – gals like Mary and Agnes of the snack counter – wouldn't be so quick to poke fun at him.

His mind made up, he turned the corner and began to follow the blood up 11th Street.

The television. He could see it now. Karen Ling on the five o'clock news. 'Byron Lewis, twenty-eight-year-old poet and part-time usher at the Elsinore theater, last night came to the aid of a mugging victim in an alley off 11th Street. The victim, twenty-two-year-old fashion model Jessica Connors, had been assaulted earlier that evening in front of the theater where Byron worked. Bleeding and disoriented, she had staggered several blocks before falling unconscious where she was later discovered by the young poet. Byron made the grisly discovery after following Jessica's trail of blood. According to paramedics, Jessica was only minutes away from death at the time she was found. Her survival is being attributed to Byron's quick actions in applying first aid and summoning paramedics. She is currently recovering, and extremely grateful, at Queen of Angels Hospital.'

Byron smiled.

Just a fantasy, he told himself. But what's wrong with that?

The bleeder will probably turn out to be an old wino who cut his lip on a bottle of rotgut.

Or worse.

You'll probably wish you'd gone straight home.

But at least you'll *know*.

Stopping at Harker Avenue, he found a spot of blood on the curb. No traffic was nearby. But Byron believed in playing by the rules. So he thumbed the button to activate the WALK sign, waited for the signal to change, then started across.

If the bleeder had left any drops on the road pavement, passing cars must have obliterated them.

He found more when he reached the other side.

The bleeder was still heading north on 11th Street.

And Byron realized, with some dismay, that he had crossed an invisible border into Skid Row.

In the area ahead, many of the streetlights were out. They left broad pools of darkness on the sidewalk and road. Every shop in Byron's sight was closed for the night. Metal gates had been stretched across their display windows and doors. He glanced through the checkered grating in front of a clothes store, saw a face at the window, and managed to stifle a gasp of alarm.

Just a mannequin, he told himself, hurrying away.

He made a point to avoid looking into any more windows.

Better just to watch the sidewalk, he thought. Watch the trail of blood.

The next time he looked up, he saw a pair of legs sticking out of a tenement's recessed entryway.

The bleeder!

I did it!

Byron rushed to the fallen man. It *was* a man, unfortunately. A man with holes in the bottom of his shoes, whose grimy ankles were blotched with scabs, whose trousers were stained and crusty with filth, who wore a ragged sweatshirt that had one empty sleeve pinned up.

No left arm.

His right arm was folded under his head like a pillow.

'Excuse me,' Byron said.

The man kept snoring.

Byron nudged him with a foot. The body twitched. The snoring stopped with a startled gasp. 'Huh? Whuh?'

'Are you all right?' Byron asked. 'Are you bleeding?'

'BLEEDING?' The man squealed and bolted upright. His head swiveled as he looked down at himself. Byron helped by shining the light on him. 'I don' see no blood. Where? Where?'

Byron didn't see blood on the man, either. But he saw other things that made him turn away and try not to gag.

'Oh God, I'm bleedin'!' the man whined. 'They musta bit me. Oh, they's always bitin' me. Why they wanna bite on ol' Dandy! Where'd they get me? They after ol' Dandy's stump again? Jeezum!'

Byron risked a look at Dandy, and saw that the old man was struggling with his single arm to pull his sweatshirt off.

'Maybe I've got the wrong person.'

'Oh, they's after me.' The shirt started to rise. Byron glimpsed the gray, blotchy skin of Dandy's belly.

'Gimme yer light, duke! C'mon, gimme!'

'I've gotta go,' Byron blurted.

He staggered away from the frantic derelict – and saw a spot of blood farther up the sidewalk.

Dandy wasn't the bleeder, after all.

'I'm sorry,' Byron called back. 'Go back to sleep.'

He heard a low groan. A voice sunken in fear and disgust said, 'Aw, looky what they's done to me.'

If only I'd left the guy alone, he thought.

Real neat play. I should've gone on home.

But he'd come this far. Besides, he couldn't turn back without passing Dandy. He might cross to the other side of the street, but that would be cowardly. And he was no less curious than before.

The drops of blood led him to the end of the block. He waited for the traffic signal to change, then hurried into the street. This time, the trail continued over the pavement. A good sign, he

135

thought. Maybe the bleeder had crossed so recently that no cars had yet come by to wipe out the spots.

I'm gaining on him. Or her.

Oh, he did hope it was a woman.

A slender blonde. Slumped against an alley wall, a hand clamped to her chest just below the swell of her left breast. 'I'm here to help you,' he would say. With a brave, pained smile, she would say, 'It's nothing. Really. Just a flesh wound.' Then she would unbutton her blouse and peel the bloody side away from her skin. She wore a black lace bra. Byron could see right through it.

He imagined himself taking out his clean, folded handkerchief, patting blood away from the cut, and trying not to stare at her breast. His knuckles brushed against it, though, as he dabbed at the wound. 'Excuse me,' he told her. 'That's okay,' she said. 'Come with me,' he suggested. 'I'll take you to my apartment. I have bandages there.' She agreed, but she was too weak to walk without assistance, so she leaned against him. Soon, he had to carry her in his arms. He wasn't huge and powerful like Digby, but the slim girl weighed very little, and . . .

'Hey you.'

Startled, Byron looked up from the sidewalk. His heart gave a quick thump.

She was leaning against the post of a streetlamp, not against a wall. She was a brunette, not a blonde. She wasn't holding her chest.

Her hands, instead, were roaming slowly up and down the front of her skirt. The skirt was black leather. It was very short.

Byron walked toward her. He saw no blood on her shiny white blouse. But he saw that most of the buttons were undone. She didn't wear a black lace bra like the bleeder of his fantasy. She didn't wear one at all, and the blouse was open wide enough to show the sides of her breasts.

'Looking for someone, honey?' she asked. Running the tip of her tongue across her lower lip, she squirmed against the light post. As her hands slid upward, the skirt rose with them. It lifted above the tops of her black fishnet stockings. The straps of a garter belt were dark against her pale thighs.

Feeling a little breathless, Byron looked her in the eyes. 'You aren't bleeding, are you?' he asked.

'What do you think?' She eased the skirt higher, but he didn't allow his eyes to wander down.

'I don't think you understand,' he said. 'I'm trying to find someone who's bleeding.'

'Kinky,' she said. 'What's your name, sweet thing?'

'Byron.'

'I'm Ryder. Wanta find out how I got my name?'

'Have you been standing here long?'

'Long enough to get lonely. And hot.' One of her hands glided up. It slipped inside her blouse. Byron saw the shapes of her fingers through the thin fabric as they fondled her breast.

He swallowed. 'What I mean is, did you just get here?'

'Few minutes ago. You like?' She eased the blouse aside, showing him the breast, stroking its erect nipple with the edge of her thumb.

He nodded. 'Very nice. But the thing is . . . did you see anyone go by?'

'Just you, Byron. How about it?' She stared at the front of his slacks. 'You look mighty sweet to me. I bet you taste real fine. I know *I* do. You wanta find out just how fine, too, I'll bet.'

'Well . . . see, I'm looking for someone who's bleeding.'

Her eyes narrowed. 'That'll cost you extra.'

'No, really . . .'

'Yes, really.' She curled her lower lip in, and nipped it. Then she pushed the lip outward as if offering it to Byron. A trickle of blood rolled down. When it reached her chin, she caught it on the tip of her index finger. She painted her nipple with it. 'Taste,' she whispered.

Byron shook his head.

Ryder smiled. More blood was dribbling toward her chin. 'Oh? Do you want it someplace else?'

'No. I'm sorry. Huh-uh.' He backed away from her.

137

'Hey now, buster . . .'

He whirled around and ran.

Ryder yelled. He understood why she might be upset, but that was no reason to call him such names. They made him blush, even though nobody seemed to be around to hear.

*I'm* hearing, he thought as he dashed up the sidewalk. And I'm not half those things she's calling me. She knows it, too. She saw.

Crazy whore.

By the time he reached the other side of the next street, she had stopped shouting. Byron looked back. She was gone.

While he gasped for air, he swept the beam of his flashlight over the sidewalk. He saw no blood spots.

I lost the trail!

His throat tightened.

It's all her fault.

He stomped his foot on the sidewalk.

Calm down, he told himself. It's not over yet. You still had the trail when you ran into her.

The DON'T WALK sign was flashing red, but Byron didn't care. After all, he hadn't even *looked* at the signal the first time across. Now, it just didn't matter.

Old Dandy'd been bad enough. But Ryder!

Running into people like that made traffic signals seem pretty trivial.

No cars were coming, so he hurried back across the street.

Nothing to it.

He smiled.

When he found a spot of blood on the sidewalk, a thrill rippled through him.

'Ah ha!' he pronounced. 'The game's afoot!'

Now I'm talking to myself? Why not? I'm holding up fairly well, all things considered.

Spying a second drop of blood, he understood how he had lost the trail. The bleeder hadn't crossed the road, but had headed to the right along Kelsey Avenue.

Byron quickened his pace.

'Gaining on you,' he said.

As he hurried along, he realized that the spots on the sidewalk were farther apart than they used to be. The distance between them had been irregular from the start – but anywhere from three to five feet, usually. Now, it seemed more like eight to ten feet from one drop to the next.

Is the wound coagulating? he wondered. Or is the bleeder running dry?

What if the blood stops entirely?

If that happens, I'll never find her.

Or find her too late – dead in a heap.

Neither outcome suited Byron.

He broke into a run.

A few strides after passing the entrance of an alley, he lost the trail again and staggered to a halt. Turning around, he returned to the alley. His flashlight reached into it, and a spot of red gleamed on the pavement two yards ahead.

Odd, he thought. In his fantasies, he'd imagined finding the bleeder in an alley. What if it *all* would happen just the way he'd pictured it?

Too much to hope for, he told himself.

But he felt a tremor of excitement as he entered the alley.

He shined his light from side to side, half expecting to find a beautiful woman slumped against one of the brick walls. He saw a couple of garbage bins, but nothing else.

She might be huddled down, concealed by one of the bins.

Byron stepped past them. Nobody there.

He considered lifting the lids, but decided against it. The things would stink. There might even be rats inside. If the bleeder was in one of them, he didn't want to know.

Better not to find her at all.

This was supposed to be an adventure with a glorious and romantic outcome. It would just be too horrible if it ended with finding a body in the garbage.

He kept going.

Ten strides deeper into the alley, his pale beam fell upon another drop of blood.

'Thank God,' he muttered.

Of course, there were several more bins some distance ahead – dark boxes silhouetted by faint light where the alley ended at the next road.

I'll find her before then, Byron told himself.

Any minute, now.

A black cat sauntered across the alley. It glanced at him, eyes glowing like clear golden marbles.

Good thing I'm not superstitious, he thought, the back of his neck tingling.

'If only you could talk,' he said.

The cat wandered over to the right side of the alley. Back hunched, tail twitching, it rubbed its side against a door.

A door!

Byron tipped back his head and inspected the building. He thought that it might be an apartment house. Its brick wall was three stories high, with fire escapes at the windows of the upper floors. All the windows were dark.

He stepped toward the door. The cat leaped and darted past him.

He almost grabbed the knob before noticing that it was wet with blood.

A chill crept through him.

Maybe this isn't such a great idea, he thought.

But he was so *close*.

Still, to enter a building where he didn't belong . . .

This might very well be where the bleeder lived. Why had she entered from the alley, though, instead of using the front? Did she feel that she had to sneak in?

'Strange,' Byron muttered.

Maybe she simply wandered down the alley, lost and dazed, and entered this door in the hope of finding someone who would help her. Even now, she might be staggering down a hallway, too weak to call out.

Byron plucked a neatly folded handkerchief from his pocket, shook it open, and spread it over his left hand. He turned the knob.

With a quiet snick, the latch tongue retracted.

He eased the door open.

The beam of his flashlight probed the darkness of a narrow corridor. On the hardwood floor gleamed a dot of blood.

He stepped inside. The hot air smelled stale and musty. Pulling the door shut, he listened. Except for the pounding of his own heartbeat, he heard nothing.

His own apartment building, even at this hour, was nearly always filled with sounds: people arguing or laughing, doors slamming, voices from radios and televisions.

His building had lighted hallways.

Hallways that always smelled of food, often of liquor. Now and again, they were sweet with the lingering aromas of cheap perfume.

Nobody lives here, he suddenly thought.

He didn't like that. Not at all.

He realized that he was holding his breath as he started forward. He walked slowly, setting each heel down and rolling the shoe forward to its toe. Sometimes, a board creaked under him.

He stopped at a corner where this bit of hallway met a long stretch of corridor. Leaning forward, he aimed his beam to the left. He saw no blood on the floor. His light reached only far enough down the narrow passage to reveal one door. That door stood open.

He knew that he should take a peek inside.

He didn't want to.

Byron looked to the right. Not far away, a staircase rose toward the upper stories. Beyond that was a foyer and the front entrance.

He saw no blood on the floor in that direction.

I'll check that way, first, he decided. He knew it would make more sense to go left, but heading toward the front seemed safer.

He turned the corner. After a few strides, he twisted around and checked behind him with the light. That long hallway made him very nervous. Especially the open door, though he couldn't see it from here. Instead of turning his back on it, he began sidestepping.

He shined his light up and down the stairway. The balustrade flung crooked, shifting bars of shadow against the wall.

*What if the blood goes up there?*

He didn't want to think about that.

He checked the floor ahead of him. Still, no blood. Coming to the foot of the stairs, he checked the newel cap and ran his light up the banister. No blood. Nor did he find any on the lower stairs. He could only see the tops of five, though. After that, they were above his eye level.

*I don't want to go up there,* he thought.

He wanted to go up there even less than he wanted to search the far end of the hallway.

Sidestepping through the foyer, he made his way to the front door. He tried its handle. The door seemed frozen in place.

He noticed that his light was shining on a panel of mailboxes. His own building had a similar arrangement. But in his building, each box was labelled with a room number and name. No such labels here.

This came as no surprise to Byron. But his dread deepened.

*I've come this far,* he told himself. *I'm not going to back out now.*

Trembling, he stepped toward the stairway. He climbed one stair, then another. The muscles of his legs felt like warm jelly. He stopped. He swept his light across two higher treads that he hadn't been able to see from the bottom. Still, no blood.

*She didn't go this way,* he told himself.

*If she did, she's on her own.*

*I didn't count on having to search an abandoned apartment house. That'd be stupid. God only knows who might be lurking in the empty rooms.*

Byron backed down the stairs and hurried away, eager to reach the passage that would lead to the alley door.

He felt ashamed of himself for giving up.

Nobody will ever know.

But he hesitated when he came to the connecting hallway. He shone his light at the alley door. Twenty feet away. No more than that. He could be outside in seconds.

But what about the bleeder?

You'll never know, he thought.

You'll always wonder.

Suppose it *is* a beautiful young woman, wandering around in shock, slowly bleeding to death? Suppose you're her only chance?

I don't care. I'm not going upstairs.

But what about that open door?

He could take a look in there, couldn't he?

He swung his light toward it.

And heard the soft murmur of a sigh.

*Oh my God!*

He gazed at the doorway. The sigh had come from there, he was sure of it.

'Hello?' he called.

Someone moaned.

Byron glanced again at the alley door, shook his head, and hurried down the corridor.

So much for chickening out, he thought, feeling somewhat pleased with himself in spite of his misgivings.

I'll be a hero, after all.

'I'm here,' he said as he neared the open door. 'I'll help you.'

He rushed into the room.

He jumped the beam of his flashlight here and there. Shot its bright tunnel into corners of the room. Across bare floorboards. Past windows and a radiator.

At his back, the door slammed shut.

He gasped and whirled around.

And stared, not quite sure what he was seeing.

Then a small whimper slipped from his throat and he stumbled backward, urine running hot down his leg.

The man standing beside the door grinned with wet, red lips.

143

He was hairless. He didn't even have eyebrows. Nor did he appear to have a neck. His head looked as if it had been jammed down between his massive shoulders.

His bloody lips grinned at Byron around a clear plastic tube.

A straw of sorts. Flecked inside with red.

The tube curled down from his mouth to a body cradled in his thick arms.

The limp body of a young man whose head was tipped back as if he found something fascinating about the far wall. He wore jeans and a plaid shirt. The shirt hung open. From the center of his chest protruded something that resembled a metal spike – obviously hollow inside – which was joined with the plastic tubing. A single thin streamer of blood stretched from the hole, across his chest, and down the side of his ribcage.

It was the streamer, Byron knew, that had left the trail of drops which led him there.

He pictured the monstrous, bloated man carrying the body block after block down city streets, drinking its blood as he lumbered along.

Now, the awful man shook the body. His cheeks sank in as he sucked. Some red flew up through the tubing. Byron heard a slurpy hollow sound – the sound that comes from a straw when you reach the bottom of a chocolate shake.

Then came another soft sigh.

'All gone,' the man muttered.

His lips peeled back, baring red teeth that pinched the tube.

He dropped the body.

The spike popped out of its chest and swayed at the end of the tubing.

'Glad you're here,' he said. 'Got me an awful thirst.'

Wrapping his thick fingers around the spike, he stepped over the body.

Byron spun around, ran, and leaped. He wrapped his arms around his head an instant before hitting the window. It exploded around him and he fell until he crashed against the pavement of a sidewalk.

He scurried up and ran.

He ran for a long time.

Finally, exhausted, he leaned against a store front. Panting for air, he looked where he had been.

Now *that's* a trail of blood, he thought.

Too weak to go on, he let his knees unlock. He slumped down on the sidewalk and stretched out his legs.

His clothes, he saw, were shredded from the window glass.

So am I, he thought.

But that thing didn't get me.

Smiling, he shut his eyes.

When he opened them again, he saw a woman crouching beside him. A young, slim blonde. Really cute. She looked a lot like the one he'd hoped to find at the end of the trail. 'You'll be all right,' she said. 'My partner's calling for an ambulance.'

She nodded toward the patrol car idling by the curb.

# Desert Pickup

All *right!*' He felt lucky about his one. Walking backward along the roadside, he stared at the oncoming car and offered his thumb. Sunlight glared on the windshield. Only at the last moment did he manage to get a look at the driver. A woman. That was that. So much for feeling lucky.

When he saw the brake lights flash on, he figured the woman was slowing down to be safe. When he saw the car stop, he figured this would be the 'big tease.' He was used to it. The car stops, you run to it, then off it shoots, throwing dust in your face. He wouldn't fall for it this time. He'd walk casually toward the car.

When he saw the backup lights come on, he couldn't believe his luck.

The car rolled backward to him. The woman inside leaned across the front seat and opened the door.

'Can I give you a ride?'

'Sure can.' He jumped in and threw his seabag onto the rear seat. When he closed the door, cold air struck him. It seemed to freeze the sweat on his T-shirt. It felt fine. 'I'm mighty glad to see you,' he said. 'You're a real lifesaver.'

'How on earth did you get way out here?' she asked, starting again up the road.

'You wouldn't believe it.'

'Go ahead and try me.'

He enjoyed her cheerfulness and felt guilty about the slight nervous tremor he heard in her voice. 'Well, this fella gives me a lift. Just this side of Blythe. And he's driving along through this . . . this *desert* . . . when suddenly he stops and tells me to get out and take a look at one of the tires. I get out – and off he goes! Tosses my seabag out a ways up the road. Don't know why a fella wants to do something like that. You understand what I mean?'

'I certainly do. These days you don't know who to trust.'

'If that ain't the truth.'

He looked at her. She wore boots and jeans and a faded blue shirt, but she had class. It was written all over her. The way she talked, the way her skin was tanned just so, the way she wore her hair. Even her figure showed class. Nothing overdone.

'What I don't get,' he went on, 'is why the fella picked me up in the first place.'

'He might have been lonely.'

'Then why'd he dump me?'

'Maybe he decided not to trust you. Or maybe he just wanted to be alone again.'

'Any way you slice it, it was a rotten thing to do. You understand what I mean?'

'I think so. Where are you headed?'

'Tucson.'

'Fine. I'm going in that direction.'

'How come you're not on the main highway? What are you doing out here?'

'Well . . .' She laughed nervously. 'What I'm intending to do is not . . . well, not exactly legal.'

'Yeah?'

'I'm going to steal cacti.'

'What!' He laughed. 'Wow! You mean you're out to lift some cactuses?'

'That's what I mean.'

'Well, I sure hope you don't get caught!'

The woman forced a smile. 'There *is* a fine.'

'Gol-ly.'

'A sizable fine.'

'Well, I'd be glad to give you a hand.'

'I've only got one shovel.'

'Yeah. I saw it when I stowed my bag. I was wondering what you had a shovel for.' He looked at her, laughing, and felt good that this woman with all her class was going to steal a few plants from the desert. 'I've seen a lot of things, you understand. But never a cactus-napper.' He laughed at his joke.

She didn't. 'You've seen one now,' she said.

They remained silent for a while. The young man thought about this classy woman driving down a lonely road in the desert just to swipe cactus, and every now and then he chuckled about it. He wondered why anybody would want such a thing in the first place. Why take the desert home with you? He wanted nothing more than to get away from this desolate place, and for the life of him he couldn't understand a person wanting to take part of it home. He concluded that the woman must be crazy.

'Would you care for some lunch?' the crazy woman asked. She still sounded nervous.

'Sure, I guess so.'

'There should be a paper bag on the floor behind you. It has a couple of sandwiches in it, and some beer. Do you like beer?'

'Are you kidding?' He reached over the back of the seat and picked up the bag. The sandwiches smelled good. 'Why don't you pull off the road up there?' he suggested. 'We can go over by those rocks and have a picnic.'

'That sounds like a fine idea.' She stopped on a wide shoulder.

'Better take us a bit farther back. We don't wanta park this close to the road. Not if you want me to help you heist some cactus when we get done with lunch.'

She glanced at him uneasily, then smiled. 'Okay, fine. We'll do just that.'

The car bumped forward, weaving around large balls of cactus, crashing through undergrowth. It finally stopped behind a cluster of rocks.

'Do you think they can still see us from the road?' the woman asked. Her voice was shaking.

'I don't think so.'

When they opened the doors, heat blasted in on them. They got out, the young man carrying the bag of sandwiches and beer. He sat down on a large rock. The woman sat beside him.

'I hope you like the sandwiches. They're corned beef with Swiss cheese.'

'Sounds good.' He handed one of them to her and opened the beer. The cans were only cool, but he decided that cool beer was better than no beer at all. As he picked at the cellophane covering his sandwich, he asked, 'Where's your husband?'

'What do you mean?'

He smiled. It had really put her on the spot. 'Well, I just happened to see that you aren't wearing a ring, you understand what I mean?'

She looked down at the band of pale skin on her third finger. 'We're separated.'

'Oh? How come?'

'I found out that he'd been cheating on me.'

'On *you?* No kidding! He must have been crazy.'

'Not crazy. He just enjoyed hurting people. But I'll tell you something. Cheating on me was the worst mistake he ever made.'

They ate in silence for a while, the young man occasionally shaking his head with disbelief. Finally, his head stopped shaking. He decided that maybe he'd cheat too on a grown woman who gets her kicks stealing cactus. Good looks aren't everything. Who wants to live with a crazy woman? He drank off his beer. The last of it was warm and made him shiver.

He went to the car and took the shovel from the floor in the back. 'You want to come along? Pick out the ones you want and I'll dig them up for you.'

He watched her wad up the cellophane and stuff it, along with the empty beer cans, into the paper bag. She put the bag in the car, smiling at him and saying, 'Every litter bit hurts.'

They left the car behind. They walked side by side, the woman glancing about, sometimes crouching to inspect a likely cactus.

'You must think I'm rather strange,' she confided, 'picking up

150

a hitchhiker like I did. I hope you don't think . . . well, it was criminal of that man to leave you out in the middle of nowhere. But I'm glad I picked you up. For some reason, I feel I can talk to you.'

'That's nice. I like to listen. What about this one?' he asked, pointing at a huge prickly cactus.

'Too big. What I want is something smaller.'

'This one ought to fit in the trunk.'

'I'd rather have a few smaller ones,' she insisted. 'Besides, there's a kind in the Saguaro National Monument that I want to get. It'll probably be pretty big. I want to save the trunk for that one.'

'Anything you say.'

They walked farther. Soon, the car was out of sight. The sun felt like a hot, heavy band pressing down on the young man's head and back.

'How about this one?' he asked, pointing. 'It's pretty little.'

'Yes. This one is just about perfect.'

The woman knelt beside it. Her shirt was dark blue against her perspiring back, and a slight breeze rustled her hair.

This will be a good way to remember her, the young man thought as he crashed the shovel down on her head.

He buried her beside the cactus.

As he drove down the road, he thought about her. She had been a nice woman with obvious class. Crazy, but nice. Her husband must've been a nut to cheat on a good-looking woman like her, unless of course it was because of her craziness.

He thought it nice that she had told him so much about herself. It felt good to be trusted with secrets.

He wondered how far she would have driven him. Not far enough. It was much better having the car to himself. That way he didn't have to worry. And the $36 he found in her purse was a welcome bonus. He'd been afraid, for a moment, that he might find nothing but credit cards. All around, she had been a good find. He felt very lucky.

At least until the car began to move sluggishly. He pulled off the road and got out, 'Oh, no,' he muttered, seeing the flat rear tire. He leaned back against the side of the car and groaned. The sun beat on his face. He closed his eyes and shook his head, disgusted by the situation and thinking how awful it would be, working on the tire for fifteen minutes under that hot sun.

Then he heard, in the distance, the faint sound of a motor. Opening his eyes, he squinted down the road. A car was approaching. For a moment, he considered thumbing a ride. But that, he decided, would be stupid now that he had a car of his own. He closed his eyes again to wait for the car to pass.

But it didn't pass. It stopped.

He opened his eyes and gasped.

'Afternoon,' the stranger called out.

'Howdy, Officer,' he said, his heart thudding.

'You got a spare?'

'I think so.'

'What do you mean, you think so? You either have a spare or you don't.'

'What I meant was, I'm not sure if it's any good. It's been a while since I've had any use for it, you understand?'

'Of course I understand. Guess I'll stick around till we find out. This is rough country. A person can die out here. If the spare's no good, I'll radio for a tow.'

'Okay, thanks.' He opened the door and took the keys from the ignition.

Everything's okay, he told himself. No reason in the world for this cop to suspect anything.

'Did you go off the road back a ways?'

'No, why?' Even as he asked, he fumbled the keys. They fell to the ground. The other man picked them up.

'Flats around here, they're usually caused by cactus spines. They're murder.'

He followed the officer to the rear of the car.

The octagonal key didn't fit the trunk.

'Don't know why those dopes in Detroit don't just make

one key that'll fit the door and trunk both.'

'I don't know,' the young man said, matching the other's tone of disgust and feeling even more confident.

The round key fit. The trunk popped open.

The officer threw a tarp onto the ground and then leveled his pistol at the young man, who was staring at the body of a middle-aged man who obviously had class.

# The Mask

The Palace Theater screened a different horror classic every Saturday at midnight. Allan Hunter hadn't missed one in over a year. Tonight, he'd watched the original *Nosferatu* with Max Schreck.

Though he owned a car, he'd always made the two-mile journey from his apartment to the Palace afoot. The trip *to* the theater was enjoyable, but it was the return trip that he craved. He knew there were dangers. A more sensible man would drive to and from the movies rather than risk a mugging, or worse. But if he drove, safe and insulated inside his car, he knew he would miss the thrill.

For Allan relished the mysteries of the night.

Apartment windows enticed him. If dark, who slept within? Or who didn't sleep, but lay awake or made love or stood at the black windows, peering out, perhaps watching him wander by? If still aglow in the deep hours of the night, who was about inside, doing what?

The shops and stores along the way, locked and deserted, intrigued him. If their fronts were barricaded by iron gates, all the better. The accordion gates tantalized Allan. They whispered of the owner's fear. He often stopped and peered through them, wondering what needed such protection through the night.

Each time a car swept past Allan on the quiet streets, he tried to glimpse who was in it, and he wondered, going where? People heading home after work, after a late film or party? A lover on his way to a rendezvous? A wife fleeing her brutal husband? A maniac on the prowl for his next victim? Often when a car went

155

by, he imagined that its brake lights might suddenly flash on, that it might swing to the curb in front of him, that its door might fly open and someone call to him – or leap out and rush him. Just *thinking* about that gave Allan goosebumps.

And so did thinking about what might lurk in the dark spaces along his route: recessed entryways and those narrow gaps he encountered where two buildings didn't quite join – and alleys. Such places gave him a delicious tingle. He always quickened his pace to get past them. Often he couldn't force himself to glance in, appalled by the possibilities of what he might find. Derelicts, or worse.

There *were* derelicts abroad. Some slept in entryways, or on bus-stop benches. Some, curled in shadows, glared at him as he hurried by. Others shambled along the sidewalks or down the streets, clutching secret prizes. Or trudged behind rattling supermarket carts piled high with bizarre shapes. Allan found no magic, no excitement, in contemplating such wrecks. They scared him, disgusted him. They hardly seemed human at all.

They were the worst thing about walking home after the midnight movies.

Whenever possible, he crossed the street or even backtracked to avoid confronting one. But sometimes he was caught by surprise and had no choice but to endure the stench, the maniacal jibbering, the whiny plea for money.

With such mad, vile creatures lurking in the night, it was little wonder that Allan rarely encountered normal people during his treks home from the movies.

Most of those he saw were in the midst of rushing to or from their parked cars. Occasionally, he spotted someone walking a dog. Once in a great while, a pair of joggers. Never a jogger out by himself, always with a companion. Sometimes a lone man hurrying along. Almost never a woman.

No woman in her right mind, he thought, would wander about the city alone at this hour.

When the woman came into sight as he walked home after *Nosferatu*, he thought she must be mad – or wildly reckless. Even

156

though she was a block away, he could see she was no derelict. Her stride was too steady as she approached the corner. Her hair, silvery in the streetlight, looked trim and well groomed. She wore a pale blouse, shorts that reached almost to her knees, white socks and dark shoes.

Certainly not a derelict.

A prostitute? Allan had never encountered any prostitutes in this neighborhood. And wouldn't a streetwalker be dressed in something exotic or scanty?

This woman looked more like a co-ed who'd wandered too far from campus. Or like one of the young teachers at the high school where he taught – Shelly Gates or Maureen O'Toole, for instance. Or like some of the women he liked to watch when he made his weekly trips to the supermarket. Casually dressed, trim and neat and clean.

Allan realized that he had stopped walking.

How strange to see someone like her roaming about at this hour!

She had come to a halt at the street corner, her head turned away. She seemed to be checking for traffic, preparing to cross the intersection.

But then she turned around.

She had no face. Allan's heart slammed.

*What's wrong with her!*

She walked briskly toward him.

No face!

He glanced at the street, tempted to race across and escape. But when he looked at the stranger again, she was closer. Close enough for him to see the shimmer of fabric that draped her face. Silver, glossy. It hung from her forehead, slotted with holes for her eyes and mouth, and fluttered below her chin.

A mask!

Allan heard himself moan. Chills chased up his back. His scalp prickled.

He leaped off the sidewalk and sprinted for the other side of the street.

*What if she comes after me?*

157

He sprang over the curb, dodged a parking meter, and looked back.

She had stopped. Her head was turned his way.

*She's watching me. Oh God, she's watching me. But at least she's staying put.*

Allan swung his eyes to the sidewalk and hurried for the corner. He didn't want to see her again, but in his mind she was crossing the street, pursuing him. He had to look again.

Checking over his shoulder, he saw her still standing motionless, still watching him.

At the corner, he rushed to the left. A few strides, and the wall of a Wells Fargo bank sheltered him from the stranger's view. He slowed and caught his breath.

Safe.

'Christ,' he muttered.

He'd walked the night streets countless times, seen his share of weird derelicts, watched hundreds of horror films, read scores of fright books.

But he'd never been spooked like this.

Spooked? Scared nearly witless.

By a piece of silver cloth no bigger than a hanky.

As he walked along, he began to feel ashamed of himself. What a coward, running like that. The woman had looked perfectly normal except for the mask. And the mask itself had been nothing hideous. A simple square of fabric. Possibly silk. Nothing to inspire panic.

She's *gotta* be a nut case, going around like that.

Nothing wrong with running away from a lunatic.

But what if she's sane? What if she only wears the mask because her face is disfigured? She walks at night when there's almost nobody around to see her, and wears her mask just in case. In case someone like me comes along. So her face won't gross me out.

And I ran away as if she were a monster.

What an awful life she must live. And I came along and made it worse.

Good going.

Allan considered turning around, going back and searching for her. But he didn't have the nerve.

He couldn't get the woman out of his mind. He thought about her constantly: that night as he lay in bed; Sunday as he corrected papers, labored on his vampire novel, read and watched television; all week long. At school, every slender, blonde student in his classes reminded him of her. So did two of the teachers, Shelly and Maureen, even though Maureen was a redhead. They all forced him to remember the woman in the mask, and his shame.

The more he thought of her, the more certain he grew that she wasn't crazy. She was a sensitive young woman cursed with a hideous face. She led a solitary, lonely life, willing to venture from her home only in the dead of night, and then with her face concealed.

He could imagine the anguish she must've felt when he fled from her.

If only he had held his ground. Smiled as she approached. Said, 'Good evening.' It was too late for that, however. The most he would ever be able to do was apologize for adding to her misery.

To do that, he would need to find her again.

But he'd spotted her some time after 1 a.m. That's when he would need to go looking. If he tried it on a school night, he'd be wasted the next day. He had to wait for the weekend.

At last, Friday arrived. Allan awoke feeling nervous and excited. Tonight, he would go out searching for her.

What would he say if he found her? How would she react? She might hate him for running away. *How could you do that, you bastard! I'm a human being, not a freak!*

Or she might indeed, after all, turn out to be utterly mad.

'Is something bothering you?' Shelly asked him during lunch.

'Me? No.'

'Are you sure? You've been acting strange all week.'

159

'I have?'

Shelly glanced at Maureen. 'You've noticed it, haven't you?'

Maureen, who rarely spoke, studied her sandwich and shook her head. 'He seems fine to me.'

'It might help to talk about it,' Shelly told him. 'You aren't sick, are you?'

'I feel fine.'

'If it's too personal . . .'

'Leave him alone,' Maureen said. 'He doesn't want to talk about it.'

'You *have* noticed!'

Maureen shrugged. Her eyes met Allan's. 'You don't have to say anything. It's none of our business.'

'Of course it's our business. We're his buddies. Right, Allan?'

He smiled. 'My buds. Right. I do appreciate your concern, really. Thanks. But it's nothing. I'm just a little bit nervous about this gal I'll be seeing tonight.'

'Ah-ha!' Shelly's eyes gleamed. 'A gal! Go for it, Romeo!'

'That's wonderful,' Maureen said.

'Anybody we know?' Shelly asked.

'*I* don't even know her. Not exactly. She's just somebody I met last weekend. At the movies. She sat across the aisle from me. We didn't even talk. But if she's there tonight . . .'

'Whoa!' Shelly held up her hand. 'Hold on. One second. She was at that midnight creepshow thing you go to on Saturday nights? And you don't know her? So where do you think you'll find her tonight?'

Allan felt heat wash over his face. This is what comes of lying, he thought. He shook his head and forced himself to laugh. 'Geez, I don't know. Guess I *won't* be seeing her tonight. You're right.'

'Boy, you must have it bad. You don't even know what day it is.' She nudged Maureen with her elbow. 'Looks like we've got a case of love at first sight.'

'I don't even know her,' Allan protested.

'She must be quite a fox.'

'Quit teasing him,' Maureen said. 'Let him eat his lunch.'

Shelly laughed. 'So what's she got that we ain't got?'

No face, Allan thought.

But he only shrugged. Then Jake Hanson came to their table and the conversation turned to obnoxious students, as it often did. When the bell rang and Allan got up from the table, Shelly said, 'Hey, good luck with the fox. Don't do anything I wouldn't do.'

Allan headed for his fifth-period class, wishing he'd kept his mouth shut.

Finally, the school day ended. On the way home, he stopped off at Blockbuster Video and picked up six tapes. Horror movies. Two of which he hadn't already seen. They would help pass the time.

He ran one during supper, but his mind was on the masked woman. He hardly noticed the movie. Then he tried to work on his vampire novel, but gave up after an hour. As he sat in his recliner to watch the next movie, he thought, What's the use? I might as well stare at the wall.

And then he had a very welcome thought.

It came in the form of Shelly's voice saying, 'So where do you think you'll find her tonight?'

Shelly was right.

Why get all worked up when I probably won't find her tonight, anyway? We ran into each other on *Saturday* night. Why not wait for then?

Yes!

I'll stay home tonight, enjoy my movies, go to bed at a reasonable hour . . .

The feeling of relief was immense.

Then Saturday arrived. The hours crept by. He told himself that he didn't *have* to approach the masked woman. He could take a different route home from the theater, and avoid her. For that matter, he could stay home.

And miss the midnight showing of *The Cabinet of Dr Caligari*? He'd already seen the film six or seven times. A shame not to watch it again, though. He could always drive his car.

161

No. I'll walk. I'll take my usual route. If I see her, I'll apologize. And that will be the end of it.

After supper that night, he sat in his recliner and watched *The Texas Chainsaw Massacre*, then *I Spit on Your Grave*. For minutes at a time, he was able to forget about the masked woman. When the movies were over, he took a shower. He shaved. He combed his hair and splashed some Chaps on his cheeks. Instead of wearing his favorite outfit for the midnight show – old blue jeans and his Bates Motel T-shirt – he put on a good pair of Dockers and a plaid sports shirt.

In the bedroom mirror, he shook his head at himself.

What the hell am I doing? You'd think I really *did* have a date.

Hey, maybe she won't recognize me dressed up like this. She couldn't have gotten a very good look at my face.

At a quarter past eleven, he left his apartment. He gave his parked car a long look as he walked by it.

So much easier if I just drive.

He couldn't.

He had to make an attempt to find her.

Tense and shaky, he walked to the Palace. He usually bought nachos and a Pepsi at the refreshment counter. But tonight he had no appetite. He took his seat. He glanced about at the familiar crowd, fearing that *she* might've come to watch the movie. Then the lights dimmed. He rubbed his sweaty hands on the legs of his trousers, and faced the screen.

*The Cabinet of Dr Caligari* began.

He stared at it. But in his mind, he saw the masked woman. Saw himself approaching her. What if she's bonkers? What if she's dangerous? What if she lifts the mask to show me her face and it's horrible? Worse than anything ever created by Tom Savini or Stan Winston? Worse than the ugliest fantasies of Clive Barker?

He tried to calm himself.

Maybe she won't show up.

He had never run into her before. Last Saturday night could have been a fluke. She might've been out on a special errand, or something.

Maybe I'll never see her again.

As much as he dreaded the encounter, however, he found himself troubled by the idea of never seeing her again. It was more than a need to set matters right. He'd known that all along, he supposed.

She frightened him, but he longed to learn her secrets.

All the mysteries of the night, so eerie and tantalizing, seemed banal compared to the woman in the mask. She was the ultimate mystery.

Mad or sane? What lurks beneath the mask? What possesses her to walk the empty streets? Does she have a tortured soul? What stories might she tell of children shrieking at the sight of her, of heartless abuse, of solitary years locked away from daylight? How does it feel to be shunned?

He could learn the answers.

Tonight.

The lights came up.

Allan walked into the night. By the time he'd walked a block, he was alone.

His mouth was dry. His heart thudded. His legs trembled.

He gave no thought to the windows above the street, barely glanced through the accordion gates of the closed shops, paid no attention to passing cars, looked into dark entryways and the gaps between buildings and the alleys for no reason other than to search for her. As he hurried along, he noticed a few derelicts. He saw them, felt neither fear nor disgust, and turned his eyes away to look for the masked woman.

Finally, he came to the block where he'd encountered her. The sidewalk stretched ahead of him, deserted. He slowed his pace. He gazed at the corner.

Where are you?

Maybe I'm early. No. If anything, *Cabinet* was five or six minutes longer than *Nosferatu*. Maybe I'm too late, then.

But if she'd come this way, we should've run into each other already.

Maybe she stayed home tonight. Or chose a different route.

He stopped. It was just about here that he'd been halted by the sight of her. She'd appeared from the right, walked to the corner and turned her back to him as if intending to cross the street. It was here that he'd been standing when she turned around.

He waited.

Dribbles of sweat slid down his sides.

I ought to just keep walking. If she doesn't show, she doesn't show.

He checked his wristwatch. One twenty-eight.

Give her five minutes.

When he looked up from his watch, she was already past the corner and striding toward him.

He gasped and staggered backward.

Cool it! he told himself. This is it. You wanted to see her, here she is.

The silver fabric shrouding her face shimmered and swayed as she walked. Her hair gleamed in the streetlights. Instead of shorts and a blouse like last week, she wore a dress. It looked purple and shiny. It hung from her shoulders by narrow straps, draped the swells of her breasts, tapered down to a sash at her waist, flared out at her hips and drifted against her striding thighs. It was very short. Her legs looked long and sleek. She wore sandals, not shoes and socks.

Allan's heart thundered.

*She's gorgeous!* Except for that damn mask. What horrors did *it* conceal?

She must be mad. No sane woman would walk these streets at such an hour – and *not* in a dress like that!

Don't just stand here, gaping at her.

He started walking toward her.

Her sandals made soft clapping sounds on the concrete. Her skirt briefly took on the shape of each thigh that swept against it. The ends of the sash swung by her side. The silken fabric clinging to her breasts trembled and jiggled.

Maybe she is a whore, after all.

If so, she might wear the mask merely to conceal her identity.

Or to make her look enigmatic. Her face might not be ghastly, after all.

Now, only a few strides separated Allan from the woman.

In the darkness behind the mask's eye slots, he could see nothing except mere specks of reflected light. A vague hint of lips showed through the slot at her mouth.

*I've got to say something. Apologize. At least.*

He was walking straight toward her, so he angled to his right.

Her head turned.

He managed a smile.

They passed each other.

He breathed in her perfume. A scent so strange and delicious it forced him to sigh, to look back at her.

She halted as if she felt his gaze.

'Excuse me?' he said. Damn, but he sounded like a scared kid!

She turned around.

'Do you remember me?' he asked.

'Oh, yes.' Her voice was low, breathy. In spite of the narrow gap at her mouth, it stirred the mask like a soft breeze.

'I . . . I guess I kind of . . . lost my cool last week. I'm really glad you came along.' He shrugged. 'I wanted to apologize.'

'Apologize? For running from me?' she asked.

'I'm really sorry.'

'What's your name?'

He hesitated. 'Allan.'

'Allan what?'

She wants my *last* name? Good God, she'd be able to look me up, find me. 'Hawthorne,' he lied. 'Allan Hawthorne.'

She stepped toward him, mask and dress glimmering, and reached out her hand. Allan shook it. But when he tried to let go, her fingers tightened. She held him in a firm, warm grip. 'I'm Ligeia,' she said.

The name surprised him. 'Really? Ligeia? There's a story by Poe . . .'

'I know,' she said in her strange, hushed voice.

'I really like Poe.'

'We have that in common, then. Come with me.' She pulled him by the hand. And kept his hand in hers as she led him slowly down the sidewalk.

'Uh . . . Where are we going?'

'Does it matter?'

'I don't know.'

'You're free to leave, if that's your wish.'

'No. No, that's okay.'

She nodded slightly, then turned her head forward.

Allan hoped to see under her mask, but it curved around the side of her face, hiding her almost to the ear. It hung from a headband, a folded scarf that was tied at the back. The way the silver cloth was tucked in over the top of the scarf, it flowed down smoothly except for a slight bump made by the tip of her nose. Her chin didn't seem to touch the draping fabric at all.

They walked in silence for a while.

He wished she would say something.

Finally, he broke the silence himself. 'I really felt awful about running away.'

She stopped and turned toward him. 'It was this,' she said. Her other hand came up. Her fingertips glided down the glossy mask, easing it inward. Ever so briefly as the fingers slid down, the mask took on the contours of her face. Though her eyes remained hidden, Allan glimpsed a veiled suggestion of slender nose and cheeks. Her lips appeared for an instant, bare in the opening. Her fingers drifted the fabric against a small bulge of chin. Then she breathed. The hints of her face dissolved behind a silver tremor.

Allan tried to swallow. He wished his heart would slow down.

'I frighten you, don't I?'

'A little,' he whispered. 'I guess.'

'We fear the unknown,' she said. 'But we're enthralled by it.'

'Yes.'

'Do I enthrall you, Allan?'

He let out a small, nervous laugh. 'I don't know. You sure . . . make me curious.'

'You wonder what the mask hides.'

'Yes. And . . . and why you walk around at an hour like this.'

'So I won't be seen.'

'But why?'

'My face, of course. Come along.' She turned away, pulling at his hand, and they resumed walking. 'I like the night,' she said. 'It holds such secrets.'

'But its dangerous.'

'Not for me. The mask protects me. People keep their distance. They take me for a madwoman.'

'I guess . . . I was afraid of that, myself.'

'I know.'

'You're not, though.'

'You don't think so?'

'Hope not.'

Laughing softly, she squeezed his hand. 'I think I like you, Allan.'

'I think I like you, too.'

'Shall we be friends?'

'Sure,' he said.

She looked at him. '*Are* you sure?'

'Yeah. I mean, why not?'

'You're still frightened of me, aren't you?'

'A little, maybe.'

'I won't hurt you.'

'It's just . . . you know, the mask. If I could see your face . . . Is it . . . is something wrong with it?'

'My face is my own.'

'How can we be friends if you're hiding behind a mask, if you won't let me see what you look like?'

She gave no answer, but led him into an alley. His mouth went dry. His heart slammed. As they left the lights of the street behind, he peered into the darkness. High walls on both sides. Dumpsters ahead. But no lurking derelicts that he could see. Though the alley appeared deserted, he trembled with dread and excitement.

167

Ligeia halted. She put her hands on his shoulders.

'Is my face *so* important?' she asked.

Oh, God! She's going to take off the mask. Now. Right here in the alley. In the dark.

'Is it?' she asked again.

'Uh. I guess not. Not really.'

'You said we can't be friends unless you know what I look like.'

'That isn't quite what . . .'

'Suppose I'm not pretty? Would you run from me again?'

'No.'

'Suppose I'm horribly ugly?'

'Is that why you wear the mask?'

'Perhaps.' Gently, she rubbed his shoulders. 'How important is my face to you, Allan? Does it need to be beautiful? Or can you accept me without . . . passing judgement on it?'

He managed to whisper, 'Yes.'

'Yes what?'

'I don't need to see.'

She glided forward, wrapped her arms around Allan and drew him close against her. He felt the heat of her body, the push of her breasts, the cool smoothness of the mask against his face. Her lips met his mouth.

Her lips felt wonderful. Warm and moist.

So long since the last time he'd held and kissed a woman. The feel of her shocked him with desire.

But she *must* be hideous, or why . . . ?

He didn't care. She smelled of strange, jungle blossoms. Her sweet breath filled him. He slid his tongue into her mouth and she sucked it in deep and writhed against him, rubbing him with her sleek body as her hands clutched his back.

His own hands roamed Ligeia's back, caressing the skin above the top of her dress, roaming lower, sliding the fabric against her, following her curves down past the sash. He filled his hands with the soft, firm mounds of her buttocks. And knew they were bare beneath the fragile veil of the skirt. Moaning into her mouth, he pulled the skirt up.

Ligeia grabbed his wrists. She forced his hands down to his sides and leaned away, shaking her head. She breathed hard. The mask clung around her mouth, wet.

'What's wrong?' Allan whispered.

'Nothing. You're . . . I've got to leave now.'

He took a step toward her. She stopped him, hands against his chest.

'I'm sorry,' she said. 'Perhaps we'll see each other again.' She backed away from him.

'Don't go.'

Without another word, she whirled and fled.

The moment she vanished from sight, Allan ran to the mouth of the alley. He spotted her to the right, dashing up the sidewalk, her shimmering dress afly, her arms pumping, her long bare legs striding out, her sandals clapping the concrete.

'Ligeia!' he cried out.

She didn't look back.

*What if I never see her again?*

Maybe that'd be for the best, he told himself. What sort of relationship could we have, anyway? She has to wear that mask. Too grotesque to go anywhere without it.

I'd be better off . . .

She darted around the corner.

'No!' he yelled into the night, and sprinted after her.

The hell with the mask, he thought as he raced up the sidewalk. Who gives a shit! Who gives a shit *what* she looks like!

He ran harder than he'd ever run before.

Pounded around the corner.

Skidded to a halt when he saw her no more than fifty feet away.

Obviously, she hadn't thought he would pursue her. She was walking slowly, head down, arms swaying limp at her sides, sandals scuffing along. She seemed lost in her thoughts, crushed by a burden of dejection.

Ligeia, Allan thought. What have I done to you?

He ached to rush forward and take her into his arms and make everything all right.

That might only make matters worse.

Is she upset because I got carried away in the alley? *She's* the one who started it. And that dress! Nothing on under it. What did she expect?

Maybe that isn't it. Suppose she's falling in love with me and knows it can't work. Maybe that's why she fled.

Whatever the reason, she was probably in no mood for Allan to put in an appearance.

He couldn't just walk away, though.

So he decided to follow her. He crept closer to the building fronts, ready to duck out of sight if she should start to turn around, and made his way forward, matching her pace.

Find out where she lives, he thought. She's bound to head for home, sooner or later.

He felt guilty, sneaking after her. Spying on her. It seemed like a betrayal. But he kept at it, knowing that if he quit he might lose her forever.

It went well for two blocks.

Then she stopped at a street corner. Though there seemed to be no traffic, she stood and waited for the light to change. As Allan watched, she began to turn around. He rushed forward, dodged into an entry way and stepped on the ankle of a derelict huddled in the darkness. The filthy old man flinched, moaned. With a gasp, Allan lurched away from him and staggered into the middle of the sidewalk.

He jerked his head forward, spotted Ligeia at the corner.

Facing him.

'Ligeia!' he called. 'Please!'

She flung herself around and leapt into the street. Without checking for traffic.

'Look out!' Allan cried.

The teenager bearing down on her yelped. Ligeia tried to lean out of his way. The teenager swerved, but not in time.

The bicycle slammed into her, tumbled her to the pavement,

twisted away and hit the curb, its abrupt stop hurling the kid against the handlebars.

Ligeia, sprawled in the street, started to push herself up.

As Allan ran to help, the kid jumped from his bicycle, let it fall, and hurried toward Ligeia. She was crouched, trying to stand, her back to him. 'Geez, lady. You okay?'

She looked over her shoulder at him. Her mask gleamed in the streetlights.

'Yeeeah!' he gasped, and bolted for his bike.

Even before he got to it, Ligeia was up and running. The kid started to pick up his bike, but dropped it and scampered out of the way when he saw Allan bearing down on him.

Allan hurdled the rear wheel.

Ligeia had already made the other side of the street.

'Wait!' he called.

She didn't look back, didn't slow down.

She was fast. Not as fast as Allan, but almost. It took all his speed to gain on her.

'Please! Stop!'

She *had* to be hurting. A patch of skin over her right shoulder blade was scraped raw. Her skirt was torn, and drooped away from the scuffed cheek of her buttock. Her pumping arms showed Allan abraded elbows. Her whole body must be afire with pain.

'Why are you *doing* this?' he gasped.

'Leave me alone!' she cried out.

'No! You need me! I need you!'

'You . . . don't *know* me!'

'I know you're lonely. I know I *care* about you. We can't lose each other. Please.'

'You'll hate me!'

'Bullshit!'

'I'm . . .'

'I don't give a flying fuck if you look like Godzilla!'

Reaching out, he grabbed her left arm. She tried to twist free of his grip. 'Stop that!' he snapped. And tugged her to a halt. Turned her roughly toward him.

171

Clutching both her upper arms, he pushed her backward and pinned her against the accordion gate of a pharmacy. It rattled as she hit it.

'Settle down.'

She quit struggling. She gasped for air. Her breath gusted out the front of her mask.

'Are you okay?' he asked.

She shook her head.

'You shouldn't have run.'

'Obviously.'

The remark made his throat tighten. He drew Ligeia gently against him. And her arms wrapped around him. He pressed his face against the mask, felt her cheek through its slick fabric. They held each other for a long time.

Then Ligeia whispered, 'I don't want to lose you so soon. Before we've even . . .'

'You won't.'

'You haven't seen my face.'

'It doesn't matter.'

'Think so, huh?' She squeezed Allan hard against her, then eased him away. 'I . . . I've got to show you.'

He nodded. He felt as if his heart might crash out through his ribcage. 'You don't have to.'

'I do. Better that you see it now, than . . .' Ligeia quit without finishing. She raised her hand to the headband across her brow. Hooked it with her fingertips. Peeled it back. The mask slid up her face.

More than her mask was coming off.

Her hair, too.

Oh God!

Her arm dropped to her side, mask and wig clutched in her fist.

Allan gaped at her.

She stared at him. She caught her lower lip between her teeth. After a few moments, she said, 'At least I'm not Godzilla.'

She let the mask and wig fall. Reaching up with both hands

she unpinned her hair. She shook her head, ran her fingers through the flowing red tresses. Her green eyes shimmered with tears.

'Maureen?'

'Don't hate me,' she said in the voice he knew so well, a voice so different from the breathy tones of Ligeia. 'Please.'

'How could I hate you? But I don't . . . Why? Why the mask? What's going on?'

'I just got tired of the buddy treatment, Allan.' A tear fell from the corner of each eye. They made silver trails down her cheeks. 'Day in, day out. You never . . . I'm not your buddy. I never wanted to *be* your buddy. So maybe it made me a little crazy and . . .'

'A lot crazy. Something might've happened to you, wandering around at night like this.'

She sniffed and rubbed away the tears. 'I just wanted you to notice me.'

'God, Maureen.'

'I wanted to show you that I'm a woman.'

His throat tightened. 'I always knew you were a woman. But it never entered my mind that you might want to . . . get involved with me. You never said anything. You never gave me any reason to suspect it.'

'I know. I know. I wanted to. I just couldn't. But then . . . I guess it was seeing *Phantom of the Opera* a few weeks ago that gave me the idea. I thought, what if he doesn't realize it's me? What if I'm a stranger he meets in the night? A mysterious, seductive masked woman. The way you're into spooky stuff, I figured it might work.'

'It sure worked, all right.'

'Too well, I guess. Back in the alley, I just couldn't . . . let it go any further. It wouldn't have been right. It wasn't me you wanted. It was Ligeia. Not plain old ordinary me.'

'She was . . . the most exciting woman I ever . . . She was fantastic.'

'I guess you must be awfully disappointed.'

173

'I don't know. I suppose so. It was the mystery, you know? I was the unknown and being afraid of who she was, what she might look like under the mask. Now that it's you . . .'

'It was always me.'

'Yeah, but . . .'

'It was. It *is*. I *am* Ligeia.' Crouching, she picked up the mask and wig. She put them on and took hold of Allan's hand.

'I don't think that'll work.'

'Won't it?' she asked, her voice low and breathy.

'I know it's you.'

'Do you?'

'Of course.'

'You know nothing.'

Allan felt a chill crawl up his spine.

She led him along the sidewalk. 'Maureen is a spineless pitiful creature of the light. I despise her.'

'Hey, come on. You don't have to do this.'

'I belong to the night.'

'Cut it out, okay? I'm *glad* you're Maureen.'

'I'm *not* Maureen. Call me again by that vile name at your peril.'

'Oh, for godsake.'

She pulled him into the darkness of an alley. She pushed him against a brick wall.

'This is ridiculous,' he muttered, his voice trembling. 'Let's get out of here.'

She lifted his hands to her breasts. He felt them, warm and firm through the slick fabric. She rubbed his palms against her stiff nipples.

'You're making me nervous. I wish you'd stop this. We're gonna have to look each other in the face, Monday morning.'

'You won't be looking *me* in the face. I'm Ligeia.'

'Come on, we both know you're not.'

She released his wrists. 'Lift my mask,' she whispered.

His heart kicked. 'What for?'

'You'll see.'

174

'I don't need to see. I know who you are.'

'Then why are you afraid to lift the mask?'

'You already took it off.'

'That was in the light. I am a woman of the darkness.'

He tried to laugh. 'You're pretty good at this. But I think we oughta get going.'

'I showed you Maureen. I didn't allow you to see Ligeia. The true face of Ligeia shuns the light. But you may look upon it now, if you have the courage.'

'I'm not afraid.'

'Then lift the mask.'

He stared at the fabric draping her face, tried to see her eyes and mouth behind the black slots. 'I know it's you,' he murmured. But he thought, *What if it's not?*

Ridiculous. Crazy.

But he couldn't force himself to lift the mask.

'Who am I?' she asked, her breath stirring the cloth.

'Ligeia.'

'Yessss.' She pulled him forward against her.

They embraced, they kissed, they squirmed breathless as they caressed and explored each other. She winced once when Allan touched the scrape behind her shoulder. He whispered, 'I'm sorry' into the warm pit of her mouth. Then he was on his back on the alley pavement. Maureen straddling him, bare to the waist. As he squeezed her breasts, she sank down and impaled herself.

Afterward, she lay on top of him and kissed him through the mouth slot of her mask.

He sighed. He'd known Maureen for three years. Three years wasted, he thought. So much missed.

'I must leave you now,' she whispered.

'No. I'll walk you home. Or we could go to my apartment.'

'Not tonight, my darling.' She pushed herself up, and Allan sighed with a feeling of loss as he slid out of her. Standing, she raised the top of her dress and arranged the shoulder straps. 'Farewell.' She turned away.

'Hey! Don't leave!'

175

She ran from the alley.

Allan knocked on the door of Maureen's classroom ten minutes before the start of first period Monday morning.

'Come in.'

He entered. She pushed back her chair and stood up, smiling. She wore a sleeveless, yellow sundress. She looked radiant. The sight of her made Allan's heart race. How could he have known her so long and never realized how beautiful she was?

Her bright green eyes watched him as he approached her desk.

'Good morning, Ligeia,' he said.

'Huh? Ligeia?'

He grinned. 'Still up to your tricks.'

She frowned with confusion. 'What?'

'Saturday night was great. The greatest.'

'Oh? You got together with your mystery woman?'

'Sure did.'

'Must've gone pretty well.'

'You oughta know.'

Her frown deepened. 'How would I know?'

'How about having dinner with me tonight?'

The frown vanished. A corner of her mouth curled up. 'Are you kidding?'

'Not a chance.'

'What about this other gal of yours? Ligeia? You just met her, and now you want me to go out with you?'

'She won't mind.'

'She must be very understanding.'

'What she doesn't know won't hurt her. I don't think we'll be seeing each other again. Not till next Saturday night, anyway.'

'You some kind of a two-timer?'

'Yep.'

The door opened. A couple of students came in.

'Look,' Maureen said, 'we can talk about this later. I've gotta get the spelling list onto the board.'

'Fine.'

176

He turned away, nodded a greeting to the kids, and paused at the door.

He looked back.

Maureen, facing the chalkboard behind her desk, wrote 'fantasy' with her right hand. Her left arm hung at her side.

Allan stared at her elbow.

She looked back at him. She raised her eyebrows. 'Is something wrong?'

'Your elbow,' he murmured.

She smiled. 'Just had a little mishap over the weekend.' She rubbed the dark crust of scab, then turned again to the chalkboard.

# *Eats*

I'm a trained investigator, so I knew right away that the dame who walked into my office had class. How did I know? She had blue hair on her head and a poodle tucked under one arm. I took my feet off my desk.

'My name is Mabel Wingate,' she said.

'Want me to stand up and cheer?' I asked through my mouthful of sandwich.

She tittered. 'Isn't he delightful!' She put the question to the pooch, chucking it under the chin. 'Do you think he might be good enough to share his sandwich?'

It was salami and Swiss on an onion roll with lettuce and onions and plenty of mayo. I'd just bought it at Lou's Deli down the block. I'd taken only one bite. I didn't want to part with it.

'This is my lunch, lady,' I said.

'You don't mind, do you?' she asked.

'Are you planning to hire me?'

'We shall see.'

I'm not an idiot. If I didn't fork over some of my sandwich to Snuggles or Snookums or whatever its name was, the old gal would find herself a different gumshoe. (I needed the work. Things have been slow lately, ever since I got on TV for plugging one of my clients. What can I say? Mistakes happen.)

'You don't watch much television, huh?' I asked.

'Please,' she said. 'The sandwich.'

'Oh, sure.' I set it down on my desk. She reached for it. 'Ah ah!' I snapped. 'Not the whole thing.'

179

'No, of course not. Excuse me.'

She waited, hovering over my desk and watching while I scooted back, slid up my trouser leg, and pulled the shiv out of my boot. I pressed its button. The blade flew and snapped into place.

'Dear me,' Mabel said. She was impressed. Her mouth looked like a doughnut.

'My toadsticker,' I told her.

'I do hope you've washed it.'

I've seen what dogs eat. Washed or not, pooch wouldn't care. I pinned the sandwich to my desk top and tried to keep its insides from slopping out as I cut. It made a real mess. 'There you go,' I said.

Mabel snatched up the biteless half. 'You're a dear,' she told me. She smiled at the dog. 'Isn't he a dear, Muffin?'

Muffin licked its chops.

But Mabel was the one who ate the sandwich.

She wolfed it down, then eyed the remains of my half. I stuffed the last of it into my mouth before she could make a grab for it.

'That certainly was tasty,' she said. 'I haven't eaten properly in ages.'

I had already noticed she was skinny, but I hadn't given it much thought. After all, it's chic to look like a cadaver.

'Have a seat,' I told her.

She sat down. Muffin licked some mayo off her chin.

'Someone,' she said, 'wants to poison me.'

'I see.'

'It's frightful. I hardly dare touch a bite. I'm withering away to nothing. You must help me.'

'I charge three hundred beans a day,' I said.

'Three hundred what?'

'Dollars.' It was double my usual rate, but I figured she could handle it. She wore diamond earrings, a pearl necklace, and eight rings. I knew that none of the jewelry was fake because of her blue hair and poodle.

'That sounds a trifle steep,' she said.

180

'You get what you pay for,' I explained. 'I'm the best.'

She rolled her eyes toward the ceiling as if she doubted my word.

'You don't want to pinch pennies,' I said, 'when your life's on the line.'

'I suppose you're right.'

'Of course I'm right.'

She set Muffin on the floor. It skittered under the desk and started chewing on one of my boots. I used my other boot to fend off while Mabel took a checkbook out of her purse. Usually, I insist on cash. A lot of my clients (back when I had clients) were deadbeats. But I figured I could trust Mabel.

She made out the check to Duke Scanlon, Private Investigator. Then she filled in the amount. I licked my lips and stopped kicking Muffin. She signed the check and slid it across the desk. I got mayo on it. 'Will that be enough,' she asked, 'to retain your services for a week?'

'Consider me retained. For starters, what makes you think someone wants to poison you?'

'I don't *think* someone wants to poison me, I *know*.'

'Has there been an attempt on your life?' I asked.

She rolled her eyes again. She was good at it. 'My dear young man – may I call you Duke?'

'Duke it is, Mabel.'

'Duke, now see here, had I been poisoned already I would hardly need your services. I would be pushing up daisies like my dear husband, Oscar.'

'What happened to Oscar?' I asked.

'Why, he died, of course. That's what happens when one is poisoned.'

'Ah-ha,' I said.

'Ah-ha, indeed. It was dreadful. He barely had a chance to swallow. One moment he was complaining that the hollandaise had curdled, and the next moment he was in it.'

'Eggs Benedict?' I asked.

'Precisely.'

'When did this happen?'

'April fifteenth,' Mabel said. 'That's over a month ago, and I haven't eaten properly since then. Whoever murdered Oscar, you see, intends to do the same to me.'

Muffin tried to climb my leg. Smiling at Mabel, who couldn't see what was going on, I bent over and patted the little cutie on the head and gave its ear a twist. It bit my wrist, then scampered away and hopped onto Mabel's lap looking pleased with itself.

'What did the police find?' I asked.

'The police? Ha! I told them and *told them* that Oscar had been poisoned, but would they listen? No. As far as they were concerned, poor Oscar simply dropped dead from a bum heart.'

'Did Oscar *have* a bum heart?'

'He most certainly did by the time *they* saw it.'

'Was an autopsy performed?'

'Of course,' she said.

'No traces of poison were found?'

'No, but I've discussed the matter with my physician and he assures me that there are several varieties of poison which might go undetected.'

'He's right,' I told her.

'Of course. He's a doctor.'

'Do you have any idea who might have . . .'

'You wouldn't have another one of those delicious sandwiches would you?' she interrupted.

'Not on me,' I said.

'Then let's discuss the rest of the details over lunch. I'm famished.'

I was all for it. Not only was I starving, but this called for a celebration. I was two thousand one hundred dollars richer than I'd been ten minutes ago, and the case would be a cinch. All I had to do was go through the motions.

Because Mabel Wingate was in no danger of being poisoned. Her late husband, Oscar, had been dropped by a faulty ticker, not Eggs Benedict. It was good enough for the cops; it was good enough for me.

182

Shrinks probably have a name for Mabel's condition – the way her mind turned things around to help her cope with the sudden shock of her Oscar's death. I have a name for it, too – bananas.

Mabel was bananas and rich.

I stood to make out like a bandit.

'Not a peep about this to the chauffeur,' she warned as we left the building.

'Yamamotos's,' Mabel told him.

He started driving. 'I'm not big on Japanese food,' I said.

'None the less, I am.'

So Yamamoto's it was. Mabel left Muffin in the limousine with Herbert the chauffeur, and we went in. 'I just adore sushi,' she said as we sat at a corner table.

'Sushi? She the waitress?'

'You have a lot to learn, Duke.'

She ordered the same meal for both of us. When the waitress left, she started right in on the case. 'One of my relatives,' she said, 'is obviously the villain. With Oscar out of the way, you see, the entire family fortune fell into my hands. Once I'm out of the way, they'll inherit oodles.'

'Who, exactly, will get the oodles?' I asked.

'According to the terms of our will, the wealth would be divided equally among our three children. We also provided handsome amounts for each of our servants.'

'So you figure one of the kids poisoned Oscar?'

'Or one of their spouses,' Mabel said. 'Or one of the servants. Or a combination.'

'In other words, you suspect everyone.'

She nodded.

'So they all have a motive. But who had the opportunity? Who was present at the time of Oscar's death?'

'They all were. Wingate Manor is a rather large estate. All of our children live there with their spouses. The servants were also in the house that morning: Herbert the chauffeur, George the

183

butler, Wanda the maid, Kirk the stable boy and, of course, Elsie the cook.'

I counted on my fingers. 'That makes eleven suspects,' I said. 'Any grandchildren?'

'Not one.'

'Well, it makes a big bunch. Maybe we can narrow it down a little.'

Before we could start narrowing it down, the food arrived. I stared at it. I wished I was back at Lou's Deli. 'What *is* this stuff?' I asked.

'Sushi, my dear.'

'It looks like dead fish.'

Mabel tittered.

I put my nose close to the plate, and sniffed. The last time I'd smelled something like it, I was a kid in a rowboat trying to grab bait out of a minnow bucket. It was a hot day, and most of the minnows were belly up. 'I'm not going to eat this,' I said.

'Oh, but you must. Until you catch the killer, you'll need to act as my food taster.'

'What are you getting at?' I asked.

'Eat,' Mabel said.

For three hundred dollars a day, I'll eat anything. So I forked a critter, held my breath so I couldn't smell it, and put it into my mouth. It tasted the way I was afraid it might taste.

Mabel watched me chew. She hadn't touched her food yet. I swallowed, and tried to wash the taste out of my mouth with water.

Mabel kept watching.

I got the picture. She was waiting to see if I'd keel over.

'Oscar didn't die in a restaurant,' I said.

'No,' said Mabel. 'But one can't be too careful.'

'Nobody's going to sneak into the kitchen of a restaurant to poison you,' I said.

'One never knows.' She pointed her fork at something on my plate that looked like an octopus tentacle.

I ate one, and gagged.

'Now that.'

*That* looked harmless. It looked like a cake of crisp rice – sort of. But it tasted like something that had been left overnight in the cloudy old water from a goldfish bowl.

Mabel watched me eagerly. I didn't keel over, but I wanted to.

'Fine,' she said. 'Now we trade plates.'

We traded, and she dug in. It made me feel sick, watching her stuff such junk into her mouth. I flagged down the waitress and ordered a double Scotch on the rocks.

The Scotch helped. I drank, and tried not to look at Mabel.

This job, I decided, was not turning out to be such a picnic.

That's how it started. After leaving Yamamoto's Sushi Bar and Bait Shop, we took the limo to Wingate Manor. It was quite a snazzy joint.

Mabel introduced me around as the son of an old school chum who was down on his luck and would be living in for the next week. The living in part came as a surprise, but I didn't complain. After all, the place was like a luxury resort complete with pool, sauna, a tennis court, stables, and a television in every bedroom. No wonder the two daughters, the son and their assorted mates weren't eager to move out.

None of them struck me as killers. That came as no big surprise, since I'd already decided Mabel's deck was short a few cards.

At cocktail hour, we all sat around the pool. George the butler passed out drinks. I wanted Scotch, but I got a vodka gimlet – the same drink as Mabel. After I took a sip, she managed to switch glasses with me. She was quite artful about switching. I don't think anyone caught on.

George passed around a tray of snacks. Canapes, Mabel called them. Since I was the guest, she said, I should be first to help myself. I ate one. It was a miniature sandwich with liver inside. I'm not big on liver, but it sure beat sushi. I didn't keel over. Mabel took one.

Later, the rest of the clan headed into the dining room. I could smell a roast. My stomach grumbled. I had one foot in the dining room when Mabel grabbed my arm and stopped me.

'Duke and I will be dining later,' she told the others. 'We have some matters to discuss.'

She led me into the study. 'I can't let them see that I've hired a taster,' she explained.

'No,' I muttered. 'I guess not.'

'They'd know I'm onto their game.'

'Right,' I said.

Bananas.

I could have used a few bananas, just then.

Finally, the dining room was cleared. Our turn. The roast was cold, but it tasted great. Mabel watched and waited. I poured gravy over my mashed potatoes. I took a big bite. She raised her eyebrows. I sipped the red wine. I ate a yucky chunk of broccoli.

We stared at each other.

'How are you feeling?' she asked.

'Starved.'

'You're doing splendidly,' she said. We traded plates and glasses.

This went on for the next five days. Breakfast, lunch, cocktails and dinner, whether we were taking our meal at the estate or at a restaurant, I tested all the food and drinks first. Then we switched, and Mabel ate her fill. Except for one return trip to Yamamoto's, it wasn't half bad.

I spent my days swimming, riding horses, and sometimes playing tennis with members of the clan. A certain son-in-law named Aaron showed a nasty streak on the courts. He liked to slam balls at my face. He was a doctor when he wasn't hanging around the estate. If I had to pick a poisoner, it would have been him.

But I didn't have to pick.

Nobody had any intention of poisoning Mabel. She didn't need a private eye or a food taster. She needed a shrink.

I knew that all along.

On Friday afternoon, four hours after our second trip to

Yamamoto's, my stomach couldn't hold out for the cocktail hour. I snuck into the kitchen. Elsie the cook wasn't around. The snacks were ready. I took a loaded tray of canapes out of the refrigerator, set it on the counter, and picked up one of the tiny sandwiches. Muffin, who had grown very fond of my boots during the past few days, was busy gnawing at my ankle. I peeled open one of the snacks and sniffed it. Liver, yuck. I tossed it across the kitchen, and Muffin went scampering after it.

The dog gobbled it down.

*Adios*, Muffin.


Muffin may or may not have been poisoned by the canape. Its ticker might've just chosen that moment to go on the fritz.

Sure.

I'm a trained investigator. I don't believe in coincidences.

Mabel wasn't bananas, after all.

In a way, that made me feel good. I'd grown fond of the old dame. I was glad to find out she wasn't a loony.

I returned the tray of poisoned snacks to the refrigerator. Then I stashed the mortal remains of Muffin in the pantry and went up to my room to fetch Slugger.

Slugger is my .38 caliber snub-nosed revolver. I don't have a permit to carry a concealed weapon (it got lifted after I dropped that client mentioned earlier), but I didn't plan to go up against a killer without my equalizer, so I tucked Slugger under my belt. I pulled out my shirt-tail to keep him out of sight, and went outside to the pool.

By five o'clock, the whole gang was there.

'Has anyone seen Muffin?' Mabel asked.

Nobody had seen Muffin. That included me.

George came out with a tray of cocktails. We took our glasses. I sipped. Mabel tried to sneak her usual switch, but I shook my head. 'Not necessary,' I whispered. She raised her eyebrows, then smiled.

She looked around to make sure nobody was within earshot, then whispered, 'Have you unearthed the killer?'

George returned with the tray of poisoned appetizers.

'Put them on the table,' I ordered.

'I'm to pass them, sir,' he said.

'Do as Duke says,' Mabel told him.

With a nod, George set the tray on the poolside table. 'Now,' I said, 'go and bring out the other servants. Everyone.' He left.

Sally, the wife of Aaron the doctor, saw George depart without passing snacks. 'What gives?' she asked.

'This gives,' I answered, and pulled out Slugger.

Everyone except Mabel started yelling at me. 'See here!' I heard. And, 'Put that away!' And, 'He's berserk!' One of Mabel's daughters covered her ears and shouted, 'Oh oh oh, he's going to murder us all!'

'Quiet!' Mabel called out. 'Duke is a private detective whom I hired to protect me.'

That shut them up. Some looked surprised, others confused, a few miffed. Aaron looked more miffed than anyone. I was glad he didn't have a tennis racquet handy.

'Line up,' I commanded.

They formed a line with their backs to the pool.

'What is the meaning of this?' Sally asked.

'You'll soon find out,' I said.

When the servants showed up, I made them stand in line with the rest of the gang.

'Mabel,' I said. 'The tray.'

She went to the table and hefted the tray.

'One canape apiece,' I told her.

She walked slowly down the line of eleven suspects, making sure that each of them took one of the little sandwiches.

'Okay,' I said. 'When I count to three, I want every one of you to eat your snack.'

'This is ridiculous!' snapped Sally.

'Just a little test,' I explained. I didn't bother playing games with the count. I rattled off, 'One two three.'

They all ate.

Except Aaron. He threw his canape at me.

'You're the poisoner!' I shouted. I aimed Slugger at his snarling face. 'Freeze!'

Aaron froze.

The other ten didn't. They dropped. Some pitched onto the concrete. Some flopped into the pool.

Mabel looked at me. 'You idiot!' she yelled.

'Oh, boy,' I muttered.

In this game, some cases are tough. Some are a lead-pipe cinch. You win a few and you lose a few. You hope it all evens out in the end, but if it doesn't . . . well, that's the way the cookie crumbles.

I wouldn't have it any other way. I'm a sleuth, a snoop, a gumshoe. I'm the guy you call when the chips are down and your back's to the wall. I'm Duke Scanlon, Private Eye.

# The Hunt

Still there. Still staring at her.

Kim, seated on a plastic chair with her back to the wall, felt squirmy. Except for the door frame, the entire front of the laundromat was glass. The florescent lights overhead glared.

To the man in the car outside, it must be like watching her on a drive-in movie screen.

She wished she'd worn more clothes. But it was a hot night and very late, and she'd postponed doing her laundry until nearly every stitch in her apartment needed a wash. So she'd come here in sneakers, her old gym shorts from high school, and a T-shirt.

Probably why the bastard's staring at me, she thought. Enjoying the free show.

No better than a Peeping Tom, the way he just sits there, gazing in.

When Kim had first noticed him, she'd thought he was the husband of one of the other women. Waiting and bored, choosing to spend his time in the comfort of his car, maybe so he could listen to the radio – and ogle her from a discreet distance.

Soon, however, two of the women left. The only one remaining was a husky middle-aged gal who kept complaining and giving orders to a fellow named Bill. The way Bill listened and obeyed, he had to be her husband.

Kim didn't think that the stranger in the car was waiting for them.

They finished. They carried their baskets of clean clothes out to a station wagon, and drove off.

Kim was the only woman left.

The stranger stayed.

Every time she glanced his way, she saw him staring back. She couldn't actually see his eyes. They were masked in shadow. But she felt their steady gaze, felt them studying her.

Though she was unable to see his eyes, enough light reached him from the laundromat to show his thick neck, his shaved head. His head looked like a block of granite. He had a heavy brow, knobby cheekbones, a broad nose, full lips that never moved, a massive jaw.

Wouldn't be so bad, Kim had thought, if he looked like some kind of wimp. I could handle that. But this guy looked as if he ate bayonets for breakfast.

She'd wanted to move away from her chair near the front. Wait at the rear of the room. Hell, duck down out of sight behind the middle row of machines.

But if she did that, he might come in.

I'm all right as long as he stays in the car.

I'm probably all right as long as Jock's here.

She didn't know Jock's name, but he *was* one. The big guy might even be a match for the stranger. He appeared to be a couple of years younger than Kim – maybe nineteen or twenty. He had so much muscle that he couldn't touch his knees together if his life depended on it. Nor would his elbows ever rub against his sides. His sleeveless gray sweatshirt was cut off just below his chest. His red shorts were very much like Kim's, but a lot larger. He wore them over sweatpants.

She watched him, now, as he hopped down from one of the washers and strutted to a nearby machine. He thumbed a button. The door of the front-loading drier swung open. A white sock and a jockstrap fell to the floor.

Kim's stomach fluttered.

*He's done*.

She forced herself not to glance out the window. She forced herself not to hurry. She tried to look casual as she rose from her chair and strolled toward the crouching athlete.

'Hi,' she said, stopping beside him.

He looked up at her and smiled. 'Hello.'

'I'm sorry to bother you, but I was wondering if you could do me a favor.'

'Yeah?' His gaze slipped down Kim's body. When it returned to her face, she knew he would be willing to help. 'What sort of favor?' he asked.

'It's nothing much, really. I just don't want to be left alone in here. I was wondering if you could stick around for a few minutes and keep me company until my clothes are finished. They're in the driers, now. It'll just be about ten more minutes.'

He raised his eyebrows. 'That's it?'

'Well, if you could walk me out to my car when I'm done.'

'No problem.'

'Thanks. I really appreciate it.'

He stuffed the rest of his laundry into a canvas bag and tied the cord at the top. Standing up, he smiled again. 'My name's Bradley.'

'I'm Kim.' She offered a hand, and he shook it. 'I sure appreciate this.'

'Like I told you, no problem.'

Kim stepped to a washer across the aisle from him. He watched as she braced her hands on its edge and boosted herself up. Watched her breasts.

Maybe it wasn't such a hot idea asking him for help.

Don't worry, she told herself. He's just a normal guy.

She slumped forward slightly and cupped her knees to loosen the pull of the fabric across her chest.

'You live near here?' Bradley said.

'Yeah, a few blocks. Are you a student?'

'A sophomore. I live off-campus, though. I've got my own apartment. Do you come here often?'

'As un-often as possible.'

He laughed softly. 'Know what you mean. Chores. I hate them.'

'Same here. Especially laundry. It gets kind of spooky here.'

Her head turned. She wanted to stop it, couldn't, kept turning until she saw the parked car and the grim face behind its windshield. She quickly looked back at Bradley.

'If you get spooked, why do you come here so late?' he asked.

'No waiting for machines.' Then she added, 'Famous last words.'

Bradley frowned. 'What is it?' He glanced toward the front, then scowled at her. 'What's the matter?'

Kim felt her mouth stretch into a grimace. She shook her head. 'Nothing.'

'Is it that guy out there?'

'No, it's . . . He's been watching me. Ever since I got here. He just sits there, staring at me.'

'Oh yeah?' Bradley glared in the man's direction.

'Don't! Jesus! Just pretend he's not there.'

'Maybe I ought to go out and . . .'

'No!'

He turned to Kim. 'You don't know who the guy is?'

'I've never seen him before.'

'No wonder you're worried.'

'I'm sure it's nothing,' she said, beginning to tremble again. 'He probably just likes to look at women.'

'*I* like to look at women. That doesn't mean I hang around laundromats like a goddamn pervert.'

'He's probably harmless.'

'Doesn't look harmless to me. Who's to say he isn't some kind of freak like the Mount Bolton Butcher?'

'Hey, come on . . .'

Bradley's face went pale. His eyes widened. They roamed down Kim, and returned to her face. 'Christ,' he muttered. 'I hate to tell you this, but . . .' He hesitated.

The change in him frightened Kim. '*What*?'

'You . . . you're a dead match for his victim profile.'

'What are you talking about?'

'The Mount Bolton Butcher. He's had eight victims, and they all . . . they were all eighteen to twenty-five years old, maybe not

194

as pretty as you, but almost. And slim, and they all had long blonde hair parted in the middle just like yours. You look so much like the others that you could all be sisters.'

'Oh shit,' Kim muttered.

'I was going with a girl who kind of fit the profile. Not as much as you do, but it had me worried. I was afraid, you know, she might end up raped and dismembered like . . . Is there a back way out of here?'

'Hey, come on. You're really . . .'

'I'm not kidding.'

'I know, but . . . It probably isn't him, right? I mean, he hasn't . . .'

'He hasn't nailed anyone in two months, and the cops think he might've left the area, or died, or been jailed for something else. But they don't *know*. They're just trying to calm people down, saying stuff like that. Have you ever been up around Mount Bolton?'

Kim shook her head. It felt a little numb inside.

'I tell you, it's one big mean wilderness. A guy could hide out for years if he knew what he was doing. So maybe he laid low for a while, and maybe now the urge has gotten the best of him, and . . . Not much of anyone goes camping up there anymore. If he wanted a new victim, he might have to come down into town for one.'

'This is really starting to give me the creeps.'

'Just sit there a minute. I'll check the back.'

Bradley walked up the aisle between the rows of silent washers and driers. He stepped past the coin-operated vending machines where patrons could purchase drinks, snacks, detergent or bleach. He tapped out a rhythm as he walked by a long, wooden table where people earlier had separated and folded their laundry. Then he disappeared into a recessed area at the rear of the room. He was out of sight for just a second.

When he stepped into the open again, he met Kim's eyes and shook his head.

Not once did he glance toward the man in the car as he came

back to her. 'Nothing but a utility room,' he said. 'The only way out is the front.'

Kim nodded and tried to smile. She felt a corner of her mouth twitch.

'You think your stuff is about ready?'

'Close enough.' She hopped off the washer. Bradley picked up his laundry bag and stayed at her side as she headed for the pair of driers near the front.

'Your car's in the lot?' he asked.

'Yeah.'

'I'll get in with you. If he thinks we're really together, maybe he won't try anything.'

'Okay,' Kim said. Both driers were still running. She could see them vibrating, hear their motors and the thumps of the tennis shoes she'd tossed into the nearer of the two.

She swung her laundry basket off the top of that machine, set it at her feet, crouched and opened the front panel. The motor went silent. Reaching inside, she lifted out a handful of warm clothes. They still felt a little damp, but she didn't care.

'If he follows us when we leave,' Bradley said, 'maybe we can lose him. But at least you won't be alone. As long as I'm with you, he'll think twice before he tries anything.'

She dropped more clothes into the basket, and looked up at Bradley. 'I really appreciate this.'

'I'm just glad that I'm here to help.'

'Do you really think he might be the Butcher?'

'I hope we don't find out.'

*What if* you're *the Butcher*?

The thought came suddenly, and seemed to turn her stomach cold inside.

No. That's ridiculous.

Looking away from him, she continued to unload the machine.

What's so ridiculous about it? Bradley seems to know a lot about the Butcher. And he wants me to take him in my car. Once we're alone . . .

For all I know, he's been lying from the start.

196

Maybe he's *with* the other guy. They might be working together.

Don't let him in the car, she told herself. Walk out with him, but . . .

'Oh shit,' Bradley muttered.

Her head snapped toward him. He was standing rigid, eyes wide as he gazed toward the front.

Kim sprang up and whirled around.

The stranger filled the doorway. Then he was inside, striding toward them.

He wore a dark stocking cap. His face was streaked with black makeup. His black T-shirt looked swollen with mounds and slabs of muscle. The sling of a rifle crossed his chest. So did the straps of a harness that held a sheathed knife, handle down, against the left side of his rib cage. Circling his waist was a web belt loaded down with canvas cases, a canteen and a holster. He wore baggy camouflage pants. Their cuffs were tucked into high-topped boots.

Bradley, fists up, stepped in front of Kim. His voice boomed out, 'Stop right there, mister.'

A blow to the midsection dropped Bradley to his knees. A knee to the forehead hurled him backward. He hit the floor sliding and lay limp at Kim's feet.

She whirled away and tried to run. A hand snagged the shoulder of her T-shirt. The fabric tugged at her, stretched and ripped as she was twisted sideways. Her feet tangled. She crashed against the floor.

The man grabbed her ankles, tugged her flat. His weight came down on her back. An arm darted across her throat and squeezed.

Kim woke up in total darkness. She lay curled on her side. Her head ached. At first, she thought she was home in bed. But this didn't feel like a bed. She felt a blanket under her. The surface beneath the blanket was hard. It vibrated. Sometimes, it pounded against her.

She remembered the man.

Then, she knew where she was.

To confirm her fears, she tried to straighten her legs. Something stopped her feet. She reached out. Her fingers met hard, grooved rubber.

The spare tire.

The car stopped. Kim had no idea how long she had been trapped inside its trunk. Probably for an hour. That's about how long it should take, she knew, to drive from town to the wilderness surrounding Mount Bolton.

Ever since regaining consciousness and realizing she was in the trunk of the man's car, she had known where he was taking her. After a period of gasping panic, after prayers for God to save her, a numbness had settled into Kim. She knew she was going to die, and there was nothing she could do about it. She told herself that everyone dies. And this way, she would be spared such agonies as facing her parents' deaths, the deaths of other loved ones and friends, her own old age and maybe a lingering demise in the grip of cancer or some other horrible disease. Has its advantages.

*God, I'm going to die!*

And she knew what the Butcher did to his victims: how he raped them, sodomized them, tortured them with knives and sticks and fire.

The panic came back. She was whimpering and trembling again by the time the car stopped.

She heard the engine quit. A door thudded shut. Seconds later, a muffled jangle of keys came from behind her. She heard the quiet clicks of a key sliding into the trunk lock. The clack of a latch. Then, the trunk lid swung up, squeaking on its hinges.

A hand pushed under her armpit. Another thrust between her legs and grabbed her thigh. She was lifted out of the trunk, swung clear of the car, and thrown to the ground. The forest floor was damp, springy with fallen pine needles. Sticks and cones dug against her as she rolled onto her back. She stared up at the dark shape of the man. He was a blur through her tears.

'Get up,' he said.

Kim struggled to her feet. She sniffed and wiped her eyes. She lifted the front of her torn T-shirt, covering her right breast and holding the fabric to her shoulder.

'What's your name?' the man asked.

Kim straightened her back. 'Fuck you,' she said.

A corner of his mouth curled up. 'Look around.'

She turned slowly and found that she stood in a clearing surrounded by heavy timber. There was no sign of a road, though she suspected they couldn't be far from one. The car couldn't have traveled any great distance through the underbrush and trees. She faced the Butcher. 'Yeah?'

'Do you know where you are?'

'Got a pretty good guess.'

'You're a tough little thing, aren't you?'

'What've I got to lose?'

'Not a thing, bitch. Look to your right. There's a trail sign.'

She looked. She spotted a small wooden sign on a post at the edge of the clearing.

'Stick to the trail,' he said. 'You'll make better time.'

'What are you talking about?'

'You've got a five-minute headstart.' He raised an arm close to his face. With the other hand, he pushed a button to light the numbers on his wrist watch. 'Go.'

'What is this?'

'The hunt. And your time is running.'

Kim swung around and dashed away from the man. She didn't head toward the trail sign. Instead, she ran for the end of the clearing. This was the way the car had come. She might reach a road.

He's not going to let me get away, she thought. This is just part of it. A goddamn game. I'm not going to get out of here alive.

*That's what he thinks.*

I haven't got a chance.

*Oh yes I do, oh yes I do.*

She dodged a bush, raced through the gap between two trees, and shortened her strides when she met a downslope.

Car couldn't have come this way, she realized. The bastard must've turned it around before he stopped. Knew I'd try this.

I'm running *away* from the road.

She wondered how much time had passed. Her five minutes couldn't be up yet.

He won't give me five, she thought. He's probably already after me.

But she couldn't hear anything back there. She heard only her huffing breath, her heartbeat, her shoes crunching pine needles and mashing cones and snapping twigs.

I'm making too much noise.

Then a foot slipped out from under her. She saw her leg fly up. Saw the treetops. Slammed the ground and slid on her back, forest debris raking her shirt up, scraping her skin. When the skid stopped, she lay sprawled and didn't move except to suck air into her lungs.

I can't run from him, Kim told herself. He'll catch me easy. Gotta sneak. Gotta hide.

Sitting up, she peered down the slope. It wasn't heavily wooded. The dense trees were off to the sides. She stood. She glanced toward the top. No sign of him yet. But time had to be running out.

In a low crouch, she traversed the slope. Soon, she left the moonlight behind. The dark of the forest felt wonderful – a sheltering blanket of night. She walked slowly, trying not to make a sound as she stepped around the trunks of spruce and fir trees, ducked under drooping branches.

The place smelled like Christmas.

Play it right, she told herself, and maybe you'll see another Christmas.

How good is this guy? she wondered. Is he good enough to track me through all this in the dark?

He wouldn't have let me go if he wasn't sure he'd find me.

There must be a way. I just have to be smarter than him.

200

He's after me by now, she thought. Even if he did wait the whole five minutes.

Kim stepped behind a tree, turned around, and scanned the woods. Except for a few milky flecks of moonlight, the area was black and shades of gray. She saw the faint shapes of nearby trees and saplings. Nothing seemed to move.

You won't spot him till he's right on top of you, she realized, recalling his dark clothes and makeup.

She looked down at herself. Her legs were dim smears, her shorts dark, but her T-shirt almost seemed to glow. Muttering a curse, she pulled it off. She tucked it into the front of her shorts, so it hung from her waist. That was better. She was tanned except for her breasts, and they weren't nearly as white as the shirt.

Turning around, Kim made her way toward a deadfall. The roots of the old tree formed a clump nearly as high as her head. Bushes and vines had grown around the trunk. She considered climbing over the dead tree, but decided to bypass it, instead.

As she neared the mound of dirt-clogged roots, she noticed a space between the trunk and the ground. Kneeling, she peered into the opening. It was exposed, but she would be out of sight if she squirmed to where a thick nest of bushes grew in front of the trunk.

The idea of being trapped beneath the dead tree didn't appeal to her. Probably a host of nasty creatures under there – ants, spiders, termites, slugs. They would crawl on her.

Besides, she told herself, if it looks like a good hiding place to me, it'll look like one to him. If he comes this way, he'll check it out. And he'll have me.

Forget it.

She hurried around the root cluster and headed to the right of the deadfall. With the barrier at her back, she broke into a run and didn't bother moving from tree to tree for concealment. She dashed as fast as she could, staying clear of trees, dodging occasional clusters of rock, circling patches of underbrush. At last, winded and aching, she ducked behind a trunk. She bent over and held her sweaty knees and gasped for air.

That little burst of speed, she thought, ought to put some ground between us. He can't run all-out, not if he's tracking me.

How can he track someone in the dark? she wondered. It wouldn't be easy, even in daylight, to follow her signs. What does he look for, anyway? Broken twigs?

Kim pulled the T-shirt from her waist band and mopped her wet face, her dripping sides, her neck and chest and belly. As she tucked the shirt into her shorts again, she wondered if the Butcher might have a night-vision device. Maybe an infra-red scope, or something.

That would explain a lot.

He seemed so sure he'd find me.

Maybe took it out of his car while he was giving me the headstart.

How can I hide from something like that?

They pick up body heat? she wondered.

What if I bury myself?

That idea seemed just as bad as hiding under the deadfall.

Sighing, Kim leaned back against the tree. Its bark felt stiff and scratchy. A quiet scurrying sound made her flinch. But it came from above. Probably a squirrel up there, she thought.

What about climbing a tree?

Even if the Butcher figured out that she had gone up a tree to hide, there were thousands. She could climb high enough to be invisible from the ground. The limbs and foliage might even offer some protection from a night scope, if he had such a thing.

If he does find me, Kim thought, he'll have a damn tough time getting to me.

He could probably shoot me out of it. That won't be easy if I'm high enough. And he might be afraid of the noise. The sound of gunfire would carry a long distance. Somebody might hear it.

Besides, I'd rather be shot than taken alive. Quick and clean.

If he doesn't shoot me down, his only other choice is to go up after me. That'll make *him* vulnerable.

'All *right*!' Kim whispered. 'Let's make it even tougher.'

She stepped out from under the tree. Crouching, she studied

the ground. Here and there, the faint gray shapes of rocks jutted through the mat of pine needles. She gathered several, choosing those that were large enough to fill her hand – large enough to do some real damage. When she had six, she spread her shirt on the ground. She piled them onto the shirt, brought up its corners, and knotted it to form a makeshift sack.

Swinging the load at her side, Kim wandered through the trees until she found a stand of five that were grouped very closely together. Their branches met and intertwined, forming a dark mass.

Perfect.

She hurried to the center tree, saw that it had no handholds within easy reach, and went to the tree beside it. The lowest limb of this one was level with Kim's face. After the first limb, it looked as if the going would be easy.

The shirt full of rocks presented a problem. Kim thought about it for a while. Then, she opened the knot and retied it so that the untorn sleeve was free. She pushed her left hand through the neck hole and out the short sleeve, then slid the bundle up her arm. With the weight of the rocks tugging at her shoulder, she swung the load out of the way against the side of her back.

She shinnied up the trunk, struggled onto the limb, stood, and began climbing carefully from branch to branch. It wasn't as easy as she had supposed. Soon, her heart was slamming and she had to fight for air. Stopping to rest, she leaned away from the trunk and peered down. She couldn't see the ground – just a tangle of lower branches.

I'm pretty high, she thought.

Damn high. Jesus.

Her throat tightened. Her stomach fluttered. Her legs began to tremble. She turned suddenly and hugged the tree. I'm safe up here, she told herself. I'm not going to fall. She reminded herself of her days on the high school gymnastics team. That wasn't so long ago, she thought. This is no tougher than the uneven parallels. I've stayed in pretty good shape.

She still had to cling to the tree for a while before she found the nerve to relax her hold.

203

Just a little bit higher. Don't look down, and you'll be okay.

She got her knee onto the next branch, crawled up, stood on i swung her foot around the trunk to another, pushed herself highe and soon the process of climbing occupied all her thought leaving no room for fears of falling.

When her movements began to sway the upper reaches of th tree, Kim knew she was high enough. She straddled a branch scooted forward until she was tight against the trunk, an wrapped her legs around it.

For a long time, she stayed that way. Then, the rocks began t bother her. The sleeve of the T-shirt felt like a hand on he shoulder, trying to drag her backward. Rough edges of roc pushed against her skin through the fabric.

Easing away from the trunk but still keeping it scissore between her legs, she swung the bag onto her lap. She draped i like saddlebags over a branch just overhead and to the right.

Relieved of the burden, she inched forward again an embraced the tree.


Kim dreamed that she was falling, flinched awake, found herse slumping sideways, and clutched the trunk. Cheek pressed to th bark, she saw that morning had come. Dust motes floated i golden rays slanting down through the foliage. Out beyond th branches, she saw the bright green of nearby trees. Tilting he head back, she saw patches of blue, cloudless sky. She hear birds singing, a soft breeze whispering through the pine needles

My Christ, she thought, I made it through the night.

She'd even, somehow, drifted off to sleep some time befor dawn.

She felt numb from the waist down. Hanging onto an uppe branch, she stood and held herself steady. Sensation returned t her legs and groin and rump, making them prickle with pins an needles. When they felt normal again, she removed her short climbed to a lower branch and urinated. Returning to her perch she put her shorts back on. She sat down, one arm around th trunk, and let her legs dangle.

Now what? she wondered.

Obviously, she had eluded the Butcher. She wondered if he'd passed this way in the night and kept on going. Maybe he'd never even come close.

Maybe he'd given up, finally, and gone away.

That's wishful thinking, Kim warned herself. He won't give up. Not this easily. A, he wants me. B, I can identify him. He isn't going to let me waltz out of here.

On the other hand, he would've found me by now if he'd actually been able to follow my signs.

Maybe he *did*, she thought. Maybe right now he's taking a snooze under the tree.

No. If he knew I was up here, he would've tried to take me.

*I lost the bastard.*

The trick, now, is to find my way back to civilization without running into him.

Trying it in daylight seemed foolhardy.

Waiting for nightfall was torture. There was no comfortable way to sit. Kim changed positions frequently, mostly sitting, sometimes standing, occasionally hanging by her hands from higher branches to stretch and take the weight off her legs.

Hunger gnawed at her, but thirst was far worse. She ached for a drink of water.

In spite of the shade provided by the upper areas of the tree, the heat of the day was brutal. Sweat dribbled down her face, stinging her eyes. It streamed down her body, tickling and making her squirm. Her skin felt slick and greasy. Her shorts felt as if they were pasted on.

For all the wetness on her skin, her mouth had none. As the day dragged on, her lips became rough and cracked. Her teeth felt like blocks of gritty stone. Her tongue seemed to be swelling, her throat closing so she had difficulty when she tried to swallow.

At times, she wondered if she could risk waiting for dark. Her strength seemed to be seeping away with the sweat pouring out of her skin. Spells of dizziness came and went. If I don't climb down pretty soon, she thought, I'm going to fall. But she held on

Just a while longer, she told herself. Again and again.

Finally, dusk came. A refreshing breeze blew through the tree swaying it gently, drying her sweat.

Then, darkness closed over the forest.

Kim began to climb down. She was ten or twelve feet belov her perch when she remembered her T-shirt. She'd left it restin, on a branch up there.

It seemed like miles away.

But she couldn't return to civilization wearing nothing but he shorts.

She began to cry. She wanted to get down. She wanted to fine water. It just wasn't fair, having to climb back up there again.

Weeping, she struggled upward. Finally, she tugged the loadee shirt off the branch. Hadn't needed the damn rocks anyway. Sh plucked open the knot and shook the shirt The rocks fell thumping against branches, swishing through pine needles. She stuffed the empty rag into the front of her shorts so she wouldn' lose it, then started her long climb down to the forest floor.

When Kim dropped from the final limb, she had no clea memory of the descent.

She found herself walking through the woods. Her hands fel heavy. She looked at them, and saw that each held a rock. Sh didn't remember picking them up. But she kept them.

Until she heard the soft, windy sound of rushing water. Ther she tossed them down and ran.

Soon she was kneeling in a stream, cupping cold water to he mouth, splashing her face with it, sprawling out so she wa: submerged, the icy current sliding over her body. She came up for air. She cupped more water to her mouth, swallowed, sighed

Kim didn't think she had ever felt so wonderful in her life.

Until she was suddenly grabbed by her hair and jerked to he knees.

*No! Not after all this!*

His hands clutched her breasts, tugging her up and backwarc against him. She squirmed and kicked as he hauled her to the

nk. There, he threw himself down, slamming her against the
ound. He writhed on top of her. His hands squeezed and twisted
er breasts. He grunted as he sucked the side of her neck.

Reaching up behind herself, she caught hold of his ear. She
anked it. Heard tearing cartilage, felt a blast of breath against
er neck as he cried out. His hands flew out from under her. He
ounded the sides of her head.

Stunned by the blows, Kim was only vaguely aware of his
eight leaving her body. She thought she should try to scurry up
id run, but couldn't move. As if the punches had knocked the
ower out of her.

She felt her shorts being tugged down. She wanted to stop
*at*, but still couldn't make her arms work. The shorts pulled at
er ankles, lifted her feet and released them. Her feet dropped
id struck the ground.

Rough hands rubbed the backs of her legs, her rump. She felt
ie press of a whiskered face. Lips. A tongue. The man grunted
ke a beast.

Then he grabbed her ankles, pulled and crossed her legs,
ipping her over.

Kim stared up at the man.

He pulled a knife from his belt. Its blade gleamed in the
noonlight. He clamped the knife between his teeth and started to
nbutton his shirt.

She stared at him.

She tried to comprehend.

He was skinny, wearing jeans and a plaid shirt. His hair was a
vild bush.

*He's not the Butcher*!

He pulled his shirt open.

A roar pounded Kim's ears. The man's head jerked as if he'd
een kicked in the temple. A dark spray erupted from the other
ide. He stood above her for a second, still holding his shirt open,
ie knife still gripped in his teeth. Then he fell straight backward.

Kim's ears rang from the sound of the shot. She didn't hear
nyone approach.

But then a man in baggy pants and black T-shirt was standing near her feet. He pointed a rifle down at the other man, and put three more rounds into him.

He slung the rifle onto his back. He crouched, picked up the body, and draped it over his shoulder. Turning to Kim, he said, 'Get dressed. I'll give you a lift back to town.'

'No way,' she muttered.

'It's up to you.'

He strode into the trees, carrying the body.

'Wait,' Kim called, struggling to sit up.

He halted. He turned around.

'*He*'s the Butcher?' she asked.

'That's right.'

'Who are you?'

'A hired hand.'

'Why did you *do* this to me?' she blurted.

'Needed bait,' he said. 'You were it, bitch. I figured he'd sniff you out, sooner or later. He did, and I took him down. Simple as that.'

'How did you find me?' Kim asked.

'Find you? I never lost you. Climbing the tree was a pretty good gimmick, I'll give you credit for that. Glad you dumped the rocks, though. Great timing. That's what brought him out of cover.'

'Why didn't you shoot him right then?'

'Didn't feel like it. Coming?'

'Fuck you.'

He left.


Kim followed the stream. Early the next morning, she came upon a two-lane road. She walked alongside it. Finally, she heard the approach of a car. Just before it came into view around a bend, she lifted the torn front of her T-shirt to cover herself.

The car, a green Jeep, stopped beside her. A park ranger leaped out and hurried over to her. 'My God, what happened to you?'

She shook her head. 'Can you take me to the police?'

'Certainly.' His eyes traveled down Kim in a way that reminded her of Bradley in the laundromat. She wondered how Bradley was doing. She wondered if she wanted to see him again. 'You look like you've had a rough time of it,' the ranger said.

'Yeah.' Swaying forward, she took a quick lurching step to keep herself from falling. The ranger gripped her arm and held her steady.

'Are you all right?' he asked.

'I'll live,' Kim said. Her lips twitched into something that felt almost like a smile. She said it again. 'I'll live.' It sounded very good.

# *Slit*

The library would be closing in five minutes. Charles knew that the last of the students had already left. He was alone with Lynn.

He saw no point in heading off into the stacks to shelve books, so he lingered beside the circulation desk, arranging volumes in the cart and sneaking glances at her.

She sat on a high stool behind the desk. Her empty loafers were on the floor. Her feet, in white socks, curled over a wooden rung of the stool. Charles could see one smooth calf, the crease behind her knee, and a few inches of bare thigh. Her legs were parted as far as the straight, denim skirt would allow. The skirt's hem looked so tight against the side of her thigh that Charles wondered if it might leave a red mark on her skin.

She was leaning forward, elbows resting on the desktop, hands on cheeks, head down as she looked through *Kirkus*. Her white blouse, tucked into the skirt, was taut against her back. Charles could see the bumps of her spine, the soft curves of her ribs, the pink hue of her skin through the fabric, the slim bands of her bra.

He squatted down and placed some books on the lower shelf of the cart. This angle allowed him to see Lynn's right breast. It was there beyond the underside of her arm, a sweet mound cupped by the tight blouse, its front hovering just above the edge of the desk.

It would look so much better without the bra. The seams, the pattern, the stiffness. All in the way.

Charles pictured himself slicing through its straps.

Lynn reached out, turned a page, flinched and blurted, 'Ow!

Damn!' She jerked her hand up. She held it rigid in front of her face, fingers spread and hooked. A gleaming dot of blood bloomed on the pad of her index finger.

Charles felt his mouth go dry. His heart thudded. Heat rushed through his groin. He moaned.

She glanced over at him. Her face was red, her teeth bared. Her eyes returned to her hand. She looked as if she didn't know what to do with it. She shook it a couple of times like a cat with a wet paw, then pressed the bleeding fingertip between her lips.

'A paper cut?' he asked.

She nodded.

'I hate those things,' he said.

A cut. A slit.

He stayed crouched, hard and aching.

Lynn took the finger away from her mouth. It left some blood on her lips. She scowled at the wound, then gave Charles a tight, twisted smile. 'It's not that they hurt so much, you know? They're just so . . .' She shuddered. 'They're like fingernails skreeking on a blackboard.' She licked the blood from her lips, then returned the finger to her mouth.

'Would you like a bandage?' Charles asked.

'Do you have one?'

'Oh, sure. I'm always prepared.'

'Like a Boy Scout, huh?'

'Yeah.' Rising from his crouch, he hoped that the books on the cart's top shelf were high enough. They were. Their tops reached up past his stomach.

He turned away from Lynn and hurried into the office behind the circulation desk. There, he took a bandage from the tin inside his briefcase. He adjusted the front of his pants to make the bulge less apparent. But it still showed. He took his corduroy jacket off the back of a nearby chair, put it on, and fastened the middle button. He looked down. The front of the jacket nicely concealed his secret.

When he came out, he found that Lynn had turned around on her stool to face him. 'It's stopped bleeding,' she said.

'Yeah, but paper cuts. You rub them the wrong way and flip back the skin and . . .'

'Yuck. I guess I will take a bandage. Would you like to do the onors?' She held her hand toward Charles.

'Sure,' he said. Trembling, he stripped the wrapper off the adhesive strip. He moved closer to Lynn, halting when the wet nd of her finger was inches from his chest. He stared down at he slit – a crescent across the finger's pad, rather like the gills of tiny fish, pink under a thin white flap. The edge of the flap was way from him.

'Do you think I'll live?'

'Sure.' His voice came out husky. He felt terribly tight and hard.

'Are you okay?' she asked.

'Yeah. Cuts make me nervous.'

'You aren't gonna faint or anything, are you?'

'Hope not.' He fumbled with the bandage, peeling the shiny apers away from its sides. He let them fall. They drifted down ke petals plucked from a flower, and settled on her shirt.

Pinching the sticky ends of the bandage, he lowered the gauze enter toward Lynn's cut.

He wanted to hurt her.

*No! Don't!*

He wanted to grab her finger and rub his thumb back, flipping the little edge of skin, making her jerk and cry out.

*Not Lynn! Don't!*

As fast as he could, he pressed the bandage to her cut and ipped the adhesive ends around her finger. He whirled away nd rushed for the office.

'Charles?' she called. 'Charles, are you all right?'

He didn't answer. He dropped onto his swivel chair, hunched ver and grabbed his knees.

It's over, he told himself. You didn't do it. Lynn can't even spect . . .

He heard her quiet footsteps behind him. She put a hand on s shoulder. 'What's wrong?' she asked.

'Just . . . cuts. They upset me.'

213

Her hand squeezed him through the corduroy. 'If I'd known . .
What is it, a phobia or something?'

'I guess so. Maybe.'

In a lighter tone, she said, 'That probably explains why yo
carry bandages around, huh?'

'Yeah.'

She patted his shoulder. 'Maybe you'll feel better if you ge
some fresh air,' she said. 'Why don't you go ahead and take off
I'll close up the library.'

'Okay. Thanks.'

He waited until she was gone, then carried his briefcas
outside. The night was dank and misty.

Feverish with memories of Lynn's cut, he lingered near th
library entrance. Soon, the upper windows went dark. He picture
her up there, alone in the stacks, lowering her bandaged finge
from the switch panel, starting down the stairwell.

His Swiss Army knife was a heavy lump against his thigh. H
slipped his hand down into his pants pocket. He caressed th
smooth plastic handle.

And savored thoughts of slitting her.

Just wait for her to come out . . .

*No!*

He turned from the library and walked quickly away.


In his apartment three blocks from campus, Charles went to bed
But he didn't sleep. His mind swirled with images of Lynn.

Don't think about her, he told himself.

You can't do her.

But it would be *so* nice.

But you can't.

Lynn was a graduate student. Like Charles, she earned a smal
stipend by working part-time at the Whitmore Library. Everyon
knew they worked the same hours. Too much suspicion would b
focused on him.

Besides, he really liked her.

But damn it . . . !

Forget about her.

He tried to forget about her. He tried to think only about the others. How they yelped or screamed. How their faces looked. How their skin split apart. How blood spilled out like scarlet creeks overflowing banks of ripped flesh, spreading and running, forming new streams that slid along velvety fields, that settled to create shimmering pools in the hollows of the body, that flowed down slopes.

So many faces. So many bodies flinching with surprise or thrashing in agony. So many flooding slits.

All belonged to strangers.

Except for the face and body and cut of his mother. Struggling to stop the confusing flood of images, fighting to keep his mind off Lynn, he concentrated on his mother. Her voice through the door. *Honey, would you be a dear and get me a Bandaid?* He saw himself enter the steamy bathroom, reach high into the medicine cabinet for the tin of bandages, take out one and step to the tub where she reclined. The water was murky. Patches of white suds floated on its surface. From her chest rose shiny wet islands, wonderfully round and smooth, each topped by a ruddier kind of skin that jutted up in the center. Looking at the islands made Charles feel strange and squirmy.

His mother held a razor in one hand. Her left leg was out of the water, its foot propped on the rim of the tub under one of the faucet handles. The cut was midway between her knee and the place where the water rippled around the wider part of her leg. *I'm afraid I nicked myself shaving*, she said.

Charles nodded. He gazed at the wound. He watched the strands of red slide down her gleaming skin. They made the bath water pink between her legs. She had a hairy place down there. He couldn't see her dingus. He stared, trying to find it even though he knew he shouldn't be looking at that place. But he couldn't help himself. He felt sick and tight.

*You didn't cut if off, did you?*

*Cut off what, honey?*

*You know, your dingus.*

She laughed softly. *Oh, darling, mommys don't have dinguses. Here.* And then she took gentle hold of his hand and guided it down into the pink, hot water. She slid it against her body. Against a cut – no, not just a cut – a huge, open gash with slippery edges. He tried to jerk his hand away, but she tightened her grip and kept it there. *Go on, feel it,* she said.

*But doesn't it hurt?* he asked.

*Not at all.*

It was almost as long as his hand. Warm and slick inside. And very deep. She squirmed a little as his fingers explored.

Her voice had a funny sound to it when she said, *I'm made this way. All mommys are.* She released his hand, but he kept it there. *That's enough, now, honey. You'd better put that Bandaid on my leg before I bleed to death.*

Then Charles had the bandage ready. As he lowered it toward the small bleeding cut on her leg, she said, *You aren't gonna faint or anything, are you?* But it wasn't his mother's voice. He turned his head. The woman sprawled in the tub was Lynn.

At dawn, groggy and restless, Charles climbed out of bed. He didn't know whether he had slept at all. Maybe a little. If so, his sleep had been a turmoil of dreams so vivid that they might have been memories or hallucinations.

He felt better after a long shower. Returning to his bedroom, he sat down and stared at the alarm clock. A quarter till six. That gave him just more than ten hours before returning to work at the library. And seeing Lynn again.

He saw her naked beneath him, writhing as he slit into her creamy skin.

'No!' he blurted, and stomped his foot on the floor.

There were ways to prevent it. Tricks. He'd worked out *lots* of tricks over the years to feed his urges – to ease the needs, to keep some control.

Weller Hall seemed huge and empty. Charles knew that it wasn't empty. But he saw no one as he eased the door shut and made his way to the staircase. Those few students and professors unlucky enough to be burdened with 'eight-o'clocks' were already snug in the classrooms, probably yawning and rubbing their eyes and wishing they were still in bed.

He climbed four creaky stairs, then stopped. He listened. Beyond the sounds of his own rough breathing and heartbeat, he heard a distant voice. Probably Dr Chitwood. Dr Shithead to the students who had to suffer through his mandatory (this being a university of Methodist origin) History of Christianity class. Known as Heist of Christ. Not only mandatory, but boring, and forever scheduled for 8 a.m.

It was one of only three classes taking place in Weller Hall on Monday, Wednesday and Friday at such an ungodly hour. Chitwoods's room was right at the top of the stairs.

Grinning, Charles pulled out his knife. He pried it open and dug into the smooth, worn wood of the banister. He carved a neat, two-inch slot down the rail's top. He scraped it clean of splinters. Crouching, he ran his thumb over a grimy stair. He rubbed his thumb against the pale cut on the handrail, darkening it with dirt, camouflaging it.

Using needle-nosed pliers, he snugged an injector blade into the slot.

He straightened up and admired his work.

The edge of the blade protruded just a little bit above the surface of the rail. It was hardly visible at all.

Shivering with excitement, Charles hurried outside. He waited on a bench and watched the entrance to Weller Hall.

This'll be great, he thought. It was always great.

But he'd never done it on campus before. He began to worry about that. He even considered returning to the stairway and pulling out the blade. He could walk into town and set up the trap somewhere else, somewhere safer.

He didn't want to do that, though. Too often, the trick ended up wasted on somebody old and ugly. He couldn't take a chance on that happening. He needed to slit a co-ed, a fresh young woman. One like Lynn.

The minutes dragged by. When people began wandering into the building, Charles feared that he might miss the event. He waited a while longer, fidgeting. Then he rose from the bench, trotted up the concrete steps, and rushed inside.

A few students were wandering the corridor, lingering near doorways, entering classrooms. Nobody on the stairs. He strolled to the far side of the hall. He removed a paperback copy of *Finnegan's Wake* from his briefcase, opened the book, leaned back against the wall, and pretended to read.

From here, he had a good view of the stairway.

The book trembled in his hands.

He held his breath when a couple of girls walked past him and turned toward the stairway. They looked like freshmen. They acted like freshmen, the way they talked so loudly and laughed and gestured.

The girl on the razor's side of the stairs held books to her chest with her left arm. Her right arm swung free. At the first stair, she rested her hand on the banister. It slid up the rail as she began to climb.

Her shiny blonde hair swayed against her back. She wore a sleeveless sweatshirt. Her arms were slender and dusky. Her white shorts were very tight. Charles could see the outline of her panties. Skimpy things.

His heart slammed.

As she stepped from the third stair to the fourth, she jerked her hand off the railing.

*Got her!*

But she didn't flinch or cry out. She simply chopped her hand through the air. Some kind of damn gesture to accompany whatever inane point she was making to her friend.

She was almost to the landing before her hand returned to the banister.

Charles sighed. He felt robbed.

It's not over yet, he told himself.

She'd been so perfect, though. Pretty and blonde and slender like Lynn. A few years younger, but otherwise just right.

I couldn't have seen the look on her face, anyway, he consoled himself.

From above came a thunder of footfalls.

Charles perked up. Heist of Christ was out, the students stampeding to escape. In seconds, the first of them rounded the landing and rushed down the lower flight. Trembling with excitement, Charles watched those near the banister. A boy in the lead. Luckily, his arm was busy clamping books to his hips. Behind him came a lithe brunette, breasts jiggling the front of her T-shirt. But she carried a book bag by its straps and didn't bother with the rail.

Coming down behind her was a fat guy in a sweatsuit. But behind him was a real beauty with flowing golden hair, her shoulders bare, her torso hugged by a bright yellow tube top. Her hand was on the banister!

*Yes!*

'Ow! Shit!'

The fat guy.

*No!*

He jerked his hand off the railing and halted so abruptly that the blonde nearly crashed into him. He lifted his hand to his crimson, stunned face. Blood dripped off, streaking the front of his sweatshirt. 'Fuckin' A! Looka this! Jeeeeez!'

Kids started to crowd around him.

Before long, someone would find the razor.

Releasing a long sigh, Charles closed his book. He tucked it under one arm, picked up his briefcase and strolled up the corridor.

Later that morning, after his seminar in Twentieth Century Irish Literature, Charles sat on a park bench along one of the campus walkways. The bench was fairly well hidden by hedges at both ends and an oak to the rear.

He took two X-Acto blades from his briefcase. Each was about an inch in length, V-shaped, with fine sharp edges. At the blunt end of each blade was a tab that could be slid into one of the

219

several handles which were part of the kit. Charles hadn't brought the handles with him.

With the blades cupped in one hand, he pretended to read Joyce. He watched the walkway. People kept coming by.

Patience, he told himself.

Before he could find time to plant the blades, a couple roosted on the bench across from him. They had bags from the Burger King a block from campus. Charles waited while they ate and gabbed. He waited while they snuggled and kissed. Finally, they wandered away, the guy with his hand down a back pocket of the girl's short denim skirt.

He checked the walkway. Clear at last!

Working quickly, he planted one blade upright in a green painted slat beside his right thigh. He scooted away from it, then dug a place for the other blade on a slat of the backrest. After checking again for witnesses, he inserted the blade.

Then he roamed across the walkway and settled down on the bench where the sweethearts had wasted so much of his time. They'd left a fry behind. He brushed it to the ground. He opened *Finnegan's Wake*, and waited.

People came by. A lot of people. Alone, in pairs, in small groups. Students, instructors, professors, administrators, ground keepers. Male and female. Slender, lovely girls. Plain girls. Slobs.

Into the afternoon, Charles waited.

Nobody sat on the bench.

Nobody.

Still, Charles waited. Over and over again in his mind, beautiful young women sat down on the bench. Their faces twisted and went scarlet. They leaped up, shrieking. They hurried away, blood from gashed buttocks spreading across the seats of shorts and skirts and jeans, blood from ripped backs staining blouses, T-shirts, flowing down the bare skin of those who wore tube tops or other varieties of low-backed garments.

In his best fantasy, it was Lynn who sat on the bench. Wearing a white bikini.

He often returned to that one while he waited.

220

Lynn stopped in front of him.

He gazed up at her, puzzled. She wasn't wearing a bikini. She wore a white cotton polo shirt, pink shorts that reached almost to her knees, and white socks and sneakers. Her huge leather shoulder bag hung against her hip.

'Hi, Charles,' she said. 'How's it going?'

He shrugged. He tried to smile. He was reasonably certain this was Lynn, not a figment of his imagination.

'Ready to head on over to the salt mines?' she asked.

He glanced at his wristwatch. Ten till four. Impossible! He couldn't have been sitting here *that* long.

'I guess it's time,' he muttered.

Lynn tilted her head to one side. 'Are you all right?'

'I didn't get much sleep last night.'

'I had kind of a restless night, myself. So, are you coming?'

'Sure. Yeah. I guess so.' He put his book away, lifted his briefcase and rose from the bench. With a last glimpse at the other bench, he started walking with Lynn.

It's Fate, he thought. He'd *tried* to direct his need away from Lynn, but his efforts had failed. They were meant to fail. He was being guided by forces beyond his control, forces that had ordained Lynn to bleed for him.

'Check out my finger,' she said as they walked along. She raised it in front of his face.

The bandage was gone. Charles saw a tiny curve of white fringe on the pad of her finger. His heart thudded. 'It looks good,' he said.

'Almost as good as new.' She smiled as her upper arm brushed against him. She lowered the hand to her side. 'If it wasn't for your first-aid, no telling what might've happened. Who knows? I might've bled to death.'

Charles knew she was joking. But his heart pounded even harder. Heat spread through his groin. 'From a paper cut?'

'Of course. Happens all the time. It's the leading cause of death among librarians and editors. Honest to God.' She looked at him. 'You *do* know how to smile, don't you?'

221

'Sure,' he muttered.

'Let's see one.'

He tried.

'Miserable,' she said. 'You know, you'd be a pretty handsome fellow if you'd smile once in a while.'

He gazed at her. He pictured how her face would look with bright red blood streaming down it. He imagined himself licking the blood from her cheeks and lips.

'That's more of a leer than a smile, actually,' Lynn said. 'But it'll do. You just need more practice.'


Even after all the books were shelved, Charles stayed in the second-floor stacks.

If he went downstairs, he would see Lynn. She would be sitting on her stool behind the circulation desk, checking books in and out, or maybe wandering the floor, cheerfully offering suggestions to students in need of assistance.

As long as I don't see her, he told himself, nothing will happen.

A few students came up. Some searched for books, while others slipped into carrels along the far wall and studied. There were girls, but he paid them no attention. It would be Lynn, or no one.

He ducked into a carrel himself. For some unknown reason, it had been placed in a corner away from the lights. That suited him well. He felt snug and hidden.

He folded his arms on the desk top and put his head down.

Maybe I'll sleep, he thought.

He closed his eyes. He pictured Lynn suspended from a ceiling beam, wrists tied, arms stretched high, feet off the floor. He had no rope, though. Too bad. Go back to his apartment and get some? The emergency exits had alarms. He couldn't leave the library without passing Lynn's desk.

Maybe use my belt, instead?

That had worked before. He'd put a loop around the girl's hands and nailed the other end high on a wall.

No hammer. No nails.

A rope would be better, anyway. Even though he didn't have one, he liked the image of Lynn hanging helpless. He knew she was wearing a polo shirt. In his mind, however, she wore a regular blouse. With buttons. And he saw himself slicing off the buttons, one by one.


Charles flinched awake when someone stroked the back of his head. He jerked upright in his chair. Lynn was standing close beside him, frowning down with concern on her shadowy face.

'You really zonked out,' she said. Her voice was little more than a whisper in the silence.

'I'm sorry. I didn't . . .'

'That's okay.' Her hand stayed on the back of his head, caressing his hair. 'I was a little worried about you, though. You just disappeared.'

'I was shelving books up here. I felt so tired . . .'

'No problem.' A smile tilted the corners of her mouth. 'I thought maybe you were trying to avoid me. You've been acting so strange ever since last night.'

'I've been *feeling* pretty strange.'

'Are you still upset because I cut myself?'

'In a way, I guess.' He stood up. The chair made a loud squawk as it was scooted away by the backs of his knees. The noise made him cringe.

'I haven't been quite myself, either,' Lynn said.

He turned to face her. 'Really?'

'Really.' Gazing into his eyes, she took hold of his hands. 'The way you acted last night . . . You were so sweet, getting me the bandage and everything, putting it on my finger even though you have that phobia about cuts. I just suddenly realized . . . how really special you are, Charles.'

'Me?'

'Yeah, you.' She lifted her hands to his face. Gently caressing his cheeks, she eased against him. She tilted back her head. She pressed her mouth against his lips. After a slow, soft kiss, she

223

looked up into his eyes. 'We're all alone,' she whispered. 'I've already locked up for the night.'

All he could say was, 'Oh.' He was trembling. His heart was punching his breath ragged. His groin was tight and the way Lynn pressed against him, he knew she must be able to feel his erection.

She stepped back to make a space between their bodies. Her hands roamed over his chest. 'I was awake all night,' she said. 'Thinking about you.'

'I was awake thinking about you, too.'

'You were?' He heard a tremor in her voice.

'Yes.'

'Oh, man.' She made a soft, nervous laugh. 'I should've cut myself a long time ago.'

Her trembling fingers unbuttoned his shirt. She spread it open. She kissed his chest.

With one hand, Charles stroked her back. With the other, he dug into the pocket of his pants. He squeezed the plastic handle of his knife.

Staring into his eyes, Lynn plucked at the bottom of her polo shirt. She pulled it free of her shorts, drew it over her head and dropped it to the floor.

Charles felt as if his breath had been sucked from his lungs. He struggled for air.

Lynn fumbled at the waist of her shorts. The garment slipped down her legs. She stepped out of it, nudged it away with her sneaker.

The plastic knife handle felt greasy with sweat.

'Do you like how I look?' Lynn whispered.

Charles nodded. 'You look . . . beautiful.'

So beautiful. Slender and smooth, naked except for her skimpy white bra and panties, her white socks and sneakers.

She had a calm, dreamy look on her face. A hint of a smile. Arching her back, she reached both arms up behind her.

'Don't,' Charles murmured.

Her eyebrows lifted. 'I was just going to unhook . . .'

'I know. Let me?'

Her smile brightened. 'Sure.'

Charles pulled out his knife. As he opened the blade, he watched Lynn – ready to grab her if she should try to flee.

Her smile went crooked. She stood motionless, eyes on the knife. 'You're kidding, right?'

'I have to.'

She lifted her gaze to his face. She seemed to be studying him. Then she shrugged one shoulder. 'Go ahead, Charles.'

'Huh?'

'If you have to, you have to. I'll buy a new one.'

'Oh.'

She put her hands on his hips. He felt them shaking slightly. They squeezed him when he cut through each of the shoulder straps. Then he slid his blade under the narrow band between the cups of her bra. She closed her eyes. Her mouth hung open. He heard her raspy breathing. He tugged, severing the band.

The bra fell away.

Lynn opened her eyes. A smile fluttered on her face. 'This is pretty kinky,' she said, her voice husky.

She shivered when he rubbed the blade's blunt edge down the top of her left breast. In the glow of the nearest florescent light, he saw the smooth skin go pebbly with goosebumps. Her nipple grew. He pressed it down with the flat of the blade, and watched it spring up again. Lynn groaned.

She tugged open his belt. She unfastened the button at the waist of his jeans, jerked his zipper down, feverishly yanked his jeans and underwear down his thighs.

Can't be happening this way, Charles thought. Never had anything like this happen. He wondered if he might be asleep, dreaming.

But he knew that he was very much awake.

Lynn's fingers curled around him.

'Do my panties,' she whispered. 'With the knife.'

He cut them at the sides. The flimsy fabric drooped, but the panties didn't fall. They clung between her legs until she reached down. A small pull, and they drifted toward the floor.

'This is so weird,' she gasped. 'I've never . . . nothing like this.'

Her soft, encircling fingers slid on him. Up, and down.

The knife shook as Charles moved it toward her chest. Just above her left breast, he pressed the point against her skin. Gently.

'Careful there,' she whispered. 'You don't want to cut me.'

'I do, actually.'

Her hand slipped away. She stood up very straight, searching his eyes. 'You're kidding, aren't you?'

'No.'

'But you *hate* cuts.'

'I'm sorry. As a matter of fact, I love them. They . . . they do something to me.'

'You mean like they turn you on?'

'Yes.'

'But that's crazy!'

'I guess so. I'm awfully sorry, Lynn.'

'Hold on, now.'

'I *have* to do it. I have to cut you up.'

'Oh my God.'

He shook his head. 'You're so beautiful, and . . . I guess I love you.'

'Charles. No.'

He stared at the knife point denting her skin. A slit all the way down to the tip of her breast . . .

Lynn grabbed his hand, twisted it. As Charles yelped, the elbow of her other arm crashed against his cheek. Stumbling backward, he heard his knife clatter to the floor. His pants tripped him. He slammed the side of the study carrel and fell.

Lynn scurried, crouched, and came up holding the knife.

Charles got to his knees. He gazed up at her. So beautiful. Scowling at him, naked except for her white socks and sneakers. The blade of the knife in her hand gleamed.

'Oh, Charles,' she murmured.

Tears stung his eyes. He hunched over, clasped his face with both hands, and wept.

'Charles?'

'I'm sorry,' he blurted. 'God, I'm so sorry! I don't know why I . . . I'm sorry!'

'Charles.' Her voice held a note of command.

He rubbed tears from his eyes and lifted his head.

Lynn stared down at him. She nodded slightly. A corner of her mouth was trembling.

She flicked her wrist. She flinched and grimaced as the blade cut a tiny slit. She closed the knife and lowered it to her side.

Charles watched the thin ribbon of blood. It started just below her collar bone and trickled down. It ran along the top of her breast, split in two, and one strand began a new course down the pale round side while another made its slow way closer to her nipple.

'Come here,' Lynn whispered.

Charles was embarrassed horribly the next day in the pharmacy.

Lynn was giggling.

She plopped three boxes of condoms down on the counter. The clerk, a young man, glanced from her to Charles. He looked amused.

'You got something against safe sex?' Lynn asked.

The clerk blushed. 'No. Huh-uh.'

Charles wanted to curl up and die.

'Ring these up, too, while you're at it.' Onto the counter, Lynn tossed three tins of adhesive bandages.

# Out of the Woods

A sound like footsteps outside the tent shocked me out of half-sleep. Another camper? Not likely. We were far from the main trails and hadn't seen a backpacker in three days.

Maybe it was no one at all. Maybe a twig or pine cone had dropped from a nearby tree. Or maybe the smell of food had drawn an animal to our camp. A big animal.

I heard it again – a dry crushing sound.

I was afraid to move, but forced myself to roll over and see if Sadie was awake.

She was gone.

I looked down the length of my mummy bag. The unzipped screen was swaying inward. A cool damp-smelling breeze touched my face, and I remembered Sadie leaving the tent. How long ago? No way to tell. Maybe I had dozed for an hour, maybe for a minute. At any rate, it was high time for her to come in so we could close the flaps.

'Hey, Sadie, why don't you get in here?'

I heard only the stream several yards from our campsite. It made a racket like a gale blowing through a forest.

'Sadie?' I called.

Nothing.

'Saay-deee!'

She must have wandered out of earshot. Okay. It was a fine night, cold but clear, with a moon so round and white you could it up for hours enjoying it. That's what we'd done, in fact, before turning in. I couldn't blame her for taking her time out there.

'Enjoy yourself,' I muttered, and shut my eyes. My feet were a bit cold. I rubbed them together through my sweatsocks, curled up, and adjusted the roll of jeans beneath my head. I was just beginning to get comfortable when somebody close to the tent coughed.

It wasn't Sadie.

My heart froze.

'Who's out there?' I called.

'Only me,' said a man's low voice, and the tent began to shake violently. 'Come outa there!'

'What do you want?'

'Make it quick.'

'Stop jerking the tent.' I took my knife from its sheath on the belt of my jeans.

The tent went motionless. 'I've got a shotgun,' the man said. 'Come outa there before I count five or I'll blast apart the tent with you in it. One.'

I scurried out of my sleeping bag.

'Two.'

'Hey, can't you wait till I get dressed?'

'Three. Come out with your hands empty, four.'

I stuck the knife down the side of my sweatsock, handle first, to keep it from falling out, and crawled through the flaps.

'Five, you just made it.'

I stood up, feeling twigs and pine cones under my feet, and looked into the grinning, bearded face of a man who bore a disturbing resemblance to Rasputin. He had no shotgun. Only my hand-ax. I scanned the near bank of the stream behind him. No sign of Sadie.

'Where's the shotgun?' I asked. Then I clamped my mouth shut to keep my teeth quiet.

The man gave a dry, vicious laugh. 'Take that knife outa your sock.'

I looked down. I was wearing only shorts and socks, and the moonlight made the knife blade shine silvery against my calf.

'Take it out slowly,' he warned.

'No.'

'Want to see your wife again? If I give the signal, my buddy will kill her. Slit her open like a wet sack.'

'You've got Sadie?'

'Back in the trees. Now, the knife.'

'Not a chance.' I pressed my knees together to keep them from banging against each other. 'You'll kill us both anyway.'

'Naw. All we want's your food and gear. See, we gotta do some camping. You understand, pal.' He grinned as if a glimpse of his big crooked teeth would help me understand better. It did.

'What did you do?' I asked, trying to stall for time. 'Rob a bank?'

'That, too. Now are you gonna get rid of that knife or do I signal Jake to start cutting?'

'Better signal Jake,' I said, and grabbed my knife.

'You sure?'

'I'm sure. Just one favor, though. Do you mind if I tell my wife goodbye?'

He grinned again. 'Go on.'

'Thanks,' I said. Then I yelled, 'Goodbye, Sadie! Sadie! Goodbye, Sadie!'

'Enough.' He came forward, holding the ax high, shaking it gently as if testing the weight of its head. All the time, he grinned.

My knife flew end over end, glinting moonlight, and struck him square in the chest. Hilt first.

He kept coming. Finally I backed into a tree. Its bark felt damp and cold and rough against my skin.

'There's no Jake,' I said to distract him.

'So what?' he answered.

I raised my hands to block the ax and wondered if it would hurt for long.

Then a chilling, deep-throated howl shook the night. A mastiff splashed through the stream. Huge, brutish, black as death. The man had no time to turn. He only had time to scream before Sadie, snarling, took him down and began to rip his throat.

# Stiff Intruders

'What are you doing here?' Charlie demanded of the dead woman.

She didn't answer. She was leaning back in Charlie's lawn chair, the very chair he wanted for himself, the chair he sat in every morning to drink his first two mugs of coffee. This was his favorite part of the day: so quiet, the air still cool and fresh from the night, the sun gently warming. But now, this!

'Hey!' he shouted.

She didn't stir. She simply sat there, hands folded on her lap, ankles crossed casually. Charlie sipped his coffee and walked around her. She wore a sleek, blue evening gown. Inappropriate wear, Charlie thought. A sun dress or swimsuit would be just the thing, but a formal, off-the-shoulder gown was unsuitable, even pretentious. Not that she could be held accountable.

Charlie went into the kitchen for a refill of coffee. As he pushed through the door to the backyard and saw her still sitting there, the injustice of it overwhelmed him. He decided to nudge her off the chair and let her fend for herself.

That's exactly what he did. The woman flopped and sprawled, and Charlie took his seat.

After a few moments, he moaned in despair. He simply couldn't enjoy his coffee in front of her.

Emptying his cup on the grass, he got to his feet and rushed into the house. He wanted to pound roughly on Lou's bedroom door. That might rub Lou the wrong way, however, so he rapped lightly.

'Knock off the racket!' Lou yelled.

'May I come in?'

'Suit yourself.'

Charlie opened the door and stepped into a room stinking of stale cigar smoke. Lou was in bed, covers pulled high so that only his face showed. The chubby face, flat nose and bulging eyes always reminded Charlie of a pug named Snappy he'd once owned. Snappy, who nipped anything in sight, generally had a sweeter disposition than Lou. Especially in the morning.

'Get up, Lou. I want to show you something.'

'What?'

'Get up, get up!'

Lou moaned and sat up. 'This better be good,' he said.

'Oh, it's not good, but you'd better see it.'

Muttering, Lou climbed from bed. He put on his slippers and robe, and followed Charlie to the backyard.

'See,' Charlie said.

'Who is she?' asked Lou.

'How should I know?'

'You found her.'

'Just because she was sitting in my chair doesn't mean I know the lady.'

'What was she doing in your chair?'

'Not much.'

'How come she's on the grass?'

'She was in my seat, Lou.'

'You shoved her off?'

'Certainly.'

'That was rude, Charlie.' Lou knelt down beside her. 'Nicely dressed, isn't she?'

'Certainly better dressed than you left yours,' Charlie said.

'I won't quibble with that.' He tipped her head back and touched her bruised throat. 'A nylon stocking,' he said. 'Maybe a scarf. Not my style at all.'

'I haven't accused you of anything,' Charlie protested.

'No, that's right. Thanks. You've gotta be wondering, though.'

234

Charlie shrugged.

'You read my book, right?'

'Certainly.'

In fact, Charlie had not read it. He hadn't read any book since *Silas Marner* in high school. But Lou was proud of *Choke 'em Till They Croak: The True Story of the Riverside Strangler in his Own Words*. He had every right to be proud. The book, written during his last two years in prison, had been a hardbound bestseller. The paperback rights went for $800,000, and Ed Lentz was signed to play Lou in the Universal film.

'First,' Lou said, 'if she wasn't a blonde, I left her alone. Second, I took the clothes home to dress up my mannequins. Third, I didn't use no scarf, I used my thumbs. That's how come they called me Thumbs.'

'Certainly, I know all that.'

'Fourth, I didn't dump 'em in other people's backyards. That's rude. I left 'em on the freeway exits.' He poked her with his foot. 'Not my style at all.'

'But the police?'

'Exactly. We've gotta get rid of her.'

'What'll we do with her?' Charlie asked.

Lou pulled a cigar out of his robe pocket. He peeled off the wrapper and tossed it into the grass. He poked the cigar into his mouth and lit it. 'What we'll do,' he said, 'we'll deposit her at the bank.'

They stored her in the trunk of Charlie's Dodge until after dark that night. Then they went for a drive. Charlie, a former wheel man who drove getaway cars during numerous successful robberies and one failure, stole a Ford Mustang from the parking lot of an apartment building in Studio City. Lou followed him in the Dodge. On a dark, curving road in the Hollywood Hills, Lou picked the lock of the Mustang's trunk. They transferred her into the trunk, and left the Mustang behind the Santa Monica branch office of Home Savings and Loan.

'That was certainly a chore,' Charlie complained afterward.

235

'I got a kick out of it,' Lou said.

Two days later, while reading the morning paper, Lou announced, 'They found our body.'

'Oh?'

' "Dancer found slain," it says. "The body of twenty-nine-year-old ballet dancer Marianne Tumly was found late Sunday night, the apparent victim of strangulation. Miss Tumly, understudy of Los Angeles ballerina Meg Fontana, disappeared Friday night after the company's performance of *Swan Lake*. Her body was discovered in the trunk of a car abandoned in Santa Monica, according to police officials." ' Lou began to mumble, apparently finding no more worth sharing.

'You don't suppose they'll connect us, do you?' Charlie asked.

'Not a chance.'

For several days, Charlie drank his morning coffee in the backyard, enjoying the fresh air, the sunlight, the silence and peaceful solitude. On Saturday, however, he found the body of a lean brunette occupying his chair.

He stared at her. She stared back.

'This is ridiculous,' he said. 'Well, you're not going to ruin my day *this* time!'

But she did.

Though Charlie sat in Lou's wicker chair, back turned so she was out of sight, he could almost feel her studying the back of his head. Irritated, he went inside to refill his mug. As he poured steaming coffee from the percolator, he got an idea. He went to the linen closet. Before resuming his seat, he covered the woman's head with a striped pillow case.

That almost worked. Unfortunately, Charlie half expected her to peek out from under the pillow case. Every few seconds, he looked over his shoulder to check. It finally became too much for him. He rushed into the house and barged into Lou's bedroom. 'Lou!' he cried. 'There's another one!'

Lou's scowl turned to a grin. 'A busy man, our strangler.'

Late that night, they put her in the trunk of a stolen Firebird.

They left the Firebird in a parking lot at Los Angeles International Airport.

Though the newspaper ran stories for several days about the disappearance of a dancer – another member of the troupe performing *Swan Lake* – her body wasn't found until Thursday night. It made the Friday morning paper.

After reading the article aloud, Lou lit a cigar. 'We did real good on that one, Charlie. If we'd wrapped her up better to hold in the aroma, she might've gone another week. Know what I'd like to do, I'd like to put the next one . . .'

'*What* next one?' Charlie demanded.

'We've had these gals two Saturday mornings in a row. Number three's gonna pop up tomorrow, you can bet on it.'

'Lou!'

'Huh?'

'Let's lay for the strangler. If he comes along tonight with another corpse, we'll nab him!'

'What then?'

'We'll make him take it away.'

Lou watched his smoke float toward the ceiling. Then he said, 'Good idea. Excellent idea. I'd like to meet the guy.'

Charlie, sitting on a stool near the backyard fence at midnight, heard a car in the alley. It stopped just on the other side of the fence. He heard the engine die, then the quiet bump of a closing door.

So this is how he does it, Charlie thought. Just drives up the alley and brings her in. But the rear gate? It's always locked. How . . . ?

Behind Charlie, something thudded against the redwood fence. He turned and looked up. A blonde woman grinned at him over the top. He heard a grunt. The woman seemed to leap. She towered over him for a moment, then folded at the waist. Charlie jumped out of the way. He gaped at her. She hung there, swaying slightly, like the body of a gunslinger draped over a saddle. Another grunt came from behind the fence. Her legs flipped high, slender and pale in the moonlight. Then she dived to the grass. She performed a somersault, and lay still.

Charlie glanced toward the garage. Its side door stood open. In the darkness of its gap was the red glow of Lou's cigar.

He motioned frantically for Lou to join him.

Quickly, he crouched at the corner of the fence. The wood jolted against his back, and he saw an arm hook over the top rail. After a gasp and a scuffling sound, a leg appeared. Then, in one quick motion, the man swung over and dropped to the grass. He landed silently on his feet, less than a yard from Charlie.

Crouching, he lifted the body. He flung it over his shoulder.

'Now,' said Charlie, 'you may kindly toss her back over the fence and take her away. Clutter someone else's yard.'

Still holding the body, the strangler turned to Charlie and said, 'Huh?'

'I said take her away!'

'How come?' he asked. He was younger than Charlie had imagined. His shaved head was shiny in the moonlight. In his tight T-shirt and jeans, his stocky body looked dangerous.

'Because,' Charlie answered in a subdued voice, 'you've been putting them in *my* lawn chair.'

'I thought you liked it.'

'*Liked* it?'

'Sure.'

Charlie was relieved to see Lou ambling toward them, puffing vigorously on his cigar.

'You took good care of 'em,' the younger man continued. 'You know?'

'Why'd you bring them here?' Lou asked.

The man spun around. Charlie dodged the woman's left heel.

'Did you know about me?' Lou asked. 'Is that it?'

'Know what?'

'I'm Thumbs O'Brien. The Riverside Strangler.'

'No fooling?'

'Did you read my book, kid?' Lou's voice was eager.

'What book?'

238

'Never mind.' Lou sounded disappointed. 'So how come you're leaving stiffs in our backyard?'

'Like I was telling this guy, you took good care of 'em. I mean, the first, I was bringing her up through the alley here. It's dark, you know. So I just heaved her over the fence.'

'How did she get in my chair,' Charlie asked.

'I got to thinking, you know? How comfortable can it be on the grass? So I hustled her over to the chair.'

'Decent of you,' Lou said.

'You guys took care of her real good.'

'Thank you,' Lou said.

'That's why I came back. I figured I'll let you take care of the others, too.'

'Tell me this,' Lou said. 'Why'd you do it?'

'I just told you, you took real good . . .'

'He means,' Charlie explained, 'why did you kill them?'

'Oh.' He grinned. 'She told me to.'

'Who did?'

'Isadora.'

'Who?' asked Lou.

'Isadora Duncan. You know, Isadora! She wants 'em for her dance troupe.'

Lou tapped a column of ash from the tip of his cigar. 'They won't do her much good dead.'

Charlie groaned at Lou's display of ignorance. '*She's* dead,' he explained. 'Isadora is. Her scarf caught in the wheel of her car. A long time ago. In the twenties, I believe.'

'No kidding?' Lou nodded at the young strangler. 'So you're fixing her up with a bunch of dancers. I get it.'

'May I ask,' Charlie inquired, 'how large a group she requires?'

'Oh, big. Real big.'

'How big?'

'Fifty-two.'

Charlie imagined fifty-two more bodies in the backyard on his lawn chair. 'I won't have it!' he blurted. 'Lou!'

''Fraid that's too much, kid.'

'Too much?'

'Yeah. Sorry.'

Charlie watched the woman fall. He watched the brief struggle. It was no contest, really. The kid didn't have a scarf handy, but Lou had his thumbs.

On a sunny, cool morning toward the end of the week, Charlie carried his coffee mug outside and stopped in surprise.

'What are you doing here?' he asked.

Lou, in sunglasses and a Dodger ballcap, was sitting on his own lawn chair. A cigar tilted upward from his mouth. Propped against his upraised right knee, he held a spiral notebook. 'How's this sound?' he asked. '*Save Your Last Dance for Me: the True Story of the Swan Lake Strangler in his Own Words.*'

'It sounds like a lie,' Charlie said.

'You gotta take liberties,' said Lou, 'when you're a ghost-writer.'

# *Special*

---

# 1

The outlaw women, wailing and shrieking, fled from the encampment. All but one, who stayed to fight.

She stood by the campfire, a sleek arm reaching up to pull an arrow from the quiver on her back. She stood alone as the men began to fall beneath the quick fangs of the dozen raiding vampires.

'She's mine!' Jim shouted.

None of his fellow Guardians gave him argument. Maybe they wanted no part of her. They raced into the darkness of the woods to chase down the others.

Jim rushed the woman.

*You get her and you get her.*

She looked innocent, fierce, glorious. Calmly nocking the arrow. Her thick hair was golden in the firelight. Her legs gleamed beneath the short leather skirt that hung low on her hips. Her vest spread open as she drew back her bowstring, sliding away from the tawny mound of her right breast.

Jim had never seen such a woman.

*Get her!*

She glanced at him. Without an instant of hesitation, she pivoted away and loosed her arrow.

Jim snapped his head sideways. The shaft flew at Strang's back. Hit with a thunk. The vampire hurled the flapping body of

241

an outlaw from his arms and whirled around, his black eyes fixing on the woman, blood spewing from his wide mouth as he bellowed, 'Mine!'

Jim lurched to a halt.

Eyes narrow, lips a tight line, the woman reached up for another arrow as Strang staggered toward her. Jim was near enough to hear breath hissing through her nostrils. He gazed at her, fascinated, as she fitted the arrow onto the bowstring. Her eyes were on Strang. She pulled the string back to her jaw. Her naked breast rose and fell as she panted for air.

She didn't let the arrow fly.

Strang took one more stumbling stride, foamy blood gushing from his mouth, arms outstretched as if to reach beyond the campfire and grab her head. Then he pitched forward. His face crushed the flaming heap of wood, sending up a flurry of sparks. His hair began to blaze.

The woman met Jim's eyes.

*Get her and you get her.*

He'd never wanted any woman so much.

'Run!' he whispered. 'Save yourself.'

'Eat shit and die,' she muttered, and released her arrow. It whizzed past his arm.

Going for her, Jim couldn't believe that she had missed. But he heard the arrow punch into someone, heard the roar of a mortally wounded vampire, and knew that she'd found her target. For the second time, she had chosen to take down a vampire rather than protect herself from Jim. And she hadn't run when he'd given her the chance. What kind of woman *is* this?

With his left hand, he knocked the bow aside. With his right, he swung at her face. His fist clubbed her cheek. Her head snapped sideways, mouth dropping open, spit spraying out. The punch spun her. The bow flew from her hand. Her legs tangled and she went down. She pushed at the ground, got to her hands and knees, and scurried away from Jim.

Let her go?

He hurried after her, staring at the backs of her legs. Shadows

242

and firelight fluttered on them. Sweat glistened. The skirt was so short it barely covered her rump and groin.

*You get her and you get her.*

She thrust herself up.

I'm gonna let her go, Jim thought. They'll kill me, and they'll probably get her anyway, but . . .

Instead of making a break for the woods, she whirled around, jerked a knife from the sheath at her hip, and threw herself at Jim. The blade ripped the front of his shirt. Before she could bring it back across, he caught her wrist. He yanked her arm up high and drove a fist into her belly. Her breath exploded out. The blow picked her up. The power of it would've hurled her backward and slammed her to the ground, but Jim kept his grip on her wrist. She dangled in front of him, writhing and wheezing. Her sweaty face was twisted with agony.

One side of her vest hung open.

*She might've had a chance.*

*I got her, I get her.*

Jim cupped her warm, moist breast, felt its nipple pushing against his palm.

Her fist crashed into his nose. He saw it coming, couldn't believe it, had no time to block it. Pain exploded behind his eyes. But he kept his grip, stretched her high by the trapped arm, and punched her belly until he could no longer hold her up.

Blinking tears from his eyes, sniffing up blood, he let go. Her legs folded. She dropped to her knees in front of him and slumped forward, her face hitting the ground between his feet. Crouching, he pulled a pair of handcuffs out of his belt. Blood splashed the back of her vest as he picked up her limp arms, pulled them behind her, and snapped the cuffs around her wrists.

# 2

'That one put up a hell of a scrap,' Roger said.

Jim, sitting on the ground beside the crumpled body of the woman, looked up at the grinning vampire. 'She was pretty tough,' he said. He sniffed and swallowed some more blood. 'Sorry I couldn't stop her quicker.'

Roger patted him on the head. 'Think nothing of it. Strang was always a pain in the ass, anyway, and Winthrop was such an atrocious brown-noser. I'm better off without them. I'd say, taken all round, that we've had a banner night.'

Roger crouched in front of the woman, clutched the hair on top of her head, and lifted her to her knees. Her eyes were shut. By the limp way she hung there, Jim guessed she must still be unconscious.

'A looker,' Roger said. 'Well worth a broken nose, if you ask me.' He chuckled. 'Of course, it's not *my* nose. But if I were you, I'd be a pretty damn happy fellow about now.' He eased her down gently and walked off to join the other vampires.

While they waited for all the Guardians to return with the female prisoners, they searched the bodies of the outlaws, took whatever possessions they found interesting, and stripped the corpses. They tossed the clothing into the campfire, not one of them bothering to remove Strang from the flames.

Joking and laughing quite a bit, they hacked the bodies to pieces. The banter died away as they began to suck the remaining blood from severed heads, stumps of necks and arms and legs, from various limbs and organs. Jim turned his eyes away. He looked at the woman. She was lucky to be out cold. She couldn't see the horrible carnage. She couldn't hear the grunts and sighs of pleasure, the sloppy wet sounds, the occasional belch from the vampires relishing their feast. Nor could she hear the women who'd been captured and brought in by the other Guardians. They were weeping, pleading, screaming, vomiting.

When he finally looked away from her, he saw that all the Guardians had returned. Each had a prisoner. Bart and Harry both had two. Most of the women looked as if they'd been beaten. Most had been stripped of their clothes.

They looked to Jim like a sorry bunch.

Not one stood proud and defiant.

I got the best of the lot, he thought.

244

Roger rose to his feet, tossed a head into the fire, and rubbed the back of his hand across his mouth. 'Well, folks,' he said, 'how's about heading on back to the old homestead?'

Jim picked up the woman. Carrying her on his shoulder, he joined the procession on its journey through the woods. Other Guardians complimented him on his catch. Some made lewd suggestions about her. A few peeked under her skirt. Several offered to trade, and grumbled when Jim refused.

At last, they found their way to the road. They hiked up its moonlit center until they came to the bus. Biff and Steve, Guardians who'd stayed behind to protect it from outlaws and vampire gangs, waved greetings from its roof.

On the side of the black bus, in huge gold letters that glimmered with moonlight, was painted, ROGER'S ROWDY RAIDERS.

The vampires, Guardians and prisoners climbed aboard.

Roger drove.

An hour later, they passed through the gates of his fortified estate.

# 3

The next day, Jim slept late. When he woke up, he lay in bed for a long time, thinking about the woman. Remembering her courage and beauty, the way her breast had felt in his hand, her weight and warmth and smoothness while she hung over his shoulder on the way to the bus.

He hoped she was all right. She'd seemed to be unconscious during the entire trip. Of course, she might've been pretending. Jim, sitting beside her, had savored the way she looked in the darkness and felt quick rushes of excitement each time a break in the trees permitted moonlight to wash across her.

The other Guardians were all busy raping their prisoners during the bus ride. Some had poked fun at him, asked if he'd gone queer like Biff and Steve, offered to pay him for a chance to screw Sleeping Beauty.

He wasn't sure why he had left her alone during the trip. In the past, he'd never hesitated to enjoy his prisoners.

But this woman was different. Special. Proud and strong. She deserved better than to be molested while out cold and in the presence of others.

Jim would have her soon. In privacy. She would be alert, brave and fierce.

Soon.

But not today.

For today, the new arrivals would be in the care of Doc and his crew. They would be deloused and showered, then examined. Those judged incapable of bearing children would go to the Donor Ward. Each Donor had a two-fold job: to give a pint of blood daily for the estate's stockroom, and to provide sexual services not only for the Guardian who captured her but also for any others, so inclined, once he'd finished.

The other prisoners would find themselves in the Specialty Suite.

It wasn't a suite, just a barracks-like room similar to the Donor Ward. But those assigned to it did receive special treatment. They weren't milked for blood. They were provided good food, not the slop doled out to the Donors.

And each Special could only be used by the Guardian who had captured her.

Mine will be a Special, Jim thought. She's gotta be. She *will* be. She's young and strong.

She'll be mine. All mine.

At least till Delivery Day.

He felt a cold, spreading heaviness.

That's a long time from now, he told himself. Don't think about it.

Moaning, he climbed out of bed.

# 4

He was standing guard in the north tower at ten the next morning when the two-way radio squawked and Doc's voice came through the speaker. 'Harmon, you're up. Specialty Suite, Honors Room Three. Bennington's on his way to relieve you.'

Jim thumbed the speak button on his mike. 'Roger,' he said.

Heart pounding, he waited for Bennington. He'd found out last night that his prisoner, named Diane, had been designated a Special. He'd hoped this would be the day, but he hadn't counted on it; Doc only gave the okay if the timing was right. In Doc's opinion, it was only right during about two weeks of each woman's monthly cycle.

Jim couldn't believe his luck.

Finally, Bennington arrived. Jim climbed down from the tower and made his way across the courtyard toward the Specialty Suite. He had a hard time breathing. His legs felt weak and shaky.

He'd been in Honors Rooms before. With many different outlaw women. But he'd never felt like this: excited, horribly excited, but also nervous. Petrified.

# 5

Honors Room Three had a single large bed with red satin sheets. The plush carpet was red. So were the curtains that draped the barred windows, and the shades of the twin lamps on either side of the bed.

Jim sat down on a soft, upholstered armchair. And waited. Trembling.

Calm down, he told himself. This is crazy. She's just a woman.

Yeah, sure.

Hearing footfalls from the corridor, he leaped to his feet. He turned to the door. Watched it open.

Diane stumbled in, shoved from behind by Morgan and Donner, Doc's burly assistants. She glared at Jim.

'Key,' Jim said.

Morgan shook his head. 'I wouldn't, if I were you.'

'I brought her in, didn't I?'

'She'll bust more than your nose, you give her half a chance.'

Jim held out his hand. Morgan, shrugging, tossed him the key to the shackles. Then the two men left the room. The door bumped shut, locking automatically.

And he was alone with Diane.

From the looks of her, she'd struggled on the way to the Honors Room. Her thick hair was mussed, golden wisps hanging down her face. Her blue satin robe had fallen off one shoulder. Its cloth belt was loose, allowing a narrow gap from her waist to the hem at her knees. She was naked beneath the robe.

Jim slipped a finger under the belt. He pulled until its half-knot came apart. Then he spread the robe and slipped it down her arms until it was stopped by the wrist shackles.

Guilt subdued his excitement when he saw the livid smudges on her belly. 'I'm sorry about that,' he murmured.

'Do what you're going to do,' she said. Though she was trying to sound tough, he heard a slight tremor in her voice.

'I'll take these shackles off,' he said. 'But if you fight me, I'll be forced to hurt you again. I don't want to do that.'

'Then don't take them off.'

'It'll be easier on you without them.'

'Easier *for* you.'

'Do you know why you're here?'

'It seems pretty obvious.'

'It's not that obvious,' Jim said, warning himself to speak with care. The room was bugged. A Guardian in the Security Center would be eavesdropping, and Roger himself was fond of listening to the Honors Room tapes. 'This isn't . . . just so I can have fun and games with you. The thing is . . . I've got to make you pregnant.'

Her eyes narrowed. She caught her lower lip between her teeth. She said nothing.

'What that means,' Jim went on, 'is that we'll be seeing each other every day. At least during your fertile times. Every day until you conceive. Do you understand?'

'Why do they want me pregnant?' she asked.

'They need more humans. For guards and staff and things. As it is, there aren't enough of us.'

She gazed into his eyes. He couldn't tell whether or not she believed the lie.

'If you don't become pregnant, they'll put you in with the Donors. It's much better for you here. The Donors . . . all the Guardians can have them whenever they want.'

'So, it's either you or the whole gang, huh?'

'That's right.'

'Okay.'

'Okay?'

She nodded.

Jim began taking off his clothes, excited but uncomfortably aware of the scorn in her eyes.

'You must be a terrible coward,' she said.

He felt heat spread over his skin.

'You don't seem evil. So you must be a coward. To serve such beasts.'

'Roger treats us very well,' he said.

'If you were a man, you'd kill him and all his kind. Or die trying.'

'I have a good life here.'

'The life of a dog.'

Naked, he crouched in front of Diane. His face was inches from her tuft of golden down. Aching with a hot confusion of lust and shame, he lowered his eyes to the short length of chain stretched taut between her feet. 'I'm no coward,' he said, and removed the steel cuffs.

As the shackles fell to the carpet, she pumped a knee into his forehead. Not a powerful blow, but enough to knock him off balance. His rump hit the floor. He caught himself with both hands while Diane dropped backward, curling, jamming her thighs tight against her chest. Feet in the air, she slipped the hand shackles and trapped robe under her buttocks and up the backs of her legs. They cleared her feet. Her hands were suddenly in front of her, cuffs and chain hidden under the draping robe.

As her heels thudded the floor, Jim rushed her. She spread her legs wide, raised her knees, and stretched her arms out straight

249

overhead. The robe was a glossy curtain molded to her face and breasts.

Jim dived, slamming down on her. She grunted. Clamped her legs around him. He reached for her arms. They were too quick for him. The covered chain swept past his eyes. Went tight around his throat. Squeezed.

Choking, he found her wrists. They were crossed behind his head. He tugged at them. Parted them. Felt the chain loosen. Forced them down until the chain pressed into Diane's throat.

Her face had come uncovered. Her eyes bulged. Her lips peeled back. She twisted and bucked and squirmed.

When he entered her, tears shimmered in her eyes.

# 6

The next day, Jim let Morgan and Donner chain her to the bedframe before leaving.

She didn't say a word. She didn't struggle. She lay motionless and glared at Jim as he took her.

When he was done but still buried in her tight heat, he whispered, 'I'm sorry.' He hoped the microphone didn't pick it up.

For an instant, the look of hatred in her eyes changed to something else. Curiosity? Hope?

# 7

'What are you sorry about, Jim?'

'Sorry?'

'You apologized. What did you apologize for?'

'To who?'

'You've gone soft on her,' Roger said. 'Can't say I blame you. She's quite a looker. Feisty, too. But she's obviously messing you up. I'm afraid someone else'll have to take over doing the Honors. We'll work a trade with Phil. You can do his gal, and he'll do yours. It'll be better for everyone.'

'Yes, sir.'

250

# 8

Phil's gal was named Betsy. She was a brunette. She was pretty. She was stacked. She was not just compliant, but enthusiastic. She said that she'd hated being an outlaw, living in the wilds, often hungry and always afraid. This, she said, was like paradise.

Jim had her once a day.

Each time, he closed his eyes and made believe she was Diane.

# 9

He longed for her. He dreamed about her. But she was confined to the Specialty Suite, available only to Phil, so he would probably never have a chance to see her again. It ate at him. He began to hope she would fail to conceive. In that case, she would eventually be sent to the Donor Ward.

A terrible fate for someone with her spirit.

But at least Jim would be able to see her, go to her, touch her, have her.

And she would be spared the final horror which awaited the Specials.

Doc had judged her to be fertile, however, so Jim knew there was little chance of ever seeing her again.

He was in the Mess Hall a week after being reassigned to Betsy, trying to eat lunch though he had no appetite, when the alarm suddenly blared. The PA boomed, 'Guardian down, Honors Room One! Make it snappy, men!'

Jim and six others ran from the Mess Hall. Sprinting across the courtyard, he took over the lead. He found Donner waiting in the corridor. The man, gray and shaky, pointed at the closed door of Honors Room One.

Jim threw the door open.

Instead of a bed, this room was equipped with a network of steel bars from which the Special could be suspended, stretched and spread in a variety of positions.

Diane hung by her wrists from a high bar. There were no

restraints on her feet. She was swinging and twisting at the ends of her chains as she kicked at Morgan. Her face wore a fierce grimace. Her hair clung to her face. Her skin, apparently oiled by Phil, gleamed and poured sweat. The shackles had cut into her wrists, and blood streamed down her arms and sides.

Phil lay motionless on the floor beneath her wild, kicking body. His head was turned. Too much.

*She'd broken his neck?*

How could she?

Even as Jim wondered, he saw Morgan lurch forward and grab one of her darting ankles. Diane shot her other leg high. With a cry of pain, she twisted her body and hooked her foot behind Morgan's head. The big man stumbled toward her, gasping with alarm. He lost his hold on her ankle. That leg flew up. In an instant, he was on his knees, his head trapped between her thighs.

Morgan's dilemma seemed to snap the audience of Guardians out of their stunned fascination.

Jim joined the others in their rush to the rescue.

He grabbed one leg. Bart grabbed the other. They forced her thighs apart, freeing Morgan. The man slumped on top of Phil's body, made a quick little whimpery sound, and scurried backward.

'Take Phil out of here,' said Rooney, the head Guardian.

The body was dragged from under Diane and taken from the room.

'What'll we do with her?' Jim asked.

'Let her hang,' Rooney said. 'We'll wait for tonight and let Roger take care of her.'

They released her legs and backed up quickly.

She dangled, swaying back and forth, her eyes fixed on Jim.

He paused in the doorway. He knew he would never see her again.

# 10

He was wrong.

He saw her a month later when he relieved Biff and began his new duty of monitoring video screens in the Security Center. Diane was on one of the dozen small screens. Alone. In the Punishment Room.

Jim couldn't believe his eyes. He'd been certain that Roger had killed her – probably torturing her, allowing the other vampires small samples of her blood before draining her himself. Jim had seen that done, once, to a Donor who tried to escape. Diane's crime had been much worse. She'd murdered a Guardian.

Instead of taking her life, however, Roger had merely sent her to the Punishment Room. Which amounted to little more than solitary confinement.

Incredible. Wonderful.

# 11

Night after night, alone in the Security Center, Jim watched her.

He watched her sleep on the concrete floor, a sheet wrapped around her naked body. He watched her sit motionless, cross-legged, gazing at the walls. He watched her squat on a metal bucket to relieve herself. Sometimes, she gave herself sponge baths.

Frequently, she exercised. For hours at a time, she would stretch, run in place, kick and leap, do sit-up and push-up and handstands. Jim loved to watch her quick, graceful motions, the flow of her sleek muscles, the way her hair danced and how her breasts jiggled and swayed. He loved the sheen of sweat that made her body glisten.

He could never see enough of her.

Every day, he waited eagerly for the hour when he could relieve Biff and be alone with Diane.

When he had to go on night raids, he was miserable. But he did his duty. He rounded up outlaw women. Some became Specials, and he visited them in Honors Rooms, but when he was with them he always tried to pretend they were Diane.

Then one night, watching her exercise, he noticed that her belly didn't look quite flat.

'No,' he murmured.

# 12

Throughout the winter, he watched her grow. Every night, she seemed larger. Her breasts swelled and her belly became a bulging mound.

He often wondered whose child she was bearing. It might be his. It might be Phil's.

He worried, always, about Delivery Day.

# 13

During his free time, he began making solitary treks into the wood surrounding the estate.

He took his sub-machine-gun and machete.

He often came back with game, which he delivered afterwards to Jones in the kitchen. The grinning chef was always delighted to receive the fresh meat. He was glad to have Jim's company while he prepared it for the Guardians' evening meal.

# 14

Spring came. One morning at six, just as Bart entered the Security Center to relieve Jim of his watch, Diane flinched awake, grimacing. She drew her knees up. She clutched her huge belly through the sheet.

'What gives?' Bart asked.

Jim shook his head.

Bart studied the monitor. 'She's starting contractions. I'd better ring up Doc.'

Bart made the call. Then he took over Jim's seat in front of the video screens.

'I think I'll stick around,' Jim said.

Bart chuckled. 'Help yourself.'

He stayed. He watched the monitor. Soon, Doc and Morgan and Donner entered the cell. They slung the sheet aside. Morgan and Donner forced Diane's legs apart. Doc inspected her. Then they lifted her onto a gurney and strapped her down. They rolled the gurney out of the cell.

'I'll pick 'em up in the Prep Room,' Bart muttered. 'That's what you want to see, right?' He leered over his shoulder.

Jim forced a smile. 'You got it.'

Bart fingered some buttons. The deserted Punishment Room vanished from the screen, and the Prep Room appeared.

Doc and his assistants rolled the gurney in.

He soaked a pad with chloroform, and pressed it against Diane's nose and mouth until she passed out. Then the straps were unfastened. After being sprayed with water, she was rubbed with white foam. All three men went at her with razors.

'Wouldn't mind that job,' Bart said.

Jim watched the razors sweep paths through the foam, cutting away not only Diane's thick golden hair, but also the fine down. The passage of the blades left her skin shiny and pink. After a while, she was turned over so the rest of her body could be lathered and shaved.

Then the men rinsed her and dried her with towels.

They carried her from the gurney to the wheeled, oak serving-table. The table, a rectangle large enough to seat only six, was bordered by brass gutters for catching the run-off. At the corners of one end – Roger's end – were brass stirrups.

Feeling sick, Jim watched the men lift Diane's limp body onto the table. They bent her legs. They strapped her feet into the stirrups. They slid her forward to put her within easy reach of Roger. Then they cinched a belt across her chest, just beneath her breasts. They stretched her arms overhead and strapped her wrists to the table.

'That's about it for now,' Bart said. 'If you drop by around seven tonight, that's when they'll be basting her. She'll be awake then, too. That's when the panic really hits them. It's usually quite a sight to behold.'

'I've seen,' Jim muttered, and left the room.

# 15

He returned to the barracks and tried to sleep. It was no use. Finally, he got up and armed himself. Steve let him out the front gate. He wandered the woods for hours. With his sub-machine-gun, he bagged three squirrels.

In the late afternoon, he ducked into the hiding place he'd found in a clump of bushes. He lashed together the twenty wooden spears which he'd fashioned during the past weeks. He pocketed the small pouch containing the nightcap mushrooms which he had gathered and ground to fine powder.

He carried the spears to the edge of the forest. Leaving them propped against a tree, he stepped into the open. He smiled and waved his squirrels at the north tower. The gate opened, and he entered the estate.

He took the squirrels to Jones in the kitchen. And helped the cheerful chef prepare stew for the Guardians' supper.

# 16

Just after sunset, Jim went to the Security Center and knocked.

'Yo.' Biff's voice.

'It's Jim. I want to see the basting.'

'You're a little early,' Biff said. Moments later, he opened the door. His mouth made a tight little O and he folded as Jim rammed a knife into his stomach.

# 17

Diane was awake, sweaty and grunting, struggling against the restraints, gritting her teeth and flinching rigid each time a contraction hit her.

Jim stared at the screen. Without hair and eyebrows, she looked so *odd*. Freakish. Even her figure, misshapen by the distended belly and swollen breasts, seemed alien. But her eyes were pure Diane. In spite of her pain and terror, they were proud, unyielding.

Doc entered the Prep Room, examined her for a few moments, then went away.

Jim checked the other screens.

In the Donor Ward, the women had been locked down for the Guardians' evening mealtime. Some slept. Others chatted with friends in neighboring beds. Jim made a quick count.

In the Specialty Suite, Morgan and Donner were just returning a woman from an Honors Room. They led her to one of the ten empty beds, shoved her down on it, and shackled her feet to the metal frame. Jim counted heads.

Thirty-two Donors. Only sixteen Specials. Generally, however, the Donors were older women who'd been weakened by the daily loss of blood and by regular mistreatment at the hands of the Guardians. The Specials were fewer in number, but younger and stronger. Though some appeared to be in late stages of their pregnancies, most were not very far along, and many of the newer ones had probably not even conceived yet.

It'll be the Specials, Jim decided.

He watched Morgan and Donner leave the Suite.

In the Mess Hall, Guardians began to eat their stew.

In the floodlit courtyard, Steve and Bennington climbed stairs to the north and west towers, carrying pots of dinner to the men on watch duty. When they finished there, they should be heading for the other two towers.

Morgan and Donner entered the Mess Hall. They sat down, and Jones brought them pots of stew.

Doc entered the Prep Room. He set a bowl of shimmering red fluid onto the table beside Diane's hip. He dipped in a brush. He began to paint her body. The blood coated her like paint.

In the Mess Hall, Baxter groaned and staggered away from the table, clutching his belly.

In the Banquet Room, there was no camera. But Jim knew that Roger and his pals would be there, waiting and eager. The absence of the usual table would've already tipped them off that tonight would be Special. Even now, Roger was probably picking five to sit with him at the serving table. The unfortunate four

257

would only get to watch and dine on their usual fare of Donor blood.

In the Mess Hall, Guardians were stumbling about, falling down, rolling on the floor.

In the Prep Room, Doc set aside the brush and bowl. He rolled the serving table toward the door. Diane shook her crimson, hairless head from side to side and writhed against the restraints.

Jim rushed out of the Security Center.

# 18

'All hell's broken loose!' he shouted as he raced up the stairs to the north tower. 'Don't touch your food! Jones poisoned it!'

'Oh shit!' Harris blurted, and spat out a mouthful.

'Did you swallow any?' Jim asked, rushing toward him.

'Not much, but . . .'

Jim jerked the knife from the back of his belt and slashed Harris's throat. He punched a button on the control panel.

By the time he reached the front gate, it was open. He ran out, dashed across the clear area beyond the wall, and grabbed the bundle of spears.

The gate remained open for him. Apparently, the poison had taken care of the Guardian on the west tower.

Rushing across the courtyard, he saw two Guardians squirming on the ground.

At the outer door of the Specialty Suite, he snatched the master key off its nail. He threw the door open and rushed in.

'All right, ladies! Listen up! We're gonna kill some vampires!'

# 19

Blasts pounding his ears, Jim blew apart the lock. He threw his gun aside, kicked the door, and charged into the Banquet Room.

Followed by sixteen naked Specials yelling and brandishing spears.

For just an instant, the vampires around the serving table

continued to go about their business – greedily lapping the brown, dry blood from Diane's face and breasts and legs as Roger groped between her thighs. The four who watched, goblets in hand, were the first to respond.

Then, roaring, they all abandoned the table and attacked.

All except Roger.

Roger stood where he was. He met Jim's eyes. '*You dumb fuck!*' he shouted. 'Take care of him, guys!'

The vampires tried. They all rushed Jim.

But were met, first, by Specials. Some went down with spears in their chests while others tossed the women away or slammed them to the floor or snapped their spines or ripped out their throats.

Jim rushed through the melee. He halted at the near end of the table as Roger cried out, 'Is *this* why you're here?' His hands delved. Came up a moment later with a tiny, gleaming infant. 'Not enough to share, I'm afraid.' Grinning, he raised the child to his mouth. With a quick nip, he severed its umbilical cord.

One hand clutching the baby's feet, he raised it high and tilted back his head. His mouth opened wide. His other hand grasped the top of its head.

Ready to twist it off. Ready to enjoy his special, rare treat.

'No!' Diane shrieked.

Jim hurled his spear. Roger's hand darted down. He caught the shaft, stopping its flight even as the wooden point touched his chest. 'Dickhead,' he said. 'You didn't really think . . .'

Jim launched himself at Diane. He flew over her body, smashed down on her, slid through the wide V of her spread legs and reached high and grabbed the spear and rammed it deep into Roger's chest.

The vampire bellowed. He staggered backward. Coughed. Blood exploded from his mouth, spraying Jim's face and arms. He dropped to his knees and looked up at the infant that he still held high. He lowered its head toward his wide, gushing mouth.

Jim flung himself off the end of the table, but he knew he would be too late.

He landed on the spear. As its shaft snapped under his weight, bloody vomit cascaded over his head. Pushing himself up, he saw the baby dangling over Roger's mouth. The vampire tried to snap at its head, but the tide of rushing gore pushed it away.

Jim scurried forward. He held the child in both hands until Roger let go and slumped against the floor.

# 20

Afterwards, the Donors were released.

They helped with the burials.

Eleven dead Specials were buried in the courtyard, their graves marked by crosses fashioned of spears.

Morgan, Donner and the Guardians, who'd all succumbed to the poison, were buried beyond the south wall of the estate.

The corpses of Roger and his fellow vampires were taken into the woods to a clearing where two trails crossed. The heads were severed. The torsos were buried with the spears still in place. The heads were carried a mile away to another crossing in the trail. There, they were burned. The charred skulls were crushed, then buried.

After a vote by the women, Doc and three Guardians who'd missed the poisoned squirrels were put to death. Jones had also missed the meal. But the women seemed to like him. He was appointed chef. Jim was appointed leader.

He chose Diane to be his assistant.

The child was a girl. They named her Glory. She had Diane's eyes, and ears that stuck out in very much the same way as Jim's.

The small army lived in Roger's estate, and seemed happy.

Frequently, when the weather was good, a squad of well-armed volunteers would board the bus. Jim driving, they would follow roads deep into the woods. They would park the bus and wander about, searching. Sometimes, they found vampires and took them down with a shower of arrows. Sometimes, they found bands of outlaws and welcomed these strangers into their ranks.

# 21

One morning, when a commotion in the courtyard drew Jim's attention, he looked down from the north tower and saw Diane gathered around the bus with half-a-dozen other women. Instead of their usual leather skirts and vests, they were dressed in rags.

Diane saw him watching, and waved. Her hair had grown, but it was still quite short. It shone like gold in the sunlight.

She looked innocent, glorious.

She and her friends commenced to paint the bus pink.

# Joyce

arbara bolted out of the bedroom and straight into Darren's
ms. He caught her, held her.

'What's wrong?' he asked. 'What is it?'

'Suh . . . somebody under the bed!'

'Oh. I'm sorry. Did she frighten you? It's only Joyce.'

'*Joyce?*' Barbara struggled out of Darren's embrace and gaped
him. 'But you told me . . . you said she was dead!'

'Well, of course she is. Do you think I would've married you
I still had a wife? It's just like I said, the brain aneurysm three
ars ago . . .'

'But you've got her under the bed!'

'Sure. Come on, I'll introduce you.'

Darren took Barbara by the hand and led her into the bedroom.
he staggered along beside him. On the floor by the bed was her
itcase, the one she'd taken with her on the honeymoon,
npacked that evening, and after her shower with Darren had
ecided to tuck out of sight.

'Luggage doesn't go under the bed,' he explained. 'I keep it
ut in the garage.'

Barbara stood there, trembling and gasping inside her new
lk kimono, trying to stay on her feet as Darren carried the
itcase over to the door. Then he knelt and slid Joyce out from
nder the bed.

'Darling, meet Joyce.'

Joyce lay stiff on the carpet, her wide blue eyes gazing toward
e ceiling, her lips curled in a smile that showed the edges of her

263

straight, white teeth. Wisps of brown hair swept across her fore head. Thick tresses flowed from beneath her head – a rich, silken banner that extended past her right shoulder. Her arms, close to her sides, were reaching upward from the elbows, hands open. Her legs were straight, parted slightly. Her feet were bare.

She wore a white negligee, a skimpy number with spaghetti straps and a plunging neckline. It was every bit as short as the nightie that Barbara had delighted Darren by wearing on their wedding night, and every bit as transparent. The way he'd dragged Joyce from beneath the bed had twisted it askew, pulling its deep V sideways so her right breast rose bare through the gap.

Smiling over his shoulder at Barbara, Darren said, 'Isn't she lovely?'

Barbara dropped.

When she came to, she found herself lying in bed. Darren was sitting on its edge, a worried look on his face, a hand inside her kimono gently caressing her thigh. 'Are you all right?' he asked.

She turned her head.

Joyce stood beside the bed, six feet away, still smiling. The nightie blew softly, stirred by the breeze from the window. Though it concealed nothing with its sheer fabric, at least it had been straightened so her breast no longer stuck out.

She has a better figure than me, Barbara thought.

She's more *beautiful* than . . .

Barbara looked away, frowned at Darren. Though she wanted to sound calm, her voice came out high and childlike when she asked, 'What's going on?'

Darren shrugged. He stroked her thigh. 'It's nothing to be upset about. Really.'

'Nothing to be upset about? You've got your dead wife *stuffed* in your bedroom . . . and wearing *that*!'

He smiled gently. 'Oh, she isn't stuffed. She's freeze-dried. I found a place that does people's deceased pets. She looks wonderful, doesn't she?'

'Oh, God.' Barbara murmured.

'And that's her favorite nightgown. I don't see why she should

264

deprived of it, but if you'd rather she wear something a bit
ore modest . . .'

'Darren. She's dead.'

'Well, of course.'

'You bury dead people. Or cremate them. You don't . . . keep
em.'

'Why not?'

'It just isn't done!'

'Oh, if I couldn't have had her preserved so nicely, I suppose
ere'd be some reason to dispose of her. But look at her.'

Barbara chose not to.

'She's as fresh as the day she died. She doesn't smell. What's
e problem?'

'The problem? The problem?'

'I don't see any problem.'

'You've had her here . . . in your house . . . all along?'

'Sure.'

'Under the bed?'

'Well, only when I expected you to come over. I was afraid
ou might not take it well, so I felt it best to keep her out of
ght.'

'Under the *bed*? When I was here? All those nights I spent
re, she was . . . Oh, God. You had this . . . this *stiff* under the
d while we . . .'

'Not just any stiff. My wife.'

'Oh, that's supposed to make it okay?'

'She *was* my wife, darling. What was I supposed to do, throw
r out like an old shoe? I loved her. She loved me. Why should we
rt, just because she stopped being alive? I would've been . . . so
nely without her. And look at it from her point of view. Do you
ink she would've *enjoyed* being put in a hole, all by herself? Or
rnt to ashes? Good Lord, who would want a fate like that?
stead, she's here in her own house where she belongs, with her
sband. Isn't that the way *you* would want it? Really? It's what I'd
ant for myself. It's what I'd want for you if, God forbid, you
ould stop living before I do. So we would always be together.'

'I suppose,' she muttered, 'it would be better than . . . tho
other things.'

'No doubt about it.'

'You should've told me, though.'

'I was waiting for the right time. I'm just sorry you had t
find out about her . . . the hard way. She must've given you qui
a shock.'

'Yeah, I'll say.'

'You've taken it really well, though. You're a champ.' Wit
that, he spread open her kimono.

'Darren!' She swept it shut. Fast. And looked at Joyce. Wh
didn't seem to be watching. The former wife's gaze was directe
not at Barbara, but toward the open window beyond the be
which she seemed to find pleasing, possibly a little amusing.

'Now, now,' Darren said. 'Relax.'

'But Joyce.'

'She can't see what we're doing. For heaven's sake, she's dead

'I don't care. Not in front of her. No way.'

'Now you're being silly.'

'Silly! Goddamn it!'

'Shhh, shhh. Calm down. It's all right. I'll take care of her.'

Darren bent low, parted just enough of Barbara's kimono t
expose her groin, kissed her softly there, then climbed off th
bed. Stepping in front of Joyce, he took off his velours bathrob
'Forgive me?' he asked. Then he draped the robe over her head.
hung down nearly to her waist.

He stepped away from her. He faced Barbara. He smile
'Better?'

'Can't you just put her out in the hallway or something?'

Darren looked disappointed. 'That wouldn't be nice. This i
her bedroom, too, you know. I can't just put her out.'

Barbara sighed. This would be their first night together in th
house as man and wife. She didn't want to make a stink. Beside
it wasn't really so bad now that Joyce's face was out of sight. 'A
right,' she said.

'I could put her back under the bed, if you'd . . .'

'No, she's fine there.' Under the bed, she would be so much ser. Directly beneath them as they made love. Awful.

Darren stepped over to the light switch.

'No, leave the lights on.'

'Are you sure?'

'I don't . . . want to be in the dark with her.'

'Whatever you say, darling.'

As he returned to the bed, Barbara sat up and took off her ono. She glanced at Joyce, then lay down and shut her eyes. Darren sank down on top of her. He kissed her mouth. 'I'm so ud of you,' he whispered.

'I know. I'm a champ.'

'You are. You truly are.'

Barbara couldn't help it: every now and then as Darren kissed and fondled her and plunged inside her, she looked over at ce. His other wife. His dead wife. Standing there shrouded a bathrobe. Which wasn't pulled low enough in front to hide v the diaphanous nightie, drifting in the breeze, brushed inst the dark tuft of hair between her legs.

He used to make love to her, Barbara thought.

Here, on this same bed.

Does she know? Does she know he's doing it to me, now, right front of her? Is she jealous?

Don't be ridiculous.

Barbara tried to shake off the notion. But couldn't.

At the proper moment, she faked an orgasm.

It took a while for Darren to recover. Soon after he was athing normally again, he whispered, 'See, it was just fine.'

'Yeah.'

'She didn't bother you at all, did she? Joyce, I mean.'

'Not really.' A lie. Why not?

'I bet she made it better for you. She did for me.'

What Barbara thought was, *Oh my God*. What she said was, 'I 't know. Maybe.'

A while later, Darren said, 'Maybe I should turn the lights off v.'

'No. Leave them on.'

'You aren't still spooked, are you?'

'Just a little.'

'Well, that's all right. I'm sure she'll take a little getting us
to.'

I'll never get used to her, Barbara told herself. Never.

Soon, Darren fell asleep. Barbara tried to sleep, but her mi
was in a turmoil. She'd just married a man who kept his de
wife in the bedroom. Liked her there. As much as admitted t'
it turned him on to have her standing nearby while he made lo

Weird. Disgusting.

But it calmed Barbara whenever she thought about how thir
would be once she'd gotten rid of Joyce. Calmed her enough
that she was almost able to fall asleep.

Each time she started to drift, however, she lurched awa
with a sickening dread and had to look. To make sure Joyce had
moved, hadn't pulled the robe off her head, hadn't crept closer
the bed.

The bitch seemed to be staying put.

Of course.

All that ever seemed to move was the nightie, blown by t
breeze so it floated against her belly and pubic curls and the tc
of her legs.


When Barbara woke up, the bedroom was bright with sunlig
She'd fallen asleep after all. Somehow. In spite of Joyce.

Joyce.

She didn't want to see her, fought the urge to turn her hea
instead gazed at the ceiling and tried to appreciate the feel of t
warm breeze caressing her body.

I can't spend another night in the same room with her, s
thought. Just can't. I've gotta make Darren listen to reason.

She turned her head toward the other side of the bed.

Darren was gone.

No! What if he took his robe with him? What if *she's* uncovere

Barbara snapped her head the other way.

Joyce was gone.

Gone where?

Barbara bolted upright. Heart thudding, she scanned the room. ɔ sign of the corpse. She blew out a shaky breath and filled her ngs with the sweet morning air.

Not here. Maybe Darren came to his senses and . . .

She went cold inside and her skin crawled with goosebumps. *He put her under the bed!*

Moaning, she flung herself off the mattress. She rushed to the iddle of the room and there, a safe distance away, dropped to ʳr hands and knees and peered into the space beneath the bed.

No Joyce.

Thank God.

But where *is* she? What's Darren done with her?

At least she's not here. That's the main thing.

Calming down slightly, Barbara got to her feet. She brushed ɱe carpet lint off her hands and knees. She was still trembling, ll shivery with gooseflesh.

I can't live like this, she thought as she returned to the bed. ᴉe put on her silk kimono, wrapped it snugly around herself and ᵉd the sash. Then she turned toward the closet. She wanted her ᴑuse slippers.

What if Joyce is in there?

She stared at the shut door. And decided it could stay shut. ᴉe could do without her slippers.

Heading for the bedroom door, she noticed that her suitcase ɪs missing. Darren must've taken it out to the garage.

Maybe he'd also taken *Joyce* out to the garage.

If only.

Fat chance.

She halted at the doorway, leaned forward and swiveled her ʳad from side to side. The corridor looked clear. She rushed for ᵉ bathroom. Its door was open. No sign of Joyce. She entered ɪd locked the door. Then had a few bad moments as she ᵖproached the tub. But the tub was empty. Barbara sighed, ɪaxed a little.

She used the toilet, washed her face, brushed her teeth, sat on the edge of the tub and tried to work up her courage for venturing out of the sanctuary of the bathroom.

This is crazy, she told herself. Why should I be scared of Joyce? She can't hurt me. Can't do anything but freak me out. And make me wonder if I'm married to a crazy man.

He's not crazy. He cares about her, that's all. Can't bear to part with her.

Jesus H. Christ on a crutch.

He damn well *will* part with her. It's her or me.

Right. What'll I do? Where'll I go? I gave up my apartment already, quit my job, for godsake. Guess I can always find . . .

Why should *I* be the one to leave? *She's* the dead one.

Just gotta talk to Darren. If he'll only listen to reason and put her away someplace, everything will be okay.

Barbara forced herself to leave the bathroom. As she walked down the corridor, someone stepped out of the bedroom. She flinched before realizing it was Darren.

He'd already gotten dressed. He wore one of the bright red aloha shirts they'd bought on Maui. It hung loose down past the front of his Bermuda shorts. His legs looked darkly tanned above the tops of his white socks. He had his Reeboks on.

'Morning!' he said, smiling as he hurried toward her. 'You sure slept in, didn't you?'

Then she was in his arms. She hugged him, kissed him. My Darren, she thought.

He felt solid and warm and comfortable.

When they released each other, he said, 'I have a surprise for you.'

'You've put Joyce in storage?'

His smile faltered. 'Don't be silly. I made a trip to the doughnut shop. Maple bars!'

He knew how she loved maple bars. But she couldn't work up much enthusiasm as she said, 'Oh, that's sweet.'

Taking her hand, he led her into the kitchen. On the counter, the pot of coffee was ready. On the table, a heaping platter

270

doughnuts, including four maple bars, waited. In the corner, smiling, staring at Barbara as she entered, stood Joyce.

Her hair was done up in a ponytail. She wore a fresh white blouse. The bra beneath it, faintly visible through the thin fabric, was black. Her blouse was tucked neatly into the elastic waistband of her glossy blue shorts. She wore white socks and blue L.A. Gear athletic shoes.

'You dressed her,' Barbara muttered.

Darren grinned. 'She didn't dress herself.'

'Why?'

'Isn't that obvious?' He laughed softly and picked up the coffee pot.

'I mean, why did you dress her?'

'Oh. Well, it wouldn't be right for her to go around all day in her nightgown.' He filled the mugs with coffee and set them on the table. He pulled out a chair for Barbara.

'I'll sit over here,' she said. And took the chair on the opposite side of the table. So she wouldn't have her back to Joyce. So she could keep an eye on her.

Darren sat down in the chair he'd intended for Barbara. He took a sip of coffee. 'Actually, I did keep Joyce in her bathrobe for a while, at first. I thought to myself, why bother putting clothes on her? It got depressing, though. There she was, day and night, standing around in her robe. It made her seem . . . oh, I don't know, like an invalid.'

Tempted to make a remark, Barbara bit into a maple bar instead.

'So then I decided to start dressing her up. Off with that tired old bathrobe, on with . . . well, whatever the occasion demanded. Nightwear at night, casual things for daytime wear, one of her pretty little bikinis for poolside . . . she always liked to join me out by the pool, though she wasn't much for swimming. For more formal occasions – a birthday, Thanksgiving, that sort of thing – a lovely evening gown. Whatever seemed right.' Smiling, he bit into a jelly doughnut.

'Like having a life-size Barbie doll.'

271

'You're my Barbie doll,' he said, his voice muffled by dough nut, white powder and red jelly on his lips. 'She's my Joyc doll.'

Joyce smiled at the top of Barbara's head.

'Isn't it . . . difficult to dress her? I mean, she's stiff, isn't she

'Oh, we manage. Some outfits are trickier to get on her th others, but we make do the best we can.'

Barbara started to take another bite of maple bar. But it wou be a muddy lump in her mouth like the first one, and tough swallow. She set down the bar and drank some coffee.

'Is something wrong with your maple bar?'

'It's fine,' she muttered.

Frowning with concern, he leaned forward slightly. 'Is Joyce?'

'Of course it's Joyce. What do you think?'

'We went through all this last night, darling. I thought y understood.'

'My God, you dress her up like she's *real*.'

'She *is* real.'

'But she's *dead*! You cart her around from room to room. Y *dress her up*! You put a *bra* on her. Probably panties too, for al know.'

'Would you prefer her *without* panties?' he asked. Raising eyebrows, smiling slightly, he bit again into his doughnut.

'I'd prefer her *gone*!'

Nodding, he chewed for a while. He swallowed. He sipped coffee. 'You'll get used to her. Once you've gotten to know h better, I'm sure you'll . . .'

'I want her out of here.'

'Out of the kitchen?'

'Out of the *house*. Preferably in a fucking *graveyard*!'

'Oh, dear. You *are* upset.' The look of sorrow on Darren's fa made her heart ache for him.

'I'm sorry,' she murmured. 'I am. I love you so much. B Joyce . . .'

'She frightens you, doesn't she?'

272

Barbara nodded.

'She doesn't bite, you know.'

'I know.'

'She doesn't *do* anything.'

'She looks at me.'

'They're only glass eyes,' Darren explained gently.

'They're not hers?'

'Hers didn't fare well in the . . . process. But if they bother you . . . Back in a sec.' He pushed himself away from the table and hurried from the kitchen.

While he was gone, Barbara studied Joyce's face. Glass eyes. They sure looked real. Too real, too bright and aware. Did it make things any better, knowing they were fake? For a few moments, she thought so.

They're not Joyce.

They're not her dead eyes. Nothing much more than a couple of shiny marbles poked into her sockets.

Sockets.

The *real* Joyce hasn't got eyes. Were they gouged out? Popped? Dragged out with forceps? Did they just shrivel away in the 'process' and fall out?

Those beautiful, lively eyes gazing at the top of Barbara's head were pieces of glass stuck into pits.

Do *they* ever fall out?

Does Darren take them out lovingly, from time to time, and polish them up?

Barbara stared at Joyce. No eyes. God! Those aren't her eyes. They're covers. Hatches put there to conceal a pair of hideous cavities.

Cringing, she looked away. Thanks for telling me, Darren. Thanks a lot.

'Here we go,' he said, bustling into the kitchen. 'This'll be just what the doctor ordered.' He kissed the top of Barbara's head, then hurried around the table.

She looked up in time to watch him slide sunglasses onto Joyce's face. They were much like those worn by the Highway

273

Patrolman who'd stopped Barbara last month for making a unsafe lane change on the Santa Monica Freeway. Wire rim teardrop shaped lenses with silver reflective surfaces.

'How's that?' Darren asked. Stepping away, he admired th effect. 'Make her look rather dashing, don't you think?'

Now I can't tell where she's looking, Barbara thought. But sh didn't want to hurt Darren's feelings. He was *trying* to help 'That's a lot better.'

Maybe it is better, she told herself. Now, at least, her eyes ar out of sight. Maybe I can forget about them. Forget they aren eyes, just socket hiders.

Darren sat at the table, looking pleased with himself. 'Fo every problem, there's a solution.'

'Guess so,' Barbara said. She picked up her maple bar an forced herself to eat it.

When Darren asked how she would like to spend the day, sh suggested going to the beach. 'Fabulous idea,' he blurted. 'It' be like we're still on our honeymoon.'

'Just the two of us, right?'

'Of course.'

'You don't want to take *her* along?'

'Joyce'll be fine right here.' He winked. 'She's really prett much a home body.'

In the bedroom, Barbara tied her string bikini into place, the covered up with a blouse and shorts, and slipped into sandal Darren came in while she was making the bed. 'I'll get the towe and things while you're changing,' she told him.

'I'll be done in a jiff,' he said, and winked.

Before they left, Darren carried Joyce into the living room He set her down on the sofa, tucked a pillow under he head an pulled off her shoes. 'All comfy?' he asked. He patted her leg then took the beach bag from Barbara's hand and led the way t the door.

It was wonderful to get out of the house. Away from Joyce. A the beach, they roamed along the shoreline, holding hands. The spread towels on the sand, massaged each other with sun bloc

retched out side by side, lay motionless under the heavy sun
nd soothing breezes.

Exhausted after a night of so little sleep, Barbara slumbered
eacefully.

Later, they explored the pier. They wandered the souvenir
hops. They rode the bumper cars. Darren sank a basketball three
mes in a row and won her a furry, pink teddy bear. They ate
ied clams and homemade potato chips on a bench high above
e ocean.

Then they returned to the sand. They spread their towels again,
y down, and again Barbara fell asleep.

She awoke when Darren kissed her shoulder. 'We'd best be on
ur way.'

Her stomach twisted, knotted itself into an icy clump.

'Not yet.'

'We don't want to burn.'

'We won't. The sun block . . .'

'Nevertheless. We should be getting back.'

'It's still early.'

He glanced at his wristwatch. 'It's after three.'

She nodded. She forced herself to smile.

Her smile became genuine as she pulled the shorts up her
gs. 'I know, let's go to a movie!'

'A movie?'

'Sure. A matinee. It'll be great!'

'Well . . .'

'Please? This is out last day together before . . . it'll be off to
ork for you in the morning. We won't have another chance to *do*
ything till next weekend. Please?'

'Sure. Why not?'

They returned to the car, drove to a parking structure near the
hird Street Mall, then went to a cineplex. Of the six movies
aying there, one was scheduled to begin in fifteen minutes.
arren bought tickets, and in they went.

Soon, the theater darkened. Too soon, the movie ended.

'It sure will be great to get home and take a nice shower,'

Darren said as they walked through the lobby. He patted he rump. 'Together.'

'Why don't we stay for another?'

'Really, darling. I think one's enough.'

'Please? You know how I love movies.'

He smiled. 'How's this? We'll drop by the video store on th way home and rent a couple for tonight.'

She sighed. She didn't want to *start* anything. 'All right. you'd rather do that.'

So they drove to a video store.

Barbara studied the shelves of tapes, shaking her hea unwilling to make a choice. Over and over again, she foun reasons not to accept videos Darren selected. She'd already see this one, that one didn't sound very good. 'Don't worry,' she sai several times. 'We'll find something. There must be *somethin* decent around here.' And they kept on looking.

She managed to stretch out their search for more than an hou Finally, Darren said, 'Let's just grab a couple. I'm starving.

Barbara grabbed two that she'd noticed when they first cam in.

Back in the car, she said, 'Why don't we have a bite to e before we go home?'

'Take-out?'

'I'd rather eat *in* a restaurant. It's so much more fun.'

'Look how we're dressed.'

'We don't have to go any place fancy. Jack-in-the-Box Burger King. Whatever.'

Darren drove to Burger King. They ate at a table. Whil Barbara slowly consumed her meal, she tried to think of anothe way to delay their return home.

Give it up, she finally thought. I've stalled him as long as can without making a fuss. We can't stay away forever. Might well get it over with.

So, when the meal was done, they climbed into the car an drove through the dusk, heading for home.

Where Joyce would be waiting.

Maybe we'll be in luck, Barbara thought, and the house burnt
.vn while we were out.

Fat chance.

They rounded a corner, and there it was. Still standing.

'Did you have a good time?' Darren asked as he swung into
driveway.

'Wonderful. I really hate for it to end.'

'Nothing's ended, darling.' He stopped the car, leaned toward
rbara and stroked the back of her head. 'Our life together has
y begun. We'll have so many fine times.'

'I suppose so.'

'No supposing about it.'

She followed him into the house. Darren carried the sack of
eo tapes into the living room and set it down at Joyce's feet.

'She won't have to watch the movies with us, will she?' Barbara
ed. 'Couldn't you . . . maybe put her in another room?'

'I could. But the sooner you get used to her the better. Don't
ı think?'

'I don't think I'll ever get used to her.'

'Oh, you will, you will. Give it time. Now, you go along and
rt your shower. I'll be along in a minute.' He winked. Then he
uched, slipped his arms under Joyce, and lifted her off the
a.

Barbara's heart slammed. 'Where are you taking her?'

'The guest room.' He grinned. 'Time to get her out of the
time attire.'

She hurried ahead of them and shut herself into the bathroom.
mbling, she took off her clothes.

The daytime attire, she thought.

He's stripping her. Then he'll be waltzing in here and putting
hands on *me*.

That's what *he* thinks.

She thumbed down the lock button, then went to the tub and
ıed on the shower.

He'll just have to choose, she thought as she adjusted the
cets. Joyce or me. He can't have it both ways.

277

What if he chooses her?

I can't lose him. Not over a damned stiff!

Sighing, Barbara stepped to the door and unlocked it.

She climbed into the tub and slid the glass door shut. The h
spray felt wonderful splashing against head and face, slidi
down her body.

His hands will be clean, she told herself. They'll be all soa
when he rubs me. They won't have Joyce on them.

But she'll be waiting when we come out.

Dressed in her little see-through nightie.

God!

Standing around in her nightie and shades while we watch t
movies. Then standing by the bed while we make love.

I can't take much more of this.

Maybe I shouldn't let him have me again till she's out of t
house.

No, he'd end up resenting me. I can't do anything to *make* hi
get rid of her. He'd hold it against me forever. It has to be h
decision.

If only she hadn't been preserved so well. If she was rotten
stinky, he sure wouldn't have kept her around.

What if I go to the market tomorrow while he's at work, pi
up some really stinky cheese, poke some into her mouth? Po
some into her *everywhere*?

Yuck! I'd have to touch her.

There are always gloves for that.

Darren will think she's going bad.

And get rid of her?

What if he probes around and finds the cheese?

Would it be worth the risk?

Barbara flinched, startled, as the shower door rumbled ope
She turned. Joyce stared in at her, smiling. No silver shades,
nightie.

'No!' She staggered backward as Joyce rose, lifted high
Darren behind her. 'Get her *out* of here!' She slipped. Her run
smacked the bottom of the tub. 'Ow!'

'Darling! Are you all right?'

'No! Get her out of here! What's the matter with you?'

'This'll be a great way for you to get better acquainted. Really.
Did you hurt yourself?'

'I'll live.' Barbara scooted backward and drew her legs up to
er chest as Darren stepped into the tub with Joyce. Holding the
ody against him with one arm across her belly, he slid the shower
oor shut.

The spray splattered off Joyce's shoulders. Water spread down
er body in shiny streamers.

'Please!' Barbara begged. 'I don't *want* to get better
quainted. Take her away!'

'You'll be fine once you've gotten to know her.'

'The water'll ruin her! You'd better . . .'

'Oh, no, she's quite durable. Stand up, now, darling.'

'Darren!'

'Is it really asking so much? Just stand up. Please.'

Trembling, breathless, Barbara struggled to her feet.

Darren smiled at her from behind Joyce's shoulder. 'Now,
ome a little closer. Be careful you don't fall.'

She took a few small steps forward, and stopped.

'Closer.'

She moved closer.

'Closer.'

'No. Come on.' One more step, and she would *meet* Joyce.

'Okay,' Darren said. He blinked water out of his eyes. 'You're
oing fine. Really. You're making great progress. Now, I want
ou to touch her face.'

'Don't make me.' Her voice came out whiny.

'I won't make you do anything. Do it for me. Do it for us.
ease. You must get over this phobia about Joyce.'

'It's not a *phobia*.'

'Then we'll be able to get on with our lives. I'm sure you'll
ven come to *like* her. She'll make a fine companion for
ou while I'm away at work every day. Now, please. Touch her
ce.'

279

Barbara raised a wet hand toward Joyce's cheek. And hesitate[d], fingers shaking.

Joyce gazed at her with merry, shining eyes.

Glass stuffed in pits.

'You're so close now,' Darren urged her. 'Don't stop now.'

Holding her breath, Barbara placed her fingertips again[st] Joyce's cheek. She prodded it gently. She stroked it. The skin fe[lt] smooth and stiff. Like a fine leather shoe.

From behind Joyce's shoulder, Darren beamed at her. 'I'm s[o] proud of you!'

Barbara lowered her arm. 'I did what you asked. Now will yo[u] take . . .'

She gasped as the body lurched forward. Its hands brushed h[er] sides. Before she could leap away, *other* hands clutched he[r]. Darren's hands. They grabbed her sides, jerked her forward. Tig[ht] against Joyce.

She turned her head just in time to avoid a collision wi[th] Joyce's face. Their cheeks rubbed.

Darren kissed her, pressed his lips against hers above Joyce['s] shoulder. Pushed his tongue into her mouth.

*He can't be doing this!*

*Not with Joyce in the middle!*

But he *was* doing this, Joyce in the middle, her hard breas[ts] shoving into Barbara's breasts, her belly and groin and thigh[s] tight and stiff against Barbara. And *moving*. Rubbing against h[er] as Darren writhed and moaned and thrust with his tongue.

Barbara chomped.

Darren cried out. His hands leaped off her.

She drove her hands against Joyce's hips and rammed h[er] away, slamming Darren against the tile wall beneath the show[er] nozzle. He grunted as his head thumped. Blood exploded fro[m] his mouth.

Barbara staggered backward to get away from the four fe[et] sliding her way.

She spit out a chuck of Darren's tongue.

She hadn't meant to bite it *off*, but . . .

Horrified, she watched the bloody slab flop onto Joyce's belly button.

I've ruined him!

'Look what you made me do!' she yelled.

Darren didn't answer. Nor did he move. During the fall, he'd slipped lower so his head was under Joyce. His arms lay limp against the bottom of the tub. His legs were stretched out to either side of Joyce's legs. His genitals showed through the crevice between her thighs.

The water cascading down on Joyce sent Darren's tongue sledding down her belly.

Barbara took another step backward. Her foot landed with a splash.

The tub was filling!

*He's gonna drown!*

Dropping to a crouch, she grabbed Joyce's ankles. She pulled. The body slid toward her. She worked her hands up the legs, scooting Joyce along beneath her toward the rear of the tub.

Darren's face came into view.

The water was up past his ears. His eyes were shut, his mouth hanging open. His mouth brimmed with blood.

'You'll be okay!' she cried. 'I'll save you!'

His eyes opened.

Thank God!

Red spray exploded like a geyser as he shrieked, 'BITCH!'

He sat up fast. His chest met the top of Joyce's head and raised her body. She came up rigid like a plank lifted at one end.

Barbara, lurching to get away from Darren, slipped.

And fell forward, her knees driving down into Joyce's belly.

*Krrrrrk!*

Joyce's head jumped forward, chin poking into her throat, face falling against her chest. Between her breasts, her head was upside down, ponytail toward Barbara, the stump of her snapped neck straight up, catching spray.

Darren roared with rage.

Barbara snatched up the head by its ponytail.

281

As Darren leaned forward and reached for her, she whippe Joyce's head against the side of his face. It caved in his cheekbon and bounced off, its glass eyes flying out and shattering agains the front of the tub. Darren's eyes rolled upward. He slumped She swung the head around and around by its ponytail, and struc him again. This time, Darren's left eye popped from its socke and dangled by a cord. The third blow mashed it. The fourth sen teeth flying from his mouth.

'Joyce is durable, all right, you bastard!'

She kept on bashing his head until Joyce's broken skull parte company with her scalp. This happened while Barbara wa winding up for another strike. Her weapon suddenly went nearl weightless. She cringed as airborne head bones crashed agains the shower door. Some bounced off and rained down on he shoulder and back.

She threw down the sodden mop of hair.

Then she tore off Joyce's right arm and used it on Darren unti it broke apart. She had to pause and catch her breath befor ripping the left arm from its socket.

She smashed it down on the collapsed rag of Darren's face.

The arm didn't last long.

It wasn't easy breaking off Joyce's legs. But she managed They proved to be well worth the effort.

# A Good, Secret Place

The new kid came up the street from the house where Eddie and Aaron used to live. We'd seen him once before, the day he moved in. Even from a distance, we'd wanted nothing much to do with him. For starters, he couldn't have been older than about twelve. For finishers, you could tell he was a dork.

So there we were, Jim and I, playing catch in my front yard on one of those really fine summer nights just at dusk. The neighborhood was so quiet about the only sound was the hardball smacking into our mitts. And this new kid came strolling up the street.

It was pretty obvious what he had in mind. He was wearing a mitt.

Not just any mitt – a first baseman's glove. Have you ever noticed that the real dopey kids of this world *always* use a first baseman's glove? I think it's because they're scared of the ball. A big leather scoop like that let's them go for it without getting too close.

Anyway, he didn't come onto the lawn. He stayed at the edge of the street, off past Jim's side, and watched us. We pretended he wasn't there. Easy enough for Jim, since he didn't have to look at the kid. He kept his face toward me as we fired the ball back and forth. Once in a while, he rolled his eyes toward the sky.

Other than being too young for us and wearing that stupid first baseman's glove, the kid was dumpy. He looked like he hadn't washed his hair for a month, and greasy strands hung down his forehead. He had a face like a pig. Fat, with little pink eyes. And a red nose that was runny, so he kept sniffing and every so

often he'd stick his tongue up to lick the snot off his lip. He wo
a red shirt with yellow flowers on it. It hung unbuttoned at tl
bottom. His belly bulged out through the gap like gray puddin
Lower down, you could see his boxers. Like he'd hitched the
up, but forgotten to hitch up his pants. They were white with bl
stripes. His pants, which looked about ready to drop, were pla
Bermuda shorts. They had huge, swollen pockets, and reach
down to his knees. Below his fat calves, he wore black socks. I
wore sandals on his feet.

I'm not joking. That's actually what the kid looked like.

He was a real prize.

I tried to keep my eyes off him, but it wasn't easy, the way I
just stood there off to the side of Jim, watching us throw. I wish
he would go away. And I felt like a jerk for ignoring him. I
didn't say anything. He just stood there, sniffing and licking h
snot, and sort of smiling.

Pretty soon, he started to sock his fist into his mitt.

I really couldn't take that. It's no fun at all, being left out
stuff.

So I called, 'Heads up, kid,' and threw him the ball. I didi
burn it in, nothing like that. I tossed it high and easy and right
him. He lit up for a second, then looked alarmed as the ball g
closer. Ducking and turning his face away, he reached up with h
huge scoop of a glove and didn't even come close. The ball fle
past him and went sailing off down the street. About the time
bounced on the pavement, he checked his mitt. He frowned, lil
he was really surprised to find it empty. Then he said, 'Sorry.'

That was the first word I ever heard him say. Sorry.

Then he went chasing after the ball.

'Good going, Ricky babes,' Jim said.

'What do you want? What was I supposed to do, ignore him

'Now we'll probably be stuck with the little creep.'

'It's getting dark, anyway. Maybe we'd better call it a nig
pretty soon.'

'Yeah, I'm all for that.'

But we had to wait for the ball. The kid took a while trying

find it. Finally, he dug it out of the flower bed in front of the
Watson house and came loping up the street. Still a ways off, he
gave it a throw.

'God!' Jim muttered. 'What is he, a girl?'

It was my ball, my fault, so I had to chase it down. I wasn't
eager to pick it up, considering it had been in the kid's hand and
was probably sticky. So I snatched it off the grass with my mitt.
By the time I got back with it, the kid was stepping over the curb,
walking toward Jim.

'Getting pretty dark,' I said. 'I guess we'd better call it quits
for now.'

'Do we *have* to?' the kid asked.

I didn't like the sound of that 'we.'

'Yeah, we'd lose the ball.'

'Well, all right.' He sniffed and backhanded some goo off his
upper lip. 'I'm George Johnson. We just moved in.' He swung a
pudgy arm out behind him. 'Over there.'

'I'm Rick. This is Jim.'

Luckily, he didn't try to shake hands with us.

'You guys sure are good.'

'It just takes practice,' I said, figuring he meant we were good
with the ball.

'You want a Twinkie?' He shoved a hand down into a bulging
front pocket of his shorts and pulled out a cellophane pack. The
twin, cream-filled yellow cakes inside looked pretty smashed.

'Thanks anyhow,' I said. 'I just had dinner.'

'Please,' George said. 'They're good.'

'What the hell,' Jim said. He stuck his mitt under his arm,
took the package from George, said 'Thanks,' and ripped it open.
He scooted one of the mooshed Twinkies off the cardboard
backing and held it toward me.

'There's only two of 'em,' I said. 'You eat it, George.'

'Oh, I got plenty. I want it to be yours.'

Well, it *had* been wrapped up. So I went ahead and took it.

Jim and I both had our mouths full when George said, 'Will
you be my friends?'

How can you say no to a kid who has just given you a Twinkie?

'Yeah, well . . .' I said.

'What the hell,' Jim said.

The next day, we made the mistake of riding our bikes pas
George's house. We were heading for the Fashion Mall, a good
place to hang out and watch the babes – especially Cyndi Taylor
She was a varsity cheerleader and didn't know we existed, bu
she had a summer job working at Music World. We could pretend
to brouse through the CDs and tapes for about an hour, and spend
the whole time scoping her out. I know, that might sound kind o
dumb. You wouldn't think so, though, if you'd ever seen Cyndi.

The only thing was, George must've been keeping a lookout
We hadn't even gotten past his house when the screen door
banged and he ran out, yelling, 'Hey, guys! Wait up!'

Jim gave me a disgusted look, but George was still in his
pajamas so I figured we were safe. We swung our bikes to the curb

'Hiya, George,' Jim said.

George stopped beside us, huffing and grinning. 'Hey, where
we going?'

'Nowhere,' I said. 'Just tooling around.'

'Great! I'll be right out!'

'That's all right,' Jim said. 'Don't you have something else
you've gotta do?'

'Nope!' And off he ran, his big butt bouncing the seat of his
pajamas.

The screen door whammed shut.

'Terrific,' I muttered.

'Let's beat it,' Jim said.

So that's what we did.

We sprinted our bikes for the corner, sped around it, then cu
down the first alley. All the way to the mall, we kept glancing
back, afraid George might be on our tails. But he wasn't.

He didn't show up at the mall, either.

He ruined everything, anyway. I couldn't quit thinking abou
him. He'd been so damn excited about coming with us. He'd

robably rushed to get dressed, and yelled something to his mom ke, 'Hey, I'm going off with my pals!' He'd probably been urrying out to the garage for his bike when he saw we were one. I wondered if he'd cried. I wondered how he explained to is mom that his friends had left him behind. I felt like a jerk.

I couldn't even work up much excitement watching Cyndi aylor glide around the music store. I'd look at her, but mostly I'd ee George. I've been ditched a few times. I know how it feels.

And it doesn't always feel much better when you're the one ho did the ditching.

To get home that afternoon, we took a back route so we ouldn't have to ride past George's house.

Every night since school let out, we'd been playing catch in y front lawn after dinner. But not that night. I cut across back-ards to reach Jim's place. He had a pool, so he also had a fence. scrambled over the fence. Jim was waiting. We shot the ball ack and forth across the length of the pool. Later on, Jim stood n the diving board. I threw just out of his reach, trying to get im to fall in. After a couple of close calls with him teetering and apping his arms, he said, 'I go in and wreck my mitt, it's your ss!'

'Language!' his mom called from inside the house.

When it was almost too dark to see the ball, someone turned n the lights. Then his sister, Joan, came out with a friend. They ere both seniors and wearing bikinis. They didn't talk to us or ything, but it was great while it lasted. They splashed around, l shiny in the water, while we fired the ball from one end of the ool to the other. I think they liked having us there. They floated ound on their backs quite a lot.

But then I guess Jim's mom noticed what was going on and ot scared we might bean someone, so she told us to quit.

We went up into the living room and played some Super Mario rothers till it was time for me to go home.

I took the front way. Off in the distance, I could see George's ouse. I realized that, somewhere along the way, I'd stopped eling rotten about ditching him.

287

When it was time to set out for the mall the next day, I sped ove
to Jim's place. He was waiting on his driveway.

'Wanta drop by George's house and see if he wants to com
along?' Jim asked, grinning.

'In your dreams.'

'The little shit.'

'You said it.'

Not only had I quit feeling sorry for the twerp, but I'd foun
myself really resenting the way he'd messed with our lives. Hel
we couldn't play catch in my frontyard, we couldn't ride our bike
past his house. We were like fugitives on our own block, hidin
from him. And *then* we felt guilty about it. I did, anyway. And
didn't like it. He had no right. So the hell with him.

We coasted down Jim's driveway. At the street, Jim swung
the right.

'This way,' I said, and swung my bike to the left.

'Are you kidding?'

'Screw him.'

We picked up a lot of speed by the time we reached George
house. Neither of us looked at it. I didn't hear the screen door sla
shut, so I figured we must've shot past too fast for the little scuz

Then I looked back.

George, hunched over the handlebars of his ten-spee
swooped down his driveway and swerved into the street. H
pumped his pedals like a madman trying to catch up.

'Oh, no,' I muttered.

Jim glanced back. 'Terrific. You and your great ideas.'

'Hey, wait up!' George yelled.

'Wanta ditch him?' Jim asked.

'God *damn* it! The hell with ditching him.' I slowed down. S
did Jim.

George closed the gap. Riding between us, he matched o
speed. 'What's up?' he asked.

'Not much,' I said.

'Where'd you guys go yesterday?'

288

'Nowhere,' I said. This hot feeling went through me. It was shame, whether I wanted it or not.

'I got a sudden case of the trots and had to go home,' Jim explained. 'Sorry we couldn't wait for you. But it would've got pretty messy on the street, you know?'

'Gosh, I'm sorry.'

'Shit waits for no man,' Jim added.

George laughed. 'So, you okay?'

'Fine,' Jim muttered, and gave me the eye.

'So, where we going?'

Jim had saved us with the trots story. Now it was my turn. 'The pool. Over at the Jefferson Recreational Center.'

George's smile faded. 'The pool?'

'That's right,' I said.

He looked confused. Frowning at Jim, he said, 'Don't you have a pool?'

Jim didn't miss a beat. 'Sure, but all the babes are at the public pool.'

'You got your trunks with you, George?' I asked.

He gave our bikes a once-over. 'Where's yours?'

'Wearing 'em,' I said, and patted the seat of my jeans. 'Underneath.'

'Oh.'

'You'd better go get your trunks,' Jim said, 'and we'll meet you at the pool.'

'I don't know where it is.'

Jim gave him directions. George listened, frowning and nodding, then made sort of a nervous smile and said, 'Okay. Guess I can find it.'

'Great,' Jim said.

'See you there,' I said.

George swung his bike around and pedaled for home.

Jim and I gave each other grins. We headed for the mall.

At Music World, we roamed up and down the aisles pretending to look at stuff while we watched Cyndi. I felt a little guilty about

289

the dirty trick we'd played on George, but forgot about it when Cyndi came over to us. It was almost too much for me, being thi close to her. The way she looked and smelled made me ache.

'Can I help you find something?' she asked.

I didn't trust myself to speak. All I could do was shake my head

'We're just browsing around,' Jim said, the way he always di when she or one of the others came over like this.

'Fine. If you need any help, be sure to let me know.'

'We will,' Jim told her.

She smiled and walked away.

'Oh, man,' Jim whispered. 'What I'd give . . .'

'Yeah.'

After she'd left, we had to settle for watching her from distance. She spent a while helping other customers, and then Bobbi Andrews came into the store. She was the head cheer leader, but nothing at all like Cyndi. While Cyndi was slende and graceful and beautiful, Bobbi was squat and had a face lik a rabbit. She was really popular, anyway. There were three reason for that: her pep and two humongous knockers. I couldn't car less about any of that. Personally, I thought she was a waste.

But she was Cyndi's best friend.

They got together near the back of the store and started talking

We figured that Cyndi was too busy with her to notice us, s we wandered down the aisle for a better view. We were prett careful about it. We pretended to be greatly interested in variou CDs and albums in the trough along the way, and got to the en of the aisle.

Cyndi was close enough to touch if I leaned forward fa enough. She stood in the next aisle, leaning back slightly. Th edge of the trough just behind her pressed a dent into her pleate skirt – into her rump, too. I could see the straps of her bra throug her white blouse. The way her head was turned, I could see th fine, downy fuzz on her smooth cheek.

'. . . by ten, I think,' Bobbi was saying when I started to listen 'No later than eleven.'

'No problem,' Cyndi told her. 'Don't worry about it. We'll jus be pigging out and watching movies.' Grinning, she nudged Bobbi with her elbow. 'At least till my parents hit the sack. You won't miss much. Just don't forget to bring that extra sleeping bag.'

'Hope Doris doesn't fart in it.'

Cyndi elbowed her again, and laughed.

Then Jim elbowed me, and we got away before they could notice we'd been near enough to hear them.

Outside the store, Jim grabbed my arm. 'Did you *hear* that?' He was flushed and breathless. 'She's having a *slumber* party. Are you thinking what I'm thinking?'

I was.

'You think it's tonight?' he asked.

I knew she didn't work at Music World on weekends. This was Friday. 'It's gotta be either tonight or tomorrow night.'

'Yeah!'

We took the back route to my house so we wouldn't have to pass George's place. When we were safely out of sight in the garage, Jim said, 'Wonder if he's still at the pool.'

'You'd think he might get the message,' I said.

'Kids like that *never* get the message.'

In the house, I asked if Jim could stay the night. Mom saw no problem with that. She suggested he stay for supper, too. Then we made a trip by the backyards to Jim's place. He got his mom's permission. After he put together his sleeping bag and overnight stuff, we returned to my house.

It didn't take long to set up the tent, toss in a couple of pads from the patio lounges, and arrange our sleeping bags.

But the waiting took a *long* time.

Nothing in the world takes longer than waiting for something really great to happen.

Finally, Dad got home from work. Finally, we ate supper. Finally, darkness came and we went out to the tent.

We had to wear our pajamas and leave our clothes behind. That was how we'd always done it in the past, and we didn't want

to make my parents suspicious by doing anything differently. [
wouldn't be a problem. They expected us to make a few tri]
back and forth to brush our teeth, use the john, that sort of thin]
Once they were off to bed, it would be a cinch to sneak o[
clothes out.

We took two flashlights into the tent with us. And a couple [
cans of Pepsi and a bag of onion-flavored potato chips. We zipper[
the fly screen, but left the flaps open to get some air. Inside, we s[
cross-legged on our sleeping bags and started snacking.

'This is so neat,' Jim said.

'The chips?'

'You know.'

'God, I can't believe we're gonna do it.'

'I just hope we can see something.'

'It's a one-storey house,' I said, 'so they sure won't be upstair[

'As long as they don't shut all the curtains.'

'They won't. They can't. It'd be too cruel.'

Jim laughed softly. 'When do you think we oughta get going[

'We'd better wait till after eleven.'

'Man, I hope we don't miss everything.'

'Bobbi won't even be getting there till then. Anyway, they [
probably be messing around all night.'

'We wanta be there in time to see 'em change.'

'Change into what?'

I wasn't the one who asked that.

*George* was the one who asked that.

We both flinched and jerked our heads toward the front of t[
tent. And saw George crouched on the other side of the fly scree[
his piggish face gray in the darkness. We shined our flashligh[
on him. He squinted and said, 'Hiya, guys.'

'What're you doing here?' I snapped.

'You having an over-nighter?' he asked, just as calm as if [
hadn't heard me.

'This is private property,' Jim told him.

'Can I have some potato chips?'

'You can't come in here,' I said. 'There isn't enough room.'

'I gave you guys my Twinkies.'

'Okay, okay,' I said. I didn't want to argue with him, just get
d of him. So I unzipped the screen and handed out the bag.
Help yourself. You can have them all.'

'Gee, thanks.'

'Why don't you take them home,' I said, 'and share with your
arents.'

'Oh, they're out.' He stuffed a handful of chips into his mouth.

'Give some to your sitter,' Jim said.

'Sitter?'

'They didn't leave you alone, did they?' I asked.

'Sure. Always do.'

'Great,' Jim muttered.

'So, where we gonna go?'

'Nowhere,' I said.

'We gonna go look in windows?'

How long had he been listening to us?

'We aren't going anywhere,' Jim said.

'I'll go with you. I like to look in windows. You get to see all
nds of neat stuff.'

'What are you,' Jim asked, 'a little pervert?'

George laughed, spraying out some potato chip crumbs.

'You'd better never be looking in *my* windows,' I told him.

'Or mine,' Jim added.

'Nah. I only like to see girls.'

'You been spying on my sister?' Jim asked.

George shook his head and jammed his mouth full of potato
ips.

'He knew about your pool,' I reminded Jim.

'Yeah. You been snooping around my house?'

'Huh-uh. Honest.'

'You better never, man.'

'I'll give you some good stuff if you let me come with.'

'You're not coming "with",' I said.

'Please?'

'Good stuff like what?' Jim asked.

'Twinkies.'

'That's no big deal. What else?'

'Cut it out,' I told Jim. 'He's got nothing we want.'

'I'll getcha some booze,' George said.

'Really?' Jim sounded interested.

'Forget it,' I said.

'What kind?'

'Anything. Pop's got a whole big bar in the den. And he's got a wine cellar.'

'You can get us a bottle of wine?'

'Sure.'

'Your old man'll kill you,' I said.

George shrugged. 'He won't know any better. 'Sides, who cares if he finds out? I'll swipe us a bottle, okay?'

'Cool,' Jim said.

'Are you nuts?' I asked.

'Are you? Come on. We can tie one on on the way over to Cyndi's.'

'Good going,' I muttered. I couldn't believe he'd spoken her name in front of a sleeze like George.

'Who's Cyndi?' George asked.

'Nobody,' I said.

'Is she the girl we're gonna spy on?'

'Go on home and get the wine,' Jim said. 'But don't come back till eleven. We aren't leaving till then.'

'Promise you won't go without me?'

'Cross my heart and hope to die,' Jim said. 'Now get going.'

George shoved the potato chip bag through the fly screen then sprang up, and ran off through the dark.

'You asshole!' I yelled.

'I know what I'm doing.'

'You *ass*hole! You told him Cyndi's *name*! You told him where we're *going*! Well, *I'm* not going. Not if that sleazy little shit's coming with us. No way. I'm not gonna have him spying on Cyndi.'

'Like he's been spying on my sister?'

That slowed me down. 'You think he's been doing that?'

294

'You think he *hasn't*? Like you said, how does he know about the pool?'

'He might've heard splashing, or . . .'

'From the street? Huh-uh. He's been snooping around. I bet he's even climbed over the fence. Joan's window is right there, man.'

'That doesn't mean he's ever looked in.'

'Hey, he confessed. He *said* he looks in girls' windows.'

'Not Joan's, though.'

'Like I'm sure he'd admit it. Get real. And what do you suppose he was doing in *your* backyard tonight?'

'Trying to find us, probably.'

'Yeah, maybe. Or maybe he came along to check out your parents' bedroom. Maybe he comes along *every* night to look in their window. Maybe he gets a charge out of watching your mom undress.'

'She shuts the curtains,' I said, feeling kind of hot and awful inside.

'Yeah, but does she shut them all the way? If there's even the tiniest open space between . . .'

'That dirty bastard better *not* be watching Mom.'

'I bet he does. Maybe my mom, too. Maybe Joan *and* Mom. And your mom. Maybe every gal in the whole neighborhood. You heard him. He *likes* to look in windows.'

'If he ever spied on my mom . . .'

'We gotta teach him a lesson. That's how come I said he can come along. You think I want his wine and Twinkies? We'll take him with us, all right. And then we'll nail his rotten Peeping Tom ass.'

We lay down on top of our sleeping bags, heads toward the front of the tent so we could keep a lookout for George, and hatched our plans.

At about ten-thirty, the light came on in my parents' bedroom. Mom stepped up to the window and pulled the curtains shut. After a while, the light went off. But a faint, trembly glow showed through the curtains. It came from their TV, which they liked to watch in bed till after the eleven o'clock news. They weren't likely to get up again except maybe to use the john.

'Ready to go?' Jim asked.

'Pretty soon.'

We waited a while longer. I was feeling awfully nervous. Not so much about sneaking into the house for our stuff. About the rest of it.

Finally, I said, 'Okay.'

We crawled out of the tent and crossed the patio to the back door. We didn't try to be quiet shutting the door and heading for the bathroom. Jim went in. I waited in the hall. When he flushed the toilet, I used the noise as a cover to rush into my bedroom. I flicked on the light, found a coil of rope in my closet and gathered up our clothes. Quick as I could, I turned the light off. Then I waited in the darkness at the doorway until Jim flushed the toilet again. While it made its gushy running sounds, I hurried to the back door. I opened it, stepped outside, checked my parents' window to make sure nobody was looking, and ran to the tent.

I kept watch through the fly screen.

Before long, Jim came out.

He crawled into the tent.

'Any problem?' I whispered.

'No sweat.'

We turned on our flashlights just long enough to sort out our clothes. Then, in the darkness, we stripped. It felt weird, being naked, feeling the warm air on my body, the sleeping bag under my rump. It might've been kind of exciting if there'd been nothing on my mind except going to Cyndi's house. But George had ruined things.

Once all my clothes were on except my shirt, I wrapped the rope around my waist. It had to go around several times. I did it carefully so the coils weren't all bunched on top of each other, but arranged flat against my skin. I tucked the ends underneath.

I'd just put on my shirt when Jim whispered, 'Here he comes.' Quickly, I fastened the buttons.

We picked up our flashlights and crawled outside.

Jim pressed a finger to his lips. George nodded, and raised the grocery sack he was carrying.

I led the way. We stopped at the side of the garage.

'You got the stuff?' Jim asked.

'Sure.' George opened the sack. He lifted out a wine bottle. 'I got the Twinkies, too.'

'Great. Put it away.'

'Don't you want some now?'

'Later.'

'We know a good, secret place along the way,' I whispered. 'We'll stop there and have a little party.'

'Neat!' George said.


The hike to our 'good, secret place' took about twenty minutes.

It was a railroad underpass beneath Jefferson Avenue.

If George hadn't been with us, Jim and I would've walked over it just as fast as possible and been mighty glad to leave it behind us.

Even in daylight, the place gave us both the creeps.

We'd never gone down there at night.

I felt jittery the whole time as we walked toward it.

Partly, I was worried that we might be spotted by cops or by someone we knew in the cars that went by. I turned my face away every time a car approached us from the front.

Mostly, though, I was scared about going down into the underpass.

We'd explored it quite a few times. From what we'd found, we knew that other people used the place. There was writing on the concrete walls, some of it pretty weird and sick. And there was always a lot of junk scattered around: empty booze bottles, smashed beer cans and cigarette packs, a ratty blanket or two, even an old, stained mattress. Clothes, too. Like a flat, dirty sneaker, a sock, somebody's old underwear, a pair of pants.

Once, we got pretty excited when we spotted a bra. Jim had picked it up. It was caked with dry mud, and one of the shoulder straps was torn loose.

Our best discovery was a copy of *Penthouse* magazine. It must've gotten soaked a while before we found it, because its pages were all stiff and swollen, and a lot of them were stuck together. We peeled them apart and got to see quite a few pictures. We took that magazine with us, and Jim kept it hidden in his room.

Our most revolting discovery was a used condom. We didn't touch that.

The creepiest thing we ever found down there, I guess, was the remains of a campfire – a circle of scorched rocks around a heap of ashes. In with the ashes were a couple of charred cans and a whole bunch of small bones. We figured they were probably turkey bones, or something. Until I found the skull. I picked it up and blew off the ashes. It had a short snout and pointed teeth. Jim said, 'God, that's a cat!' I yelled and dropped it. The skull hit a rock and shattered.

After that, we'd stayed clear of the underpass.

I sure didn't look forward to going back tonight.

I would've chickened out except for one thing: it was the perfect place for making George wish he'd never messed with us.

Too soon, we got there.

Jim halted just short of where the bridge's guard rail started. We stood there, silent, and waited for a car to pass. When it was out of sight, another set of headlights showed in the distance. Jim must've figured the driver couldn't see us yet. He whispered, 'This way, quick,' and stepped off the sidewalk.

'Where we going?' George asked.

'It's a great place,' I told him. 'Nice and private.'

Before the car got much closer, we followed Jim into the trees. We were hidden by the time it whooshed by. We crept past a few trees, then began climbing down a steep, bushy slope toward the tracks. To the right, the tracks stretched off across an empty field, shiny in the moonlight. To the left, they vanished in the black mouth of the underpass.

A couple more cars sped by, but they didn't worry me. We were low enough for the guard rail to prevent anyone from seeing us.

The weeds were dewy. They made my jeans wet to the knees. I slipped once or twice. George landed on his butt once. But finally we made it down the slope and climbed a small embankment to the tracks.

'That's our place,' I told George.

'Under there?' He didn't sound thrilled.

Jefferson Avenue was four lanes wide, so the dark area beneath it looked like a tunnel. We could see the gray of moonlight at the other end, but it was too dim to show us much of anything in the underpass.

'Hope nobody's there,' I muttered.

'Keep your eyes peeled,' Jim said. 'And get ready to run like hell.'

'Can't we just stay here?' George asked.

Jim shook his head. 'Somebody might see us from the road. Let's go.'

'I don't know,' George said.

'You wanted to come along,' I reminded him.

'Yeah, but . . .'

'Hey,' Jim said. 'If you want to run around with the big guys, you've gotta do what we do.'

'Or you can go on home,' I said. 'It's up to you, but *we're* going in there.'

He hung back while Jim and I stepped over a rail and started walking down the middle of the tracks toward the underpass. I really hoped George would chicken out. I didn't want to go under there, didn't want to nail him, wanted only to have him out of our lives so we could hurry on to Cyndi's house.

But he shrugged and came after us.

There were two sets of tracks. They ran side by side, several yards apart. Ahead of us, broad concrete supports stood between them.

We waited until we were just under the edge of the bridge, then switched on our flashlights. George dug into the paper sack and came up with a big, six-volt lantern.

'All *right*,' Jim whispered.

We shined our beams into the darkness. George's was reall huge and bright. We swept our lights all over the place befor going any further.

'Looks okay,' Jim murmured.

It didn't look okay. Not at all. But at least we didn't spo anyone.

Jim aimed his beam at the nearest support. The concrete wa scrawled with names and dirty words and dates and drawings The drawings were pretty crude. The biggest was an old one tha I'd seen plenty of times before. It showed a cartoonish gal wit huge tits and her legs spread apart. Jim and I used to call he 'The Beave.' Since the last time we'd been here, somebody' added a mammoth erection just underneath her. It was aime between her legs, and squirting like a geyser.

Normally, we would've had a good time studying the artwor and making remarks. But George was with us. And we were in hurry to get to Cyndi's. And this was night.

Neither of us got cute.

'Check the other side, George,' Jim said.

'Me?'

'You got the good light. Make sure nobody's hiding behin those things.'

'Aw, geez.'

'Just do it,' I told him. 'We don't want some damn win jumping us.'

George moaned, but did as he was told. He crept past th support, shined his lantern behind it, raised the light to check th backsides of the other three supports, and swung it every whicl way. 'Okay over there,' he said, his voice shaking. He hurrie back to our side of the tunnel. 'Want me to open the wine?'

'Might as well,' Jim said.

George squatted, set down his sack, and lifted out the bottle He stood up with it. Jim held his light on its neck while Georg picked at the foil with a dirty fingernail.

I took the opportunity to look around. I stayed put, but swep my light here and there. It gleamed off the glass of an empt

300

bottle a few feet away. Over near the wall was a rag, maybe a shirt. It was surrounded by broken glass, cans, mashed cigarette packs. Halfway up the wall was an enormous black Swastika. I'd seen it before, but the drawing beside it was new to me – a rump with a hard-on shoved into its hole.

I decided to quit looking around.

George had the wine bottle clamped between his legs, a Swiss Army knife in his hands. He pried out the knife's corkscrew, then bent over and started twisting it into the top of the bottle.

Once it was in deep, he started pulling and grunting.

'Awful tight,' he muttered.

'Why don't you give it a try,' Jim said to me.

George handed over the bottle. I set my flashlight on the ground, pinned the bottle between my legs the same way he'd done, and tugged on the knife.

At first, the cork wouldn't give.

'Hurry it up,' Jim said. 'We don't wanta be late to Cyndi's.'

It moved just a little.

Then it slid out fast. As it popped free, Jim shot an arm across George's chest, whipped a leg behind him, and flung him back-wards. George yelped with surprise. Grunted when he slammed the ground.

I knew this was what we'd planned, but Jim's sudden attack probably surprised me as much as George.

I put the knife and bottle down fast.

George, wheezing for air, didn't struggle as Jim rolled him over and dropped onto his rump.

I pulled up my shirt. I unwrapped the rope. By the time I was on my knees beside them, Jim had both George's arms bent up behind him.

'Guys!' George gasped. 'What're you . . . ?'

'Shut up,' Jim snapped. 'We aren't gonna hurt you.'

I started tying George's hands together.

'Hey!' he said. 'Don't! Don't!'

'Calm down,' Jim told him.

'Is . . . is this . . . some kinda 'nitiation?'

'Sure,' Jim said.

'Is not!' I said. 'Why'd you wanta say that? He'll think he's . . . It's no initiation, George. You're not joining something. We just wanted to be left alone, damn it, but you wouldn't get the message. You're *not* our friend. You're a fat, grubby little pain in the ass!'

George started blubbering.

'*And* a Peeping Tom!'

'Yeah!' Jim joined in. 'You been spying on my sister, you dirty pervert!'

'Who else you been spying on?'

'Nuh . . . nobody!'

'I bet,' Jim said.

'Yeah,' I said. 'And you think you're gonna go with us to Cyndi's, you got another thing coming!'

Jim climbed off him, grabbed him by the feet and shoved his legs up till his calves were mashed against the backs of his thighs. Done with the hands, I looped the rope around his ankles, pulled it taut, and tied his feet together.

By the time I finished, George was bawling.

'You'd better cut that out,' Jim warned him. 'Somebody might hear you.'

'They might *come* for you,' I added.

'Puh . . . Please!'

'I'd be *very* quiet, if I were you,' Jim said.

'From now on,' I said, 'you just stay away from us.'

We stepped back. Jim turned off George's lantern and picked up the wine bottle. He took two packs of Twinkies out of the sack. I twisted the cork off George's knife and put the knife on the ground a couple of yards away from him. Then I picked up my flashlight and stuffed it into my pocket.

'If you're still here when we get back,' I told him, 'we'll untie you.'

'*If* we come back,' Jim added.

As we hurried out into the moonlight, George blurted things like 'Please!' and 'Don't leave me here!' and 'Come back!' But

302

he cut it out when we were about halfway up the slope.

'Here,' Jim said, and offered me a pack of Twinkies as we walked across the bridge.

I shook my head. 'I don't want to eat his stuff. I mean, we double-crossed him.'

Jim grinned. 'Got him good, huh?'

'Maybe we oughta go back down and let him go.'

'Are you nuts? We've already wasted enough time. Besides, the little dork would probably *still* wanta come with us. He'll think we were joking or something, and we'll be right back where we started.'

'Yeah, I guess so.'

'Anyhow, he'll probably get loose and be outa there in five minutes.'

'I don't know. I tied him pretty good.'

'So maybe it'll take him ten. Don't go feeling sorry for him. He asked for it, he got it.'

'Yeah. Maybe he'll stay out of our face after this.'

'And stay away from our windows. I ever catch him spying on Joan or Mom, he'll think he got off easy tonight. I'll cut off his dick and make him eat it.'

'Oh, gross.'

'Give him a Hostess weenie.'

I elbowed Jim, and laughed.

He made me hold the wine bottle while he unwrapped his Twinkies. 'You don't know what you're missing,' he said through a mooshy mouthful.

Watching him, I could almost taste the things. Pretty soon, I said, 'He owes us, you know.'

'Huh?'

'For all the crap he put us through.'

'Damn right.'

'Besides, he ate our potato chips.'

'Sure did.'

I took the other package from Jim, gave him the bottle back,

tore off the cellophane and started eating. I was about halfwa
through my first Twinkie when Jim took a drink of the wine.

He sighed. 'Good stuff.'

He passed the bottle to me. I had a couple of swallows. I
made my mouth pucker. When it hit my stomach, it seemed t
turn into fire. 'Thlightly impertinent,' I said.

That got a big laugh out of Jim.

We walked along, taking slugs of wine and bites of Twinkie
swinging the bottle out of sight every time a car approached from
either the front or the rear. Once we got away from Jefferson
there were a lot fewer cars. By then, the Twinkies were gone an
the bottle was almost half empty. I was feeling pretty great.

'Let's save the rest,' Jim said.

'What for?'

'For us, stupid.'

We yucked it up.

After calming down, Jim said, 'Hey, we don't wanta ge
polluted.'

'Speak for yourself.'

'Where's the cork?' I gave it to him, and he squeezed it int
the bottle's neck. 'We'll save it for the return trip.'

That sounded like a fine idea.

He carried it the rest of the way to Cyndi's house.

Except for a lamp at the end of the driveway, Cyndi's hous
was dark. Not even the porch light was on.

'What gives?' Jim asked.

'I don't know.'

'This is her house, isn't it?'

'Sure.'

We'd both been there before. Three times, we'd followed he
home after school, first to find out where she lived, then late
just because we liked to watch her walk, books clutched to he
chest, hair golden in the sunlight, skirt swinging.

'Sure looks like her house,' Jim muttered.

'That's because it is.'

'Maybe they're around back.'

So we hurried across the frontyard and made our way alongside the house. The windows there were dark. So were those in the rear, and those along the other side. I was shaking pretty badly the whole time, scared of getting caught, thrilled by our search for the girls. I could see why a guy like George might get a kick out of sneaking around like that. It was a real charge. But the charge died when we got to the street.

'Well, shit,' Jim said.

'We must've gotten here too late.'

'Thanks to George, the little shit.'

'Damn it!'

'This *is* the right house, right?' Jim asked.

'Of course it's . . . hey! Maybe we've got the wrong night! Maybe it's *tomorrow* night. All we did was guess, remember?'

'Yeah! Bet it is tomorrow night.'

'All right! So no big deal. We'll come back.'

We turned away from Cyndi's house, and started walking.

'Tomorrow,' Jim said, 'we won't have to waste time fooling around with George. He won't come anywhere near us from now on.'

'Right. And we'll get away earlier. Mom and Dad are going out. They won't be getting home till really late.'

'Man!'

'We can leave at like ten or something!'

'Fantastic! This calls for a drink!'

We passed the bottle back and forth a couple of times. We probably would've polished it off and gotten ourselves really smashed, except the bottle got smashed first. Jim stumbled on a raised section of sidewalk. He went lurching forward and the bottle flew. It exploded on the sidewalk in front of us.

Scared that somebody might've heard the noise, we ran two blocks and didn't stop till we reached Jefferson.

When the guard rails of the bridge came into sight, my stomach went kind of cold. The last thing I wanted to do was go down to the underpass.

'Wonder how Georgie-porgie's doing,' Jim said.

'I guess we'll have to find out.'

'I bet he's already home.'

'Yeah,' I said. 'I hope so.'

'I just hope he's learned his lesson. It'd sure be a pain if we had to go through this again tomorrow night.'

'When he sees us coming from now on,' I said, 'he's gonna run the other way.'

''Less he liked it down there.'

'Nobody could like it down there.'

'I don't know. He's a pretty weird kid.'

'No kid's that weird. It's too damn creepy.'

Jim laughed. 'Hope he crapped his pants, the little shit.'

At the other side of the bridge, we ducked into the trees and started down the slope. I only looked once at the underpass. The idea of George being tied up in that dark, awful place made me feel kind of sick.

Jim and I both fell on our cans a few times before we got to the bottom of the slope. The wine might've had something to do with that.

Finally, we got to the tracks.

We walked between the rails, our flashlights off. With every step, I felt shakier. I told myself that George probably *had* gotten loose and run home. We wouldn't need to go under there, at all, just shine our lights in, make sure he was gone, and leave.

He'd probably left my rope behind. It could stay right where it was. I sure didn't need the rope badly enough to go in after it.

Just where the tracks disappeared into the darkness, we stopped and turned on our flashlights. The shiny rails gleamed. About twenty feet ahead, the rail on the left was draped with rope.

My rope. It had to be.

George *had* worked himself loose.

Now, we could go home.

Jim's flashlight swung away from the rail, away from the rope, off to the side where we'd left George.

Just as I'd expected, George wasn't there.

But he wasn't gone.

Jim's light found him a couple of yards closer to the wall.

We both gasped. I felt like I'd been kicked in the belly.

We ran toward George, our beams jerking all around as we tried to spot who'd done it to him. We saw no one.

We stopped by his body but didn't look down at him. Darted our lights everywhere else. We were both panting, even though we hadn't run very far. Jim made these weird whiny sounds every time he sucked in a breath.

'See anyone?' I asked.

'Huh-uh.'

'Maybe . . . they're gone.'

I swept my light across the center supports. Four broad, concrete walls. A crazy or two or three might've been lurking behind every one of them. I knew one of us should go to the other side for a look. I didn't have the guts to do it, though.

'Let's . . . get,' Jim whimpered.

'Can't leave him.'

We shined our flashlights down at George. He lay sprawled on his back, his shirt wide open, his boxer shorts and Bermudas hanging off one foot. He was bloody all the way down to his knees.

'What'd they . . . *do* to him?'

I shook my head.

George's eyes were shut. One was swollen so it looked like a hardboiled egg with a slit across it. I'd seen a boxer on TV one time who had an eye like that after going eleven rounds with the heavyweight champ.

George's neck was shiny red, but I didn't see any wounds on it.

He was so fat and dumpy that he actually had tits. I thought about how the other guys probably gave him grief about them when he had to dress for gym class. Then I thought how there wouldn't be any more gym classes for him. Because of us.

I moved my light down his fat belly.

307

He looked so lonely and pitiful.

'Where'd all the *blood* come from?' Jim whispered. Stepping behind my back, he moved sideways past George's hips. Then he froze. The pale beam of his light slanted down between George's legs. He let out a terrible groan, staggered out of my way, whirled around and started to puke.

I pointed my flashlight at George's groin.

And knew where all the blood had come from.

Blood *still* trickled out of the raw open slot where his dick should've been.

I went numb and started to sway. I thought I might pass out, and hoped I wouldn't fall on *him*. Then my arm got grabbed. I yelped. But it was only Jim.

I started to cry. 'Look . . . look what we did.'

'We didn't.'

'They cut off his dick,' I sobbed.

'No.'

'They *did*! Look! Didn't you see?' I pointed my light at the bloody opening.

'They didn't cut off his dick, you dope. He never had one. George is a girl. They didn't cut off nothing. They banged her.'

'What?'

'She's a *girl*. Georgina or something.'

'Oh, my God.'

'Don't know why she'd sneak around spying on Joan, but . . .'

'Didn't.'

I flinched so hard it made every bone in my body hurt. Jim actually jumped and cried out. Then we shined our lights on George's face. Her eyes were open. One eye was, anyway – the one that wasn't swollen shut.

She pushed herself up with her elbows. 'Spying on you guys,' she said. 'You're who I looked at. You two, not girls.'

'You're . . . alive!'

'Yeah.'

'Why'd you make us think you were dead?' Jim demanded.

'Just wanted to hear whatcha had to say.'

'Shit!'

'I'm just glad you're alive,' I said. I wiped my eyes with my shirttail, but couldn't stop crying. I dropped to my knees beside her and put a hand on her shoulder.

'It's okay,' she said.

'No it's not! God, I'm so sorry! If we'd known . . .'

'How bad are you hurt?' Jim asked. He crouched down next to me.

'My face don't feel too good.'

'Is that all?'

' 'Cept for my twat.'

'They raped you?' Jim asked.

'Yeah. *He* did. Just one. He really stank. You shoulda smelled him.'

'We never should've left you here,' Jim said. 'We never would've, if we'd only known you were a girl.'

'If we'd gone to the pool today like we told her . . .'

'Aw, I didn't show up anyhow,' she said. 'You woulda found me out.'

I sniffed, and wiped my face again.

'I only just wanted to be your friend,' she said, her voice going higher.

'You can be our friend,' I said.

'Sure,' Jim said.

'Honest?'

'Yeah, honest,' I told her. 'This *was* an initiation. I was just lying about all that stuff I told you.'

'Really?'

'Yeah.'

'From now on,' Jim said, 'we'll never ditch you again.'

'You guys sure had me going. I was starting to figure you hated me.'

'Naw. We were just kidding.'

Her bloody face smiled. She sat up.

'You'd better not move,' I said. 'We'll have to get you an ambulance or something.'

'I'm okay.'

'You can't be okay,' Jim said. 'All that blood.'

'Oh, I was a virgin. But not anymore.' She looked at each o
us. 'You guys wanta bang me? You can if you want, now we're
pals.'

I went kind of speechless.

'Not tonight,' Jim said. 'Thanks anyway.'

I nodded.

'You sure? I'm kinda sore, but if you want . . .'

'Some other time,' Jim told her.

'Well, okay.' She sighed as if she were a little disappointed
then got to her feet. She shook her foot clear of the tangled boxer;
and Bermuda shorts. 'Wanta see something cool?' she asked.

'We oughta just get out of here,' I said.

'You guys gotta see this.' She stepped over to her lantern, ben
over as if she didn't mind us looking at her butt, picked up th
lantern and turned it on. 'Come on,' she said.

We followed her across the tracks.

Joined her on the other side of the nearest concrete support.

Where she shined her light on a bum.

He was slumped against the support, shirt open, pants dow
around his ankles. His head was down. Cradled in his arms was
pile of loose guts.

George grinned at us. 'Knew he didn't get far.'

'Holy shit,' Jim muttered.

Crouching, George plunged her hands into the guts. The
squirmed around like a bunch of wet snakes. Pretty soon, sh
came out with her knife. 'Didn't wanta lose this,' she said. Sh
stood up and cleaned the knife on the front of her shirt. 'Betch
didn't figure he'd get into my initiation, did you?'

We shook our heads.

We walked back to the other side of the tracks. There, Georg
stepped into her boxers and Bermudas. As she pulled them up
she said, 'So, what're we gonna do tomorrow?'